More Than He Bargained For

More Than He Bargained For

*The Story of a Country Bachelor, and
the Amish Girl Who Captured His Heart*

Copyright © 2023 Karen Whalen Gouker
All rights reserved
ISBN: 9798858895749

Dedication

This book is dedicated to my husband, Ron, in sincere appreciation for your encouragement and patience. Thanks for helping me imagine this work of fiction, inspired by the true-life love story of your grandparents. I wish I'd had the privilege of knowing them.

Acknowledgments

I would like to publicly thank and acknowledge the following:

My husband, Ron, for your enduring support and love throughout this creative process. This book would not have been possible without you.

Michelle Enfield, my daughter, for the cover photo – thanks!

My close personal friends and family, who never tired of listening to my many frustrations, and were always ready with sound advice.

The Stormy Night Writer's Society, for your consistently enthusiastic encouragement, and insightful critiques. Our bond has evolved from that of being a group of people sharing a common interest, to a cadre of true friends.

To The Word Weavers: Ladies, what can I say? Each of you has been, and continues to be, an inspiration to me. I confess to feeling in over my head when I first joined your ranks. Thank you for so kindly taking me under your wings.

CONTENTS

Chapter 1 1

Chapter 2 8

Chapter 3 14

Chapter 4 21

Chapter 5 27

Chapter 6 32

Chapter 7 37

Chapter 8 44

Chapter 9 50

Chapter 10 56

Chapter 11 63

Chapter 12 71

Chapter 13 76

Chapter 14 83

Chapter 15 91

Chapter 16 98

Chapter 17 105

Chapter 18 112

Chapter 19 118

Chapter 20 124

Chapter 21 130

Chapter 22 135

Chapter 23 141

Chapter 24 147

Chapter 25 153

Chapter 26 160

Chapter 27 166

Chapter 28 173

Chapter 29 179

Chapter 30 186

Chapter 31 192

Chapter 32 198

Chapter 33 207

Chapter 34 214

Chapter 35 221

Chapter 36 230

Chapter 37 237

Chapter 38 246

Chapter 39 252

Chapter 40 258

Chapter 41 264

Chapter 42 271

Chapter 43 278

Chapter 44 284

Chapter 45 291

Chapter 46 297

Chapter 47 304

Chapter 1

Lagrange County, Indiana – 1899

There was no blinding flash of strike-a-man-down lightning, nor explosive thunder sending every living creature within miles running for cover. Indeed, there was nothing about the day to give John Hartman warning of what lay ahead, not a hint that his entire life was about to be forever altered. To the contrary, he felt no need to be on guard, to protect himself. He had no idea that this day was the singular axis upon which the remaining wheel of his life would turn.

As usual, the invigorating air and crystalline light of November combined to sharpen the man's senses and focus his mind. It was a time for reflection and taking stock of one's life. The month heralded a lull in the farming year as the cycles of planting, cultivating, and harvesting resolved into the comparative restfulness of winter. This year would prove the exception.

The whole family had been busy since midsummer preparing for the auction sale of the Hartman farm. John had been born here, and this was the only home he'd ever known. All of his childhood memories had taken shape around the Shipshewana area, and it hadn't been his idea to leave. His parents, James and Susanna, made that decision when they purchased 150 acres along the Fawn River, just north of the Indiana-Michigan state line. The deal was done and there was no turning back. Today's auction would settle the disposition of their Hoosier homestead.

Sale bills had been printed, and widely distributed throughout the area. John had every reason to expect a good turnout for the auction. The weather was perfect, and the long line of horse drawn wagons and buggies winding along the drive was an encouraging sight as prospective buyers arrived. Of course, an auction attracted others, too. Some folks came to socialize, and some ventured out merely to satisfy their curiosity.

John had asked his youngest sister, Rose Ellen, to be especially attentive to their mother today. Although she usually kept her emotions in check, John sensed his mother was privately grieving the necessary abandonment of a small grave in Forest Grove Cemetery. Carved into stone, scant words and numbers capsulized the details of a brief life: *Alfred L, son of J & S Hartman. Died December 16, 1878, age three years, nine-months, four days.* John's younger brother had affectionately been called 'Alfie' by the family, and the loss of this adored little boy was still keenly felt, even twenty-two years after his passing.

Long ago, John had vowed to honor his brother as namesake for one of his own sons, but John's present prospects cast doubts for the naming of any son, or daughter either, for that matter. Not one to take his responsibilities lightly, the protective older brother to three sisters found little time to pursue a marriage partner. Still, the handsome, thirty-year-old bachelor yearned deeply for a wife and family of his own.

The aroma of freshly brewed coffee wafting on the breeze, reminded John that some of their Amish neighbors were selling food and drink today. He followed his nose to join those already gathering to patronize the concession.

"Ditcher! Hey Ditcher!" John, curious to discover who was hailing him by a name he'd not answered to in years, pivoted and scanned the growing queue behind him. The culprit, a lean Amishman wearing a wide grin, approached with an easy, loping stride and extended hand.

Laughing, John returned the man's hearty handshake. "Danny Byler? I hadn't expected to see you here today."

"Well, I wouldn't have missed it. I couldn't let you get away without sayin' goodbye. Things surely won't be the same hereabouts without the Hartmans around. Chances are, it will probably be quieter with my old friend, Ditcher, on the other side of the state line."

"Do me a favor, Danny. Will you forget that nickname from my reckless youth? Trying to explain to my folks why some of the boys are calling me 'Ditcher' is proving to be a little awkward."

"What? You don't mean to say they've not heard before now what a first-rate pugilist their son was? Why, I can personally bear witness to the fact that more than a few rowdy scrappers were put in their place by 'Ditcher' Hartman." Danny struck a boxer's stance, fists raised.

"They don't know about it," John said, "or not all of it anyway, and I'd like to keep it that way. Thank goodness all that nonsense is behind me now, and best forgotten. I guess I've outgrown the impulse to settle disagreements with my fists, or maybe I'm just getting too old to mix it up with hotheads wanting to fight."

Danny shook his head, suggesting he had his doubts. "You may be older, but I'm willin' to bet you could still handle yourself pretty well if you had to."

John changed the subject. "Enough about ancient history, Danny. How are you? Tell me, are you still married to Lovina, or has she finally come to her senses and left you?" John easily deflected the playful punch Danny threw his way.

"Lovina's the happiest woman in the whole world, and why wouldn't she be? She's been my missus for ten years now, and mother to six, growin' boys, each one as good lookin' as their dat. And what about yourself, John? Did you ever manage to get happily, or hopelessly, entangled in the bonds of matrimony?"

"Not yet. My sisters have been tireless in their efforts to fix me up with their friends, but I'm holding out for that one special girl. She just hasn't come along yet, but I'll know her when I see her."

Placing a restraining hand on his friend's arm, Danny

said. "Whoa, hold up a minute and let me get a peek inside your ear. Yep, I'm pretty sure I see daylight from one side clean through to the other. In case no one's told you, Ditcher, you can't just wait around twiddlin' your thumbs, you got to go lookin' for a gal. Maybe I should help you find a wife."

"No thank you, Danny. I'm not that desperate yet. Let's talk about something else, and if this line doesn't start moving, I'll have to come back later. Father will be needing my help with the horses."

As they waited, the two men reminisced about their years as classmates in the one-room schoolhouse situated halfway between the Hartman, and Byler farms. Both Amish, and non-Amish, referred to as 'Englishers' by the Amish community, had attended the Van Buren Township School, where many enduring friendships were formed across cultural divides.

The four Hartmans: John, Isabel, Musetta, and Rose Ellen, had been pupils there. At the same time, the Byler family's lively brood of ten children represented about one-fourth of the school's enrollment. Although the years spanning those long-ago school days had diminished John's instant recollection of all their names, he had known each one. Some of them he would never forget, like Anna. She was closest to his own age, and he'd had a serious crush on her in his third year at school. Of course, the fact that Anna always shared cookies from her lunch pail with him probably contributed to his unflagging devotion. Betsy was the only other one of Danny's sisters whose name he could readily bring to mind. He'd enjoyed a much closer relationship with the Byler boys. There was Jonas, Christian, Joel, Val, and of course, his best school chum, Danny.

Seeing his old childhood friend today prompted other recollections from John's growing up years to come flooding back. So many good times with friends and neighbors. One of the most indelible memories from those years was that of a pretty little girl atop the sharply rising hill upon which stood the Byler family home. Nearly every time he'd traveled that county road as a lad, she had been there. It always seemed to him that the girl was just watching, and waiting for him to pass by. She'd smile and wave, until he waved back. In his childish imagination he'd somehow conjured up the idea that she needed rescuing, and one day he'd made an impulsive promise to his mother as they drove past the Byler place. "Someday Mama, I'm going to get that little girl down off that hill!"

Danny's voice broke into John's wandering thoughts. "Is Rose Ellen here today?"

He'd had to repeat the question before John responded. "Yes, she's here. Why do you ask?"

"My sister, Katie, was hoping to see her."

"Katie, Katie," John repeated thoughtfully. "That's it! I'd forgotten her name. She and Rose Ellen were just starting school as I was leaving to farm with dad. Wasn't Katie a shy and quiet little thing?"

An incredulous look passed over his friend's face. "Shy? Quiet? You must be thinkin' of someone else. Katie's the spoiled and petted baby of the whole family. Now, don't get me wrong, John. She's not a bad girl, nor meanspirited either. Katie is loads of fun, and to be honest, I'd have to say she's my favorite sister, but she's certainly *not* what you'd call quiet or shy. Neither is she of a mind to settle down. She's broken as many hearts as I can count on all my fingers and toes. I probably shouldn't be tellin' you this, but Katie's betrothed to Emmon Hostettler. They're supposed to marry at the end of this month. Now Emmon's an old friend, and I feel downright sorry for him 'cause he don't have the least notion of what's comin' his way. If I were a bettin' man, I'd wager that Katie won't go through with this marriage. If she does, I'll eat my hat!"

John was clearly baffled listening to Danny as they inched forward with the line. No matter how hard he tried, he couldn't reconcile his impression of an angelic six-year-old, with his friend's description of a mischievous, free-spirited young woman. He was just about to say so when a soft voice in honeyed tones intruded, ". . . and, what can I get for you, John?"

Glancing toward the speaker, John found himself at a complete loss for the answer to her question. It's true, the voice had been captivating, but even so he was unprepared for the vision that met his eyes. John's first impression was that of a shapely, feminine form, crowned with shining, chestnut brown hair, swept up and under a modest prayer cap. A closer inspection revealed exquisitely arched brows framing warm, dark eyes he would never tire of gazing into, and lips that could surely restore life to a dying man.

A variation on the original question was being posed by the lovely girl in front of him. "John, do you know what you want?" She waited patiently, but he was dumbstruck.

The singular response resonating in his consciousness was -- *the only thing I'll ever want is you*. For one terrible moment, John believed he'd actually verbalized his answer, but apparently, he'd lost the ability to speak.

Sensing a crisis of some sort, Danny quickly inserted himself into the stalled exchange. "John, this is my little sister, Katie. Do you remember John Hartman, Sis?"

She smiled, never taking her eyes from John's. "I could never forget Rose Ellen's big brother."

After some difficulty, John found his voice. "It's a pleasure to see you again, Katie."

Danny plowed ahead with the business at hand. "Katie, we'll have coffee and pie, custard, if you have any." After paying, he cupped John's elbow, guiding him away. "C'mon John, sit down and catch your breath. She'll bring our order out when it's ready."

While attempting to gather his wits about him in order to portray a convincing semblance of normalcy, John mentally reprimanded himself. 'Get a grip old boy. Katie must be all of ten years your junior, and even if the age difference wasn't a problem, she's Amish, *and* marrying someone else this month!'

John was abruptly recalled from his altered state of awareness by the previously unknown mind-reading ability of his friend. "Oh Ditcher, you haven't gone sweet on Katie, have you?" Solicitously patting John's shoulder, Danny continued. "Now don't misunderstand, there's no one I'd like better for a brother-in-law than you, but . . . well, you know the obstacles same as I do."

"What?" John protested. "Sweet on your baby sister? No! No, you're mistaken. I was just caught off guard, seeing her all grown up. I mean, Katie sure is, she's . . ." He faltered and checked his pocket watch. "Would you look at the time? I need to meet Father over at the horse barn. See you later." He hurried off, calling over his shoulder, "thanks for the pie and coffee, Danny."

"Sure," Danny addressed John's departing back while chuckling to himself, *even though you didn't stick around long enough for either one.*

Katie arrived bearing a tray. "Where's John?" Her brother casually angled his head in the direction of the horse barn as Katie put their order down.

"Oh," a note of disappointment betrayed her interest.

"Say, isn't that Emmon Hostettler makin' his way over here," Danny asked?

"Who," Katie responded, only half listening? Her attention was focused on tracking John's path across the barnyard.

"Yep, that's pretty much how I had it figured," Danny said under his breath as he lifted the steaming cup to his lips with a knowing smile.

Emmon's glance rested on the pie and coffee on the table, as he lowered himself onto the bench across from his future brother-in-law. "Is someone joining you?"

"Well now," Danny drawled, "it don't appear so after all. You're a lucky fella, Emmon. Dig in, boy, it's all yours."

Nodding happily, Emmon paused with the fork halfway

to his mouth to acknowledge Katie. "Got a minute to sit with us?"

"No," she said curtly, "too busy." Turning on her heel, she fled back to the tent.

Chapter 2

The grandfather clock chimed twelve, sonorous tones into the silence that had fallen over the house. It was a familiar and reassuring conclusion to the bustle and busyness of the day. The sale had been a whirlwind of activity, eliciting a wide range of emotions from the family. There was excitement as the auctioneer's banter provoked a frenzy among those vying for the highest bid, and a twinge of regret, as the gavel's decisive blow signified the finality of walking away from their Indiana home. The joy of seeing old friends and good neighbors at the auction provided consolation, tempered by the knowledge that it could be a long while before they might see some of these dear ones again. But every ending was a beginning too, and held out the possibility for new happiness.

When the sales figures were finally tallied, the proceeds far exceeded the expectations of John's father. The winning bidder was taking possession of the property as soon as the family could vacate, and now the real work would begin in earnest. The coordinated efforts of all the family, and several hired hands, would be required to move the horses, farm equipment, remaining livestock, and household belongings to the new place. Early Monday morning they would finish loading the wagons, and bid a last farewell to the old home before setting out for Scottsburg, Michigan.

John knew he needed to get some sleep if he was going to be at his best for the challenges ahead. He wanted to sleep, and drifting off should have been easy, except for one thing. He could not stop thinking about Katie Byler. She appeared whenever he closed his eyes, whether he wished her to be there or not, and every time he tried to push her out of his mind, some remembered glimpse of her from the day would return to him.

Katie and Rose Ellen, arms around each other, giggling again like the schoolgirls they'd once been. Katie, going out of her way to help his mother with bundles of yard goods being readied for packing. Katie, balancing trays as she served up her sunny smile, along with pie and coffee. His eyes had continually sought her out at the auction. He couldn't help himself. It was as if he had to convince himself she was real, and not some fantasy he'd dreamed up. He had watched her throughout the day, but she'd never once given any indication of being aware of his eyes on her. Nor had she returned his gaze to signal the slightest interest in him. But then again, he reasoned, why would she? Katie had found her one and only, the man with whom she'd spend the rest of her life. John tried to not begrudge Emmon Hostettler his good fortune. Katie would be Emmon's wife at the end of this month, just four short weeks away. John wished . . . well, there was no point in wishing, was there? He closed his eyes, trying to banish Katie from his mind, and give himself up to sleep. It was an exercise in futility. He must force himself to think of something else.

With an effort, John turned his thoughts to the farm outside of Scottsburg, ready and waiting for its new owners. The stately, two-story red brick house with a welcoming porch ranged across the front, was situated at the summit of a broad rise. To the west, there was an array of outbuildings: hay and livestock barns, a hen house, as well as wagon and tool sheds. The privy could be found at a discreet distance, downwind of the family's new home. To the east, a spring house had been built into the sloping bank of Trout Creek. Water from the stream was piped inside to a stone trough where milk, butter, eggs, and cream would stay cool during the hot summers. Apple and pear orchards would house the beehives, and next to the woodlot was a small cabin, the farm's original homestead.

There could be no disputing that it was a beautiful property, but its acquisition had set him to wondering what his parents had been thinking. They were getting on in years, and there would be only the three of them, with hired help, to run the farm. John had never before questioned his father's dealings, but his curiosity was piqued at the beginning of summer, when he was told of their plans. He had, in fact, dared to ask his father, *why*? After a convoluted attempt to explain the decision, his father finally gave up and admitted. "It was your mother's idea." Then, he'd refused to say anything more on the subject.

What was even more perplexing was the conversation between John and his mother, later that very week. She'd cornered him one day while he was cleaning horse stalls. "Son, I have something to tell you." He felt suddenly apprehensive, as he always did when she called him "son" instead of using his given name. Leaning the barn shovel against a wall, he stood patiently, waiting for her to seat herself on a bale of straw. Once composed, hands resting in her lap, she spoke. "You deserve a better answer than the one Father gave you when you asked about the purchase of this farm."

John objected. "Mother, that's not necessary. You and father don't owe me anything, much less an explanation for whatever decisions you see fit to make."

"Be that as it may, I will have you know the *why* of it." She took a breath and straightened her back. "A year ago, I had a dream." She paused, shaking her head. "No, if I'm to be honest with you it was more than that. It was a vision. This house and farm appeared to me as real as anything I'd ever known, and it seemed the whole of it spread out beneath me, like I was a bird soaring overhead. The property was filled with activity. A man, his wife, and their many children were contentedly going about the business of life."

"Now you can imagine it was not an easy thing for your father to accept this revelation for what it was. He doubted the existence of such a place as I described. Then, early this year we drove to Scottsburg for a consultation with a doctor there, and taking a different route on our way home, we came upon the very manifestation of my vision. Seeing a man approaching along the road, we asked about the property, and learned he was the owner. We made our interest known, and began negotiating with him then and there."

"Son, your father and I feel the hand of time weighing heavily on us. We would see you settled in your own place, with your own family before much longer." She hesitated, "John, this place was purchased with you in mind . . . you were the man in my vision. You *are* that man. Just wait and see, the others will come in time."

Without another word she'd stood, wrapped her arms around his waist and laid her head briefly on his shoulder before leaving the barn.

Thinking about what his mother had shared with him months ago, John struggled to make sense of it. Not that he doubted her abilities as a seer. Susanna Hartman's second sight was well known to the family. Some called her prescience a gift, others a curse, but many times over it had been proven that she could accurately visualize events before they happened. She declared she had seen him with a wife and children, *many children!* At any other time, his mother's psychic foreknowledge of the future might have reassured John that his desire for a wife and family would be realized. But Katie Byler had so completely captured his heart today that he couldn't imagine himself with anyone else . . . and she was as good as married to Emmon Hostettler!

Muttering a plea for sleep, he turned toward the window and closed his eyes. Less than three miles away, someone else was having a restless night, too.

Katie's tossing and turning had so entangled her legs in the disheveled bedclothes that she was sure she knew how a moth must feel when caught in a spider's web. She was lonely in this room she used to share with her four, older sisters. As children, they'd all slept together, their spindly arms and legs overlapping like puppies snuggled together in a basket. A second bed was added as they grew. The two older sisters occupied one, while the three younger ones slept in the other bed. In the natural way of things, Katie's older sisters all left the nest for families of their own. Sarah was first, followed in quick succession by Anna and Mary. Betsy had been the last, leaving Katie alone. Katie missed them more tonight than she usually did. The girls had shared their hopes, dreams, joys, sorrows, and secrets throughout childhood and adolescence, and Katie longed once again for the comfort and counsel of a sister to quiet the turmoil in her heart.

The encounter with John Hartman at the auction today had produced an unexpected response in her. She had recognized him as he advanced toward the concession tent with Danny, and perceived the opportunity for a little harmless flirtation. Surely, John wouldn't remember her, but the deep gaze they'd shared in that brief moment after she called him by name had been intense. She'd been acutely aware of her pounding heart, breathlessness and blushing face. Katie was certain he'd felt the stirring of emotion, too. She had noticed John staring at her throughout the day, and hoped he hadn't caught her stealing glances at him in return. The contemplation of their mutual attraction only added to the other, more imminently troubling reason for her sleeplessness.

For months, Katie had been wrestling with her decision to marry Emmon. She knew if she went forward with their wedding it would be a mistake. A big mistake, and once made, beyond correction. But what could she do? Her options had run out. She would celebrate her twentieth birthday in two days. It was time to accept the inevitable. Her family was fast losing patience with her fickleness. Amish girls were expected to marry within their faith, and settle down to being a wife and mother. She'd avoided her fate as long as she could, before agreeing to Emmon's proposal.

Katie had known from the beginning that she didn't love him, any more than she had a string of other young fellows who'd asked for her hand and been refused. So, why had she accepted Emmon? The simple answer was that her folks would be sorely disappointed if she turned him down. He was the youngest son of her father's best friend, and their families were close, even within the bonds of the tightly-knit Amish community. Certain that the weight of her parents' disappointment, Emmon's unhappiness, and everyone's disapproval would be harder to bear than her own everlasting regret, Katie had resolved to see this courtship through to its inescapable conclusion.

Yet, reliving those moments with John today was calling into question the strength of her resolve. It was impossible to deny the magnetic pull that drew them together. This attraction was unlike any she'd ever experienced before. She reflected too, on her conversation with John's sister. After Rose Ellen had spoken glowingly about her marriage to Edward Carson, Katie cautioned her about viewing the world through 'Rose' colored glasses, and the girls laughed. Katie was happy for her old friend, and hoped Rose Ellen's marriage would prove to be a long, fulfilling one.

Could Katie honestly say that she wanted to spend the rest of her life with Emmon? No! There was no doubt in her mind about that. She simply didn't have that kind of feeling for him. And what of John Hartman, where did he fit into all of this? Wanting with all her heart to believe otherwise, she had to face the truth. John didn't fit, not in the least. He was an Englisher, and by all accounts, a confirmed bachelor. She and John lived in different worlds, and as much as Katie wanted to pretend the possibility existed for a future with him, she knew it was an impossible dream. Acknowledging to herself the painful reality that she couldn't have John, she decided she *wouldn't* settle for Emmon. There was only one other choice open to her. Tomorrow she would tell her folks, and Emmon, that she couldn't go through with the marriage. She'd remain a spinster, content to be of service wherever she was needed within the family.

A palpable relief about making the choice to end her

engagement washed over her, and she felt at peace. Yet, even as Katie told herself she'd be able to sleep now, the memory of what she'd read in John's eyes caused tears to pool in her own, and spill onto the pillow as she mourned the loss of what could never be.

Chapter 3

Mamm's noisy rattling around in the kitchen woke Katie, alerting her to the fact that she'd overslept. The small, cloudy mirror she kept hidden in a drawer, revealed red eyes and a puffy face, evidence of last night's torrent of tears. She'd lain awake for hours before sleep finally claimed her. The clatter from downstairs grew louder, and Katie hurriedly washed her face and dressed. She was relieved that today was an off-Sunday, fewer people would be scrutinizing the dark circles under her eyes, and jumping to conclusions that might raise suspicions of something amiss.

Obviously, Mamm's powers of observation were operating at peak performance when Katie entered the kitchen. "Katie, your face! Whatever is wrong, child? Are you coming down with something?"

"No, Mamm, I'm fine. I just didn't sleep very well, and since you asked, there is something . . ."

"Oh good," Mamm cut her off abruptly. "Give me a hand getting this food on the table. Dat will be hungry when he comes in from the barn."

Katie's intention had been to inform her folks at the first opportunity that she was breaking it off with Emmon, but now she was having second thoughts about the timing. Dat liked to linger over breakfast and savor his food on these quiet, off-Sundays. She didn't want to be responsible for giving him indigestion, and rationalized that maybe it'd be better to wait before hitting her folks with news they wouldn't welcome. Katie picked at the ham and eggs on her plate while waiting for them to finish. One of Mamm's favorite sayings kept repeating in Katie's head, *good intentions come to nothing, unless they are put to action.* She might as well get this unpleasant business over with now.

Dat pushed his chair back from the table, as if preparing to rise. Katie cleared her throat, but before she could speak, Dat said, "Katie, tomorrow is your twentieth birthday, the last birthday you'll celebrate in your childhood home. Some *big* changes are ahead for you, and for us too. Mamm and I have asked all our children, and their families, to join us today to hear about our plans for the future."

He could almost see the questions forming in his youngest daughter's mind, and reacted to quickly forestall them. "No more will be said on the subject until everyone is together." Then he rose from the table and left the room while Mamm began clearing away dirty dishes.

"Mamm . . ." Katie began.

The look on her mother's face stopped Katie dead in her tracks. "Now you heard what Dat said. We'll talk later. The furniture could stand another going over with the dust cloth, and you can sweep the floors again while I tend to things in the kitchen."

Katie recognized a dismissal when she encountered one. She was being told in no uncertain terms to keep herself busy, and out of Mamm's way. Clearly, this was meant to prevent Katie from pestering Mamm for details about the momentous news alluded to by Dat. Well, so much for *her* expectations of the morning.

Katie's thoughts strayed to Emmon. As a rule, he came calling on these Sunday afternoons. Sometimes they went for a buggy ride, or they might head to the creek to fish and talk. Actually, Emmon did most of the talking while she listened. Katie supposed this was just part of the prescribed training for wives-to-be. Emmon did seem to appreciate her amazing ability to unsnarl the lines he inevitably snagged on submerged tree roots. Would there be any opportunity for them to get away from the others today? Katie couldn't possibly admit to Emmon that she'd changed her mind about marrying him with upwards of fifty people milling around within earshot.

She was frustrated -- nothing about this day was going according to plan. Last night it had all seemed so simple and straight forward, but ever since she got up, the whole order of events, as she'd envisioned them, had been derailed by Dat's cryptic declaration hinting at *big changes* ahead.

Katie's siblings, along with their spouses and children, began arriving shortly before eleven o'clock. By noon, the entire clan had gathered, and the house was filled with the chatter, teasing and laughter of Abe and Barbara Byler's very large, extended family.

The little cousins were so happy to see each other they could hardly contain their excitement. All they were interested in was playing together. It took some doing to settle the youngsters so dinner could be served. After the sumptuous meal was devoured, the children were turned loose to romp outside under the watchful eyes and supervision of the more responsible older girls. Mothers with babies lulled them to sleep, while the women unencumbered of such a happy excuse, washed the dishes and caught up on all the latest gossip. The men, as usual, took their ease and visited while waiting for the women to join them in the large, sitting room.

From his place near the massive wood-burner, Abe clapped his hands to get everyone's attention, and then he began to speak. "Almost forty years ago in Somerset, Pennsylvania, Barbara Teis became my wife and we embarked on life's journey together. Striking out with other like-minded young people looking to join the newer Amish settlements farther west, we felt led to put down roots in Shipshewana. Mamm and I have traveled many long roads together since our wedding day, experiencing joy and sorrow, good times and bad, but always sustained along the way by our shared faith and a deep, abiding love for each other. When we began our life together, Mamm and I couldn't have come close to imagining all of this, all of *you* here today." Abe spread his arms wide to encompass all those before him in the impression of an embrace. "We are truly humbled at God's goodness to us. Our family is a blessing from above, and we want to fully appreciate that gift as long as we are granted time to do so.

"Mamm and I are growing older by the day, and taking care of the farm has become more than we can manage. After lots of soul-searching and prayer, we approached Danny with the proposal that he, Lovina, and their half-dozen boys take over our place. There's plenty of room to fill this large house as their family grows, and Mamm and I feel their smaller property is much better suited to us. A swap is what it is, if you want to call it that. So, with fewer demands on our time and energy we'll be able to see more of all our children, and precious grandchildren. Of course, no moving will be taking place until after Katie's wedding at the end of this month."

After Abe finished speaking, a momentary silence lay over the room before being dispelled by applause, and exclamations of relief and approval from his children.

"You had us wondering if something was wrong when we were all summoned here. What a relief!"

"Thank God, you've decided to slow down! Both of you have been working too hard, for too long!"

"Amen to that!"

"It's about time Dat. What took you so long?"

"We'll all help you move, and get settled."

"The grandchildren will be so happy to see more of you."

One of the older brothers observed, "now we have two reasons to celebrate – our folks taking life a bit easier, and Katie's wedding!"

Abe exhaled a sigh of relief, and swiped at the moisture accumulating in his eyes. Harmony within the family was of the utmost importance to him.

Katie, meanwhile, had begun to feel light-headed when Dat mentioned her wedding. Her mouth was dry as powder when she tried to swallow. Before she could excuse herself for a drink of water and some fresh air, Katie was arrested by the clip-clop of horse hooves on the drive, the harbinger of a new arrival. A familiar buggy was seen coming to a halt outside, and one of her brothers said, "that must be Katie's intended now." A ripple of good-natured laughter echoed around the room. Even though the identity of courting couples was supposed to be a closely guarded secret until the marriage banns were announced, knowledge of a sibling's *special friend* was almost always known in advance. Katie's eyes were fixed on the buggy outside the window. But it wasn't Emmon that exited the rig. It was his father.

Abe had been watching too, and hurried to greet his old friend at the kitchen door. Jacob Hostettler declined the invitation to stay, slowly withdrawing an envelope from the inside of his jacket. Handing it to Abe, he said, "it's from Emmon, to Katie. Tell her we're sorry. We can't understand what's gotten into our boy." Jacob lowered his head and with heavy steps walked out to the buggy. A small noise behind Abe betrayed the presence of someone else in the room. Glancing back, Abe saw Barbara, framed in the kitchen doorway. She had overheard, and interpreted Jacob's comments as a sign of bad news. "I'll get Katie."

Danny was watching as Katie got to her feet in response to Mamm's beckoning finger, and quietly asked, "do you want some company?" She nodded gratefully, and they left the room together.

Reading the look on Dat's face, Katie braced herself, standing straight with knees locked. Her hands were trembling as she took the envelope and opened it:

Katie,

I hope you can find it in your heart to forgive me. I wouldn't want to hurt you for anything in the world, but I just can't go through with this wedding.

By the time you get this message I will be gone. I'm taking the train to Pennsylvania, and I don't plan to return.

You deserve someone better, Katie. Someone who loves you.
Emmon

The room began spinning, and Katie's legs buckled. Catching his sister, Danny lowered her carefully into a chair. Mamm placed a glass of water in front of her, and Dat asked, "what is it? What does he say?"

Katie unclenched her fingers and offered up the crumpled paper. The note was passed among the three of them. Mamm's gasp was one of surprise, or indignation, or maybe both. Dat rested a big hand gently on his daughter's shoulder. "I'm so sorry Katie. I would never have thought Emmon capable of running off like this."

"Why don't you go upstairs and rest awhile," Mamm suggested? "I'll see that no one disturbs you."

Danny was left alone with Katie after their parents returned to the living room. He squeezed her hand before rising to follow them.

Katie reached out to stop him. "Danny, please wait a minute! There's something I need to say."

He seated himself beside her. "Go ahead, Baby Sister, you know you can tell me anything."

Stumbling a little over her words, she began. "I . . . I think the note from Emmon is what might be called my comeuppance." He started to protest, but she stopped him. "No, let me finish. I was ready to tell the folks this morning that I was calling off the wedding. Then I planned to break the news to Emmon this afternoon. Danny, it never once occurred to me that he wanted to end our relationship as much as I did. I guess we never really talked about why we were getting married in the first place. Now I feel like such a fool. Everyone will assume I'm heartbroken and grieving over Emmon's leaving. Truthfully, I'm just relieved, and more than a little embarrassed. So, I guess I had this coming."

With his finger, Danny tipped her chin up so they were looking at each other, eye to eye. "Baby Sister, you and Emmon were never right for each other from the beginning. I could see there was no spark between the two of you. My guess is that your betrothal was encouraged to unite the families of old friends." Danny paused for a full minute before going on, "Emmon was right about one thing though."

Surprised, Katie asked, "what was that?"

Danny quoted Emmon's words back to her: *You deserve someone better, Katie. Someone who loves you.*

Putting his arm around her shoulder, he hugged her. "Don't lose heart. That *someone* is out there, just biding his time."

Chapter 4

On his second visit to the Scottsburg General Store, John was once again impressed with the sheer inventory and variety of goods lining the shelves, as well as the welcoming feel of the establishment. Glowing red, the potbelly stove radiated a cozy warmth. Empty chairs arranged in a semi-circle before the wood burner were ready for the old-timers who'd soon trickle in to warm their bones and tell tall tales for the amusement of their fellows. Most of these men were Civil War veterans, members of the Grand Army of the Republic, better known as the G.A.R. After they tired of light-hearted repartee, their talk inevitably drifted to battles fought, and the comrades who'd not returned home. It was a history lesson told by the men who had lived it. The last time John was here, he'd made the acquaintance of three brothers, Job, George and John Bellows, all survivors of the terrible conflict. He was disappointed the old soldiers weren't here today, and discovered that he missed them.

Jake Evans, the proprietor, was a tall, lanky man with unruly red hair, hazel eyes and a ready smile for all who entered. He had the gift of making every customer, old or new, feel right at home. The Scottsburg store also served as the post office for the surrounding area, and Jake handed John several letters while inquiring about the health of his parents.

"Thank you for asking, Mr. Evans. We're all well, and glad to be settled before the worst of winter's fury arrives. You remember the old saying, *When the days begin to lengthen, the cold begins to strengthen?*"

The storekeeper's smile grew wider. "Yes indeed. Those old adages are as true today as ever. I guess that's why they endure. Now, feel free to call me Jake. We don't hold with formalities around here. Say, those books you ordered arrived on the early train. I'll just fetch them out of the back room for you." He was back in minutes, setting a stack of books on the counter. "How about a copy of *The Scottsburg Sentinel*? We're proud to claim it as our weekly newspaper, and they say it's a wise man that keeps abreast of the local news. Some of it can even be downright entertaining from time to time."

"Then I guess I better have a copy," John replied with a smile. After rummaging through his pockets, he produced his mother's shopping list and passed it to the shopkeeper.

Jake scanned the items, reading aloud, "coffee beans, tea, flour, and sorghum molasses. Yep, I can fix you right up. Will there be anything else?"

"Do you have a good restorative tonic? Father mentioned to me yesterday that he feels as weary when he wakes in the morning, as he did when he went to bed."

"You've come at just the right time, John. Earlier today I took delivery on a patent medicine that's guaranteed to cure whatever ails you." Jake pulled a bottle out of an open crate. "Here, look this over while I get your order together. It will be ready in a minute."

"Take your time, Jake. There's no hurry."

The bell over the entrance jangled, announcing another shopper's arrival. The man struggled to close the heavy door against a blustery wind. After recovering from the effort, he prophesied loudly. "This unrelenting gale purports to foretell an onslaught of frigid weather." Striking an authoritative pose, his index finger raised, he exclaimed. "*When the wind is in the east, 'tis good for neither man nor beast. When the wind is in the north, the old folks dare not venture forth.*"

Jake and John stifled their laughter at the man's theatrical entrance, and exaggerated recitation. Then Jake greeted his venerable customer. "Good day, Reverend Bailey. If I didn't know better, I'd accuse you of eavesdropping. My friend here was just quoting some weather lore himself. Let me introduce you to John Hartman, one of the newest members of our community. He and his folks, James and Susanna, moved into the old Reynolds place on Union Road about six weeks ago. John, this is Reverend Franklin Bailey. He's the interim pastor at Scottsburg's Methodist Church, and he's also been known to auctioneer from time to time." The two men shook hands as Jake moved off to fill Susanna's order.

John addressed the clergyman respectfully. "It's a pleasure to meet you, Sir."

"Your most humble servant, young man," the reverend boomed.

"Is it not possible," John posed, "that the congregation might wish to make your position here a permanent one? Having spent considerable time serving on a selection committee, I know the process to find a new minister can often be a lengthy one."

The man of God spoke. "It seems we've had the same experience then, and I would not disagree with your conclusion about the time required to complete such a daunting task. Finding the right man to lead a church requires a considerable commitment of time and prayer, and the willingness to sufficiently compensate the chosen man. Scripture tells us in First Timothy 5:18 *Thou shalt not muzzle the ox that treadeth out the corn. The labourer is worthy of his reward.*

"I will admit the pulpit has been offered for my consideration, but for myriad reasons I must decline. Therefore, until the search for a suitable replacement is concluded, I will faithfully exhort and shepherd the Scottsburg flock. Sunday morning service commences at nine o'clock. You and your family would be most welcome to join us for worship."

John thanked him for the invitation, moving to the counter in response to Jake's signal that his order was ready. After paying, he bid both men a good day, and departed. John urged the team toward home, never suspecting that he was the subject of a continuing conversation inside the mercantile.

The reverend spoke first, "Jake, I find myself compelled to become better acquainted with Mr. John Hartman. What do you know of him?"

Shrugging his shoulders, the proprietor replied, "nothing much, other than what he's told me. It's just himself and his folks on the farm. I understand there are three married sisters living in Indiana."

Franklin digested that information for a moment before remarking, "he certainly makes a good first impression. It would be apparent to any casual observer that the man is fastidious, respectful, and well mannered. A very agreeable fellow to be sure, but not someone, I surmise, to be trifled with or easily manipulated."

"What are you getting at, Reverend," Jake asked?

"Oh, nothing to concern yourself with Jake. I venture to say a timely visit to the Hartman family may be incumbent upon me in the pursuit of my Christian duty. But now to more immediate business. Do you have any packages from New York for my wife and daughter?"

"As a matter of fact, yes," Jake replied, pulling several bulky parcels out from under the counter. "The total due for this order is twelve dollars, Reverend Bailey."

"Be a good fellow, and just add that to my account, won't you?" Without waiting for Jake to reply, the cleric swept the packages into his arms, and hurried out the door. As an afterthought, he called over his shoulder, "God bless you, Jake."

A powerful, gusting wind slowed John's progress on the way home. The rough road was bordered on either side by huge trees, and more than once he had to guide the horses around fallen limbs, blocking the way. Encouraging the matched pair of Belgians on, he kept a tight rein on the team and cast a wary eye on the branches whipping wildly overhead. John hoped his parents weren't worried for his safety in this gale. It wouldn't be good for either of them to be anxious on his account.

Maybe his response to Jake's inquiry about his folks hadn't been entirely truthful where their health was concerned, although John tried to convince himself they *were* fine, or would be with enough rest. The physical demands of the move had obviously taken its toll on both of them. His father seemed to require more rest than usual. Always her husband's polar opposite, Susanna exhibited an unflagging energy, suggestive of her nerves being overstimulated. She couldn't sit for more than a few minutes before jumping up to attend to one thing or another. Just yesterday, John found his mother in the kitchen, taking rapid, shallow breaths while pressing a hand to her chest. He'd wanted her to see a doctor, but she vowed to slow down. John knew her promise was only an attempt to appease him.

John decided that if the bottle of Universal Elixir purchased from Jake proved beneficial, he would definitely get more. The idea of losing either of his parents wasn't one he was ready to contemplate. He loved and admired both of them, even admitting to a bit of envy at their closeness with each other. What he wouldn't give to make such a match himself! The sense of something, or *someone,* missing from John's life had been intensifying over the last few years. He knew he could continue to get along on his own if he had to, but what joy was there in that? John envisioned a marriage where each partner fulfilled the deepest desires of the other. Whenever he contemplated finding a mate these days, his thoughts led unwaveringly to Katie Byler. Then, with a sharp pang of regret John would remember that Katie Byler no longer existed. She was Katie Hostettler now, Emmon's wife, and although he didn't know how to go about it, he knew he must find a way to make a life without her.

Nearing the end of his journey, John mused over the person of Reverend Bailey, and acknowledged to himself that he much preferred the temperament and humble nature of his own pastor. Unlike Franklin Bailey, Theodore Smith was down-to-earth and unpretentious. John supposed he could understand how Reverend Bailey's lofty manner and dramatic oratory might appeal to some folks, but he wondered about the man's true calling. It was somehow easier to picture him as an auctioneer, rather than a man of the cloth. There was little doubt in John's mind that Franklin could manage the fever pitch of an auction crowd to the seller's advantage, as well as for his own benefit.

At last, the house came into view ahead, and John turned into the drive toward the welcoming lamplight from the kitchen window.

Chapter 5

Katie's life had turned upside-down since Emmon's unexpected departure. It was almost shocking to consider that if events hadn't transpired to prevent their ill-fated marriage, she would now be Emmon's wife. It had taken some time for her to realize that his declaration about being unable to go through with the wedding, had unwittingly saved her from being the one responsible for ending the relationship.

Dat, spared the expense of time and money for a wedding, no longer had any reason to postpone his plan for swapping houses with Danny. Her brother and his family moved into the old Byler homestead, and Mamm and Dat settled into the smaller property. Katie went to live with her sister and brother-in-law, Betsy and Peter, in Clear Springs. She could have stayed with her folks. In fact, it was all but taken for granted that she would do just that, but Providence intervened. At the family gathering in November, Betsy had confided to Katie that she was expecting a baby in June of the coming year. Knowing her sister was anxious after miscarrying during her first pregnancy, Katie volunteered to move in with the expectant parents. She would take on the lion's share of housekeeping until after the baby was born, and Betsy could manage on her own. Mamm readily endorsed this plan, giving it her stamp of approval.

It turned out that being in a new community, able to make a fresh start away from the local busybodies, was just what Katie needed. There was a liberating atmosphere about Clear Springs that gave her an optimistic outlook for the future. Maybe it was all in her mind, but it seemed to her the sun shone brighter during the day, and likewise, the moon and stars at night. She reached the conclusion that a change of scenery was good medicine for body and soul.

The church in Clear Springs had welcomed Katie, and made her feel like she belonged. There were a number of unmarried people here, and although she tried to be at least open to the possibility of finding a special someone, none of the district's unattached young men had ignited in her more than a casual interest. Occasionally, she thought about Emmon, wondering whether or not he'd found whatever it was he was searching for.

As for John Hartman, questions about the bachelor persistently plagued her mind. *What was he doing? Would she ever see him again? Was he courting someone? Did he think about her? And where, exactly, was he living?* Katie had learned at the auction that Rose Ellen's parents, and John, were moving to a farm in Michigan. At the time, it hadn't occurred to Katie to ask *where* in Michigan. Well, she reasoned, wherever it was that John had moved, it might as well be on the other side of the world for all that separated them.

Fortunately, her sister's pregnancy was progressing normally. There was nothing out of the ordinary to raise any cause for concern. Katie hoped that would continue to be the case. Betsy deserved the joys of motherhood. She was a loving soul, and the most even-tempered person Katie knew, weathering the ups and downs of life with perfect equanimity, taking everything in stride. She would be a wonderful mamm, and Peter, . . . well, he would be the kind of dat any child would choose, if such a thing were possible. He was simply the biggest kid of all, disguised as a grown-up. Katie was very fond of her brother-in-law, despite his being an insufferable tease, and prone to boasting. Impending fatherhood had gone to his head, and Peter strutted around, proud as a peacock, telling everyone that he was sure the baby was a boy. Hooking his thumbs under the suspenders that kept his pants from falling off his skinny behind, Peter would inflate his chest and pronounce. "Yep, it's a boy! Couldn't be nothin' but a boy." Katie thought if he was proved right, his crowing would be beyond her ability to bear with good grace. Maybe that's why she took a perverse pleasure in provoking him, adopting strictly feminine pronouns whenever she mentioned the baby in Peter's company.

On orders from the midwife, Betsy napped every afternoon. To avoid disturbing her sister's rest, Katie occupied herself during this time with quiet pursuits. This afternoon, Peter was in the sitting room with her, studiously pouring over the almanac, engrossed in the long-range weather forecasts, moon phases, and planting calendars, while Katie concentrated on her needlework. Though it was mean of her, Katie gushed while hand stitching a tiny garment. "I can't wait to see my niece in this sweet little gown. She will be the prettiest baby girl ever!" Katie knew her brother-in-law well enough to know he couldn't let this statement go unchallenged and as expected, he rose to the bait.

"You mark my words, it'll be a boy," he said confidently, and then surprisingly, Peter made a rare concession. "But if you want to nitpick, it's only fittin' to say that nobody but the good Lord knows for certain whether Betsy and I will be bringin' a son or daughter into the world. So, tell me Aunt Katie, what makes *you* so sure it's a girl anyway?"

Katie laughed. "Well, Peter Christner, I know one thing for certain . . . it won't be *you* bringing the little one into the world. It will be my sister doing all the bringing that's to be done. Besides, I can tell you'll have a daughter by the way Betsy is carrying the baby, *high for boys, low for girls*. Or is it low for boys, high for girls?"

"See," Peter triumphed? "You don't know as much as you think you do."

"We'll just see about that when the time comes, won't we," Katie retorted?

"My goodness," Betsy interrupted, entering the room to stand between the warring parties. "What is all this bickering about? Are you still arguing whether the baby is a boy or a girl? Guess I'll just have one of each, and then you'll both be right."

Katie rose from the rocking chair. "Here Betsy, you sit

and mind Peter while I get supper. You can put the time to good use by practicing your mothering skills." Katie rolled her eyes and made a face at Peter as she left the room.

"That sister of yours . . ." Peter began in a huff, but Betsy placed a warning finger on his lips. After pressing a kiss on that appendage, he quickly amended what he'd been about to say. "That sister of yours has been a godsend to us both, and I say, bless her for takin' on the housekeeping during your confinement. Now, my sweet wife," he cajoled, catching hold of Betsy's hand, and pulling her closer. "Come and sit on my lap."

Katie fetched a jar of pickled relish from the cellar, then sliced a loaf of bread, some cheese and a cold, smoked ham. A bowl of sauerkraut, and one of applesauce, along with molasses cookies for dessert would nicely round out their evening meal. After setting out dinnerware, glasses and utensils, Katie added a pitcher of milk to the food already on the table.

Calling Betsy and Peter to the kitchen for supper, they sat and bowed their heads in silent prayer before partaking of the light meal. Talk around the table turned to preparations for the coming spring and summer.

Even though it was months away from being a possibility, Peter was just itching to get into the fields to work the soil and plant crops. Betsy and Katie spent considerable time reviewing their garden plans, and speculating whether or not they might need to purchase some seed from the general store to supplement the cache Betsy had saved from last year. Warmer weather couldn't come fast enough to suit any of them. Anticipation was already building for the enjoyment of wild asparagus, morel mushrooms, and juicy blackberries, foraged from the nearby woods.

As always, thoughts of the baby were uppermost in all their minds, and no evening ended without a review of the projects that must be completed before the little one's arrival. Peter had yet to put the finishing touches on a chest he was constructing for the baby's clothes. Betsy and Katie had made several baby quilts, and were sewing and knitting a quantity of other items necessary for the care of a newborn. As they talked, the sisters began clearing away the supper dishes and Betsy stifled a yawn. Katie nudged her sister while taking the stacked plates from her hands. "Go to bed, Betsy. You need your sleep." On his way out the kitchen door, Peter assured his wife he'd return as soon as he made certain all was safe and secure for the animals in the barn. He was back within half an hour, wishing his sister-in-law goodnight before climbing the stairs to join Betsy in their room.

After Peter's footsteps faded away, Katie took pleasure in the peacefulness that blanketed the house. This quiet time was the sacred benediction to her day. Since joining Betsy and Peter's household, Katie had made a surprising discovery about herself. As much as she delighted in the companionship of friends and loved ones, there were times she very much liked being alone. She'd lived all her life in the close company of others. Being part of a large family, and the youngest child as well, offered few opportunities for solitude, or contemplative thought.

After the kitchen was in order, Katie draped a heavy, woolen shawl around her shoulders, and ventured out into the darkness. It was so cold that taking a deep breath caused sharp, stinging sensations in her nose. Exhaling produced a frosty vapor, visible on the air. Although the night was moonless, the snowy landscape reflected the brightness of the stars filling the winter sky. It was a beautiful sight to behold. Long ago, Dat had acquainted her with several constellations, and now she easily found Orion, the mighty hunter of Greek mythology. He was right where he should be at this time of year, positioned to the southwest in his never-ending pursuit of the Pleiades. When Katie began shivering, she reluctantly returned to the warmth of the house.

Before slipping between the blankets, she knelt beside the bed and prayed for her family. Living so far from Shipshewana and her parents had taken some getting used to, but while she missed them, she couldn't say she was homesick. What Katie was actually, was happy and contented in Clear Springs, Michigan, a small Amish settlement on the outskirts of Scottsburg.

Chapter 6

Blast! Danny thought ruefully as he examined the horse's right forefoot to confirm his suspicions of a thrown shoe. *Of all the rotten luck! The day had begun so auspiciously. Well,* he chided himself, *you should have expected the roads to be a muddy mess after the recent thaw.* January and February had deposited heavy snows across northern Indiana and southern Michigan, making travel throughout the region nearly impossible during the first two months of the year. Then, March came in like a lamb, and the mild weather proved an irresistible temptation for a trip to Clear Springs, especially since Danny was eager to deliver a very special gift to his sister Betsy, and her husband.

After moving into the old Byler homestead this past December, Danny had found a forgotten treasure while rummaging through cast-off furniture in one of the unused bedrooms. A handsome cradle, expertly handcrafted in an earlier century had been tucked away in a back corner. When he'd asked Mamm about the origin of the cradle and its history, she told Danny the story of how it had been passed down through the family. Her parents, Valentine and Katarina Teis, had brought it all the way from Switzerland on the 1833 voyage that carried them across the Atlantic. The captain of the ship had strayed far north of the route he'd intended to sail, and his deviation from the charted course meant that the long voyage became longer still, and more treacherous. Many of the passengers grew alarmed when icebergs were sighted, floating in the water. Valentine's wife, and the wife of another immigrant were both heavily pregnant, each with their first child. After Katarina was safely delivered of a son, the other woman gave birth to a boy as well, but the little mother died in the process, and was buried at sea. Katarina nursed this motherless newborn, along with her own baby boy. Barbara marveled at the risk her parents had taken in their quest for a better life in America. A faraway look was on her face while she lovingly stroked the smooth wood, and Barbara grew pensive as she spoke to Danny.

"Abe and I never used this cradle for any of our children. He wanted to personally build one that would hold only Byler babies. When your brother, Joel, and his wife gave us our first grandchild, Dat gave them the cradle he'd made. It troubles me to think my family heirloom should be going to waste in this old house. This precious cradle should be put to use, rocking a new generation of babies to sleep. Will you take it to Betsy and Peter for me?"

Danny readily agreed. After being cleaned and polished, the cradle was loaded with jars of pickles, jams and relishes nestled in among piles of homemade diapers for Abe and Barbara's coming grandchild.

Deacon, Danny's horse, whinnied and pawed the ground bringing his master back to their present predicament. Taking in his surroundings, Danny considered his options. The farrier in Scottsburg wasn't that far away, probably only a mile or two down the road, but he didn't want to risk Deacon coming up lame from pulling the buggy any farther. Turning back now was out of the question, too. He could unhitch the horse and walk him to the blacksmith shop in Scottsburg, although he didn't like the idea of leaving the buggy with its precious cargo unattended alongside the road. The oft repeated words of his father came to mind, "Son, when you don't know what to do, that's when you know . . . it's time to pray." Danny thought it was sound advice, and bowed his head. He looked up at the sound of someone approaching. A man on horseback was drawing near to the intersection of Union and Pigeon roads, and as the rider came close enough for a better look, Danny waved. "Ditcher, it's about time you got here!"

"Sorry to keep you waiting," John Hartman countered, while reining his horse to a stop and dismounting. "Now what kind of trouble have you gotten yourself into?"

The two friends greeted each another warmly as Danny laid out his dilemma. He'd been on his way to the Amish settlement of Clear Springs to visit his sister and brother-in-law when Deacon had most inconsiderately thrown a shoe.

John pondered Danny's problem, searching for a solution. "Well, here's an idea. How about we hitch Blaze to the buggy and tie Deacon off the back? When we get to Scottsburg, we'll leave your horse with the blacksmith and travel on to Clear Springs in the buggy. You can collect Deacon on the return trip. What do you think?"

"What do I think? Here's what I think -- we're standing around burnin' daylight here, let's go! But wait, it's clear you have your own plans. I won't ask you to change them, and disrupt your whole day. If you could just see us as far as the blacksmith, I can wait there until Deacon can be shoed."

"It's no bother Danny, and you didn't ask me to do anything, I offered," John said. "I was just on my way to the library, but it's nothing that can't wait. Our chance meeting is just the opportunity I've been hoping for to catch up on all the latest news from Shipshewana."

Without further delay, John's suggestion was put into action. After leaving Deacon at Barton's Smithy in Scottsburg, the two men were soon headed in the direction of Clear Springs. While enjoying the fine day and each other's company, they talked about the weather, farming, and the waning nineteenth century, speculating on what changes might lie ahead. As they covered the miles, John kept hoping Danny might say something about Katie. Determined not to ask outright, John craved any word of her, still unable to think of Katie as Emmon's wife.

When they came upon the sign announcing their arrival at Clear Springs, Danny abruptly removed his hat and handed it to John. "Notice anything different about my hat?"

"Such as," John asked, turning the brim around in his

hands? "It looks just the same as it was before."

"Exactly! And do you happen to remember what I said about my hat at your folks' auction?"

"Not particularly," John said disinterestedly, handing the black, broad-brimmed hat back to its owner.

"I was sure you'd remember what I said I'd do if a certain younger sister of mine went through with her marriage to Emmon." Danny prompted, "just think about it!"

John felt like he'd been transported back to the classroom and was being quizzed by an impatient schoolmaster. Obediently, he applied his full concentration to finding the right answer, and dutifully recited from memory: "you said: *If I were a bettin' man, I'd wager Katie will never go through with this marriage, and if she does, I'll eat my hat!*"

"Right! Give the scholar a passing mark! So now tell me, John, do you see any signs of nibblin' there?"

Suddenly speechless, John became aware that his heart rate had cranked up several notches, and he could hear it pounding in his ears. "Are you saying that Katie isn't married? Not to Emmon? Not to anyone?"

"I never figured you to be so slow on the uptake, Ditcher. That's exactly what I'm sayin'."

"But, wait just a minute," John said. "Why are you telling *me* this? Aren't you the one who warned me away from your sister with all that talk of *obstacles* barring the way of any possible relationship between us?"

"Well, yes," Danny admitted, "I did mention obstacles, but maybe I don't exactly view them as insurmountable anymore. And, bein' an interested party to the outcome of all this fuss and bother, there's a couple reasons I figured you should be informed as to the present state of affairs. First of all, Emmon ran out on Katie in November, leavin' a cowardly note tellin' her he couldn't bring himself to go through with their marriage. It was a shock to the whole family. Then, Katie told me that she'd already made up her mind to call off the engagement, but Emmon beat her to the punch. Now, it's for sure and certain I never saw any sign of tender feelings between those two, but that day at the auction, I witnessed a spark catch fire when you and Katie locked eyes with each other. It's as clear as day to me that you and my little sister belong together, despite the fact that she's vowed to remain a spinster for the rest of her life. If you care for Katie like I believe you do, you have my blessing to court her."

"And it's just that easy," John asked, arching his right eyebrow? "What about that little impediment of my not being Amish? Wouldn't the shunning she'd have to endure be an insurmountable obstacle for Katie?"

"I never said it would be easy, John. But if the idea of her being shunned is the only thing holdin' you back, I hope you won't let it stand in your way. Fact is, Katie hasn't joined the church yet, and until a young person makes that binding covenant, shunning wouldn't be applied. Now, that don't mean you both won't meet with some strong resistance, but Katie wouldn't be the first, and she won't be the last, to listen to her heart and marry for love. Most of my Amish brethren would consider the advice I'm giving you an act of heresy, but come what may, I'll stand by you."

"Well Danny, your loyalty is downright commendable," John said. "Although now you've got me wondering what it might actually be like to have *you* for a brother-in-law? And while I'm wondering, what's the second reason for cluing me in on your sister's *eligible-for-courting* status at this particular moment in time?"

"I think I may have forgotten to mention," Danny said with a grin, "that Katie is stayin' in Clear Springs with Betsy and Peter for the next several months. So, look sharp, John! In two shakes of a lamb's tail, you and Katie will be comin' face to face with each other for the first time since November."

Chapter 7

From the kitchen where she was stirring a pot of soup, Katie heard the front door open and close. An instinctive wariness about who had entered the house, was instantly dispelled when she identified the unmistakable voice of her favorite brother. After carefully moving the heavy pot off the hot burner, she wiped her hands on her apron, and hurried to greet Danny.

Katie called out while entering the room, "Hey! We didn't know you were . . ." she stopped mid-sentence, recognizing John Hartman at her brother's side.

"There's no need to be shy, Katie. You know John. Why, if he hadn't come to my rescue today, I wouldn't be here now."

"It's a pleasure to see you again, Katie," John said.

"And you, too . . . both of you." Katie pointed to a large, unwieldy bundle they'd placed on the floor. "What's this, Danny?"

"It's a surprise for Betsy and Peter. Where are they?"

"They went calling on some neighbors, but they'll be back shortly. I told them dinner would be ready soon," Katie answered.

Danny sniffed appreciatively. "Somethin' smells mighty good, I hope we get a dinner invitation. Do I detect the aroma of your apple pie?"

"Yes, you do. I baked two pies earlier and have two more in the oven. And, of course you'll stay for dinner," Katie assured him. Turning, she addressed her next remark to John, "I hope you like Dutch apple pie."

"It's my favorite," he said, his eyes focused on a slight smudge of flour, adorning one of her rosy cheeks. John imagined reaching out with his fingers to caress her soft skin while brushing away the telltale evidence of baking.

"Well, I hope my recipe doesn't disappoint," Katie said retreating to the kitchen. "Excuse me while I check the oven and set the table."

In the privacy of the kitchen, Katie quickly ran a hand over her face, and shook out her apron to remove any traces of flour. There were butterflies in her stomach, and seeing John again made her feel light-headed. He was even more handsome than she remembered. She was anxious to learn how he had rescued Danny.

Finding the pies done to perfection, she removed them from the oven, replacing them with a pan of cornmeal muffins. After adding two more plates and bowls to those already on the table, she squeezed a kitchen stool between two of the four chairs. Freshly churned butter, and a jar of strawberry jam were set out within easy reach. There being nothing more that required her immediate attention, she returned to the front room just as Peter and Betsy came through the door.

"We wondered who was here," Peter said. "How are you, Danny? Did you buy a new horse?"

"No, that's Blaze, John's horse. You remember 'Ditcher' Hartman from our old school days, don't you?"

Peter nodded and clasped John's hand. "Of course, I do. Always good to see you again, Ditcher. I guess the last time we saw each other was at the sale of your family's farm last November."

"Yes," John agreed, "time flies, doesn't it? Now that we live close to Scottsburg, we're practically neighbors. I didn't know you lived in Clear Springs. You and Betsy have a nice place here."

"Good of you to say so, John. We consider ourselves blessed. How did it happen your horse is pullin' Danny's buggy?"

"That's a long story, Peter. One that will probably get even longer by the time Danny's finished with it."

Danny took John's remark as a cue to begin his tale. "Well, I started on my way here before daybreak to make a special delivery, and it wasn't long before I found myself in a real quandary. I hadn't taken into consideration just how sloppy the roads would be. Then, Deacon threw a shoe somewhere along the muddy roads outside of Scottsburg, leavin' me at an impasse. Not wantin' to drive Deacon any further, I wasn't sure how I could complete my mission, until John came ridin' along -- in answer to my prayer it should be said. He turned out to be my good Samaritan today. It was his brilliant idea to hitch Blaze to the buggy, and leave Deacon with the blacksmith while we drove on to Clear Springs. I owe him a debt of gratitude."

"A special delivery," Betsy asked? "What is it?"

"Well, I'm not goin' to tell. You can guess if you want to, or you can open it."

Betsy peeled away layers of protective wrapping to reveal the cradle, laden with a treasure trove of smaller gifts. Danny recounted in detail his discovery of the cradle, and shared with his listeners the history of its incredible journey across the ocean. Betsy wiped away a tear when he talked of their mamm's desire to see the heirloom passed down to her and Peter. After the cradle had been thoroughly admired, Betsy asked Peter and Danny to carry it upstairs. Leading the way, she warned her husband and brother to be careful on the steps, and suggested John and Katie take the jams, relishes and pickles into the kitchen.

While they were putting the jars into a jelly cupboard, John gathered his courage. "Danny told me you'll be staying with Peter and Betsy to help out around the house, and with the baby when it comes. That's very kind of you."

"I'd do anything to help Betsy, or any of my sisters," Katie asserted, taking a quick peek into the oven to check the muffins. Satisfied that they were ready, she set them out to cool on the surface of a large wooden butcher's block.

John took a deep breath. "I hope I'm not being too forward, Katie, but with your permission, I'd like to call on you while you're in Clear Springs. Would you be agreeable to spending some time with me? You see, Danny thought it would be a good idea if we got to know each other better. How do you feel about that? I could drive you to Scottsburg someday, and show you around the town. Would you like that? Or, we could just go driving around the countryside. What do you think, Katie?"

In the absence of any response from her, John felt himself foundering as he rambled on. Wasn't she going to say anything? Maybe he should just shut up. It occurred to John that if Katie didn't put him out of his misery soon by giving him an answer, he might derive great satisfaction from inflicting some pain on her brother during their return trip.

Finally, after a silence that seemed to last for hours, Katie said. "I don't know what to say, John. I'm flattered by your attention, but I need time to think it over before giving you an answer. Is that all right?"

"Of course, take all the time you need. I don't mean to rush you, especially after the breakup with Emmon. Danny told me all about it, but I can't say I'm sorry you aren't married."

"I appreciate that," she replied. "John, could I ask you to do something for me?"

"Anything Katie, just name it. What can I do?"

"Would you let the others know that dinner is ready?"

John felt his jaw clench involuntarily. "Be happy to," he muttered, and nearly collided with Danny in the hallway while fleeing the kitchen.

Danny flattened himself along the wall to avoid being run down. "Whoa Son, somethin' got you spooked?"

"Just coming to announce that dinner is ready," John replied, frustration evident in his tone and gritted teeth.

"Well now, Betsy and Peter are right behind me so you'd best turn around before you get stampeded. It's not a good idea to dally on the way to the table. You'll soon see for yourself that Katie's cookin' is second to none." Danny linked his arm through

John's and towed him back to the kitchen.

Peter sat at the head of the table, the girls on his left, Danny on his right and John directly across from him. There was a minimum of small talk, and after everyone had eaten their fill of soup and muffins, Katie cleared away the bowls while Betsy cut one of the still warm pies.

John was sure he'd never enjoyed a tastier apple pie, and he savored every sweet, spicy bite. Sweeter still, he thought, was the smile he received from Katie after he praised her baking.

After the meal, Peter offered to show John the newest project he was working on in his toolshed. According to Danny, Peter prided himself on being an inventor, and he was always tinkering with something. His latest undertaking sat prominently on the workbench, displayed in pride of place. The contraption bore a questionable resemblance to a cage, but was constructed of old bed springs, rusted cast iron window sash weights, door hinges, and a crank handle that was immoveable. John studied it over, first from one angle and then another, while Peter stood with his arms crossed over his chest, a self-satisfied grin on his face. When it was impossible to restrain himself any longer, Peter blurted out. "Ain't it somethin'? I bet you never seen one like it before, John."

"No, I can't say as I have, Peter. What is it? That is, what does it do?"

"Well, I don't rightly know, but it must do somethin' useful, and even if it don't, then it's just inspirin' to look at!"

"What do you call it? Do you have a name for it?"

"Nope. I give each one of my creations a number. This is number twenty-two. I don't mess with names."

"Numbering sounds like a well-organized system, Peter. So, you've thought up twenty-one inventions before this one?"

"Shucks no. There must be about forty up in the loft. When I make a new one, I just pick a number I ain't used before. Would you like to climb up and see the rest?"

"Well, I wish I could Peter, but I have to get Danny back

to the blacksmith so he can be on his way home. Maybe another time."

"You'd be welcome anytime, John. And, I think my little sister-in-law would be happy to see you, too."

Danny was sharing all the latest family gossip with his sisters when Betsy asked if he'd take a letter she'd written to their folks. She just wanted to add a note of thanks for the cradle. He nodded, and while she rushed upstairs to add the postscript, Katie cornered her brother.

"John asked if he could call on me," she whispered. "He said *you* told him it would be a good idea for us to get to know each other. Did you really say that?"

"Yep, I'm guilty as charged," he confessed. "Look, there's no point pretendin' there's not somethin' between the two of you, and I think you should find out what it is. So, what was your answer?"

"I said I needed time to think about it," she replied.

"What? When were you ever the cautious one? Well, don't think too long, Baby Sister," he advised in mock sincerity, "you're not gettin' any younger, you know."

Katie playfully swatted his arm and their confidential conversation was cut short as Betsy descended the stairs. "Here's the letter, and thanks for delivering it," she said, handing him the sealed envelope.

When the little group gathered outside before parting, Betsy noticed that Katie was nowhere to be seen. Just as Danny offered to find out what was keeping her, she breezed through the front door, carrying a covered basket. He smiled broadly, extending his arms to receive the basket, but Katie walked deliberately past him, stopping in front of John. "You deserve a special reward for coming to Danny's aid today. Please accept this pie as a token of my gratitude. I hope you enjoy it."

As they drove away, Danny asked his friend, "so what did you think of Peter's machine?"

"Well Danny, it's hard to put into words. I can't make

any sense of that helter-skelter conglomeration of his, but that doesn't prove anything. Peter might be an eccentric genius for all I know. You never can tell."

"Now you're just bein' kind, John. Peter's one of my favorite people, and Betsy adores him, but let's face it, the man is as mad as a March Hare. He's a little crazy, but perfectly harmless. I just pray he lets Betsy name the baby. She says he wants to call it whatever number the day of the month is when it's born. Can you imagine?"

"Oh, come on now, Danny. You're pulling my leg."

Stopping in front of the blacksmith shop, John unhitched Blaze while Danny settled his bill, and led Deacon outside to be harnessed. After Blaze was saddled, John reached inside the buggy to snag the basket Katie had given him, but found another hand holding onto the handle. He promptly manacled Danny's wrist in an iron grip. "Mine," John warned with a growl.

With a devilish twinkle in his eye, Danny released the pie basket to his friend. "Well, you can't blame a guy for tryin,' Ditcher."

Chapter 8

The two men parted in Scottsburg, each one continuing separately on his homeward journey. Twilight deepened gradually, until even the faintest trace of light was nearly lost in the falling night. The way ahead was dark, lit only by the moon and stars overhead. John knew most folks avoided traveling these country backroads after the sun went down, but he embraced the feeling of having the whole world all to himself. He took pleasure in the solitude and peacefulness, broken only by the sounds of nocturnal creatures. An owl's haunting calls, or the chatter of a family of racoons were commonplace noises. Tonight, the distinctive chirping of spring peepers, combined with the sharp, green scent of the new season was a fitting accompaniment to the lightness of his heart.

The refrain, "Katie isn't married, she isn't married, isn't married," played over and over in his head, like the chorus of a happy song. He couldn't keep a smile from his face as he remembered how she had carried that pie straight over to him, much to Danny's surprise and chagrin. When Katie presented the basket to John, lifting it reverently like an offering, the answer to his earlier question about calling on her, shone clearly in her smiling eyes. The realization of her cleverness dawned on him then, as the necessity for returning the empty basket was implicit in his acceptance of the gift. He was emboldened to think that her heart was his for the asking, and although Katie may not know it yet, she already possessed John's, and would hold it forever.

Danny said he'd seen sparks fly between John and Katie in November. He wasn't about to quibble with Katie's brother over that analogy, but for him the most apt description of that initial contact was like being hit by a thunderbolt, leaving him unable to think or speak. Was that the moment he fell in love with Katie, or had he always loved her? What he believed for certain was that a Higher Power had a hand in bringing the two of them together from their first encounter with each other as children.

Something else Danny said came back to John, a reference to his old friend's being an *interested party* to the outcome of their courtship. That gave him pause. What, he wondered, would it be like to have Danny for a brother-in-law? How about a whole boatload of Amish in-laws, would they all be *interested parties,* too? If so, the number of people in that category was staggering. It looked like his life was about to get a lot more interesting, so he'd better get ready.

Of course, he hadn't proposed to Katie yet, but John wanted to get married as soon as possible. Now that she was free of Emmon, John wasn't about to take any chance of someone else swooping in to claim her. All at once, he was overwhelmed by the thought of everything that must be accomplished before they could even set a date. There was so much to do, it was difficult to know where to begin. The farm work had to take priority at this time of year, there was no getting away from that, but it wasn't too early to take on a couple hired hands to start working in the fields.

It was also time to open the beehives to ensure that the remaining stores of honey in each hive were adequate for that colony's survival until plants and trees were producing nectar and pollen for the bees to forage. Honey and beeswax were high demand, quality commodities, and John had plans to expand the apiary in coming years for increased production.

Another item at the top of this list he was compiling in his head, was an evaluation of the original homesteader's cabin. Its dilapidated appearance aside, John hoped that if the humble shelter wasn't too far gone, it might serve as he and Katie's first home. Tomorrow he would assess its condition and structural soundness. Maybe it wasn't as bad as it looked from a distance.

Most importantly, he would make sure to allot all the time he could spare for courting. That would be the sweetest and easiest labor of all. When he returned the basket, Katie could tell him what day and time would be best for his visits. Even though John already knew he loved Katie with all his heart, Danny was right, they needed to get to know each other better. She personified his ideal woman: feminine, caring, intelligent, attractive and self-assured. It was everything he *didn't* know about Katie that intrigued him. Discovering the nuances of her personality was something he looked forward to, and where John thought he might be in for some surprises.

John was so absorbed in the contemplation and appreciation of Katie's finer points, that if Blaze hadn't turned into the drive of his own volition, John would have passed right by the house.

Halting a moment by the kitchen stoop, John lifted the basket off the saddle horn and entered the dimly lit kitchen to set it on the table for safekeeping. After leading Blaze to the barn, John removed the tack and vigorously applied a brush to his horse's coat. The stallion expressed his approval with a nod and John stroked the powerful neck. "You did me proud today, boy. I hope you're prepared for more trips in the coming months."

John was not surprised to find his mother standing beside the cookstove when he walked back into the kitchen. "If you're hungry, I can make something for you to eat," she offered.

"No. Thanks anyway. I think I'll just turn in." John moved toward the back stairs, knowing she would momentarily call him back to satisfy her curiosity about where he'd been all day. When the expected summons didn't come, he turned to look at her, and saw a teasing grin on her face.

"I unpacked the basket and put your pie away, John. In the morning, you can tell me all about the sweet, young thing who baked it for you."

Confound it all, he thought as his head hit the pillow, there's no keeping anything secret from that woman.

Though John's last conscious thought before sleep had been of his mother, memories of Katie dominated his waking awareness of the new day. She was his inspiration, and the motivating force for his future. John rose early, anxious to get a head start on his work. He'd begin with a thorough inspection of the old homestead after downing some coffee and a cold biscuit. When a plate of bacon, eggs, fried potatoes, and hotcakes was placed before him, the notion of a hasty breakfast was quickly forgotten. "Where's Father?" John asked, reaching for the pitcher of maple syrup as his mother brought him a cup of steaming coffee.

"He's in the barn, breaking in the new hired hands before planting time."

John's eyebrows raised, "I didn't know he'd already taken on some farm help."

"He hired them yesterday," his mother replied, "while you were occupied elsewhere. And speaking of yesterday, are you going to tell me all about it, or will the details be left to my overactive imagination? I thought you were going to the library."

John's defenses went up, and he avoided her eyes. "Well, if you must know, I just happened to run into Danny Byler on his way to visit his sister and brother-in-law over in Clear Springs. His horse had thrown a shoe, leaving Danny stranded along the road. So, I hitched Blaze to the buggy, we left Deacon with the blacksmith, and I drove Danny to his destination. We stayed for dinner, visited awhile, and that's what happened. Now you know all there is to know," he finished smugly, raising the cup to his mouth.

"Hmm, yes, I think I see. You got sidetracked in the performance of a good deed. That is most admirable, and I am proud of you. It's said that kindness is its own reward. Still, you have to admit it was very nice of Katie to send that pie home with you."

John almost choked on his coffee, "Katie! Who said anything about Katie?"

She laughed at his discomfiture. This verbal sparring between mother and son was a style of communication exclusive to the two of them, and normally enjoyed by both.

His mother said, "*I* mentioned Katie – and then *you* got all flustered. You know she really is the sweetest girl. I so appreciated her help on the day of the auction. Now finish your breakfast, John, and quit dawdling. You've got plenty of work to do before you make Katie my daughter-in-law."

Staring at the old homestead, John's first thought was that anyone in his right mind would consider the primitive structure a blight on the landscape, and set it ablaze. John resisted the urge to adopt that conclusion as his own. Instead, he cast a practiced eye over the rustic dwelling while painstakingly picking his way through a thicket of prickly brambles and locust saplings that threatened to reclaim this space for wilderness. At least twenty trees in close proximity to the cabin would have to come down. John inspected the roof as much as he was able from his vantage point on the ground, promising himself an up-close look later. The cedar shakes that had been used to shingle the roof had aged to a silvery gray, and though weathered, they looked to be intact. No obvious damage was visible to either gable end, and it pleased him to see that all the vertical components of the building's construction were plumb. A massive, stone chimney had been laid up along the west end of the cabin, and it too, looked to be in sound condition. Wooden shutters covered the window openings. Those would have to be removed, in order to see what they were hiding. It was a bit of luck that the fieldstone foundation had been largely protected by broad overhangs. As a result, only minimal tucking and repointing of mortar would be necessary. The biggest concern about the condition of the exterior was an invasion of honeysuckle growing too near the cabin. It had established a foothold, and would need digging out. The vines had run riot over the porch and along the front of the little house, which he guessed to be constructed of chestnut logs.

Before commencing an inspection of the interior, John

took his hammer and pry bar in hand to pull nails from the wide, flat planks that had been used to secure the shutters. Tossing the rough sawn timber off to one side, he opened the shutters, latching them alongside each window, allowing light to penetrate the darkness inside. After removing the boards nailed across the front door, he pushed down on the handle's lever, and forced the door open with a hard shove of his shoulder. A cloud of dust raised by the action of the door sweeping inward, made him sneeze.

To his left, a large, open room ran the full depth of the interior from front to back. It was bordered on the west wall by a wide hearth, and on the east side by a wall with two doors opening into small bedrooms. The front half of the spacious area next to the fireplace was obviously the main gathering place. The kitchen took up the back third of the room. Tucked into a corner by the back door was a narrow staircase leading to an open loft built over the bedrooms. A miscellany of discarded objects left by the former occupant, gave evidence of the loft's use as a storeroom.

He found the layout of the cabin to his liking, and the condition actually much better than what he'd been expecting. Once it was thoroughly cleaned, little else would be required to make the cabin inhabitable once again. A few homey touches here and there, might even make the place charming.

Satisfied with his findings, John formulated a plan, and was methodically gathering up his tools when the frantic clanging of the dinner bell startled him. He sprinted toward the house, aware that this tolling of the bell was not the usual signal for mealtime. It was an alarm! Something was terribly wrong!

Chapter 9

The scene that met John's eyes when he raced into view of the house, could only be described as one of complete and utter chaos. Two frightened and crying children were being shepherded through the kitchen door ahead of his mother as she tried to comfort and shield them. Only steps away, his father, and sister, Musetta, were engaged in a desperate struggle with a woman who was keening loudly, and flailing wildly about as they attempted to restrain her. John realized with a shock, that the woman fighting fiercely to free herself from their grasp was Isabel. His beautiful sister was almost unrecognizable in her anguish. He moved quickly behind her, telling his father and Musetta to release their hold when he counted to three. One! Two! Three! They staggered away, spent from the tussle, and in one swift movement John pinned Isabel's arms alongside her body, imprisoning her within his strong embrace.

Calling over and over to her in a calm, controlled voice, he strove to break through whatever agony was holding his sister in its thrall.

"Belle, Belle! Isabel, listen. It's me, John. I'm right here with you. Hush now, hush. I'm not going to leave you. Please don't struggle, Belle. You'll only wear yourself out. Listen to me, Belle. Listen. You are safe, no one can hurt you. I've got you, Belle, it's all right, it's all right. Close your eyes, Honey, and breathe. Breathe, that's a good girl."

Isabel's breathing moderated to ragged, body-wracking gasps. Trembling violently, she slumped against her brother, her strength gone. She fell into unconsciousness, and John lifted her gently. His father and Musetta followed as he carried Isabel upstairs to a bedroom where he lowered her limp body onto the bed. Musetta quickly pulled a quilt from the linen press, and laid it over the still form of her sister.

"She'll be all right now, John. I'll stay with her until Henry return for me."

Father lowered his voice to a whisper, leaning close to John. "Come, let's go to the parlor where we can talk."

John held his desire to learn what catastrophe had befallen Isabel in check, until after the pocket doors closed. "What happened?"

Motioning his son to take a seat, John's father restlessly paced the floor before giving his account of the dire circumstances.

"I was just coming in from the barn when Henry Kline careened off the road, driving his team hell-bent-for-leather, right up to the kitchen door. Isabel was delirious, screaming that she wanted to die, and Musetta was being buffeted about as she tried to prevent Isabel from throwing herself out of the wagon. Johnny and Eliza were paralyzed with fright, crying as they witnessed their mother out of her mind, raving like a mad woman. That's when Mother rang the dinner bell to call you back to the house. Between us, Henry and I managed to get everyone safely out of the wagon, and before he left to go for Rose Ellen and Edward, he told me what happened."

"Friedrich Bachman was killed in a horrible accident at the mill this morning. If that news wasn't bad enough, the fool dispatched to inform Isabel of her husband's death spared her none of the gory details in his telling. Mercifully, she and the children weren't alone when she was informed of Friedrich's death. Henry and Musetta were visiting, and when the messenger persisted in his graphic narrative, Henry grabbed the man and hauled him outside, threatening to contact the mill's owner."

"Poor Belle," John cried, "and the children! How did this accident happen? Did Henry have any more details to share with you?"

"No. There wasn't any time to discuss it further. If he knows more on the subject, we'll have to wait for his return to hear it."

At the sound of doors sliding open, Father paused to see who was entering the parlor. Wiping her eyes, Mother sat beside him, and rested her head against his shoulder.

"Johnny's worried about his mama, and begged to see her. He said he had to know she wasn't dead, like their father. It broke my heart when he said that, and I let both of the children peek into the room so they could see her. I've just come from giving them a small dose of laudanum and putting them to bed. They're young, and will recover from this loss, but my greatest worry is for Isabel. She has such a fragile psyche; I don't know how she will handle this terrible blow. She cannot be left to manage on her own right now."

"No, that is out of the question," John agreed. "I think she and the children must make their home with us."

Father nodded. "Let's get them moved here as quickly as possible. When Henry returns, he and I will make plans for loading up all their things."

Withdrawing a wallet from an inside vest pocket, he handed John several folded bills. "I believe we may assume Friedrich's body is at the mortuary in Vistula. John, I know this is a lot to ask of you, but would you take care of the necessary arrangements?"

Without any hesitation, John agreed. "Of course. You can count on me to take care of everything there. I'll just change clothes and be on my way."

Anxious to get this unpleasant task over and done with, John set out with Blaze at a brisk gait. On the road he thought about his sister. There were only eighteen months separating them in age. She was his first sibling, and he'd laid claim to her from the moment he saw her. Only a toddler himself when she was born, he'd immediately disliked the hissing sound of the name their parents had bestowed on his little sister, and promptly shortened it to *Belle*. From then on it remained his special name for her. She was born with stars in her eyes, and a song in her heart. Belle grew quickly into a trusting, carefree child, ready to believe whatever she was told, however far-fetched or fanciful. From early on John recognized that his sister would need protection in this world, and stoutly declared himself her defender.

He and Belle seldom disagreed about anything . . . until Friedrich appeared on the scene years later. John's sister gained renown as a ravishing beauty. Belle and Friedrich met at the home of a mutual acquaintance, and the dashing older man, possessed of polished manners and a smooth, continental charm, effortlessly swept Belle off her feet. John was wary of this smooth talker, and learned after making discreet inquiries that Friedrich was known to have a weakness for hard liquor and gambling. He'd also been implicated in the ruin of a formerly respectable young woman's reputation. Although John tried to caution her against a hasty marriage, Belle refused to hear him out. As a last resort, he confronted Friedrich privately, going so far as to threaten the man with physical injury if he didn't leave his sister alone. Friedrich's only response had been to laugh in his face. John knew then which of them held the winning hand. Although John was confident that he could physically best this sorry excuse for a man, it would be impossible to overcome Belle's blind devotion to Friedrich.

The couple married seven years ago after the briefest of engagements, and without Father's blessing. Johnny was born two years later, and Eliza arrived on her brother's first birthday. From all outward appearances, the little family was living a life of domestic bliss.

John knew the darker reality of the heartache hidden behind the smiling face his sister presented to the world. Increasingly when he called, she and the children were found without adequate heat or food in the house. The light in Belle's lovely eyes had been extinguished and replaced with a dull, haunted expression. His vivacious and free-spirited sister appeared more diminished each time he saw her. Finding it useless to ask questions she refused to answer, he gave up prodding for information, and simply insisted she take the money he pressed into her hand.

Though John felt no sorrow to learn of Friedrich's death, it pained him greatly to witness Belle's suffering, and he prayed that one day she might be blessed with a full measure of peace and joy in her life. In Vistula, he dismounted and tied Blaze to the railing outside of Ferrin and Sons Mortuary. When greeted by an attendant, John introduced himself, stating his business with the funeral home. He was ushered into Mr. Ferrin's office to consult with the gentleman. After confirming that Friedrich's body had been received by the undertaker, John stated the family's desire for a modest funeral to take place the day after tomorrow. A simple casket, and graveside service would be all that was required. When asked for particulars of the deceased's date of birth and parentage, John could provide only sketchy biographical details. He knew Friedrich had immigrated from Germany about twenty years ago, and to the best of John's knowledge, he had no living relatives, apart from his wife and children. After reaching an agreement for the cost of services, John paid the deposit. Then, he asked to see the body, and requested that all personal effects be released to him.

"I regret to say that no personal belongings were discovered on his person," Mr. Ferrin replied.

A little warning bell sounded in John's head. "Am I to understand you found nothing? Not a folding knife, coin purse, or pocket watch in his clothing? Nothing at all?"

"That is correct. Mr. Bachman's apparel was damaged beyond salvaging, although his shoes are still in our possession."

"So," John persisted, "you didn't think the absence of personal belongings at all suspicious?"

"Unusual perhaps, but suspicious? You understand, of course, that we have no control over the body until it is delivered to us. For all I know, any belongings on his person may have been removed before he came into our care."

John demanded, "I think I must see the body now."

"That is your right, Mr. Hartman, but I strongly advise against it. Mr. Bachman sustained severe damage in the accident."

"That is beside the point, Sir. As my sister's representative in this matter, I insist on viewing the remains."

Reluctantly, Mr. Ferrin acquiesced. Together, they traversed a warren of hallways before entering a cold, stark room, reeking of formaldehyde, and other disagreeable odors. The undertaker directed him to the side of a table, and whisked back the sheet to reveal what was left of Friedrich Bachman. The sight of a corpse, mangled beyond recognition, caused John's gorge to rise in his throat. Swallowing hard while taking shallow breaths, he forced himself to scrutinize the body for anything that might confirm his brother-in-law's identity. No conclusion could be drawn from the man's ruined features, but John's gaze lingered on the hands.

"Friedrich wore a distinctive gold and diamond ring on his right hand, but there is no ring there now. I've never seen him without it."

Bristling, Mr. Ferrin took offense. "I hope you are not suggesting any impropriety on my part, or that of anyone in my employ?"

"It was not my intention to infer anything of the sort, Mr. Ferrin," John explained. "I was merely making an observation. I know the man never removed that ring."

In a somewhat mollified tone, the mortician suggested, "perhaps he took it off before going to work at the sawmill?"

"I think it unlikely," John replied. "He was a purchasing agent, not a sawyer."

"Then," Mr. Ferrin concluded, "it would be my recommendation that you talk to his former employer."

The hour was too late to find anyone at the mill, so John reined Blaze toward home. As he rode, words from scripture came unbidden to his mind, "Sufficient unto the day, is the evil thereof."

Chapter 10

Immediately after returning from the funeral parlor, John checked on Isabel and the children. He found his sister's condition much the same as when he left, and a quick glance into the room where Johnny and Eliza were sleeping revealed his mother, keeping watch. She held a finger to her lips, cautioning him not to speak as she rose quietly to join him in the hallway. Whispering her intention to maintain vigil for a while longer, she told John his father was waiting for him downstairs. After kissing her cheek, he headed toward the parlor.

James Hartman listened carefully to all John had to say about his visit with the undertaker, becoming increasingly disturbed by the account his son was giving.

"I don't like it, John. Something isn't adding up as it should, and since Mr. Ferrin claims not to know what happened to Friedrich's personal belongings, we have no recourse but to investigate the matter ourselves. I've made plans with Henry and Edward to help me move Isabel's things here tomorrow. It's up to you to deal with Friedrich's employer."

Early the next morning, John traveled to the sawmill, timing his arrival so that he would be waiting when the owner made his appearance. Someone here had to know something, and he was going to get answers to his questions. It soon became apparent that John was about to be sorely disappointed in his expectation of getting a thorough recounting of the accident.

Jasper Gosling's temperament was not improved when the businessman arrived to find John Hartman waiting for him. Not bothering to hide the irritation he felt at having his schedule interrupted, he revealed his displeasure with a scowl at the receptionist after being informed of the reason for his visitor's call. Mr. Gosling stomped into his office, leaving the door ajar, and calling out impatiently, "I haven't any time for questions this morning, Mr. Hartman. Due to Friedrich Bachman's untimely death, I find myself at a disadvantage without a lumber buyer."

Fighting to control his temper at the man's rudeness, John covered the distance between them in a few, long strides, and faced the mill owner seated behind his desk. "How very unfortunate for you, Mr. Gosling, losing a lumber buyer. My sister and her children are only deprived of a husband and father."

"Yes . . . well," Mr. Gosling fumbled, "feel at liberty to give my condolences to Friedrich's family. Now, what is it you want with me?"

"To begin with, I'd like an explanation of how the accident happened."

"How does any accident happen," Mr. Gosling parried? "It's just the unfortunate coincidence of being in the wrong place at the wrong time.

Yesterday, while I was talking to Friedrich, some drifter from Ohio came in looking for work. When I told the man he could start right away, Friedrich volunteered to take him to the cutting shed. As they passed through the yard, a bundle of logs suspended overhead from a rigging wire, fell when the sling failed. It was Friedrich's fatal misfortune to be directly beneath the free-falling load. I understand that the new fellow barely escaped, scrambling out of the way. The yardman said the lad was so badly shaken he lit out running, and no one has seen hide nor hair of him since."

"There were witnesses then" John asked?

"A couple of workers on the crew saw everything."

"I would like to interview them."

"There's no need for that. I just told you what they reported."

"What about Friedrich's things? Did he leave any personal belongings in his desk?"

"No, I looked through his desk myself. Nothing of a

personal nature was found there. Now, I have business that requires my attention." Mr. Gosling concluded their meeting in a dismissive tone. "Good day, Mr. Hartman, you can show yourself out."

"I'm leaving, Mr. Gosling, but perhaps you will be more cooperative when the village constable investigates this incident." John was bluffing, and they both knew it. The local authority was known for being a man easily influenced by a bribe, or a bottle.

The house Friedrich had rented for his family was only a short distance from the mill, and John rode there in a matter of minutes. He found his father and brothers-in-law loading furniture, and other household goods, into a couple of wagons. As the men finished tying down the cargo with ropes, a stylish carriage pulled off the road and stopped in front of the property. An older gentleman stepped out. John and his father walked over to introduce themselves to the man, who identified himself as Maxwell Reid, the property owner.

Accepting Isabel's house key from James Hartman, Mr. Reid said, "I regret the intrusion. My real purpose for stopping by was to express my sympathy, and ask how Isabel and the children are coping. I trust they are being cared for by your family?"

"Yes," James replied, "they are living with us."

Mr. Reid exhaled an audible sigh of relief. "You cannot imagine what a consolation that knowledge is to me. I am only too well aware that Isabel suffered many hardships, financial and otherwise, due to her husband's willful neglect. Forgive my presumption to use her given name, but I will *not* utter his. Isabel is a fine young woman, and a wonderful mother, although she refuses to believe the truth of that. She blames herself for their domestic troubles, although nothing could be further from the truth. Please convey my sincere sympathy to her, and tell her that she and the children are daily in my prayers."

Respectfully, John detained Mr. Reid as he was about to return to his waiting driver. "Please sir, will you tell me to what extent Friedrich was in arrears on the rent?"

Straightening to his fullest stature, Mr. Reid met John's eyes. "I decline to answer, except to say you may rest assured there is no outstanding balance in my account book against your sister. Indeed, I find myself in her debt for the kindness and friendship she has shown me over the last several years. I wish you both a good day, gentlemen."

They watched as he walked away, leaning heavily on his cane.

Isabel was coming to terms with the reality that she must accept the new circumstances of her life in order to survive, and care for her children. The sharp edge of pain from yesterday's tragic events, was being dulled by the gradual understanding that she must cope with the situation, and move on. She would not be a burden to her parents, but would somehow find a way to provide for herself and her little family. But first, she had to get through today, and tomorrow, and each day after that. Staying close to her mother, she helped with the household chores and looked after her children.

Musetta and Rose Ellen had come early to help Isabel get settled. They began cleaning three of the unused bedrooms upstairs. Dust and cobwebs were wiped from the corners, windows washed, fresh draperies hung, and floors swept and mopped. It was decided that the largest room would be shared by Isabel and her daughter Eliza, leaving Johnny to bunk alone in the smaller one. When the work was finished, the oak floors gleamed, and the windows sparkled. Once the beds arrived, and were set up, they would be covered with warm colorful quilts, making the rooms cozy and comfortable. The two women prayed their older sister would find healing and sanctuary here.

When the wagons pulled up to the door, the hired hands were waiting, ready to unload Isabel's household belongings. The bedsteads were erected, and furniture that wouldn't be used was stored in the third bedroom. Isabel would be kept busy for days, sorting and organizing her possessions.

Everyone was weary after the long day, contributing to

the unusual quietness that settled over those gathered for supper. Isabel had joined the rest of her family at the table, and thanked them for their help. She even managed to eat a little of what was on her plate. When Musetta and Rose Ellen began clearing away the dishes, John offered to take charge of the cleanup so they could go home with their husbands. Everyone would need rest ahead of tomorrow's funeral. Isabel surprised John by volunteering to wash the dishes. When he protested and tried to refuse her help, she insisted on doing her share. He decided her stubbornness was a good sign. Their parents retreated to the parlor, taking Johnny and Eliza with them.

As John and his sister attacked the pile of dirty plates, John told Isabel about meeting Mr. Reid at the rented cottage. He conveyed the old gentlemen's message that she was daily in his prayers. "He regards you very highly, Belle, and extends his sympathy."

Smiling, she said, "Mr. Reid was always kind to me, and he adored the children. He loved to rock Eliza to sleep while I read stories to Johnny. When I told him the money you gave me should be applied to the rent, he refused to take it, saying I needed it more than he did. I tried to argue, saying I wouldn't accept charity from him. So, he found small things for me to do, inconsequential tasks, such as filling vases or dusting his books." She took a deep breath. "Did he tell you how much I owe for the unpaid rent?"

"Mr. Reid said you owe nothing. In fact, he feels himself in your debt." John replied, watching a lone tear trail slowly down his sister's cheek.

They worked side by side in silence for several minutes before she spoke again, "John, I can't thank you enough. Father told me you made the funeral arrangements after Friedrich was killed at the mill. Did you see his body when you were at the undertaker's?"

John hoped she hadn't noticed the involuntary shudder that passed through him at her question. "Belle, please don't ask me . . ."

"I have to know, John. Was it terrible, did he suffer greatly?"

John took her hands, drying them with the towel he held, and turned Belle to face him.

"I am sure it was over so quickly there was no time for suffering. Friedrich probably never knew what happened." He folded her close then, his chin resting on her bowed head. "You may not believe this now, but the day will come when you'll be happy again. Everything will be all right, Belle. I'll always be there for you and the children. I promise."

She attempted a light-hearted reproach. "You shouldn't make promises you can't keep, big brother." No sooner were the words out of her mouth than she dissolved into tears. "It's just that I feel responsible somehow, like the fault for our failed marriage, even his death, lies with me. I disappointed Friedrich so many times. There was nothing I could do to make him happy, and there was nothing about me that pleased him."

John shook her gently. "Belle, stop! I won't let you take the blame for this. None of what has happened is your fault. Come on now, I hear mother putting Johnny and Eliza to bed, let me walk you upstairs so you can kiss them good-night."

The morning was bleak and bitterly cold, and its pale light revealed a dusting of snow on the frozen ground. It seemed an appropriate setting in which to say goodbye to Friedrich. Mother remained at home with the children, making it a small, solemn assembly that flanked the open grave at the cemetery. Isabel shivered, standing close beside the casket, while John and Father supported her on either side. Musetta and Rose Ellen huddled together behind their older sister, with Henry and Edward closing ranks around the hurting family.

John's attention was suddenly captured by a couple of coarsely dressed men, loitering around some headstones a little distance away. He had the uneasy feeling they might be some of Friedrich's former acquaintances. His suspicions were confirmed as the unsavory pair began making their way directly toward his sister after the final "amen" was pronounced by the minister. Handing Isabel off to their father, John was joined by Henry and Edward as they intercepted the men.

Stale breath fouling the air, the coarser of the two interlopers spoke brazenly. "We're not lookin' for trouble with you. Our business is with the widow. We done a job for Friedrich three days ago, a big dirty job, and he didn't never give us our money. Now we reckon his woman better pay up."

Adopting a deceptively mild tone, John warned, "you're making a big mistake. You are not welcome here. I'm telling you, and your friend, to leave."

The bold intruder smirked. "And who's gonna make us? You think we're scared? What's the woman to you anyhow, your new bed warmer?"

John drove his fist hard into the man's face, then shifting his weight he delivered a powerful left hook to the body. It was supremely satisfying to watch the man crumble to the ground.

Having witnessed his companion's punishment, the other man tried to run away, but found he was hemmed in by Henry and Edward. As they pushed him to his knees, John hovered over him. "Look after your friend, and don't either of you ever trouble my sister again."

Chapter 11

Several weeks had passed since the funeral, and life was slowly beginning to resume its normal routine. As a consequence of the disruption caused by Friedrich's death, John had delayed his return to Clear Springs. He was eager to set out this morning for what he hoped to be the first of many calls on Katie Byler. Returning the basket and empty pie plate, gave him a good reason to justify his unexpected visit today. While hitching Blaze to the buggy, a reedy voice piped up from somewhere behind him. "Where are you going, Uncle John? Can I go with you?"

He turned, ready to dissuade his young nephew from tagging along, but the hopeful expression he saw on the boy's face caused John to waver.

"I don't know when I'll be back. It might be past your bedtime."

"Please, please Uncle John."

John could hardly deny this boy who'd just lost his father. "Well, if your mama says you may go . . ."

Not waiting to hear more, Johnny ran into the house, yelling for his mother. Minutes later Belle walked out, holding firmly to her son's hand.

"John, are you sure about this," Belle asked her brother?

After receiving an affirmative nod, she leaned down to kiss Johnny goodbye. The lad wriggled impatiently, anxious to free himself from this embarrassing display of maternal affection. Isabel issued a cautionary word to her bachelor brother. "I hope you know what you're getting yourself into. Don't blame me if he talks your ears off!"

She released Johnny, who straightway launched himself into his uncle's waiting arms.

"Can I drive Uncle John? I know how. Can I?"

Belle laughed. "Don't say I didn't warn you."

Standing between his uncle's knees, Johnny proudly held the lines as he navigated the length of the drive. They hadn't gone far before John realized his sister had not been exaggerating. This youngster was a natural born chatterbox. He wondered briefly if it *might* be possible to have one's ears talked off, but mostly he enjoyed the child's amusing banter.

After several miles, the conversation took on a more serious tone. "Uncle John, do you have a little boy of your own?"

Not sure where this line of questioning was going, John answered. "No, Johnny, I don't."

"Well, don't you want one?"

"Sure, I do, and someday I hope to have one."

Taking a breath to bolster his courage, Johnny asked hesitantly. "Well until you do . . . until you do have one, Uncle John, couldn't I . . .? Could I be your little boy?"

John's breath caught in his throat at the earnestness in his nephew's voice. Pulling off to the side of the road, he opened his arms. "Come here, son." He felt the child's tense body relax against his chest. "You're almost like my own boy, Johnny. Why, we even have the same first name. Did anyone ever tell you that your mama named you after me? I want you to always come to me if you need help, or if something's bothering you, or if you just want to talk. Do you understand?"

Listening as he snuggled closer, Johnny nodded, then shifted back slightly to look up at his uncle. "And you know what, Uncle John? I'm glad my mama gave me your name."

"Me too, buddy. Now just take it easy for a while. We'll be coming to Clear Springs soon."

Betsy was hanging clothes out to dry, when from the corner of her eye she saw someone pull up to the hitching rail. It was John Hartman! Then a blur of movement streaked across her field of vision. Her husband, a frisky collie romping at his side, was already on his way from the barn to greet their visitor. Peter called over his shoulder to Betsy, "better let Katie know we'll have one more for dinner . . . no, make that two," he amended, as John lifted a little boy from the buggy. A certain look passed between husband and wife, and Betsy knew what that glance signified. The two of them had put their heads together after Danny and John's visit in March, concluding they'd not seen the last of John Hartman.

"Good to see you again, John, and who's this fine fellow?"

"This is Johnny, my sister Isabel's son."

"Pleased to meet you, Johnny. I'm Peter Christner, and this pup jumpin' round my knee is Charley."

Reacting to his name, the collie gave a sharp bark. Seeing his nephew stiffen in response, John asked, "you're not afraid of dogs, are you, Johnny?"

The boy rejected that suggestion at once. "I'm not afraid, Uncle John! I'm almost six . . . and six-year-old boys, aren't scared of anything!"

"Ain't that the honest truth," Peter said with a laugh? "Johnny, you make me wish I was six-years-old all over again!"

Pulling Johnny closer to his side, John crouched beside the dog. "Let's make friends with Charley, shall we?"

At Peter's command, Charley sat and behaved himself like the gentleman he was, while Johnny ran his fingers through the dog's long, silky coat. Charley forgot his manners only once, thoroughly licking Johnny's face.

"Come on fellas, let's go in and see what's cookin'." When they reached the house, Peter ordered. "Stay Charley." Obediently, the collie dropped to his belly on the path outside his master's door. Petting the dog's head, Peter said "Good Boy." A little voice echoed, "Good Boy." Charley looked at his new friend and wagged his tail.

Betsy and Katie made a great fuss over Johnny, saying how pleased they were to have him visit. Giving John a warm smile, Katie thanked him for bringing his nephew along. Her smile set his mind at ease, and he was glad she'd made Johnny feel so welcome. In fact, it seemed Katie was actually quite taken with the boy. Announcing that dinner wouldn't be ready for another 30 minutes, Betsy asked if everyone would like to play a game while they waited.

"Oh yes," Johnny cried out excitedly. "I know! Let's play *Huckle, Buckle, Beanstalk!*"

"I love that game," Katie exclaimed, clapping her hands together.

Huckle, Buckle, Beanstalk, John thought? This can't be happening! Decidedly not a devotee of parlor games, John was sure Peter would intervene quickly with some excuse to keep them from getting ensnared in this childish pastime. After the raised eyebrow he aimed at his friend went unheeded, John provided the cue Peter must be waiting for. "Peter could probably use my help outside while the rest of you play."

"Well . . ." Peter seemed to be stalling. "Why don't you help me look for something in the other room?" He led the way to a small chamber off the front hall and John followed without question, until the door closed behind them.

"What's going on, Peter? You can't be serious about *Huckle, Buckle, Beanstalk,* can you?"

"It's a trick, John. One of their wily, female tricks. I know it sounds crazy, but if you want the upper hand in courtin' you got to humor your girl's foolishness once in a while. Like now with this silly game. Mark my words, you'll regret it if you don't just go along. Take it from someone who had to learn the hard way. Otherwise, there'll come a time when you and that gal you're sweet on, are sittin' under the kind of moon made 'specially for sparkin' and just like that," Peter snapped his fingers to demonstrate, "she's ready to go home." Rummaging through the pigeon holes of a desk, Peter found the object of his search, a large, shiny marble. "I'm only trying to help you, John. Come on, we better get back."

As John trailed after Peter, he suddenly recalled from childhood his mother's voice reading *Alice's Adventures in*

Wonderland. Now, he asked himself, what kind of rabbit hole have I just fallen into here?

"Betsy," Peter handed the marble to his wife, "I thought this would make a dandy prize to hide."

Holding it up in her fingers so everyone could get a good look, she reviewed the rules of the game. The person who was 'it' would be left alone to hide the object, and when the prize was secreted away the others were called back to begin the hunt. The first one to discover the hidden item, and call out "Huckle, Buckle, Beanstalk" was the winner. Katie volunteered to be 'it' and after the others had vacated the room, she purposely chose a hiding place at their youngest player's eye level. Arranging the marble where it was clearly visible in a potted fern, she summoned the players. And though it was concealed in different places for each of the following rounds, predictably Johnny was the only one able to spy the marble.

At the kitchen table, Johnny wormed his way in between his uncle and Katie, monopolizing the young woman and basking in the warmth of her undivided attention. By the end of the meal, John was way past regretting his decision to allow Johnny to accompany him today. He certainly didn't need any competition from a fearless, and irresistible, six-year-old rival.

"Hey, I almost forgot," John blurted out when he managed to get a word in, "your basket and pie plate are still in the buggy."

Before anyone else could respond, Peter leaned back in his chair, stretching his long legs out, and drawled. "Is that so? Well, why don't you and Katie go for a drive? She could bring it in when you return. Be a real shame to let such a beautiful day go to waste. Johnny and I might throw sticks for Charley to fetch while you're gone." He looked down at the boy. "How 'bout it, partner?"

"Can we? I'd like to play with Charley!"

Alone at last, and settled cozily in the buggy, John noticed that Katie had turned suddenly shy as they drove along the winding, country roads.

"You're awfully quiet. Has the cat got your tongue?"

"No," she demurred. "I was just thinking about your nephew."

"Johnny? Don't you think he's a little young for you? Maybe you should consider someone closer to your own age?"

"Well, I don't know," Katie teased. "Johnny *is* awfully sweet. Tell me, how did he happen to be with you today?"

John explained that Isabel and her children had moved in with their folks after her husband was killed in an accident. Glimpsing a lake ahead, he turned onto the access lane and stopped in a grassy area overlooking the water.

"Katie, there's more than meets the eye to my sister's circumstances, but we'll talk about that another time. Right now, I want to talk about you." He reached over and took her hand in his. She didn't look at him, but neither did pull her hand away. In an unsuccessful attempt to hide the blush flaming her cheek, she shyly lowered her head.

"Katie?" When she raised her eyes to meet his, he held her gaze. "What are you going to do after the baby's born, and Betsy's able to get along without your help?"

She shrugged. "Well, I suppose there will always be someone in the family needing help. Danny and Lovina certainly have their hands full with six boys."

John rephrased his question. "What I mean is, what do *you* want to do? Just for a minute, don't think about what someone else needs, or wants, from you. Have you given any thought to your desires for the future?"

Her eyes widened in surprise at the question, "I don't know. No one's ever before asked me what *I* want. Do you know what you want, John?"

"Yes, I most definitely *do* know what I want." John squeezed her hand before releasing it, "and maybe you'll figure out what you want before we take another drive next Friday. Now, let's walk down to the lake."

Later, back at the house, John lifted Katie down from the buggy, pulling her close to him as he did so. He wanted to kiss her, but resisted the temptation, brushing his lips against the silken hair at her temple instead.

Seeing his uncle's return, Johnny knelt beside Charley and gave the collie a hug before walking with Peter to the buggy.

John exchanged a handshake with Peter. "Thanks for everything, Peter. It was good of you and Betsy to keep Johnny for me."

"It was our pleasure. That boy's more entertainin' than a county fair. You're both welcome anytime."

Holding Katie back when she would have followed her brother-in-law to the house, John asked quietly, "I'll see you Friday then?"

Before she could even so much as nod her head, Peter spun round and raised his hat to John. "Come early and stay for supper, why don't you?"

Katie rolled her eyes. "That man could hear grass grow." Feeling a tug on her skirt, she looked down and saw Johnny beckoning her. Bending at the knees, she balanced easily on her toes beside him. Cupping his hands around her ear, he whispered something to her. In response, she wrapped Johnny in her arms, pressing a kiss on his cheek. It nettled John more than a little to see that coveted kiss wasted on his nephew. How is it, he thought, this same boy who'd chafed earlier at his mother's caresses, now seemed reluctant to leave Katie's embrace?

Hustling his nephew onto the driving seat, John climbed up and took the reins in hand. "I'll see you next week, Katie. Good-bye until then."

She was still waving as they turned onto the road.

"Thanks for letting me come with you today, Uncle John. I liked Peter and Betsy, and Charley, too."

"Aren't you forgetting somebody? You sure seemed to like Katie."

"I liked her most of all. She's lots of fun, and pretty, too."

John's curiosity got the better of him. "Say, what did you whisper in her ear?"

"Can't tell! It's a secret. Are you going to marry Katie, Uncle John?"

"I plan to," John replied, "if you don't beat me to it!"

Positioning himself against the solid comfort of his uncle's shoulder, Johnny had the final word. "Good luck, Uncle John!"

Chapter 12

Despite the chilly breezes swirling about the countryside, Spring arrived with vibrant color and riotous noise. Hepatica, marsh marigold and bloodroot bloomed in the woods and wetlands around Clear Springs, and all kinds of birds were single-mindedly constructing nests in which to raise this year's clutch. The scolding of Blue Jays filled the air with jeers that sounded like rusty hinges. Katie smiled and thought that they were a raucous, but handsome bunch of rowdies.

It was time to search the woods for tender fiddlehead ferns, wild asparagus and highly prized morel mushrooms. Katie was well acquainted with foraging, planting, harvesting and preserving food, and she found great satisfaction in these pursuits. Her neck and shoulders warmed under the late April sun as she pulled a perfectly straight furrow in the freshly turned earth with the hoe. She'd had her feet in the dirt since she was old enough to walk, and loved being outdoors, in harmony with the natural world. Working in the garden was more than the physical exertion required to put meals on the table. It was something akin to worship. She saw the stooping, kneeling, pulling and lifting movements as the ordered steps of an ancient dance honoring the giver of life.

Normally, Katie's sister would be at her side, but advancing pregnancy was hampering Betsy's ability to bend forward with ease. The midwife suggested during her last visit, that the baby's size likely meant a delivery in May, rather than June. Excitement was building daily for the baby's coming. If all went well, Katie reckoned by the end of August, Betsy would probably be ready to manage without her help. And, what then?

Katie thought about the last time she'd seen John. When he'd asked her what she wanted to do after her commitment to

Peter and Betsy was fulfilled, she'd found herself unnerved by the question. To her way of thinking, the very idea of considering her own wants or desires smacked of selfishness. She'd been raised with a clear understanding of what the church and her parents expected of her: obedience, baptism, marriage, and a family. What else was there, but to submit to a life of service? Other than accepting one suitor over another, Katie could think of no other significant choice women might make for themselves.

For the first time, Katie recognized that apart from her identity as Amish, and her connection to others, she couldn't describe herself, except in terms of relationship. She was first and foremost Amish, then a daughter, granddaughter, sister, niece, aunt, sister-in-law, and probably someday, a wife and mother. By occupation; she was gardener, cook, baker, housekeeper, quilter, mender, child-tender and so on. But wasn't there more to her than that? Who was Katie Byler all by herself, and what did she want? She was starting to get a headache when Peter's voice intruded on her thoughts.

"Katie? Katie, are you in there," he tapped lightly on the top of her head? "I'm tryin' to talk to you."

"Oh! Sorry Peter," she answered. "I didn't hear you. I was thinking."

"Well, there's the problem right there. Thinkin' is something women should stay clear of. It's too much for 'em. Like I'm always tellin' Betsy, leave the thinkin' to us men, that's why God put us in charge."

Katie flung the hoe down with all the force at her disposal, and threw her hands upward in exasperation. "Men!"

Flabbergasted at her reaction, Peter tugged at his beard and watched her stalk back to the house. "Now, what do you 'spose has gotten into her?"

"Is that you Katie," Betsy asked, hearing the back door swing shut? "It's past time for a break. Come and sit with me."

Raising her eyes from the blanket she was knitting, her hands stilled and she nearly dropped a stitch in alarm.

"Katie, what is wrong? Are you crying?"

Drawing the back of her hand across her eyes, Katie replied. "No, it's just a headache, Betsy. I'm going upstairs to lie down for a while."

Alone in her room, she closed the door, lowered the blinds and removed her shoes before curling into a tight ball on the quilt-covered bed. Katie's muffled sobs vibrated through the bedframe. After several minutes, the door opened and Betsy came in bearing a tray. "I've brought something to make you feel better. Just stretch out on your back with your eyes closed and lie still."

Betsy set the tray with its tumbler of amber liquid, a basin of water, and a folded cloth on the bedside table. After wetting the linen and wringing it out she applied the damp compress over Katie's forehead and eyes. Then pulling a chair closer to the bed, she sat and waited, humming softly.

The cloth, faintly scented with lavender, was cool and soothing. Katie felt it lifted, and then replaced on her brow after being refreshed in the water. Soon, she pushed herself up, resting her back against the headboard. "You're so good to me, Betsy. I feel much better now, thank you."

Betsy handed the glass to Katie, who sniffed its contents before taking a swallow. "I thought the cider was all gone."

"Peter just opened the last keg a few days ago. It may be starting to turn, so go easy. Do you feel like talking?"

Katie eyed her sister over the rim of the tumbler. "I just don't understand men!"

The corners of Betsy's eyes creased as she laughed. "Well, join the party. I'm bound to say every woman since Eve has uttered those very words. So, tell me, did Peter say something to upset you, or is John the one responsible for your distress?"

"Both! Well, Peter got me riled up this morning, but I ought to know what to expect from him by now. What really has me in a tizzy is something John said to me the last time I saw him."

"Yes . . .?"

"He asked me what I was going to do after the baby comes and you don't need my help any longer."

"And, what did you say?"

"Well, I said there's always someone in the family needing help. Then he made me understand he was asking what I *wanted* to do, not what I thought I *should* do. It's confusing, Betsy. Aren't we supposed to want to do what we should do, what we're expected to do? Doesn't our faith teach us to put others ahead of ourselves?"

"Katie, I think you're misunderstanding what John was trying to say. Unless I'm mistaken, he wasn't criticizing your willingness to help others, nor was he suggesting that selfishness is a virtue." Betsy hesitated, "may I speak plainly?"

Katie nodded.

"If it has somehow escaped your notice, Little Sister, let me make it clear to you. John Hartman is a man with deep feelings, and serious intentions for you, but he's not one to take getting what he wants for granted. Some men don't concern themselves with what a woman thinks. Some don't care, and some don't even believe a woman capable of rational thought. John is not one of those men. He is interested in everything about you, including your mind. If he asks . . . no, *when* he asks you to marry him, giving an answer based on what you think he wants, or expects to hear, is not going to be enough. He has to know what's in your head and heart, and he needs to know that you want him for the man he is, apart from any offer of marriage and all that entails."

"Betsy! I thought you said you didn't understand men?"

"No, that's what *you* said. My observation was that every woman has probably expressed that same sentiment." She brushed her fingers gently across her sister's cheek. "The truth is, women *do* understand men, but sometimes we forget what we know. Sometimes we get so busy caring for everyone else, we disregard the intuitive wisdom God gave us. And even though you're barely twenty, you know more than you think you do, Katie. What you must answer for yourself is, do you love John, and do you *want* him?"

"Do you think men understand women, Betsy?"

"The best ones do, Honey." Betsy gathered her things together and went downstairs.

Katie admitted to herself that John Hartman had stolen her heart and captured her imagination. It was easy to dream about being his wife, and indulging in these pleasant fantasies seemed harmless enough. But it wasn't harmless, and it wasn't fair. Katie thought about everything her sister had said, and knew that Betsy's intuition about John was right. He was courting her in earnest, and he was challenging her to know her own mind about what she wanted for the future. It would be wrong for her to continue seeing him if she wasn't willing to honestly entertain the idea of marriage. The hurdle requiring Katie to make a leap of faith in this regard wasn't how she felt about John, it was living with the consequences that would follow. What would her family say, and how would they react? No doubt some of them would be more understanding than others, but those sympathetic souls would likely be in the minority. She had never considered being joined in matrimony with someone outside her faith. If she were no longer Amish, what would she be? As she pondered this proverbial fork in the road, a startling new thought presented itself. If she said 'No' to John, how could she ever live the rest of her life without him?

Chapter 13

"Hello," Isabel's voice rang out as she entered the cabin? "Are you here, John?"

"Coming," her brother answered, making his way down from the loft. "I didn't hear the dinner bell. It's not time to eat already, is it?"

"No, that's not why I came for you. We have visitors, or, you do anyway."

John's head jerked up as he brushed dirt from his clothes. "What? Visitors you say? Why on today of all days? I'd wanted to work on this place while I have a break from planting spring oats. Well, who is it?"

"It's a gentleman caller who says he's a friend of yours, and he's brought his daughter with him."

"Could you be more specific, Belle? I don't have time for guessing games."

She quickened her pace to keep up with John's long legs as they headed toward the farmhouse.

"Ouch! Someone's a little prickly today. What's bothering you?"

"Sorry Belle. I don't mean to take my frustration out on you. Farming demands so much of my attention right now, and I'm trying to snatch any bit of time I can to work on this old homestead."

"I know, John," she said sympathetically. "You've been working from sunup to sundown. Are you losing weight? Your clothes are hanging off you."

He shrugged. "When I'm in the middle of something, I just don't think about eating, and the next thing I know, my pants are loose. I'm sure you know how it is."

"Oh yes," she quipped with obvious sarcasm. "I'm

forever having to take in the seams of my britches!"

"Okay, okay. Can we move on? Who is this mysterious visitor?"

"He introduced himself as the Reverend Franklin Bailey."

John stopped dead in his tracks, although his momentum threatened to pitch him off balance.

"That's odd. I met the man only once, about four and a half months ago at the Scottsburg General Store. I wonder what he wants?"

"He didn't say. You can ask him yourself while I help Mother prepare dinner."

Balancing the linen towel and pitcher of hot water his mother had ready for him in the kitchen, John took the back stairs two at a time on the way to his room. Pouring water into a basin, he shed his work clothes, and drenching the towel in water quickly washed and dressed in clean apparel. In scarcely ten minutes John was entering the parlor to relieve his father from the onerous task of extending hospitality to strangers.

"Reverend Bailey, I trust you are well, sir. It's been a while since we first met in Scottsburg. I do apologize that I wasn't here to introduce you to my parents."

The portly reverend heaved himself to his feet and shook John's hand. "It is a pleasure to see you again, young man. Your father has been a most attentive host, and the good woman of the house insists we share your noon meal." The reverend was interrupted by a guttural croaking emanating from the woman of indeterminate age seated by the front window. "But forgive me, I am remiss by ignoring my favorite traveling companion. John, allow me to introduce my daughter, the lovely and talented Miss Brunhilda Ophelia Bailey."

Miss Bailey didn't bear the slightest resemblance to her father. Where he was of considerable proportions, she was thin and angular in the extreme. Dressed in what John assumed to be the latest fashion in cosmopolitan areas, she accentuated her outfit with an expression of haughty superiority.

He took the limp, gloved hand she extended to him for a brief clasp, "I am very pleased to make your acquaintance, Miss Bailey."

A shrill, whining voice assaulted his ears and grated on his nerves. "Please call me Hildy. My father speaks very highly of you, and says we are sure to become the best of friends."

It taxed John's imagination to think he might share anything in common with this person sufficient to warrant the commencement of a friendship. He cast about in his mind for an appropriate rejoinder to her assertion, but finding none, he fell back on the reverend's introductory remarks.

"Your father made reference to your being accomplished. What, may I ask, is your particular talent?"

Even as he posed the question, he felt vague misgivings. John silently begged God's mercy that Miss Bailey might not claim any notable skill requiring the use of her voice. Perhaps she was adept at needlework or basket weaving. But he was to have no such luck.

In helpless and appalled fascination, John watched as Miss Bailey underwent a startling physical transformation. Stretching out her neck, she lifted her head, pulled her shoulders back, stiffened her spine, and crowed an F major scale that resolved itself three notes above high C. The force, and nasal quality of her singing, left John dizzy. He felt at risk of being rendered unconscious. Glancing quickly over at his father, he saw the good man was similarly affected by Miss Bailey's performance.

Reverend Bailey on the other hand, was swelling with paternal pride. The elder Mr. Hartman quickly excused himself on the pretense of supervising the hired men, and nearly ran headlong into Isabel who was rushing into the parlor, concern written plainly all over her face.

"Is everyone all right? It sounded like someone was in pain!"

Before John could correct his sister's assessment of the

situation, Miss Bailey fixed a scathing look upon her.

"Obviously *you* have no ear to appreciate a trained voice. I am widely acknowledged to be the best lyric soprano between Peoria and Poughkeepsie."

Seeking to smooth his daughter's ruffled feathers, the reverend said, "now, now dearest, you mustn't excite yourself. I am reasonably sure Isabel meant no offense. After all, it can hardly be expected that any of the local inhabitants hereabouts would have been privileged to experience the performance of a true prima donna, such as yourself."

"Oh Papa, what a consolation you are to me," Miss Bailey purred while leaning on her father's arm for support. Then, she addressed Isabel. "Of course, I *am* willing to forgive, if you will apologize."

An expression of disbelief flitted across Isabel's face before she recovered and composed her features. "Miss Bailey, I scarcely think there is anything I can add to what your father has already said about my ignorance. However, even without benefit of your privilege, and an ear to recognize operatic excellence, I must admit your voice is original and without equal. I've never heard anything like it. Please accept my sincere apologies for mistaking your vocalizations to be the cries of an injured person, or the death throes of a wounded animal. I assure you, Miss Bailey, it was an innocent mistake on my part."

Brunhilda felt she'd been outmaneuvered by Isabel, but couldn't quite work it out. She hadn't liked that part about 'a wounded animal,' but then again, she *had* received an apology, hadn't she? The more she considered it, the more confused she became. Nothing but a new summer wardrobe from Bloomingdales could assuage the insult to her pride. Hildy would convince her mother a shopping trip to New York was in order as soon as they returned home from this forsaken backwater. She turned condescendingly to Isabel. "Well, I don't suppose you knew any better. I accept your apology."

Susanna Hartman entered the room, looking for her

daughter. "Isabel, the children are waiting for you in the kitchen, and I would like to get better acquainted with Miss Bailey."

Summoning Brunhilda to her with a wave, Susanna said, "Let's walk in the garden. The tulips and jonquils are at their peak for viewing."

Wiping his brow with a large handkerchief, Reverend Bailey breathed a sigh of relief. "Whew! In parlance of the common man, *that was a close shave*. John, you must understand that Brunhilda, like most artistes, is high-strung, and can become rather theatrical when provoked. Surely Isabel did not mean any harm, although her remark about 'the death throes of a wounded animal' leads me to believe she is a clever fox. Fortunately, Isabel's inference seems to have passed over Brunhilda's head. Now, all is forgiven and we will say no more about it. If I may, I would like to get to the reason for my call."

"Yes," John agreed, "I should like to know that myself. Please continue Reverend Bailey."

"John, you made a favorable impression upon me from the moment Jake Evans introduced us at his store. I marked you as a young man likely to succeed at anything you might attempt. So, although you are currently engaged in farming, I believe you have the potential to aspire to a loftier career. One that promises to support you and a future family in grand style. Have you ever considered politics? I mean, take a look at Honest Abe . . . he had humble beginnings and look to what heights he ascended! I have connections all over Michigan, even extending to surrounding states, and might be persuaded to help you on your way. Think of all the good you could do for people. Think of . . ."

"Excuse me, Reverend Bailey, but I have never entertained any desire to run for public office, and cannot think of a single reason why you should wish to encourage me in such a venture."

"I'll be blunt then, John. Hildy is our only child and almost beyond marriageable age. While she can be challenging, and her propensity for opera, society and fashion is not universally appealing, she lays claim to an advantage many young women lack. A sizeable dowry passes to her husband on their wedding day. I hope you will not take umbrage at my framing this proposition in terms of a financial transaction, but if you were to consider marrying Hildy, I can assure you the return on your investment would be most profitable."

John was aghast. "What you are suggesting is quite impossible, Reverend Bailey."

Refusing to be so easily defeated, the reverend asked, "is there, perhaps, another young woman already in possession of your affections? If that is the case, let me issue a word of caution. Often these liaisons fail to result in matrimony. Especially if the parties are of disparate backgrounds. Think it over. Should you find yourself later at liberty to accept this proposal, you have only to say the word."

While Reverend Bailey was attempting marital negotiations in the parlor, another drama was unfolding in the garden. As Susanna led Brunhilda through a flower bed of bright yellow and red blooms, they were joined by Johnny and Eliza, returning from an exploration of the fishing hole. The eager lad was carrying a small pail in one hand and a fishing creel in the other. His excitement was evident.

"Look! Look at what we found," he said, handing the pail to his grandmother. She and Brunhilda peered into the water to see a quantity of tiny, aquatic creatures with short, plump bodies and broad tails swimming about.

Drawing back, Brunhilda asked fearfully, "what are those things?"

Eager to impress their guest, the boy scooped up a handful and joyfully exclaimed, "polliwogs! Do you want to hold some?"

"No! No! Get those creatures away from me!"

"Show them what else we got," prompted Eliza, pointing to the creel. "It's magic! If you kiss it, it'll turn into a prince!"

Realizing what was about to happen, Mrs. Hartman tried

to stop Johnny from opening the creel but she was too late. A large bullfrog was lifted out, and Miss Bailey went into hysterics, screeching at the top of her voice. The startled frog leaped from Johnny's slippery grasp onto the bodice of the young woman's dress. Brunhilda promptly fell to the ground in a dead faint.

When she came to, she was reclined on a fainting couch, and Mrs. Hartman was waving smelling salts under her nose. Rudely pushing the glass vial away, she demanded that her father take her home at once.

John and his sister watched the Baileys leave, and Belle dramatically passed the back of her hand across her forehead.

"Whew! Goodbye and good riddance! I am sorry if you had your heart set on a political career, with Brunhilda Ophelia Bailey thrown into the bargain for your wife. But having her for a sister-in-law would be more than I could stand."

"Belle," John accused, "you were eavesdropping!"

"Well, just who do you suppose sent those children after frogs and polliwogs?"

Catching her round the waist, John lifted her in a wide arc. "Thank God for my meddlesome, interfering sister!"

Chapter 14

"It must be Friday," Peter remarked, coming in from chores to join his wife at the table. "Katie's smile is always brighter on courtin' days, and I 'spect we'll be seein' John Hartman soon enough."

"Now, Peter, don't start teasing," his wife admonished.

"That's all right, Betsy," Katie said, putting a plate of hotcakes and sausages in front of her brother-in-law. "I'm not paying him any mind, but are you sure you can manage the whole day without me?"

"Of course. I'm feeling just fine. The midwife has assured me I have at least two weeks before this baby comes, though if you're going to have a day off, you better do it sooner than later."

"What's all this 'bout a day off? Is Katie goin' somewhere?"

"You know very well John's taking her to visit his family today. Katie, leave those dishes, I'll take care of them."

"All right Betsy, but at least let me gather eggs for you then," Katie said while snagging a basket off the hook by the kitchen door. "Be back in a few minutes."

After he finished eating, Peter reached around his wife as she stood at the sink, placing his empty plate in the dishpan. Leaning down he nuzzled her neck and cradled her rounded belly in his arms. "So, we'll be by ourselves, unsupervised all day? I don't know if I can behave myself without a chaperone."

"You're forgetting I'm here to keep you in line," Betsy said with a girlish giggle. Possibly in reaction to its mother's laugh, the unborn child landed a powerful kick against Peter's hand. He raised his eyebrows, "that boy kicks like a mule."

"You know, Peter, it could be a girl."

"With a wallop like that? Not likely."

Returning from the henhouse, Katie emptied the egg basket and packed one of the pies she'd baked yesterday for John's family. She ran upstairs to change, and while putting on a clean dress, Katie reflected on the conversation she'd had with Danny last Saturday when he and his family were visiting.

Her brother hadn't wasted any time on small talk before he broached the subject on his mind, "Peter tells me John Hartman's a regular caller these days. Have the two of you sorted out your feelings for each other?"

"You don't beat around the bush, do you, Danny?"

"Well, it's not likely we'll have much time to talk without bein' interrupted."

Katie acknowledged the truth of this, "yes, you're right. So here is what's troubling me. If John proposes marriage and I accept, what will Mamm and Dat have to say about that? Won't it be a terrible disappointment to them? And what about the rest of the family, and our friends?"

Danny studied the dear, familiar face across from him. He held her gaze and stroked his thumb absently along his jaw line. "Katie, I think you know the simple answer to your questions, but let me give you something else to think about. Perhaps being the youngest, you haven't given much thought to the fact that our folks aren't always goin' to be around. None of us knows how long we have on this earth and when it comes right down to it . . . the only life you can live is your own. No matter what you decide, not everyone will be happy 'bout it. It's been my observation that when someone closes a door, it's usually closed forever. Now, might be another door will open, but it won't be the same one. Time only moves in one direction Baby Sister, and we have to go with the flow."

Charley's bark drew Katie back to the present. Pulling the window shade aside, she saw John and hurried downstairs to meet him.

He'd had to rein in the impulse to gather Katie into his arms as she walked toward him with bright eyes and rosy cheeks.

"It's wonderful to see you again, Katie. I've been looking forward all week to bringing you home with me."

"It will be good to see your family again."

Blaze signaled his impatience with a toss of his head as Peter came jogging up with the basket Katie had left behind in the kitchen. "Hey, you 'bout forgot somethin.' As I recall, John's partial to your Dutch Apple pie."

Taking the basket in his left hand, John shook Peter's hand. "Thanks, you have a good day. It might be late when we return but I'll bring Katie home safe and sound."

"No worries on that account," Peter replied.

Absent her former reserve, Katie was chattier and more animated than usual, seeming at ease to be alone with John. He sensed a sea change about her and dared to hope she was coming to know her own mind about him. Emboldened, he laid his hand on top of the one she'd rested on the seat between them, and waited for a reaction. Instead of ducking her head, as she'd done when he first touched her, she met his eyes with a level gaze and smiled. He tugged her closer to him, and for the rest of the trip they remained side by side, each taking pleasure in the nearness of the other.

A flurry of activity greeted them as they arrived at the Hartman home. John jumped lightly down from the buggy to help Katie out, and at once she was enveloped by the enthusiastic greetings of his family. John's parents, having lived for years in close proximity to the Bylers, were familiar with the family and extended a genuinely warm welcome to Katie. Isabel was used to Katie orbiting the periphery of her life as younger sister Rose Ellen's best friend. She wrapped Katie in a quick hug before Johnny pushed his way forward to stand before Katie, eager to serve as her personal escort. Only Eliza hung back, waiting to be introduced to this new and strangely dressed person in their midst. When she attempted to hide in her mother's skirts, John lifted his niece and held her securely. "Don't be shy, Eliza, this is Katie. She is here to visit for the day."

"Hello Eliza, I'm happy to meet you. What is your baby's name," Katie asked, patting the little girl's doll?

"Her name is Sally," Eliza whispered.

"Such a sweet name. If you think Sally would like a new blanket, I'll make one for her before I see you again."

"Would you," Eliza asked? "She'd like that a lot."

Isabel reclaimed her daughter from John. "Why don't you show Katie around, while mother and I are busy in the kitchen?"

Johnny saw an opening, and was quick with a suggestion. "Hey Uncle John, we could look at the baby ducks on the pond, and . . ."

James Hartman interrupted his grandson, "maybe later, Johnny. Right now, I need your help with something. Come along."

As his family obligingly scattered, John gave Katie a tour of the farm. They worked their way through the outbuildings, past the fish pond, toward the orchard and farther on, ending up at the old cabin. He had recently cleared away the rampant overgrowth on the exterior, and refurbished the small stable.

"What's this place," Katie asked when they entered the little clearing?

"It's the original homesteader's cabin. I live here now. Would you like to see inside?"

"May I? It looks like a storybook cottage."

"Then close your eyes and don't open them until I say so." Standing behind her, he unlatched the door, placed his hands on her shoulders, and walked her over the threshold. Once inside he said, "open your eyes."

Accustomed to the plain starkness of unadorned rooms, Katie felt overwhelmed. Everything seemed to be competing for her attention, and though scarcely able to take it all in, she was drawn to the colorful warmth of the interior. Cushioned chairs and a settee were arranged on a large rug in front of the fireplace. A three-stack barrister bookcase held John's leather-bound volumes, many of which bore proof of having been read often. A few good hunting prints hung on the wall, along with some smaller portraits. There was even a glass-fronted curiosity cabinet displaying fossils, arrowheads, relics and other found objects.

He led her through the rest of other rooms, relating how his sisters had joined forces one day to surprise him while he was working in the fields. They had cleaned the little house from top to bottom and filled it with some of the family's old furnishings and kitchen wares. The finished result pleased him so much that he'd moved in the following day. That had been a week ago and he'd found the peaceful seclusion of the place entirely to his liking.

The homey atmosphere of the cabin worked its magic on Katie, too, and she hesitated at the door, glancing back into the room. Neither of them wanted to leave.

"It's beautiful, John. It looks like your sisters thought of everything. I can't see a single thing missing."

Placing his hands at her waist, he pulled her in closely and she rested her arms naturally against his shoulders, hands clasped behind his neck.

In a voice husky with emotion, John said. "The only thing lacking to make it a real home is you, Katie. You will forever be the heart of my home."

It was a memorable first kiss. He lowered his head slowly, breaking eye contact with her only at the last moment, when with a gentle but determined intention he took her mouth, and stole her breath. Her eyes closed as she felt herself falling into the embrace. Always a tactile person, touching was one of her most elevated senses, and her hands were never still. Whether caressing a child's soft cheek, kneading pliable bread dough, or scratching a dog's rough head, touching was a compulsion with her and one of the most frequent means of expressing her affection. So, it was only natural that Katie's fingers, of their own accord, threaded and tangled the thick strands of hair curling on the nape of John's neck. It was strange, she thought later, reflecting on what might otherwise have been an insignificant detail in her memory, except for John's response to the touch of her fingers. He'd groaned softly as he ended the kiss, breathing heavily before suddenly holding her at arms' length from him.

"Katie, I'm too old for long engagements and courtship rituals. I love you, and want to marry you. I pray God puts it in your heart and mind to love me back." Before she could respond, John placed a long finger against her lips. "Don't give me your answer yet, but when you're ready, I want honesty from you above all else."

Compelled to lean closer to catch her breathless voice, he heard her say, "I'll always be honest with you, John."

He smiled, and for just a moment she was able to breathe normally again until he whispered. "We'd better get back to the others while I can still remove my hands from you."

After closing the door behind them, John saw Isabel hurrying along the path, a worried look on her face. "Come quickly, Mother says it's urgent!"

The three of them ran abreast the remainder of the way to find the larger buggy ready and waiting with Susanna Hartman seated inside, her bag of folk remedies close by. "Hurry, John. There's no time to waste!"

After lifting Katie onto the backseat beside his mother, John vaulted to the driver's bench and slapped the reins against the horse's back.

Suddenly afraid, Katie looked to the little woman at her side. "What is it? What's happened?"

Clasping the younger woman's hands in her own, Susanna comforted the wide-eyed girl. "Nothing's happened yet dear, and God willing all will be well, but Betsy and her baby need some help. Now don't worry I've delivered more than a few babies in my time; we'll get her safely through this."

Katie's mind was racing as she tried to calm herself, *surely Peter would have gone for the midwife at the first sign of any trouble. If only she had stayed home with her sister today.* She prayed silently for Betsy as they neared Clear Springs.

When John drove into the yard, Peter was leading a horse from the barn, his face revealing the fear and worry he felt for his wife.

"I'll drive," John insisted. "Get in, Peter."

Katie jumped out, turning to help Susanna alight. Then she took the reins from Peter's hand and ran his mount back to the barn while John's mother raced to the house. Minutes later Katie was at her sister's bedside, watching her writhe in pain. John's mother issued commands in a firm voice. "Katie, get soap and hot water, along with plenty of clean cloths."

Reassured by the older woman's presence, Betsy had calmed down by the time Katie returned to the room with everything Susanna required.

Betsy squeezed her sister's hand, "I'm glad you came back when you did. Everything happened so quickly. I was scared and Peter didn't want to leave me alone."

"Oh Betsy, I shouldn't have left you today."

"Enough of that talk, girls, it's time to get down to business and bring this new life into the world."

In a shorter time than any of them would have believed, Betsy was delivered of a hefty baby boy. The little fellow was sleeping peacefully in his mother's arms when his father's frantic voice was heard downstairs, calling out for his wife.

Katie met him at the foot of the stairs, holding up a hand in warning. "Not so loud, Peter. I've got something to tell you."

"No! Is it Betsy? Is she all right? Why is it so quiet? Tell me what happened. No! Don't tell me!" The knuckles of Peter's clenched fists were white, and his face was ashen.

"Betsy's fine, but she says if you wake the baby and he starts bawling, you'll have to answer to her. Congratulations, Peter, you got your boy."

Peter swept Katie up in a hug, swinging her into the room before planting a big kiss on her surprised face. Then he was off, clattering up the stairs, hollering at the top of his voice, only to be answered by a wail of impressive volume coming from his son.

Katie stood where Peter had deposited her and saw John waiting across the room. He walked over to stand in front of her. "The midwife wasn't home and we couldn't find her anywhere, but I knew everything would be all right with my mother here."

Katie couldn't ignore the question begging to be asked. "John, how did your mother know what was happening here?"

"She just knows, Katie. We don't understand it, and she has no explanation other than its God's gift to her. Any other questions, Bright Eyes?"

"Bright Eyes, is it? I kinda like that." She braced her hands on his strong shoulders and stood on tiptoe to whisper in his ear. "No other questions, John, just an answer. It's 'Yes,' now and always."

Chapter 15

Every afternoon while Betsy napped and Peter was busy with chores, Katie had baby Joshua all to herself. It was a precious hour she looked forward to each day. Waltzing the baby slowly around the room, she wondered how one little person could fill such a big space in her life, occupying a void she never knew existed before. Today, her nephew was wide awake, staring intently into her eyes as she held him close to her body. He made cooing sounds, struggling to work his mouth into just the right position, as if to tell her something of great importance. Katie gave a low laugh as she lightly caressed his head. "Josh, I have the feeling that once you're able to talk, you'll never run out of things to say. You might find it hard to keep up with your dat, but I bet you'll give him a good run for his money."

"Better not let Peter hear you say that."

Katie looked up, her heart pounding. "Where did you come from, John? I didn't hear the door."

"Well, I can be a very stealthy stalker when the situation calls for it," he said, placing himself behind her for a better view of the baby. Taking advantage of this position, he folded his arms around her waist, bending his head over her shoulder to press a lingering kiss on that tender spot, just below her ear.

"John! What are you doing?"

"I should think it's pretty obvious. Do you want another demonstration?" Seeing a spark of fire in her eyes, he lifted his hands in surrender. "Okay, I know that wasn't fair. Here, let me hold my nephew."

"Joshua's not your nephew."

"Well, he will be soon enough. Come on, I won't drop him."

She reluctantly handed Josh over, missing at once the

warmth and weight of the baby's body as she transferred him to John. Crossing her now empty arms in front of her to compensate for the loss, Katie noticed the ease with which John held the little one. "What brings you here today?"

"I'm running an errand for father. He's repairing some equipment and sent me after parts. I figured as long as I was this close to Clear Springs, the neighborly thing to do would be to see if there was anything Peter or Betsy might need from Scottsburg."

"Really? Considering we're on the other side of Scottsburg it seems that besides making extra work for yourself, this *neighborly* call takes you out of your way. Not that I'm complaining, you understand."

The guilty look on his face gave him away, "I can see you're already onto me. It's going to be hard getting anything by you. If you want the plain truth, I just had to see you today. Do you forgive me?"

With an impish grin, she responded with a dose of his own medicine. "I suppose you're forgiven, although for someone who claims to value honesty so highly, you might wish to apply those same standards to yourself. And, now that you've generously offered your services, I'll see if Betsy needs anything from the general store. I don't know about Peter, he's probably in the barn."

Katie ran lightly up the stairs while John settled down to rock Joshua, reflecting on the tableau that met his eyes when he'd quietly entered the room. He'd been deeply moved by the sight of Katie swaying slowly with the baby in her arms. There was such tenderness on her face. It made him wish he was an artist, and able to capture the moment on canvas. In his imagination he pictured her holding their own little one. "Someday," he promised himself, "someday."

As he studied Joshua's face, John thought the little one appeared to be assessing him, as well.

"Hello Josh Christner. Remember me? You'll get to know

me as Uncle John. We met on your birthday. What are you thinking, little fella?" John lapsed into the soft humming of a half-forgotten lullaby, rocking rhythmically until Joshua's eyes closed.

The sisters came downstairs together, and Betsy took her son from John's arms. "Good to see you again, John. There are a few things I could use from the store. Would you mind if Katie goes along to shop for me?"

He stood, "I'd be glad to take her off your hands for a while. Let me find Peter to see if he needs anything. Then we'll be ready to go."

Peter couldn't think of a single thing he wanted, except for a packet of licorice mints. "Betsy craved 'em all the time she was carryin' Josh . . . and now I'm the one that can't get enough of 'em." Peter held out a coin, which John refused.

Katie had been to the Scottsburg General Store several times before, but never with John. If Jake was surprised to see them together, he didn't let on that it was anything out of the ordinary to see an Amish girl keeping company with an Englisher. Katie went briskly about the business of filling her market basket while John and the proprietor engaged in small talk before Jake was called away to help another customer. John let Katie know he was going next door to pick up the part for his father, and he'd be back soon. It had been quiet in the store, but Katie was suddenly aware she'd drawn the attention of three teenage girls, whispering and giggling as they moved closer. They raised their voices to ensure Katie would overhear their hurtful remarks.

"Will you look at that, girls? As I live and breathe, it's a Pilgrim . . . right here in Scottsburg. And, it's not even close to Thanksgiving!" Their laughter carried a mocking undertone.

"Wait a minute, maybe she's a Quaker. Ask her if she says *thee* and *thou*?"

"You ask her! Besides, don't Quakers wear big, shiny buckles on their shoes?"

"I think she's one of those Amish from over in Clear Springs."

"All I know is I'd rather die than dress like that! Dark, plain colors, that strange cap, no buttons, no jewelry, and those ugly shoes!"

Jake appeared out of nowhere. "That's quite enough, young ladies. If you're just loitering around to embarrass my customers, you'd best leave."

He watched them flounce through the door, noses in the air.

"I am sorry Katie. I only wish I'd been here when they started harassing you."

She *was* embarrassed now. If there was anything she disliked about being Amish, it was how dressing 'plain' caused her to stand out from others. Although the distinctive garb and other aspects of Amish life served to visibly mark their separation from the world, Katie had a natural aversion to being the center of attention.

When John returned and joined Jake and Katie at the cash register, he immediately sensed that something had happened to charge the atmosphere. "Is something wrong, Katie?"

Before she could reply, Jake told how she'd been subjected to some rude comments from a few spoiled, inconsiderate girls. He again expressed his regret over the whole episode.

Katie didn't want to hear any more about the unfortunate encounter. "Jake, everything is all right. Please don't be concerned on my account, I've heard worse."

Those words, *I've heard worse*, echoed over and over in John's mind on the way back to Clear Springs. He was outraged by the pure meanness of some people.

Katie couldn't help but notice that the knuckles of his fisted hands were white.

"John, you're not still thinking about those girls back at

the store, are you?"

"No," he lied. "I'm thinking late October, or early November would be a good time for our wedding. I guess I should talk to your father soon."

"Are you nervous about that, John?"

"No," he lied a second time. "Should I be?"

"Well," she took a deep breath, then blew it out. "I know he won't like it, but we'll talk to him together, and when he understands how we feel about each other I think he'll accept our decision. And, if he doesn't . . ." she paused, and they finished the sentence in unison. "We'll cross that bridge when we come to it."

Katie smiled. "Fall is the perfect time for a wedding."

"Well, I'm not taking any chances when it comes to presenting my case to Abraham Byler. I think I'll pay your brother a visit in the next few days for his advice about how best to approach your dat."

"That's a good idea. You can always count on Danny for some words of wisdom."

After a restless night, John decided he might as well head straight to Shipshewana to see his old friend.

Lovina answered the door. "I suggest you scout out the area around Willow Pond if you're looking for Danny." Sure enough, at the end of a well-worn path, he saw Danny reclined against the grassy bank, knees bent with one bare foot crossed over the opposite knee. A straw hat covered his face, and in the grass beside him lay a fishing pole.

"Hey, Lazybones! How's the fishing? Are you catchin' anything . . . besides forty winks?"

Danny sprang up to clasp hands with John. "Well, if it ain't my old Pal! I was just thinkin' about you. What do you say we build us a raft and float down the river?"

"That sounds mighty tempting, but I've never been one to run away from my problems."

"You got problems, John?"

"Just looking for some advice. Katie and I want to ask for your dat's permission to marry. We thought you could tell us how to get started off on the right foot with him."

Danny considered quietly for a few minutes. "So, you're gonna beard the lion in his lair, are you? You're a brave one. I've heard it said there's strength in numbers, but it wouldn't do for him to feel like you're gangin' up on him. Don't let Katie say too much, John. You take the lead, and try to understand how Dat's gonna feel. I can tell you for a fact it won't be welcome news."

"What do you think he'll say, Danny?"

"That's anybody's guess, but I think you should be prepared for some stiff resistance. Generally speaking, his bark is worse than his bite, but he can bark with the big dogs. Now, I can't imagine he'd actually forbid the marriage, but we're talkin' about a father seein' his baby girl breakin' away from her folks, and rejectin' their way of life. It will feel like a betrayal to him."

John's voice took on a sarcastic tone. "Gee, thanks for the encouragement, Danny. I can't tell you how much better I feel."

"I'm just tellin' how it is, brother. Wasn't it Shakespeare wrote: *the course of true love never did run smooth?* You got to consider the worst that could happen. So, let me ask you, what are you going to do if the fair maid's father locks her up in the castle tower?"

John answered quickly. "I suppose like any worthy knight who has rescued captive lady, I'd breach the walls and carry her off."

"Bravo! Spoken like one of King Arthur's own. Now, for what it's worth, here's my advice in a nutshell. Hope for the best, but prepare for the worst."

To say it was not going well was an understatement, when one week later, John and Katie approached her folks. The young couple made every effort to be respectful, and considerate of her parents' feelings, acknowledging the difficulty for their acceptance of the situation. Abraham Byler listened in stony silence as John asked the patriarch's permission to wed his daughter.

"Katharine, leave the room with your mother. I will talk to you later."

Katie was rooted in place, not sure who her father was addressing, until Mamm began pulling her by the arm.

"Wait!" She looked at John, her eyes pleading for his intervention.

"It's all right, Katie," he said, trying with his gaze and tone of voice to convey more reassurance than he felt. "Everything will be fine."

When the men were alone in the room, Abe spoke, "I do not doubt that you and my daughter have feelings for each other, but a lasting marriage is built on much more than that. The two of you have no future together, and I will never consent to your marrying my daughter. If you truly care for Katie and want what's best for her, you will never see her again. In fact, something has happened that would make a union between you and Katie impossible. I am telling you to bow out gracefully. Have I made myself clear?"

"You've been plainspoken in what you've said," John answered, "but you left a lot unsaid, and I feel entitled to an explanation. Why would it be impossible for Katie and me to marry?"

"You're not entitled to anything, but I'll tell you anyway. Emmon Hostettler called on me yesterday. He repented of abandoning Katie last fall, and was seeking my permission to wed her as soon as possible. I've given my blessing, and it's all been settled. After their marriage, she will immediately accompany her husband back to Pennsylvania."

"And what about Katie? Does she have nothing to say in this matter?"

"Don't interfere in things that are none of your business. You can show yourself out, I don't want to see you again." Dismissing John, Abe strode out of the room, leaving the dejected suitor alone, with a reeling head and breaking heart.

Chapter 16

Katie heard the low murmur of voices rising from the room below, although couldn't decipher the words. It wasn't right that she'd been sent away. She should be part of this conversation, but Mamm was standing in front of the bedroom door to block Katie's leaving. Then, a summer storm swept in with a sudden, violent fury, and all other sound was drowned out.

Barbara Byler had been afflicted with a paralyzing fear of thunder and lightning since childhood. She trembled at every deafening rumble, and streaking flash of light. Her breathing grew rapid and shallow. Katie inched closer to the window to look outside. Rain pelted against the glass, obscuring her vision. For a few brief seconds the rain abated, and she was able to see clearly. What she saw terrified her. John was outside, struggling to control Blaze as he untethered the frantic animal from the hitching rail, and leaped into the buggy. A blinding bolt of lightning struck the massive oak in the yard, causing a huge limb to fall.

What was happening? Where was John going, and why was he leaving without her?

"John, come back! Wait for me!" Pushing Mamm aside, Katie threw open the door. Dat, caught off balance in the act of turning the doorknob, stumbled headlong into the room. Without stopping, Katie rushed past him, running down the stairs and out of the house.

Buffeted by strong gusts and lashed by stinging rain, Katie found it impossible to maintain a straight course as she ran the gauntlet of thorny raspberry bushes bordering the drive. Their canes were thrashing whips, catching and tearing her clothes. Bowing her head, she leaned into the wind, plodding two steps forward before being driven one step back. When she finally stood by the roadside there was no sign of John, only a trail so littered with storm debris it was hard to imagine that anyone could have passed through unscathed.

Katie was drenched, and her teeth chattered with cold and fear. The realization that her father had banished John to the peril of this storm, cut her to the quick. She would never forgive Dat if anything happened to John.

While clambering over a downed tree, Katie's progress was hampered by her torn, sodden dress. Stopping to work her fingers through a hole in the fabric, she ripped away several inches of the skirt's hem. After tearing the limp prayer cap from her head, Katie flung it away, shaking her hair free as she attempted to follow John.

Abruptly, the wind stilled, shrouding everything in an eerie silence while the storm's energy built to unleash even more power. The sky grew ever darker and more menacing. Wind whistled shrilly, wailing through trees, and bending long-standing giants until they broke, splitting the air with a sound like the firing of rifles. Hair swirling upwards, Katie felt like she was about to be lifted into the air, and pulled into the black cloud overhead.

Managing at last to flee to the imagined safety of an open space away from the trees, she reached the edge of a cornfield, pausing to catch her breath. Moments later, a heavy blow struck the back of her head, and the world went dark and silent.

John's thoughts were in turmoil, but he was strangely grateful for the wild storm that mirrored the one raging in his heart. He was more than ready for a fight, and welcomed the physicality of combating the elements. It had taken every ounce of willpower he possessed to overcome the impulse to carry Katie away with him, but in the end, reason prevailed. A hasty action now might ruin everything later. There were plans to be made, and he must find a way to talk with Katie.

Blaze was uncontrollable, screaming and rearing up to slash the air with his hooves. Fearing for the safety of his horse,

John stopped beside a fenced pasture. His shoulder and arm muscles burned from the effort of restraining Blaze. After struggling to open the pasture gate, John let the fear crazed stallion run free. Answering to its primal instincts, the normally compliant steed thundered away, leaving its rider on foot, and at the mercy of the elements. Scanning his surroundings, John's eyes settled on a drainage ditch bisecting the adjoining field. Hoping to spy a footbridge somewhere along its length, he was rewarded by the sight of a rudely-built construct of rough, wide planks spanning the small gulf. There was barely room to huddle against the bank under one end of the structure, but it provided him some meager cover while waiting out the storm, and worrying about Katie.

Recovering his footing after stumbling into the room, Abe wheeled around to pursue Katie, but then his attention was drawn to Barbara. His wife was in distress. Her face was pale, and she was gasping for air. He immediately helped her to their bed, promising to stay by her side. Abe knew the crisis was over when Barbara's breathing resolved to its regular, even rhythm, and the haunted expression left her eyes.

He thought about Katie while the storm held him housebound. He was so angry with her. No, he amended, he wasn't angry with *her*, it was that man. That John Hartman, boldly asking for his daughter's hand. Had he really expected Abe to agree? His Katie was Amish born, and Abe was determined she would marry one of her own people. All his other children had found suitable Amish mates, and she would, too.

In the past, Abe had pitied some of his friends whose children had strayed, bringing shame on their families by taking non-Amish husbands or wives. Though he hadn't like admitting this, he knew he'd have been humiliated too, if he'd been in their shoes. That thought pricked his conscience, making him wonder whether *shame* and *pride* weren't two sides of the same coin. Was it because of his pride that he would feel shame? He knew that Katie, not having joined the church yet, wouldn't be shunned if she married John, and neither would her family be forbidden contact with her. Still, Abe believed it would be damning evidence of his failure to preserve the family's bloodline, untainted by marriage with an outsider.

Thankfully, Emmon had returned yesterday, wanting Katie back. Once she understood this, Abe was certain she'd be happy to forgive Emmon. Surely his daughter had only fallen for John because she was heartbroken and vulnerable after Emmon left her.

Emmon had been excited to report that when he returned to Pennsylvania with a wife, certain conditions for him to inherit the large, prosperous farm of his childless, widowed uncle would be met. This knowledge brought Abe peace of mind about his youngest daughter's future. Yes, he assured himself, everything would work out as it should. As if in confirmation of this thought, the sun broke through the clouds and shone resplendently over the countryside. Now, it was time to find that willful, rebellious daughter of his.

The damage Abe surveyed after walking through the back door was staggering. He searched the barn, assuming Katie had taken refuge there, but no answer came to his repeated calls. When at last he looked upon the impassable roadway, his heart hammered in his chest. Where was his little girl?

John emerged from the ditch to find Blaze nearby, in the company of a small herd. He checked his horse for signs of injury. Thankfully, finding none, he set off in the direction of the old Byler home. Danny almost didn't know him upon answering the door, and was shocked when recognition came.

"John, are you hurt? Come in. What are you doing here?" The answer presented itself in an instant. "Don't tell me! This is the day you and Katie went to talk to Dat?"

John nodded his head as Danny peered around him. "Well, where is she?"

"Your father kept her there, and sent me away. He's dead set against our marrying, won't even consider it. Did you know

Emmon's returned? He wants to wed Katie as soon as possible, and he has your dat's blessing."

"What?" Danny asked, plainly unaware of this turn of events.

"Lovina! Get John a change of clothes and something to eat. I'm going to check that everyone is all right at Dat's, and then I'll be back."

"Wait, Danny," John said, "you're not going without me."

Danny shook his head. "Trust me, John. It's better this way. I won't say that I've seen you. Stay here until I return."

As Danny was nearing his destination, he saw Dat at the end of the drive, gesturing him to hurry. Something small and white was fluttering from his hand. "Danny, come quick!"

Abe thrust the flimsy material at his son. "This prayer cap was under a branch in the road. I think it belongs to Katie. You've got to help me find her. She was here today with John Hartman. He wanted to marry her, and I sent him away. Then she ran off."

Danny noticed bleeding cuts and scratches on his father's hands. "Slow down, Dat. I'll find her. You stay here with Mamm in case Katie returns. I'll get a search party together and start looking. We won't stop until we find her."

Neighbors were already gathering to clear the road, and clean up the storm's aftermath. It was agreed they'd watch for Katie as they slogged their way down the roadway. Danny hurried through the fields, back to his place.

Judging that Katie couldn't have gone far in the storm, the search concentrated along the one-mile stretch of road between Danny's home and his parents' house. Progress was impeded by the necessity of stopping to clear the way as they searched. Later in the afternoon the searchers regrouped at Dat's house for a break. Hours had passed with no sign of Katie, and night would be falling soon. There was talk of calling off the search until morning. Danny said he wasn't quitting, but every man should do as he thought best. There was no question as to John's decision, he would continue by lantern light until she was found, searching all night if need be. A few others volunteered to keep looking, and the rest promised to return in the morning.

John made a suggestion. "Let's start with this field, closest to your folks' house. We know she was somewhere behind me, and might have left the road to find shelter, as I did myself."

Crops had been flattened to the ground, concealing everything underneath. It looked like a hopeless task, searching for a needle in a haystack. Still, they raised their lanterns time and again to broaden the circles of light playing over the ground. Suddenly, Danny's lantern swung wildly. "Be careful here, John, I nearly tripped over this fallen tree."

John turned toward the sound of Danny's voice. "Where? Just a minute, don't move. Hold your light steady. I think I saw something under the tree." Placing his feet deliberately, he advanced to where Danny was waiting, and swore softly under his breath. A closer look elicited a louder response. "Oh God! Oh God! She's here, Danny, trapped under these branches!"

Danny found a stout length of wood to serve as a lever, using it to raise branches off Katie's body while John pulled her free. She was cold to his touch, and unresponsive. Lifting her into his arms, John began running toward the house.

"Wait John. Let me light your way so you don't fall."

Abe heard their shouting as they entered the yard, and met them at the door. Worry for his daughter hid any other emotion his face might have revealed. He motioned John to lay Katie on a small bed. Barbara rushed in carrying extra blankets. The sound of multiple shots reverberated through the air, and they knew Danny was discharging a shotgun to let the other searchers know Katie had been found.

John and Danny set out to Dr. McKinley's house, about a quarter of a mile away, bringing the physician back with them. After he finished examining his patient, the doctor offered little in the way of an encouraging prognosis.

"Miraculously, she doesn't seem to have any broken bones, though there are plenty of bruises. What's most concerning is the nasty blow to her head. There's no way of knowing exactly how badly she's injured right now. I must caution you that it's possible she may have some memory loss when she regains consciousness. Obviously, nothing to eat or drink while she's in this state, although wetting her lips and giving minuscule sips of water, if she's able to swallow, would be advisable. Keep her comfortable in a quiet, dimly lit room. I will stop by tomorrow, but send someone for me at once if her condition worsens."

"Is there anything else we can do," Dat asked?

"Yes," the doctor said, "you can pray. And while you're petitioning the Almighty, you might want to give thanks for the men who found her. They probably saved her life."

After the doctor left, Dat addressed John. "You have my gratitude for finding Katie and bringing her back, but that doesn't mean I've changed my mind about anything."

John held Abe's gaze. "May I have a moment alone with her before I leave?"

There was a pause while Dat considered John's request. "Against my better judgment, I will allow it, but the door remains open and I'll be just outside."

Alone with Katie, John leaned over and kissed her softly. "Katie, I love you . . . please come back to me."

Chapter 17

Straightening to his full height, legs planted squarely apart and arms crossed over his chest, Danny faced his father in the kitchen. "It's been three days, Dat. Katie's not responding to anything, not the sound of a voice, the touch of a hand, or even the aroma of Mamm's cooking. She's barely surviving with the little bit of water spooned past her lips. You heard the doctor, she can't go on like this without lasting harm, or even dying. I want to bring John here to see her. It's worth a try."

Abe studied Danny's posture. The dominant stance conveyed an unmistakable message. He was being challenged by his own son.

"No! No, I won't have him here. Emmon was over just this morning, his second visit in as many days, and when he paid his respects to Katie, there wasn't any reaction from her. If his presence had no effect there's no reason to believe a call from John Hartman would produce different results."

"Don't talk to me about Emmon, Dat! He paid his respects? You make it sound like he was attending her funeral! And tell me, Dat, where was Emmon when Katie was lost, and lying unconscious out in the storm? He couldn't even be bothered to join those of us searching for her."

"Well, . . . ah, I asked about that, and he said that he thought he was coming down with a bad cold, and couldn't risk catching pneumonia."

"That's not a reason, it's an excuse, and we always have to make excuses for Emmon, don't we?"

"There *is* no excuse for Emmon," a woman's voice answered. "No excuse at all."

It took both men a moment to realize Mamm had been there at her stove the whole time, invisible to them, as she usually was.

"What did you say," Abe asked, incredulously?

"I said, there's no excuse for Emmon, yet you continue to believe every lying word he says." Barbara stamped her foot on the word 'lying' for emphasis.

Abe was stunned. Until this very moment, any hint of disagreement between himself and his wife had been discussed in private, not in public, and certainly never in front of one of their children.

This stranger, masquerading as his wife continued. "It might interest you to learn what Franny Hostettler had to say to me when she was here with her son this morning. It seems Emmon's in a mighty big hurry to get back to Pennsylvania with a wife in tow, and he's not waiting around to see if Katie recovers, or if she doesn't. Did you know that, Abe?"

When he didn't reply, Barbara said, "I didn't think so. You see, Abe, although Katie was his first choice, he had a substitute in his pocket, just in case. Franny wouldn't tell me the girl's name, but said the young woman and Emmon were tying the knot this afternoon, and leaving directly afterwards on the train. Franny and Jacob are heartbroken. This was the final straw for both of them.

"If you ask me, which no one has, I think Danny makes a good point. Let John Hartman come over, and we'll see what happens. When John and Katie were here last week asking for your blessing to marry, the love they have for each other was plain to see. And if you can't accept Katie's choice for a mate, whether he's Amish or not, then I feel sorry for you, husband."

Abe hadn't seen this coming. He'd been backed into a corner by the two people he trusted most. It was bad enough to have his authority challenged by Danny, but it was unthinkable for Barbara to rebel against him. It was mutiny, and a blow to his manhood. Abe was grudgingly coming to accept that in order to save face in this matter, a compromise might be made, but if either of them expected a total capitulation, they could just think again.

"Enough!" He raised his hand as if issuing a decree. "This is my decision. John may see Katie tomorrow, but not without someone else present as chaperone. And regardless of what, if anything, happens during the visit, it will be the last time he sets foot in this house. You make sure he understands that, Danny."

Having said his piece, Abe gathered up the remnants of his wounded pride, and retreated to the barn to lick his wounds.

Deciding early the next morning to make himself scarce before any unwelcome company arrived, Abe hitched up the buggy and left. Relations between himself and Barbara had been strained since yesterday, and despite having vowed as newlyweds not to let the sun go down on their wrath, they had yet to make peace with each other. Abe had been certain that he knew Barbara so intimately there was nothing new left for him to learn about her. He'd been wrong. She'd taken him by surprise, openly scolding, and stating her opinions in front of Danny, without consulting him first. A wife ought not do that to her husband. This lack of respect reflected poorly on him.

Why, Barbara had been downright feisty and spirited! Normally, Abe would only use those words to describe the attributes of a fast horse. He blushed at the unseemliness of the comparison, but reconsidering, he had to admit that Barbara *had* made quite the picture with her tossing head, snapping eyes, and slender foot striking the floor. Abe hadn't reckoned she still had that kind of fire burning inside. Absent the steely display of will she'd shown yesterday, he would have compared her to smoldering embers, capable only of giving off a benign warmth. Then she had stood up to him, and he'd seen flames hot enough to scorch his fingers.

Who was this fiery female, and what had happened to his meek, submissive wife? Come to think of it, when was the last time he'd really noticed what a fine figure of a woman Barbara was? So, what if her dark hair was streaked with silver, and she'd grown a little thicker about the waist after ten children? She was still as beautiful to him as the first time he'd seen her. Suddenly, Abe was dismayed to realize he'd been taking her for granted, and he wondered if it was too late to make amends.

Barbara, who'd kept watch at Katie's bedside all night, was yawning when John arrived with his mother and sister Isabel. She rose to greet the women as John went directly to Katie's side.

"I'm glad you're here Mrs. Hartman. Betsy told me what a godsend you were when Joshua was born. I've heard you have a special gift for healing, and it may be there is something you can do for our Katie."

"Please call me Susanna. We should be on a first name basis, don't you agree, Barbara? There are some things I'd like to try if you have no objection, just simple, common-sense measures, like massage to stimulate circulation, and letting in some fresh air and sunlight. I know this flies in the face of the doctor's advice, but after four days with no improvement, it may be time to change course."

"Yes Susanna, I completely agree, and trust Katie to your care. What can I do to help?"

"Why don't you rest? I can see you've been up all night."

Barbara relented. "I could use some sleep, but call if you want anything. There's something simmering on the stove if Katie wakes and is hungry. Please help yourselves, too."

Susanna was bossing John and Isabel around the dark, stuffy room when Danny arrived, and found himself drafted into her service too.

"Danny, you and John open all these windows to allow for some light and cross ventilation. Isabel, fetch my medicine bag from the buggy, and bring in that potted rosemary plant, too." Making a quick search of the dresser and washstand, Susanna found a hair brush, flannel cloths and a clean gown. After the two men finished with the windows, she sent them after pails of water.

"Now, let's move Katie's bed to the middle of the room,"

Susanna directed, "away from that dark corner." They complied with her order. "That's good. Raise her up so her back is propped against the pillows and headboard. That's right, Isabel and I can manage on our own now. I'll call if you're needed."

Susanna closed the door after them while Isabel unpacked a shallow, bronze dish setting it on a small table, nearer the bed. A tied bundle of sage, rosemary and juniper was lit, and placed on the dish to burn. Susanna pushed up her sleeves and began massaging Katie's arms and legs, gently at first, and then more vigorously. She started with rubbing alcohol, and finished with scented oil. Isabel stood behind the low headboard, and applied a boar's bristle brush to Katie's scalp, pulling it with steady strokes through the length of her hair. When the strands were shining and free of tangles, Isabel twisted them into a loose knot at the back of Katie's head. Together they rolled Katie onto her stomach and Susanna began a deep massage of her shoulders and back.

When her mother began to tire, Isabel spelled her, commenting as she kneaded slack muscles. "I can feel her coming back, Mother. She was limp as a rag doll when we started, but her color's returning and her breathing is deeper."

Turning Katie over, they slipped a fresh nightdress on her, and left her to rest undisturbed.

The room had been transformed into a space of light and air. Leafy shadows from the trees outside danced across the walls, and a small curl of aromatic smoke rose upward. When it was time to open the door, John and Danny rushed in, sitting on either side of the bed.

"She looks better, Susanna. When do you think she'll wake up," Danny asked?

"I can't say when, Danny, but I believe with all my heart it will happen. Talk to her, boys, I'm sure she hears you."

Danny stayed several minutes, encouraging his sister before touching John's shoulder and leaving the room.

John's heart was too full for words. Never mind his

mother's presence, he must let his actions speak for him. Leaning over Katie, he gently pressed his lips to hers. Not expecting a response, his eyes flew open and he pulled back slightly when he felt her arms encircle his neck.

"Oh John," Katie whispered. "You came back for me. Don't ever leave me again."

He squeezed his eyes shut to prevent tears of relief from falling, and held Katie closer to him.

Susanna left them alone in the room, closing the door behind her. Holding a hand over her heart, she turned to Isabel. "She's awake, she's talking. Thank God, I believe Katie's going to be all right!"

While the two embraced in relief, Susanna remembered Danny and Barbara. "Is Danny still here?"

"He went upstairs to look in on his mother. I'll run up and tell them the good news."

Susanna heard buggy wheels in the drive, and opened the door to admit Doctor McKinley. "Mrs. Hartman! I didn't expect to see you here."

"Come in Doctor. Come in, your patient is awake."

"Are you sure about that," he asked?

The sound of feet trooping down the stairs made further conversation impossible. Doctor McKinley intercepted the little group making for Katie's room. "Please! I must ask you to wait here with Mrs. Hartman while I look in on my patient."

The doctor was amazed on two accounts, first to see Katie conscious, and second to see her in John Hartman's arms. Evicting the earnest suitor, the physician took Katie's pulse. Satisfied with the strong, if rather fast, steady throbbing, he smiled.

"I am happy to see you are showing signs of recovery. Have you eaten anything since you've been awake?"

"No, I'm not very hungry."

"Katie, it has been days since your last meal."

"But that can't be right, you must be mistaken, Doctor

McKinley."

Without correcting her, he asked. "Do you remember what happened during the storm?"

"I . . . I saw John driving away in all that thunder and lightning. He was leaving me behind and I didn't know why. We're going to be married." Some confusion crept into her voice. "I ran outside to call him back, and he must have heard me, because he's here now."

The physician held her hands. "Katie, I don't want to alarm you, but it seems there's a lapse in your memory, just some bits you've forgotten. I'm sure everything will come back to you in time. Now, it's nothing to worry about, but you should ease slowly back into your regular routine, be patient with yourself, okay?"

"I don't understand, what did I forget? What happened that I don't remember?"

"You've been unconscious for several days since the injury. It's my medical opinion that you've experienced some degree of retrograde amnesia caused by a blow to your head. The important thing now is to get your strength back. Your family and friends are anxious to see you. I'll allow a brief visit before you have something to eat."

The house was uncommonly quiet when Abe opened the door two hours later. Barbara had been waiting for him, and looked up expectantly, her face wet with tears. Neither one waited for the other to make the first move, but rushed forward to meet in a strong embrace.

"I'm so sorry Abe, I was wrong, I . . ."

"No Barbara, hush, hush. Will you forgive a stubborn, old fool? You are the brightest light in my life. Don't cry. Are you alright?"

"Yes, I'm fine now that you're home, and Katie . . . oh, oh, Abe!"

She opened the door to the room where Katie was sleeping, and told Abe how she'd regained consciousness. Abe walked over to gaze down at his daughter's peaceful face, and wiped a tear from his eyes.

"God is good, Barbara. God is so good."

Chapter 18

"So, there you have it, John. Dat is thankful for Katie's recovery, although the lingering smell from the herbs your mother burned made him wonder if some hocus pocus spells might have been cast. Mamm was able to convince him otherwise. Dat still has a long way to go before he's willin' to admit he's fightin' a losin' battle. Just remember, Lovina and I are on your side."

"At least I've got that going for me," John replied, handing Danny a book which concealed a note for Katie, hidden inside. "Did she send a reply to my last letter?"

Danny held out a slim novel, pulling it back as John reached to take it. "It's crossed my mind that I really should be gettin' some compensation for my services. How much do you figure my time and trouble's worth?"

"Your time and trouble? You'd spend all your time fishin' if Lovina would let you, and trouble is your middle name. Anyway, I couldn't pay you what Katie's letters are worth to me."

Danny surrendered the book. "Just thought I'd ask. Say, I'm in no hurry if you want to read that letter aloud."

"Forget it. You've got a message to take back, and when you deliver it, I hope you don't subject Katie to the same torment you give me."

"Define the difference between *torment* and *tease*," Danny asked, neatly knocking John's hat off before making his getaway?

Resisting temptation, John stashed the book under his pillow for safekeeping until later, when he'd have time to savor every word.

In spite of Dat forbidding all contact between John and Katie, a scheme had been hatched to keep the lines of communication open. Danny had worked out a regular schedule for the conveyance of messages between the sweethearts. Considering that Abe wasn't much interested in reading, except for the Bible, or the Amish newspaper, it was assumed the odd book lying round the house wouldn't tempt him to thumb through its pages.

It was no accident that Danny's pick-up and delivery at the Hartman farm coincided with the big, noon meal served at their table every Monday. Since that was Lovina's wash day, the Byler family had to make do with cold leftovers for lunch. Raising six growing boys, it was every dog for himself at the table, and sometimes Danny just didn't feel up to fending off the young pups. The return trip to Shipshewana put him in Mamm's kitchen during supper preparations, where he was sure to find a tasty morsel to whet his appetite for supper.

Danny was just admiring a new glow on Mamm's face when Katie breezed in from the garden. Seeing the book in her brother's hand, Katie snatched it away, retreating to her room. Danny smiled, "I'd say she's back to normal. Don't you think so, Mamm?"

"That's for sure. Katie's doing more than her share around here, and can't be persuaded to do less. She really misses Peter, Betsy and little Joshua though. Did I tell you they're coming to visit this Friday? All the family is invited."

"Lovina mentioned it. Do you think there's any chance Katie will be allowed to return to Clear Springs?"

"No. Dat insists she stay right here, where he can keep an eye on her. I've never seen him like this with any of our other children, but of course, she's the last. He's afraid he'll lose her to John, but he will accept it in the end."

"Are you *sure* about that Mamm?" Danny noticed the bulge of a small object hidden under the neckline of her dress. Every time she touched it, a shy smile played over her lips.

"Yes Danny, I'm sure."

After he left, Barbara allowed herself a few moments to reflect on the evening she and Abe had argued, . . . and made up.

The fierceness of her outburst when reproaching him had shocked them both. She hadn't known what to expect on his return, but it certainly wasn't an apology, or the velvet-covered box she saw lying on her pillow that night as she stood brushing her hair.

"What is this, Abe?"

He'd looked up from his side of the bed, hands under his head, elbows bent. "I guess you'll have to open it if you want to find out. Just remember, *curiosity killed the cat.*"

"*But satisfaction brought it back,*" she replied, opening the box. A beautiful, cloisonné enameled heart, strung on a thin, black ribbon was revealed. Barbara's eyes grew wide at the sight.

"Abe! It's beautiful! So lovely, but how can I wear it without violating church rules?"

He'd gone to her then, and fastened the little heart around her neck. His breath had warmed her skin while he concentrated on the task.

Abe let his hands rest on her shoulders. "Barbara, if a husband can't adorn his wife as he sees fit, without breaking restrictions made by other men, then I say *hang the rules.*"

She'd given no thought to removing it since then, although she knew prying eyes might detect the telltale sign of something under her dress. A small disparity perhaps, but enough to set tongues wagging. There were always those eager to find fault, and make accusations. Well, so be it. Abe's defiance had sent Barbara's heart soaring, as much as his gift of the little pendant. It was his personal declaration that the sacred covenant between husband and wife, transcended the unquestioning adherence to rules formulated by mortal men. She had loved him then.

After supper, Abe settled back in his chair, reading the news from Amish communities scattered around the country. Katie insisted Mamm leave the kitchen dishes, and take some time for herself.

Barbara gratefully obliged, retreating to the bedroom

where she lifted a hinged, wooden case from beneath layers of quilts in the blanket chest. This was her treasure box, the repository of a priceless hoard. It had been a long while since she'd opened it, but she could still name every little thing inside.

Many years ago, she'd made ten drawstring bags to hold keepsakes of her children, objects only a mother's heart would hold dear. It was an odd assortment of acorns, autumn leaves, first attempts at quilt blocks, notes, poems, sketches, and other items, found or fashioned by little hands. As is often the way in families, some youngsters are more imaginative than others, appreciating beauty in unusual things. The perfect example being Danny's birthday gift to her one year -- a discarded snake skin! She still had, and loved it. To each child's sack, she'd added a small, folded and sealed paper that contained a lock of hair, and that son or daughter's first baby tooth.

She wondered if any of her daughters were saving vestiges of their children's growing up years? And what about her sons? She didn't typically think of men being sentimental in that way, but maybe they were.

At least one man could answer that question. Throughout the day, knowledge of that unopened letter kept John motivated to finish his work as soon as possible. No matter how dog-tired and ready for bed, sleep could wait until after he'd read Katie's message several times over. Then it would be added to those already hidden in a box in his dresser.

Slipping his hand under the pillow, John pulled out Belle's worn copy of *Little Women*, riffling through the pages until a folded paper fell out.

July 1900

My Dear John,

   It's impossible to say how much I miss you and long to see you again. Each day is an eternity, from the moment I open my eyes until they close again in slumber. I pray every night to dream of you, but on those nights when I lie awake, the book that's shielded your message consoles me.

Keeping myself always busy is how I get through the days, imagining every little task a labor of love undertaken in our own house. Chores leave little time in which to bemoan my present circumstances. Of course, it is satisfying to know my work lightens Mamm's burdens. Soon enough she will have to manage without my help. I am counting down every day of the three months and two weeks until our wedding, and hoping Dat will become reconciled to our marriage so it might not prove necessary for us to elope.

If only he had agreed to let me return to Clear Springs. Then our courting could have resumed in the usual way. Truly John, Dat is not unkind, but he still refuses to entertain any thought of your calling on me. I am not allowed to venture anywhere away from the house on my own, or even in Danny's company, maybe especially in Danny's company as the friendship between the two of you is no secret. It seems all my comings and goings are monitored.

You know I was raised to honor and obey my parents, submitting to my father's authority as long as I live under his roof. Yet I feel imprisoned, held against my will.

The following is a poor attempt to express how I would feel, if I were in your keeping.

Surrender

Never a captive more willing
To be taken, and bound so complete.
The cords of your love – soft, entwining,
My heart dismisses retreat.

Your weapons are all so disarming,
Eyes that gently entreat,
A touch, full of tender caressing,
Surrender – exceedingly sweet!

I must close for now. Write as often as you're able. I know you *must be busy with the first hay cutting of the season. Give my greetings to all your family. Tell Eliza I haven't forgotten about the little blanket for her baby doll, and have it nearly finished. Let Johnny know I have a new game to teach him. My regards to your father, and of course to your mother and Isabel. The debt I owe them for tending to me while I was injured is one beyond my means to repay.*

With all my love ~ Katie.

John could hardly get past Katie's romantic verse, returning to it again and again, until it was committed to memory and imprinted on his heart. He recalled thinking months ago, that as he got to know Katie better, he might be surprised by some facets of her personality. But never would he have imagined his unassuming, Amish sweetheart to be the writer of such passionate poetry! He placed the letter under his pillow, falling asleep to dream of Katie.

Chapter 19

On the morning after wash day, Lovina Byler did something she hadn't done in longer than she could remember. She overslept! The sun, illuminating a beam of dust motes as it shone through the window and into Lovina's eyes, caused her to squint against the light. Disoriented, she sprang out of bed. How had she not heard Danny get up?

Hurriedly dressing, she stumbled to the boys' room to see if they were awake. The beds were empty. Where were her sons? The smell of something burning stung her nose.

In the kitchen, Danny was engulfed in a smoky cloud billowing from a skillet full of sputtering grease and blackened strips of bacon. Absorbed in loosening burned hotcakes stuck to the griddle, he was cheerfully oblivious to all else around him. The boys, all six of them, sat around a lake of spilled milk and maple syrup, flowing across the breakfast table.

"Mama! Mama!" A chorus of voices hailed her appearance in the doorway.

"Oh no!" She reached for a dishrag to mop up the mess. "Danny, why didn't you wake me?"

Nonplussed, he answered. "Because, Sweet Pea, you looked plumb wore out. I thought a little sleep would do you good."

Her throat was so tight and full of swallowed tears, that Lovina couldn't trust herself to speak. She blinked her eyelids rapidly until the lashes were heavy with salty wetness. What could she say? After all, Danny *had* meant well, wanting to let her stay in bed. How had he phrased it? *I thought a little sleep would do you good?* There was no way the man could possibly comprehend the meager amount of sleep that was her portion every single night. She was weary to the bone.

The youngest was fussing and squirming on his highchair. Lingering in his vicinity, was an unmistakable odor, and Lovina immediately knew the cause of his discomfort. "Why don't you and the rest of the boys wait in the other room, Danny? I'll get this little fellow cleaned up, and then I'll make breakfast."

Lovina and Danny had been married for ten years, and they'd been good years, but her naive miscalculation for the amount of energy required to raise six children, and manage a household, was becoming clearer to her all the time. Today was her thirtieth birthday, and she felt more than twice her age.

As she labored over the stove, sounds of laughter and rambunctious wrestling floated in from the front room. Lovina kept reminding herself that the blessings of home and family outweighed the challenges. Danny was a wonderful husband and father, and their sons were all happy, healthy boys. Nine-year-old Amos was a natural born leader, already bossing his five brothers around, albeit with mixed results. Just a year younger, Benjamin was their adventurer, often striking out on his own in pursuit of some exciting quest. He most definitely was *not* a natural born follower. The twins, Caleb and David, had come along two years later. Lovina and Danny joked privately that they should have named them *Calamity* and *Disarray*, to describe the aftermath of their antics. There was no denying that they were double trouble, and whatever mischief one didn't think of, the other one did. Four-year-old Eli was next in line. Luckily, keeping track of him was as easy as pinpointing Danny's whereabouts. Eli's devotion to his dat was evident in the youngster's already perfected impersonation of his hero. He routinely engaged in the annoying habit of echoing Danny's words, reminding Lovina of a talking parrot she'd once seen at the county fair. Bringing up the rear, so to speak, was ten-month-old Felty. Lovina had yet to figure him out. In fact, he was a bit of a conundrum to all of them. With his dark hair and hazel eyes, he didn't even resemble the rest of the family. His given name was actually Valentine, after Danny's youngest brother, but everyone called him *Felty*. Derived from the South German pronunciation of 'Velte,' the nickname was a shortened version of Valentine. Danny had thought it an inspired choice, since they'd needed an 'F' name to follow 'E.' It had, of course, been Danny's idea to name their children in alphabetical order.

Lovina had no desire to use all twenty-six letters at their disposal, but she was pretty sure the letter 'G' would be up for consideration before the new baby arrived in mid-December. She hoped with every fiber of her being that 'G' might stand for *girl*. For the time being, Lovina was keeping the news of an addition to their family all to herself.

After breakfast, Danny took all the boys, minus Felty, outside for chores. He got them busy feeding chickens, collecting eggs, and cleaning out the hen house. Then, the two older boys mucked out horse stalls, and the twins put down fresh bedding. Eli reprised his usual role as Danny's little shadow.

It was nearing eleven o'clock when a party of women drove up to the hitching post, and began unloading an assortment of bags and baskets. Shouts of recognition erupted from the five boys as they raced to greet Grandma Miller, Aunt Loretta Beachy and older cousins, Sarah and Veronica. Danny welcomed the visitors and began toting their cargo inside.

Looking through the window, Lovina observed her mother, sister and twin nieces approaching the front door.

"Come in, come in. Don't mind the mess, I got a late start this morning. To what do I owe this unexpected pleasure?"

After hugs were exchanged, her mother answered. "Well now, we are part of your birthday surprise."

Danny averted his eyes away from Lovina, trying to sneak past her. Calling after him, she demanded. "What do you know about this, Danny?"

Loretta interrupted her sister, "you can scold him later, Lovina. Right now, you might want to freshen up and fix your hair. Go on, scoot!"

Clearly outnumbered, Lovina resigned herself to doing as

she was told. When she reappeared a few minutes later, Danny took her hand in his. "C'mon birthday girl, your royal carriage is waitin'."

After helping her into the buggy, he pulled onto the road, heading north and then east. It was a picture-perfect summer's day, and Lovina felt her fatigue lessen with each mile they put behind them.

She couldn't resist asking, "where are we going, Danny?"

"Niagara Falls! I've been wantin' to try my luck at goin' over the falls in a barrel. Won't that be excitin'?"

Lovina rolled her eyes. "Seriously Danny, where are we going?"

"That's for me to know, and you to find out."

Knowing it was useless to expect a straight answer from him, she settled back and enjoyed the passing scenery as he serenaded her with silly songs. Rhythmically tossing his head in time with Danny's syncopated beat, the horse seemed to especially appreciate his master's rendition of a rather bawdy drinking song. Honestly, Lovina marveled, she had no idea where her husband picked up all the tunes and tales in his vast repertoire. Obviously, most of them were garnered from outside their church district, and would no doubt, have met with the bishop's stern disapproval. Somehow, the threat of censure or discipline had never proved a deterrent to Danny.

After persuading Lovina to join him in several choruses of *Row, Row, Row Your Boat*, Danny halted near the shores of Stone Lake. They alighted, and he handed Lovina a blanket before producing a basket from behind the buggy's bench. Soon a picnic lunch of cold chicken, pickles, crackers and cheese, and a jar of mint tea was laid out before her.

"Oh, Danny! This *is* lovely. How long can we stay?"

"Long enough to row across the lake and back, after we finish eatin'."

"That sounds wonderful, but aren't you forgetting that we don't have a boat?"

"A minor detail, Lovina. Just close your eyes, and I'll conjure one up with a magical spell."

She humored him, hearing his footfalls move away toward the wooded area where they'd tied Deacon. Then, there was the sound of something heavy being dragged across the sand.

"No fair peeking! Are you ready to be amazed? *Abracadabra! Alakazam!* A boat for my lady! Look Lovina, it worked!"

She had to laugh at the phony expression of surprise on Danny's face as he gestured grandly to a rowboat. Lovina applauded as he bowed. She folded the blanket, holding it under her arm while Danny returned the basket to the buggy.

An idyllic hour-and-a-half slipped by while they were on the water. Sunshine glinting off the mirror surface of the lake, broke into a million dazzling points of light. A cool breeze played with errant tendrils escaping Lovina's prayer cap, tempting her to let her hair down. Deep contentment stole over them, and the companionable silence they shared was a peaceful interlude from the usual distractions of their busy lives. Too soon, it was time to row back across the lake. The soothing warmth of the sun, and the boat's gentle gliding motion through the water was lulling Lovina to sleep. Unable to keep her eyes open, she curled up on a canvas tarp at the bottom of the boat, resting her head on the blanket. Danny covered her face with his hat to shield her from sunburn.

She didn't awake until he was pulling the craft onto the beach, and she felt sand grating against the boat's underside. Rubbing her eyes like a child suddenly roused from a nap, Lovina allowed Danny to lift her out of the boat, placing her on solid ground. She waited in the buggy while he returned the boat to its owner.

"Thank you for the most wonderful birthday, Danny. It was exactly what I needed to make me feel like a new woman."

"I'm glad it made you happy. We should do this again sometime, maybe before the new baby arrives."

"How did you know?"

"Come on now, Lovina. We've been married ten years, and had six children together. Did you really think I wouldn't notice all the signs?"

"You don't miss a thing, do you Danny? I guess I just wasn't ready to admit the truth out loud yet. Some days it's all I can do to keep up with you and the boys."

"Well, that's where you'll be really excited about the rest of your birthday surprise. Until school starts, Sarah and Veronica are going to stay with us to help with the housework, and the children. Once school is in session, it will just be Eli and Felty to care for until the older ones return home. How does that sound?"

"It sounds too good to be true. Won't Loretta be needing her girls' help at home? I don't see how she can spare them even for a few weeks."

"Well, you'll have to take that up with her, because having the girls stay with us was her idea."

As they continued homeward, Danny steered the conversation to a subject near and dear to his heart. "Let's talk about names. It's never too early to decide what we're going to call this little chap." Reacting to her raised eyebrows, he quickly added, ". . . or little lass. I hadn't exactly ruled out that possibility." Proving he had considered that remote chance, Danny took a deep breath and began reciting a list of names: "How about Gunther for a boy, or Greta for a girl? Gunther and Hans, if we have twin boys. Greta and Heidi for twin girls. And hey! This thought just came to me. If we have a mixed set of twins, are you ready for this, Lovina? We'll name the girl Gretel and the boy, Hansel. You know, like *Hansel and Gretel?*"

Putting her head in her hands, Lovina groaned, "Oh Danny!"

Chapter 20

Carrying his son proudly into Abe Byler's house, Peter Christner came face to face with a formidable line of Amish women waiting to relieve him of little Joshua, forcibly if necessary. Grandma Barbara was first, followed by Betsy's sisters, sisters-in-law and nieces. Katie offered to go last, thinking she wouldn't have to relinquish Joshua once she got her hands on him. When it was her turn, she found a rocking chair in the quietest corner of the room, settling down to make up for lost time with her youngest nephew. It was amazing how much he had grown in only two months.

A crowd of youngsters gathered around her to get a close-up look at the family's newest addition. Smitten with Joshua at first sight, all the little girls stroked his soft cheeks, kissing his forehead, and pronouncing him the sweetest baby ever. The boys' mild interest was satisfied with a quick glance, before they dashed outside to play. Amos, Ben, Caleb and David Byler spent considerably more time assessing Joshua's potential, huddling together briefly before arriving at a verdict.

Amos was blunt. "Ain't he awful weak and puny, Aunt Katie? He looks like the runt of the litter. I mean, there's just not much to him. Uncle Peter is so long and tall, we thought his son would take after him."

"Give Joshua time, boys. He's only a couple of months old. Someday he might be bigger and taller than all of you."

"Might be," Amos conceded, stroking an imaginary beard on his jaw. "Might be, but you can't hardly expect us to wait around for him to get big enough to play with? He's too small . . . even for Felty!"

"Yeah," Ben piped up, "as far as I can see, the only thing he's got going for him is that he's not a girl." Four heads bobbed in total agreement.

The twins didn't hold back either. Caleb said. "If our dat caught a fish that small, he'd, -- ." David completed his brother's sentence. "He'd throw him back."

Leaning forward, Katie craned her neck around, as if searching for someone. "And just where is your dat? We'll see what he has to say about your opinions."

At once the four scallywags turned tail, running outside as if the Furies were after them. They'd no sooner disappeared than Katie heard a strange, strangling sort of noise. Danny staggered around the corner toward her, arms wrapped tightly around his mid-section in an attempt to quell the laughter overtaking him. Then his knees folded, and he was on the floor bellowing with hilarity. Eli, never far behind, mimicked his dat's faltering gait, giving vent to a nasal snort as he collapsed on top of Danny.

Lovina was mortified by the behavior of every male in her household, with the exception of Felty, who was soundly asleep on her shoulder.

Stepping over her brother and nephew, Katie began to console her sister-in-law. "Oh Lovina, you poor thing. Let's put Felty down on my bed, and I'll make you some tea. Don't fret. Nobody holds you responsible for your crazy husband. Most of us have known Danny longer than you have, and we still don't understand him."

Betsy, who'd appeared to reclaim her son, readily agreed. "That's the truth."

Peter reached a hand down to help Danny to his feet while Eli scrambled up, and the men who'd witnessed the whole scene, applauded.

"Looks like them apples didn't fall far from the tree," Peter remarked.

"Just wait until Joshua gets older. You never know what youngsters will say or do, but you can be sure it will be embarrassin' sometimes."

Peter clapped his brother-in-law on the back. "I just hope you and your boys don't end up sleepin' in the barn tonight."

Taking Eli by the hand, Danny started for the door. "I guess a little talk with those rascals is in order, before I try to get back in Lovina's good graces."

Betsy joined Katie and Lovina in the bedroom. "Do you mind if I lay Joshua down beside Felty? It's nice and quiet in here."

Lovina pressed a handkerchief to her eyes. "Oh Betsy, I can't tell you how sorry I am for what my boys said about Joshua. And then Danny, carrying on like he did."

"Don't apologize, Lovina. Your boys aren't any more mischievous than their cousins. Well, not much anyway. And, as for husbands, take a look at mine why don't you? Sometimes Peter's pranks get the best of me, too."

"Are you feeling all right, Lovina? You look wrung out."

"I have been feeling more tired than usual, but my nieces are staying with us to help out for a while. Sarah and Veronica were working in the garden when we left, but they should be here soon. I'm sure you've both probably already guessed that I'm pregnant."

Betsy and Katie pulled their sister-in-law into a hug. "We're so happy for you," Betsy said. "When will the little one be making its appearance?"

"In December."

Katie reminded her. "I'm just down the road if you need anything, and I hope you get your girl this time, Lovina."

They were interrupted by a knock on the door, and when it was opened, a repentant Danny was standing there. "I'd like to speak to my wife. Alone, if you girls don't mind."

As his sisters passed him in the doorway, Danny remembered something. "Katie, it nearly slipped my mind, but I have something for you in the buggy. A friend of mine dropped by unexpectedly yesterday and left a book you might enjoy. I'll get it for you before we leave."

Katie grew flustered at this news. "A book? Oh, a book! Fine, that will be fine, Danny."

Betsy teased her sister while the water heated. "Danny had an unexpected visitor who left a book for you? I think that sounds suspicious, but don't worry Katie, your secret's safe with me."

Sarah and Veronica arrived shortly before dinner, just in time to corral the Byler boys and keep them out of further mischief.

The families began leaving ahead of evening chores, until only Danny, Lovina, her nieces and the boys remained. When it was time for Danny to hitch Deacon to the buggy, Katie said she'd walk out with him for a breath of fresh air.

"I wasn't expecting another book so soon Danny. I have nothing to send back today, but I'll have something ready on Monday."

Her brother's eyes twinkled. "Well, my friend was certainly moved by your last message. He couldn't wait until Monday to reply."

Katie blushed and Danny laughed. "I never told you this before, but when I encouraged John to court you back in March, I said I was *an interested party to the outcome of all this fuss and bother,* and are things ever gettin' interestin'. I'm right in the middle of a real love story! Sometimes I imagine myself as Cupid, the wingèd messenger of Venus, goddess of love."

"Danny Byler as Cupid? I'd say you have a lofty imagination, brother. A messenger you may be, but forget the cherubic image, and think of yourself as a homing pigeon."

Walking toward them with Felty on her hip, Lovina caught the end of their conversation. "What about homing pigeons?"

"Katie's just given me a great idea. I'm going to build a pigeon roost; get some birds and we'll be in business."

"What?" Katie began to protest, "I never said . . ."

Raising a hand, Lovina shushed her. "Here come the

boys. Now Danny, don't you dare say anything about homing pigeons in front of them. We'll talk about this harebrained idea of Katie's later."

"But it wasn't my idea," Katie insisted.

At that moment a heaving tangle of boys approached, grunting, tussling, arms and legs knotted together. They gravitated as a single entity toward their parents. Looking a little dazed, Sarah and Veronica remained a safe distance behind. Asking permission to walk back to the house, the girls cited their concern for overcrowding the buggy.

Lovina handed Felty to Danny. "That's a great idea, girls. I think I'll join you." Without another word, Lovina, and her nieces strode off down the drive.

Danny sighed loudly, motioning Amos to the front seat. Then he plopped Felty down on Amos's lap. "Settle down boys, or it's a trip to the woodshed when we get home." His sons seldom heard threats of that nature, and were shocked into silence. Glancing at each one, Danny was satisfied to see a look of trepidation in their anxious eyes.

As her brother began leaving, Katie realized he'd forgotten to give her the book from John.

She ran to catch up with him. "Wait, wait! What about the book?"

"Oh! Yes, I have it here for you."

"Thanks Danny. And don't be too hard on the boys, okay? They just got carried away."

"Well, shiver me timbers," Danny roared in a thick brogue, winking at Katie. Lovina had let it slip earlier that Danny was reading a tale of pirate adventures to the boys. "Don't be too hard on 'em she says! I say let 'em beg for mercy. They'll all walk the plank 'afore day's end."

"You know," she whispered, "if the bishop gets wind of what you're reading to your sons, you could be in big trouble."

"Look who's talking," he countered, a wicked grin on his face.

Entering the house, Katie felt the stillness press heavily on her. It was always like this after everyone left. The house, echoing with riotous gaiety earlier, seemed to be almost mournful in the absence of any voices to break the silence. Since there was no sign of her folks, she assumed they'd retired to their room for a nap. Walking through the house on tiptoes to keep from disturbing them, Katie opened the door to her room, and spied a child-sized lump under the quilt on her bed. Setting the book aside, she lifted the covers. It was Eli! The poor little tyke had been overlooked and left behind. Katie gently tousled his flaxen hair and kissed his cheek, knowing someone would return for him as soon as he was missed.

Making herself comfortable at the small writing table, she opened the letter that had been hidden in the book, and read.

My darling, Katie,

After reading your letter I wanted nothing more than to fly to your side. As for the poem? There are no words adequate to praise your gift for poetry. How long have you been writing verse? You must write more! I am the happiest man in the world.

It seems so long since I held you in my arms that when I am finally able to do so again, I'm afraid I'll never let you go. So, you will always be a captive, but know too that I am yours, now and forever. I could go on endlessly professing my love for you, but if I am to get this to our messenger yet today, I must conclude my note.

It would be negligent of me if I did not convey greetings to you from all my family. Isabel and mother are concerned about your health, and continue to keep you in their thoughts and prayers. The two of them are up to something, and spend every spare moment on some secret undertaking in the sewing room, to which I am strictly forbidden access.

My father sends his regards, and says I am to let you know he is willing at any time to intercede for us with your father, if you think that would be of any help. Personally, I believe that course would be unwise.

My news concerning the children is as follows: Johnny was beside himself with excitement at your mention of a new game. He's driving me to distraction to know what it might be. Eliza is anxious for her dolly's blanket, worried that Sally might get cold without it.

I love you with all my heart, and until we meet again, I remain, Your John

Chapter 21

Lovina enjoyed walking with Sarah and Veronica. She'd missed the daily camaraderie between herself and others of her gender after marrying. Being in the company of her nieces reinforced the hope that this next child might be her first daughter.

"Aunt Lovina," Veronica asked, "what was it like growing up with our mamm?"

Lovina appeared to carefully consider the question before answering. "It was wonderful, except when she was being the bossy oldest girl in the family."

When the twins got over the astonishment of their aunt speaking so candidly to them, they snickered at her response.

"So," Lovina asked them in return. "What's it like having my sister for your mamm?"

Sarah thought for a moment, "pretty much what you said, except that in our case it's a bossy mother instead of a sister. To be fair though, you expect your mother to be telling you what to do and what not to do. I guess that is their job after all."

Walking between her two nieces, Lovina put an arm around each of them. "Let me tell you something about your mamm, and my sister Loretta Miller Beachy. It was my good fortune to have her as an older sister. I used to think she was too hard on me sometimes, but her influence and example are something I've come to appreciate more every day. She helped prepare me for the responsibilities of becoming a wife and mother. Being the oldest girl meant she carried the added weight of looking after all the younger ones, which you both know firsthand is no easy task. That's why I am so grateful that she's allowing you to help me out for a few weeks. I know what it's costing her to do without you girls, even for a little while.

But let me be clear. I'm not saying my sister was all work and no play, all starch and no sass. We had plenty of fun times together and got into our share of trouble, too. In fact, I remember once we snuck out at night after everyone else was in bed, and, . . ." she caught herself in the nick of time. "Well, I'll just say she could make me laugh harder than anyone else. At least until Danny came along."

The mention of her husband set in motion a train of thought upon which the minds of teenage girls were frequent travelers. Veronica sighed. "It must be awful nice to have a husband who is so much fun. Our dat is strict and serious, but things are never boring at your house. If I could have any wish come true, I'd wish to marry someone just like Uncle Danny."

"Me too," Sarah wistfully agreed.

Lovina started giggling so hard she had to stop and wipe her eyes. "Be careful what you wish for girls. You just might get it."

She'd recovered her composure by the time Danny passed them on the road, leading his scurvy crew in a chorus of *Yo Ho Blow the Man Down*. Lovina just shook her head, wondering about this husband of hers, a man she'd describe as only marginally Amish in the day-to-day expression of his beliefs.

Danny was unhitching Deacon, and the boys were engaged in mock swordplay, as Lovina and the girls came on the scene to rescue Felty from the raging battle.

Lovina couldn't put her finger on it right away, but something was missing. "Where is Eli?"

Danny wasn't concerned at her question. "Well, he's right over . . . he's right . . ." Suddenly his head swiveled one way, then the other and his hands stilled. "Boys, what have you done with Eli?"

The battle paused as the brothers looked at each other, then lifted their shoulders in perfect synchronization. "We don't know where he is," Amos said.

"But, didn't you notice whether or not he was missin'

when we left Grandma's?" Danny's voice betrayed an edge of impatience.

"No, we thought he was with you," Amos replied.

Lovina had a sick feeling in the pit of her stomach that was not in any way attributable to her condition. "Danny, how *could* you forget him? I only hope he didn't wander off somewhere by himself."

"Now don't start worryin' Lovina. We're talkin' about Eli here, not Ben, the intrepid explorer. I'm sure Eli is safe and sound at the folks, and I'll head right back there to get him."

Katie had read John's note several times over before putting it away. She'd added the finishing touches to the doll blanket for Eliza, wrapped it in paper and tied up the package with string. She loved sewing, and thought about how much she was going to enjoy making clothes for her own family someday. Then, it dawned on her that while she would certainly be sewing, she would not be making the simple, plain garments of the Amish. Katie had never thought about that before! She had a lot to learn about living in the 'English' world.

"Help," a little voice squeaked!

She moved to the bedside. "It's all right, Eli, Aunt Katie's here."

"But why am I here? Where is everybody? Do I live here now?"

"Of course not, silly goose, you just got tired and fell asleep in my bed."

A horse whinnied outside. "Time to get up, it sounds like your dat is here for you."

Katie picked up the package containing the doll blanket, and led Eli into the kitchen where they met Danny. She'd expected the boy to run eagerly to his dat, but Eli seemed uncertain about taking his next step.

Lowering himself to one knee, Danny met Eli's gaze and felt his heart constrict, seeing the child's protruding lower lip begin to quiver.

"Eli, what is wrong, son?"

Sniffling, the boy asked, "am I in trouble? When I woke up and you were gone, I thought you didn't want me anymore."

"What? Our family wouldn't be the same without you. We didn't leave you behind on purpose."

At the tender sight of her nephew rushing into his father's arms, Katie turned her head and blinked tears from her eyes.

She handed Danny the wrapped parcel, mouthing, "for John." He nodded, and left with Eli clinging closely to his chest.

You would have thought the prodigal son had returned when Eli was restored to the bosom of his family. Lovina swept him up in her arms and shed a tear or two of relief, while staring daggers at Danny. After Eli was set down, his older brothers patted him on the back, and congratulated him for having a real adventure all by himself. Even little Felty gave Eli an awkward hug, while spouting some unintelligible gibberish.

After Danny and Eli had departed, Katie decided to go berry picking. The blackberry bushes closest to the house had already been stripped clean, but she knew more berries could be found along the lane that led to the woods. The afternoon was waning, but there were still a few hours of daylight before nightfall. Taking a gallon-sized pail from the storeroom, Katie walked out into the sultry air.

The wider world outside the stillness of the house was alive with the humming of bees, and the singing of indigo buntings. Monarch butterflies danced across a patch of milkweed near the pasture gate. Setting out across the yard, Katie noticed the tamest of the barn cats falling into step behind her. Pittypat had started life as the scrawniest runt from the last litter produced by the family's ancient mouser, Cleopatra. Having survived against all odds, Pittypat was now a mother herself, and the terror of any rodent foolish enough to cross her path.

It wasn't long before Katie saw the heavily laden blackberry bushes in the thicket ahead and quickened her steps, eager to fill the pail. The berries were easily as big around as her thumb and nearly as long. At the slightest touch of her fingertips, berries spilled into her hand. She popped the largest one into her mouth. Rich, purple sweetness burst on her tongue, releasing an intoxicating perfection! Concentrating on harvesting this bounty, Katie was vaguely aware of the orange tabby weaving itself back and forth between her ankles. The ping of berries raining into the pail filled the air with drumming, until the container's bottom was covered, muting the sound. A catbird scolded loudly overhead, presumably expressing outrage at having his berry patch pillaged, but caught up in the joy of her task, Katie disregarded the warning.

Suddenly, a sharp hissing sent a shudder up Katie's spine. Her scalp tingled and she felt the hair rise on her arms. Pittypat, back arched, was staring at something in the lane. Katie followed the direction of the cat's gaze, and her own eyes settled on a large, tawny cougar about fifty yards away. Time stopped while the predator stared back without moving, before finally slinking slowly off into the trees. Turning back toward the barn, Pittypat sailed over the ground with long, bounding leaps. Katie's legs felt leaden, but she willed them to move as she ran home in the falling twilight.

Abe was waiting on the back step when she arrived breathless, at the edge of the yard. He took in her stained, scratched fingers, and blanched face. "Are you all right, Katie? You look like you've seen a ghost."

"I was just picking blackberries." Holding up her nearly full pail, she said, "let's go inside."

Mamm was thrilled with the berries, saying she'd been wanting to make some blackberry cordial for winter. Over supper, Katie told her parents about the cougar, giving Pittypat credit for alerting her to the presence of the big cat. Mamm was alarmed at the news of a cougar, but Dat consoled her. "All's well that ends well," he said, promising to check with the neighbors to see if other sightings had been reported.

Chapter 22

Birthdays weren't usually observed with much fanfare in the Hartman family, but plans were made to celebrate Isabel's twenty-ninth birthday with a surprise party. Maxwell Reid had masterminded this subterfuge, writing Isabel weeks earlier to request her help organizing souvenirs from last winter's trip to Florida. He'd insisted the only day on his calendar available for such a project was August first. Unaware his real mission was a diversionary one, Isabel quickly agreed to accommodate his schedule.

On the appointed day, Johnny and Eliza kept watch from the yard for Mr. Reid's fancy carriage. Their old friend arrived promptly at nine o'clock to collect his guests. Leaving his lofty perch, the driver assisted Isabel and her children into the carriage.

"Isabel," Mr. Reid declared, "it does my old heart good to see you looking happy and well. Johnny and Eliza have grown so much I hardly know them."

"It's good to see you too, Mr. Reid. The children and I have missed you. You're looking hale and hearty, sir."

"Please call me Maxwell. We've been friends a long time. I appreciate your comments pertinent to my improved health. The last time we saw each other I'd just returned from my trip, and was still recovering from travel fatigue. I find Florida quite to my liking, and plan to undertake the arduous journey again this year to overwinter in its warmer climate. But enough about me, how are you faring? I was very worried for you after your husband's death."

"Thank you for your concern, Maxwell. We're adjusting, and doing as well as can be expected. I remember we talked briefly about your Florida sojourn when you returned home at the beginning of March. You must have much more to tell us."

"I certainly do," agreed the old gentleman with a twinkle in his eye, "but my tales will keep until we arrive at my home."

Once they were all settled comfortably in the solarium at Bramble Briar Lodge, the housekeeper carried in a tray of cookies and lemonade, placing it within easy reach of Maxwell's guests. The earlier humidity of the day had been swept away by an advancing front, replaced with a soft breeze to set the scene for Maxwell's description of Mount Dora. His words painted a tranquil picture of orange groves, saw palmetto trees, and live oaks hung with ghostly Spanish moss. The sight had been a welcome relief after the rigors of his trip. Reaching this picturesque destination had been no small undertaking for the elderly man. He'd traveled first to New York, from which point the Atlantic Coastline Railway conveyed him to Jacksonville, Florida, and thence via the Jacksonville, Tampa and Key West Railway to Sanford. The last twenty-nine miles were traversed on the Seaboard Coast Railway. Mount Dora's railroad depot was within a stone's throw of The Lake House, an establishment of some renown. The current owner and proprietress of the inn, Miss Rathbone, was a spinster lady from Boston, well versed in hotel operation. She greeted Maxwell warmly, making him feel at home.

During his stay at the hotel, he often joined other guests to participate in bird watching expeditions, and hunting parties. Lake Dora attracted fishermen from near and far for its abundance of bass and catfish.

Maxwell held his visitors enthralled with stories of the alligators, wild hogs, and snakes that abounded in the area. He related one occasion where he'd witnessed a fearsome 'gator attack. An aged mother sow, and three of her young were drinking at the water's edge, when a powerful thrust of the alligator's tail hurled two of the piglets into the lake. Splashing into the lake behind his prey, the 'gator feasted on the unlucky little porkers.

Johnny was on the edge of his seat, hanging on Mr.

Reid's every word, but Eliza's expression betrayed her anxiety over the piglets' fate. Isabel decided to intervene. "I do think it's time we were about our business, Maxwell, or our visit will be over before we've made any progress. Perhaps the children could occupy themselves in the library while we work?"

"An excellent idea, my dear, but first I have a surprise for each of them." Bearing down heavily on his cane, he stood and walked stiffly across the room to a cabinet, from which he pulled two packages. The bulkiest one he held out to Eliza. All smiles now, she tore the wrapping off to reveal a large, stuffed camel. "Thank you, Mr. Reid. Thank you."

Johnny patiently waited his turn, and Mr. Reid did not disappoint. "I selected this especially for you, knowing you'd appreciate it. One adventurer can always spot another of his tribe."

The boy was speechless after unwrapping his gift. In his hands he held a handsome, leather-bound book, its cover embossed with fierce looking jungle inhabitants.

"Of course, your mother will help with the reading until you've mastered that skill for yourself."

Isabel was moved by her friend's generosity, "Maxwell, you really shouldn't . . . "

"Shouldn't what," he interrupted? "It makes me feel good to give your children a little happiness. Goodness knows they should have some."

The next hour was spent sorting postcards, seashells, and other knickknacks into covered boxes before the driver appeared to announce that all was in readiness for their return home.

Even before turning into the drive, Johnny noticed several of his cousins chasing each other around long tables set up in front of the house. "Mother! Why is everyone here?"

Isabel had no answer, but Mr. Reid remarked innocently. "It appears to be some sort of celebration."

John helped his sister out of the stylish conveyance as cries of *Happy Birthday Isabel* filled the air. Maxwell alighted next, and was greeted by James and Susanna Hartman.

Isabel was formally seated in the place of honor, surrounded by those who had gathered to celebrate her birthday. When dinner was served, everyone gave their attention over to the freshly caught and fried fish, ripe tomatoes, green beans, new potatoes, and blackberry cobbler.

The afternoon passed pleasantly, and after she got over being the center of attention, Isabel enjoyed it very much. She was touched by this demonstration of her family's love for her, and their optimism for a happier future after the mistreatment she'd endured from her late husband.

As shadows lengthened, parents began rounding up children for travels homeward, and evening chores. Maxwell handed Isabel a package bound with satin ribbon, and kissed her cheek before climbing into his carriage.

After Johnny and Eliza were put to bed, Isabel sat with her folks in the parlor, thanking them for such a memorable birthday.

"You've had enough sadness in your life," her mother replied. "We wanted to make the day special."

Carrying the still unopened gift from Mr. Reid into the room, John placed it in his sister's lap. "I found this on the sideboard. Aren't you curious about what's inside?"

"To be honest, I'm a bit nervous to find out. Maxwell is generous to a fault with his money, and if it's something extravagant, people will gossip. I don't wish to be the cause of any distasteful speculation about the nature of our relationship."

"Oh, let them talk," her mother advised. "What can be said about Mr. Reid, except that he's an honorable old gentleman?"

Isabel untied the ribbon, removing the wrapping to reveal two jewelry cases. She picked up the smaller one, obviously a ring box, and opened it. Holding the gold and diamond men's ring between her thumb and index finger, she marveled. "Wherever did he find this? I never expected to see Friedrich's ring again!"

Holding her breath, Isabel lifted the hinged lid of the other case. There, on its bed of ivory silk lay a coiled rope of stunning, amber beads.

She gasped. "Great-grandmother's amber necklace! What do you all know about this?"

John was the first to confess. "At the mortuary, I'd noticed Friedrich's ring missing from his hand, and thought it strange. I learned later from Mr. Reid that Friedrich had pawned the ring, and the amber necklace."

Isabel brushed tears from her eyes. "I was ashamed to tell anyone about that. Just days before he was killed, I surprised Friedrich as he was removing the necklace from my jewelry drawer. He claimed we were deeply in debt, and he needed the amber beads to pay off a loan. When I objected, he struck me hard across my face with the back of his hand. As for his ring, I know he still had it then, because it left a mark on my cheek."

As he listened to his sister, John's hands clenched into fists. He was ready to bolt to his feet when James Hartman laid a hand on his son's knee. "What's done is done, John. We're all saddened and outraged by what Isabel endured in her marriage, but it seems clear that better days are ahead for her and the children."

"God willing," Susanna interjected with an undercurrent of concern in her voice.

James cast a sideways glance at her. "With your permission, I will continue where John left off?"

He turned to Isabel. "John and I met Mr. Reid while moving your belongings from the house Friedrich had rented. Your landlord asked us to convey his sympathy to you. After a brief conversation he left, but hadn't gone far when he turned back, remembering something he wanted to tell us. Maxwell said he'd stopped by to call on you two days before Friedrich's death, and immediately noticed the cut and bruises to your cheek. After imploring you to reveal how you sustained the injury, you admitted Friedrich was responsible. Maxwell also remembered your saying that Friedrich must have gotten rid of his ring that day, since it was gone from his hand the next morning."

Susanna spoke, "Maxwell said that after pondering everything over in his mind, he concluded the only lender likely to do business with Friedrich was a pawnbroker. He searched every pawn shop in two counties before finding the ring and necklace. The shop's owner confirmed that the man pawning the items matched Friedrich's description, and spoke with a German accent. He'd never returned to redeem his pawn, so the items were for sale. After purchasing them, Maxwell shared with us his desire to return your lost property. We decided a surprise birthday party would be the perfect finale to our little plan."

Isabel held her hands over her heart. "Just knowing that someday I'll be able to give Johnny his father's ring, and pass the amber necklace on to Eliza, means the world to me. Thank you with all my heart."

After their parents retired, John and Isabel sat together in the parlor, engaging in small talk. After mentioning his interest in learning how to play the mandolin, John asked if she had any inclination to take up the instrument.

"Goodness no! There are already too many demands on my time. I've finally overcome my procrastination about going through Friedrich's things, and have packed his clothes to give away. What is missing though, is his best pair of shoes. Didn't you say the undertaker gave those to you?"

"That's right. You were in no condition to deal with that at the time, so I put his shoes in the upstairs storeroom. Shall I get them for you?"

Isabel stood. "I'll walk up with you, then it will be convenient for me to put them with his other things."

When John found the bag, he hesitated before opening it. "I haven't looked inside and don't know their condition. Do you want me to look first, Belle?"

"No. Let's just make certain the shoes are good enough for someone to get use of them."

After the footwear was pulled from the satchel, John and Isabel stared in disbelief at a pair of worn, blood-stained work brogues that were much too large to have ever been worn by Friedrich.

Chapter 23

Belle clutched her brother's arm. "John, does this mean what I think it means?"

In his mind, he recalled the events of the day Friedrich died. The sights and smells assaulting his senses as he'd stood beside the corpse, returned now in startling clarity. John thought he might retch. The body had been so severely damaged that John struggled to identify his brother-in-law with any degree of certainty. His most significant observation at the time was that Friedrich's ring was missing. If he'd known then that his brother-in-law had pawned it, John might not have thought that to be of any consequence, but there'd been something else about that hand that troubled him. What was it? Now it came back to him, the surprise he'd felt at seeing freckles scattered across the back of the hand. Was it possible the dead man was not Friedrich? Had Belle's husband faked his own death? If so, he could hardly have acted alone. And who then, was the poor unfortunate buried in the graveyard?

John hadn't liked Friedrich from the moment Belle had introduced him to the family. The man's ingratiating demeanor and shifty eyes, instantly put John on guard. Friedrich was a charlatan, and slick as hair oil, but capable of murder?

Belle was tugging at his sleeve. "Do you think he's still alive?"

John instinctively pulled her into a comforting embrace. "I don't know Belle, but living or dead, Friedrich has no power to hurt you ever again. You, and the children are safe here. Now, go to bed and don't worry." After leaving his sister at the door to her room, John set out on the path leading to his cabin.

It was late, but he kept mulling over the suspicious details of his brother-in-law's fatal accident. Friedrich had needed money, needed it so desperately he'd pawned his ring and Belle's amber beads for a tidy sum. He would have come away from the transaction with more than enough to settle his delinquent rent, but had the possibility of securing his freedom tempted Friedrich to murder? He'd have had enough to pay off an accomplice or two, and start over somewhere else with a new identity. If the man had only wanted to free himself from his financial responsibilities, why hadn't he pursued a legal remedy? The only conclusion John found plausible was greed. Friedrich would have eschewed the expense of a lawyer and court costs, choosing abandonment of his family, under the guise of an accidental death. If this was the case, the cowardice he'd stooped to may have saved Belle from the stigma of divorce, but now everyone believed she was a widow, and legally free to marry again.

John said a special prayer for Belle and the children, and then he prayed for Katie. He missed her more every day they were apart. How much longer could he force himself to honor her dat's wishes? Couldn't Abe Byler see he was jeopardizing a future relationship with his own daughter because of his stubbornness?

The next morning at the breakfast table, John found himself alone with his mother. "Where's Father? I need to talk to both of you. It's important."

"Your father took Isabel and the children to Clear Springs on some business. Sit down and tell me what's on your mind while I fix your plate."

"It can wait until they return."

"If this is about Friedrich, and your suspicions that he's still alive, Isabel's already told us."

"You don't seem surprised at that possibility," John remarked, as a plate of biscuits and gravy was set down in front of him.

"I've actually wondered about it before now, especially after Father told me about the two men who showed up at Friedrich's funeral, insisting he owed them money. I understand they were threatening to collect on the debt from Isabel." While speaking, his mother lowered herself onto the chair across from him. "Do you think Isabel and the children are safe here?"

John thought for a moment before getting up to pour himself more coffee. "I think she is safer here than anywhere else. Let's not borrow trouble before it comes calling. Tell Father I'm in the orchard when he returns."

Feeling frustrated, Katie crumpled another sheet of paper, adding it to the others piling up on the floor as she struggled to express her feelings. It was going on six weeks since Dat sent John away. How much longer would they have to wait to see each other again? John's passionate letters spoke of his love and devotion, his longing for her, his dreams for their future together. She'd read each letter many times over, and felt her own ardor ignite at his words. But words, however lovely on paper, couldn't replace a lover's physical presence. Katie yearned to see John's face, hear his voice, feel his touch. Did he share her frustration, or was it possible he was content with the distance between them? Was this nothing more to him than a safe, undemanding flirtation? In her imagination, she saw herself years from now, an old maid with a box full of ribbon-bound love letters, engaged in a never-ending correspondence with John.

It was time to face facts. Dat had vowed he'd never consent to their marrying. When Katie had dared bring up the subject for discussion, he had turned his back on her and walked away. A sense of indignation rose within her. Why should she have to confront Dat alone? Where was her suitor, her champion? Maybe John found their situation tolerable, but she was running out of patience. A stalemate could last forever without the impetus to break it, and somebody had to make the first move.

Katie impulsively scribbled a terse message on the paper before her, slipping it between the pages of the book that would be returned to John. She went in search of Mamm, finding her in the storeroom. Katie asked permission to call on their widowed neighbor, Phoebe Trueblood. Mamm gave her assent, pressing a loaf of freshly baked bread for the elderly woman into Katie's hands.

Phoebe was a Quaker. Like most members of The Society of Friends, she was industrious, considerate, and peace-loving. She valued a simple lifestyle, service to others and equality for all mankind. Katie called out a greeting to the small figure busily at work in the flower bed. "Hello Phoebe, I have a loaf of bread for you from my mamm."

"Katie! I was just wishing for company. Would you take the bread to the kitchen? After I finish routing out this stubborn goutweed, we will sit and visit."

After doing as she was asked, Katie lent her efforts to the age-old battle between gardeners and weeds. As they worked, she confided her fears and frustrations to the wise old woman. "Phoebe, why can't Dat just accept that John and I love each other? That we belong together? Shouldn't he want me to marry the man I love, instead of making that choice for me?"

"Katie, although growing up may be a natural process, it's not an easy one, and parents sometimes harbor expectations for their children that make it even more difficult. Abe probably took it for granted that all his children would marry within the church, and now he's judging himself a failure. Good parents want to raise children capable of making sound decisions, and living independently. At least that's what we tell ourselves, but granting them that liberty is often painful for parent, and child."

Katie absentmindedly pulled on the ties of her prayer cap as she listened. "I know what you're saying, but I don't want anyone to be hurt."

Phoebe took one of Katie's hands in her own. "Someone always gets hurt. In this world there is no escaping the fact that we all hurt each other, and ourselves, too. I'm not talking about wickedness. I'm saying that despite our best intentions, it happens, and sometimes we are even complicit in our own wounds. Forgiveness and restoration are always what we hope for, but if that doesn't happen, you must move on."

After they finished weeding, Katie followed the little woman into her house. Before Katie left, Phoebe gave her a jar of blackberry preserves. On her way home, she thought about the hasty note she'd impulsively scrawled to John, and regretted the tone she'd used. The message was abrupt, impersonal and subject to misinterpretation. It could almost be construed as the prelude to an ultimatum. Absorbed in her thoughts, she jumped, nearly dropping the jar when she felt a furry tail rub against her legs. "Pittypat! You always appear when I least expect it. I envy the liberty that allows you to come and go as you please. Just watch out for that cougar while you're wandering afield." She rubbed Pittypat's little head, and was rewarded with a deep, thrumming purr emanating from her feline confidante.

Leaving the preserves with Mamm, Katie hurried to her room to dispose of the note she'd penned earlier. The tidiness of the writing desk indicated that someone else had been there, and cleared away the pile of crumpled paper from the floor. The further realization that the book was gone caused color to drain from her face as she hurried back to the kitchen. "Mamm, I can't find the book I was reading. It was in my room. Have you seen it?"

"No Katie, I haven't seen it, although I threw away some crumpled papers. Come to think of it, Danny might have picked it up. He usually comes on Mondays with a new book for you, but something unexpected came up, and he must have taken the old book with him today."

"Oh no! I need to see if I can catch him at home. May I leave for a while, just long enough to get that book?"

Mamm studied Katie's face. "Go on then, it just seems like a lot of fuss over a book."

Katie set out at a fast walk, before raising her skirt and breaking into a run as she passed beyond view of anyone watching from the house. She was breathless when she arrived at Danny and Lovina's. Katie noticed her sister-in-law, pacing nervously on the porch.

"I saw you running, Katie. What's happened? Is anyone hurt?"

She regretted causing Lovina worry. "Everyone is all right, I'm sorry if you thought otherwise."

Sinking into a rocker, Lovina motioned Katie to settle herself in another chair. "Sorry? Well, I should say so! Here I was imagining all sorts of terrible things that might have befallen the folks, or that you were being chased by that cougar that's been roaming around. Never scare me like that again! What is the matter with you?"

"Forgive me, Lovina. I was hoping to catch Danny at home. He came to the house earlier today while I was with Phoebe. He took a book from my room. Is he here?"

"A book? That's what this is all about? It must be some story for you to run all the way here, and for nothing, I might add. Danny left ages ago, said he was going to Michigan, and he'd be back in time for supper."

Hearing this news, Katie lowered her head in defeat. "It's too late then. I won't take up any more of your time, Lovina. Mamm is expecting me back."

Chapter 24

It was one of those days when John became so engrossed in his work, that the clanging of the dinner bell represented an intrusion, rather than a welcome break from his labor. He never felt the need for food when caught up in a productive and satisfying job. Eight bushels of pears were arranged around the base of the tree he was picking, and there were almost enough in his bag to fill the ninth. This afternoon he would load up the wagon and move the pears from the orchard to the root cellar to undergo a period of cooling. Later, this harvest would be relocated to the fruit shed for ripening. John judged the pears would be ready for market by mid-September.

A tuneless whistling issued from the direction of the orchard path, and John cocked his head toward the sound. From his vantage point atop the ladder, he spied a familiar straw hat approaching through the trees. Executing the fastpitch he'd perfected years ago; he called out a warning. "Heads up, Byler!"

Reacting instinctively, Danny tilted his head back, raising both hands to catch the pear speeding toward him.

"Nice lookin' Bartletts," he said, joining John at the bottom of the ladder.

"I'll send a bushel home with you."

"Thanks, Lovina will like that. She makes a really good pear pie, although I have to say Katie's pear pie is the best I've ever eaten."

"Is that right? Not that your word isn't good enough for me on that subject, but I can hardly wait to sample one for myself. What brings you here today?"

"We got news late yesterday that Lovina's second cousin, once removed, is comin' for a visit. Magdalena Kauffman arrives at the Shipshewana Depot on Monday, with plans to stay in the area for an unspecified period of time, movin' from one relative's home to another. A bunch of us menfolk drew straws to see who'd be pickin' her up at the station, and I lost."

"Oh, come on now, Danny. How much of an inconvenience can one cousin be for a week or two?"

"John, it's not without good reason that the family calls her 'Looney Lena.' And who knows how long she'll be with us? I can tell you this, the first time I met Lena was before Lovina and I were married, and it made me think twice about whether or not I wanted to join up with that bunch."

"Now I know you're pulling my leg."

"You don't understand, John. When the moon is full, that woman goes outside to howl, and I'm not talkin' about some little yip-yappin' either. It'll raise the hair on the back of your neck." At the expression of disbelief on John's face, Danny added. "May lightnin' strike me dead if I ain't tellin' the truth!"

John surreptitiously glanced at the sky, backing a few paces away from Danny. "Okay now, take it easy. You're starting to scare me, and I'm fearless. Come on, Danny, it's time for dinner, and don't forget those pears."

An unfamiliar barking announced their arrival to the open yard surrounding the house. The family was gathered in a semi-circle around a handsome collie. Johnny saw his uncle and called out. "Guess what? I got my very own dog, and his name is Rex."

As they moved closer, John's father explained. "Mother and I thought it might be a good idea to have a dog on the place. Johnny's always talking about Peter and Betsy's collie, so we paid them a visit to find out where we could get one just like him. How did we do?"

Setting the bushel of pears down, and dropping to one knee, Danny petted Rex. "He's the spittin' image of Charley. They must be brothers."

John held his father's gaze briefly, and nodded. "I think having a dog around here is a great idea."

Belle waved her brother toward the house. "You and Danny wash up. We're waiting dinner for you."

"We'll be right there," John assured her, following his friend to the Amish buggy.

After Danny loaded the basket, he pulled a book from under the seat. "Katie wasn't home when I stopped by the folks, but I could see she'd slipped a paper between some pages, and before you ask, no, I didn't read it. Tell Isabel I'll take a rain check on the dinner invitation. Thanks again for the pears, John. I'll see you a week from Monday."

As John walked toward the kitchen door, he noticed a corner of the note peeking out from the book. It was odd that Katie hadn't sealed her letter in an envelope. He stopped a moment to pull the paper out, and take a quick look. The whole of her message consisted of only two, very brief sentences. The first was a statement, the second a command.

Becoming aware of his sister's voice calling, John shoved the paper into his pocket and hurried into the house. He tried to be attentive to Johnny's excitement over the dog, but his attempts were in vain. Unable to focus his mind on anything other than the message, he began to question whether or not Katie had even written it. The penmanship was not her usual, graceful style. By comparison, this was a harsh, scribbling hand, and the language was abrupt, void of any tender emotion.

After ten minutes of pushing food around on his plate, John excused himself. "I'm taking the wagon to the orchard." Without waiting for a response, he strode off in the direction of the barn, his mind clearly occupied with a matter of great concern.

Isabel was in the process of rising from the table, when her father stopped her. "If you're planning to follow John, don't do it."

"Maybe he would like a sympathetic listener, Father. Something is obviously bothering him."

"I know the look of a man who doesn't want to talk

about his troubles," her father answered. "Leave him be. He'll either figure it out on his own, or he won't, but that stubborn set to his jaw tells me he wants to be left alone."

"Your father's right, Isabel. Let's clear away the dishes. We still have time to work on our sewing before suppertime."

The wagon was loaded with twenty bushels of pears when John drove up to the entrance of the root cellar. His father was waiting for him. "That's a fine-looking harvest, John. They should fetch a good price at the market. How many bushels do you figure are left to pick?"

John removed his hat, wiping the back of his neck with a handkerchief, "probably twice what I took off the trees today."

"Tomorrow, after the hired hands have finished harvesting cucumbers, I'll send them to the orchard," his father said. "Do you want me to take the wagon back to the barn for you?"

"No. After I unhitch the wagon team, I'm saddling Blaze. There is someone I need to see later, and I can't say when I'll get back."

"All right, Son."

John had tried all afternoon to distract himself with physically demanding work, leaving his mind free to consider what his response should be to Katie's message. If he were to form an opinion from its two short lines, he'd have to conclude she was extremely upset, or in some kind of trouble. Why hadn't she given him something of substance to go on? He wasn't a mind-reader. All he knew was that neither of them would have any peace until they could talk face to face. By the time John changed clothes and got on the road, it was almost twilight. There were miles to go before he'd reach his destination, and it'd probably be too late to find anyone awake when he arrived, but that couldn't be helped.

Night had fallen, and the inky sky was studded with bright stars when John rapped on the door of the darkened house. It was a perfect night for lovers to gaze at the heavens, and into each other's eyes. Abandoning that kind of thinking, he raised his fist to knock again, almost hitting Danny in the face when the door suddenly swung open.

"John! What in the world is wrong? Come in, come in."

"I won't even apologize for the lateness of the hour, Danny, but you've got to help me. I have to see Katie. I need to see her now."

"Well, I'll do what I can, but everyone will be in bed. What's happened?"

John took the note from his pocket and held it out to Danny. "Read this. I don't know what it means, but I'm not waiting a week to find out."

Danny unfolded the paper, holding it so the light from his lamp illuminated the words. **We need to talk. Meet me behind the schoolhouse, next Wednesday morning at ten.**

A footstep sounded on the stair, causing both men to turn their gaze in that direction. Lovina, a blanket thrown over her shoulders, walked purposefully toward them. "Let me see that."

"Lovina, there's no reason for worry. It was only John Hartman at the door. Go on back to bed, honey."

"I'm not worried and I can see just fine who was at the door. Now show me what you have in your hand."

Any protest Danny was going to make was forgotten as he looked at his wife. There was nothing for it, but to surrender the message into her open palm. She read it, looking at John. "When did you get this?"

John cut his eyes sideways toward Danny before stammering, "I ah, I received it earlier today."

"That's what I thought. Both of you come into the kitchen, and sit down."

Now they were in Lovina's territory, and her authoritative manner left no doubt in either man's mind about who was in charge.

"Hmmm," Lovina rolled her eyes toward the ceiling,

drumming the fingers of her right hand on the table. "Katie was here after you left today, Danny. She was looking for that book you took from her room, and she was upset to learn you'd gone to Michigan. Maybe she hadn't intended that note to be delivered to John. The only way to know for sure is to ask her. So, what's your plan?"

John repeated his earlier plea. "I have to see her, Lovina."

"Well, *you* can't show up at Abe Byler's, asking to see Katie, especially at this hour of the night. Danny might be able to pull it off, though."

Her husband thought he'd misheard her. "Exactly what are you talking about, when you say *pull it off?*"

"Obviously we need to get Katie here, so she and John can talk. Tell your parents I am having a restless, troublesome night, and it would be a great comfort to me if Katie could stay over with us."

"Let me get this straight, Lovina. You're asking me to lie to my folks?"

"First of all, Danny, it's not like you, and the truth are always on speaking terms. Secondly, what you'll be saying is not a lie. I *have* been experiencing a sleepless night, ever since John got here."

John had been watching the exchange between the two with fascination, and a growing admiration of Lovina. She was clearly her husband's match. Clearing his throat, John dared to make a suggestion. "Maybe I could stable Blaze, and hitch up the buggy while Danny's getting dressed?"

Handing him a lantern, Lovina pronounced his idea an excellent one.

While waiting impatiently for Danny to return, John stood hidden in the shadows of a tree. He was counting on Danny's talent for persuasiveness to succeed in delivering Katie to him. The buggy halted a few steps away, allowing Katie to alight before Danny drove to the barn. She stifled a scream as a figure blocked her path to the house. "John! What are *you* doing here?"

"Your message said we needed to talk, so here I am."

Katie's response died on her lips as John swept her into his arms and stole her breath away with a kiss.

Chapter 25

The heady fragrance of sweet rocket and evening primrose permeated the air, while John and Katie lay on a blanket blinded by love, and galaxies of stars spilling out of the vast upturned bowl of the sky. Wrapped in each other's arms, they had talked for hours before Katie fell asleep, her head resting on John's shoulder. She'd slept, oblivious to his study while he committed every feature, angle, curve and line to memory, until he felt sure he could sketch her from memory.

With the opening strains of the dawn chorus, John conceded that it was time to leave. He woke Katie with a soft whisper. "Good morning, Beautiful."

Her eyes fluttered open. "I thought last night was just a dream, but here you are." She walked to the barn with him, holding the lantern while he saddled Blaze. The screen door at the back of the house swung shut with a bang, and they saw Danny coming toward them.

"Good mornin'! Lovina will have breakfast on the table as soon as I finish milkin'. How about keepin' me company, John? Blossom's not much for conversation this time of day."

Katie excused herself, leaving the men alone. "I'll help Lovina in the kitchen,"

Inside, she ran upstairs, dashing water on her face, and rearranging her hair before joining her sister-in-law in the kitchen. Katie carefully set out plates, cups and flatware. "Lovina, I don't know how to thank you and Danny, for making last night possible. I won't forget the big risk you took so John and I could be together."

After sliding a pan of biscuits into the oven, Lovina draped her arm over the younger woman's shoulders. "Let me ask you something, Katie. Why are you and John determined to wait until November to marry? Do you really think Dat will come around and welcome John as his son-in-law? Because I don't see that happening. Maybe you ought to think about eloping."

Katie was saved from answering as John and Danny entered the back porch, where they made use of the soap, hot water and towels laid out on a bench for them.

Danny quickly took his seat at the table, but John lingered in the doorway.

Lovina waved him into the room. "John, don't even think about leaving without some breakfast. I won't hear of it."

Knowing when he was licked, John took the chair beside Katie, giving her hand a squeeze under the table. After a silent prayer, platters of fried potatoes, ham and scrambled eggs were passed around. Katie stood to fetch the coffee pot. "Where are the children this morning, Lovina?"

"Still in bed, and sleeping, I hope. It won't be long now until school takes up again, and my nieces return home. I will miss those girls. They've been such a help to me, and I'm not sure how in the world I'll manage after they're gone."

"Say," Danny said casually to Lovina, as if the idea had just popped into his head. "Say, maybe Dat would let Katie stay with us a couple of days a week, considerin' your delicate condition and all."

John bit his tongue to keep from smiling. He could hardly imagine any other woman as capable as Danny's missus, whether pregnant or not.

Lovina smiled, nodding approvingly. "That's a wonderful idea, Danny. In fact, some extra help would be especially appreciated with my cousin coming to visit. I'd almost forgotten Lena is arriving on Monday."

"*I* hadn't forgotten," Danny said, wryly.

"It's all settled then," Lovina said, ignoring her husband's sarcastic tone. "Danny, I want you to work everything out with your folks when you take Katie home."

Danny stood, saluting Lovina with an exaggerated bow.

"Your wish is my command, my Lady."

Her Highness rewarded this display of fealty with a rap on his head and the parting words, "get a move on then, I hear the pitter patter of little feet upstairs."

At the end of the drive, John reined Blaze north, as Danny and Katie turned to the south.

Mamm met Danny's buggy at the kitchen doorstep. "I've been so worried. How is Lovina this morning?"

"She's feelin' fine now. I have to say she slept much better with Katie at our place last night. As a matter of fact, we were wondering if Katie could stay over at our place, one or two nights a week to help out with the boys?"

"I'm sure Dat will have something to say about that," Mamm said, not meeting her son's eyes. "Why don't you talk to him? He's in the toolshed this morning."

Balanced on a stool, his legs splayed apart, Abe was whittling a toy horse as a pile of shavings accumulated on the floor. It was Dat's habit to carve a farm animal for each new grandchild, and because he wanted them to know they were special, every sibling within a family was given a different kind of animal. He'd started with the usual horses, cows, pigs, sheep, and chickens, but as the number of grandchildren grew, the range of animals expanded. Soon oxen, goats, dogs and cats were added to the menagerie. Doing a quick calculation in his head, Danny figured the total number of grandchildren must now be close to fifty. He was amazed the man had time to do anything besides whittling.

Dat looked up at him. "How is Lovina?"

Danny leaned his shoulder against a supporting upright, crossing his arms. "She's doin' the best she can, probably better than most, considerin' all she has to contend with right now. Her cousin is comin' for a visit on Monday. You remember Lena Kauffman, don't you Dat?"

Abe's hand trembled, and he lost his grip on the knife. It fell from his hands. Bending forward to pick the blade up from the floor, he answered Danny's question. "I do for a fact remember Lena. She's pretty unforgettable. How long is Lovina's cousin going to be stayin' around here?"

"I'm guessin' that she'll at the least want to stay through huntin' season. I never saw anyone who could track deer like Lena. Sometimes I wonder if she was raised by wolves. Anyway, I just wanted to give you fair warnin' that a strange woman might be wanderin' through the woods."

Abe muttered under his breath, "in my opinion, all women are strange."

Danny ignored the remark. "Dat, we were wonderin' if you'd allow Katie to stay over with us one or two nights a week. Lovina could use the help."

"Seems to me Lovina's got plenty of help," Abe answered. "Besides, Katie has more than enough to keep her busy here, and she'll soon have something else with which to occupy her spare time."

"How's that, Dat?"

"I'm inviting a widower over to have supper with us soon. Katie is just what Moses Zook needs in his life. No doubt he'll be grateful to have a wife, and mother for his children."

"I'm assumin' this plan of yours will be news to Katie?"

"Danny, let me tell you something before you get on your high horse with me. Don't presume to second-guess the choices I make for Katie. I want what is best for her. Maybe someday you'll understand. Fact is, I'm praying your new baby will be a girl, and do you want to know why? Because until you're the father of a daughter, you're never going to grow up and fully understand the God-given responsibility men have for the weaker sex. Remember it was Eve, not Adam, that was deceived by the serpent in the garden. Women, by their nature, are easily led astray. It's our duty to protect them from their own selves, as well as those that would take advantage of them."

"Dat, are you sayin' that the worst man, so long as he's

Amish, would be a better choice for Katie than John?"

"Not a better choice, the only choice. My objection to John Hartman has nothing to do with his character. I would gladly approve his courtship of your sister if he were one of us, but things being what they are, I cannot allow it."

Disgruntled, Danny turned to leave, but stopped when Dat called after him. "I know you and John have been friends since childhood, but you need to ask yourself how cozy you ought to be with those outside our faith. Certain members of the church are taking note of your comings and goings with worldly people. And one last thing, any effort on your part to further the relationship between John and Katie needs to stop now. That's all."

Summarily dismissed, and smarting under Dat's rebuke, Danny left.

Katie attended to her regular chores, but Mamm noticed she was unusually quiet and listless all day. After supper, Mamm insisted Katie go right to bed, convinced the girl was coming down with a summer cold.

Abe made himself comfortable in his chair and picked up the paper, resuming his reading where he'd left off the night before. "That was a fine meal, Barbara. Can't say as I've ever had a better one in all the years you've been putting a plate in front of me."

"I'm glad you liked it Abe, but all the credit goes to Katie tonight. She cooked this afternoon while I finished piecing a quilt top."

"Did she now? Well, she'll make some man a good wife one of these days."

"You seem pretty sure about that. Got any idea how that will come about, Abe? You know as well as I do, who she wants, and you won't even allow him to call."

"We're not talking about *him*, Barbara. I forbid it. Anyway, I met a likely prospect at the horse sale. A solid, respectable Amishman who'd be perfect for our Katie."

"And who might that be?"

"Moses Zook. Maybe you saw him at the Schmuckers' place last week during church? He's only recently moved his family here from Ohio."

"Surely, you don't mean that widower? The one with all those children? He must be more than twice Katie's age, hardly a suitable match for our daughter. Besides, she loves John, and he loves her, Abe."

"I know what's best for Katie. She can just forget John and get used to the idea of marrying Mose. A person can get used to anything, if they put their mind to it. We'll have no more discussion on the subject. Now I'm going to bed, Barbara. You've spoiled a perfectly good evening for me."

"Abe," he halted midway up the stairs at the tone of her voice. "If Katie marries John Hartman and you turn them away, I hope you'll be able to live with your decision, because I'll never forgive you." They each stared at the other, neither one willing to be the first to admit defeat in this battle of wills. Abe opened his mouth as if to say something, then changed his mind, and stomped downstairs instead. Looking past her, he walked out of the house slamming the door behind him.

The noise woke Katie, and she peeked out of her room. Tears were streaming down Mamm's face. "What's wrong? Are you and Dat arguing?"

"I'm sorry, I shouldn't have raised my voice. Sit with me, Katie. I have a story to tell you. It's about someone who will always hold a special place in my heart. You've heard me talk about my three, older brothers? They were all dead before you were born. I was the last one of our parents' children to survive. Only that's not the truth. I had a younger sister, named Sarah. She was caring, kind, and my best friend. Everyone who met her loved her, including Nathaniel Miller, the son of a local shopkeeper in Somerset. There was just one problem with the young man, and it was a big one. He wasn't Amish. Sarah was forbidden to see him. Our folks warned her of the consequences if she disobeyed, but Sarah followed her heart, and eloped with Nathaniel. She was shunned, cast out of our family and the church. I never saw her after that. Later, I learned she and Nathaniel had moved to Bonner Springs, Kansas. I don't know if she's still alive or not, but if she is, I'd give anything to see her again.

"Katie, if you and John marry, I will never turn my back on you. I'd rather be cut off from the church myself than to never be a part of your life."

Chapter 26

At the Shipshewana Depot, Danny was waiting for Lovina's cousin. He honestly wasn't looking forward to Lena's visit, but family was family whether by blood or by marriage.

Lena had been born in Sugarcreek, Ohio to Crist and Magdalena Kauffman. She was their only daughter, and was named for the mother who'd lived only a month after giving birth to her. Left without a wife, Crist had no idea how to raise a girl, and so he brought the child up just like another one of his sons. Lena knew how to hunt, fish, and do a man's work by the time she was thirteen.

Fortunately, a sympathetic schoolmarm helped Lena navigate the mysteries of puberty, and her adolescent years. All her brothers had by then started families of their own, leaving her alone on the farm with their dat. In time, the old man became ill, and Lena spent the next ten years caring for him until he breathed his last. The farm passed to the oldest of Crist's boys, and for a time Lena was shuttled from one brother to another, earning her keep and little else besides. Most recently she'd been hired to care for a dying woman, an old schoolmate who would be leaving behind a husband and eight children. When it was all over, Lena felt unwanted and unwelcome.

The train was already thirty minutes behind schedule, and the waiting crowd was growing restless. At last, several shrill blasts from the locomotive's whistle rent the air to announce its imminent arrival. A steady stream of passengers flooded from the train to be welcomed by family or friends. Danny stayed in the background, searching for Lovina's cousin. Then he saw her. Clutching the handles of a large traveling bag, Lena was the last wayfarer to step down onto the platform. Discounting her whipcord leanness and towering height, with a good imagination you could *almost* have mistaken her for any other, forty-something Amish spinster.

At first, Lena gave no visible sign that she'd seen him. There was no energetic waving of the hand or toothy grin, although she struck out on an unwavering course in his direction. "Danny Boy," she exclaimed in a booming voice! "I was hoping you'd be the one to meet me!"

'Danny Boy' winced at the moniker by which she persisted in addressing him.

He acknowledged her with a respectful nod, hands clasped tightly together behind his back, as memories of her bone-crushing handshake were painfully recalled.

The next thing he knew, he was snatched up and lifted clean off his feet in a suffocating bear hug. It took him a moment to recover his breath and balance after landing back on terra firma. Danny coughed to cover his embarrassment. "Well, Lena, are you ready to go?"

"All in good time, Cousin. There's my luggage to collect first."

"Luggage," he asked in confusion, taking in the oversized bag at her feet? "Are you sayin' there's more?"

"Trunks and barrels! I hope you brought the wagon."

He hadn't, blissfully unaware that he was going to need it. After cramming in as much of Lena's cargo as the buggy could hold, there remained a considerable number of crates, trunks and bags, spilling out of a railway baggage cart. Danny could read the handwriting on the wall. What was supposed to have been a *little errand*, was not only going to require a second trip, with the wagon, but it would take up his whole day. The mental strain of collecting Lena, and all her paraphernalia, was beginning to wear thin on Danny's inherently good humor.

He couldn't keep the sarcasm from his voice. "Did you bring everything you own, Lena? I always thought you liked to travel light. This *is* only a visit after all, isn't it?"

"Yes and no."

"What do you mean, *yes and no?*"

"Just what I said. Yes, I packed everything I own, . . . and no, this is not just a visit."

It felt like a great, wild bird was beating its wings against his rib cage in order to break free from the confines of his chest. The reins dropped from his hands, and were neatly recovered by Lena.

"Hey, are you all right, Danny Boy? You seem sort of surprised. Didn't Lovina tell you I was moving to Shipshewana?"

"Uh, I guess it must have slipped her mind," he answered, covering for his missus by speaking what he knew to be a bold-faced lie. Lovina's mind was like a steel trap, and her memory rivaled that of an elephant's. Darned if he wasn't going to find out what Lena and Lovina had cooked up between the two of them. Lena and Lovina, the very cadence of their names sounded to him like the headline of a vaudeville act. He slapped the reins against the horse's back, and fumed silently the rest of the way home.

When Danny deposited Lena on the doorstep, his missus had their little clan neatly assembled and waiting. The boys stood in awe, eager to be introduced to this peculiar giantess, while Sarah and Veronica got reacquainted with their distant cousin. Danny was dutifully unloading the buggy, trying to capture Lovina's attention, but she seemed intent on avoiding eye contact with him.

"Lovina," he projected at a volume that couldn't strictly be called shouting, but was definitely heading in that direction. "Where do you want these?" With an exaggerated sweep of his arm, Danny indicated the pile of bundles and bags alongside the buggy.

Lovina quickly called Sarah and Veronica to her side while cautiously approaching her husband. "Girls, will you help Uncle Danny carry Cousin Lena's things upstairs? Take everything to the farthest bedroom." Lovina spun round to retreat in the direction of the house, but Danny Boy was ready for her. He clamped his hand like a vise just above her elbow. She wasn't going anywhere.

He addressed their nieces. "Girls, you go on and start without me. Auntie Lovina and I need to have a few words." Pulling his wife around to a shade tree in the back yard, he turned her to face him, releasing her arm. Danny glowered, assuming an offensive stance, elbows out and hands planted on his hips. He was steaming. "Is there somethin' you forgot to tell me about your cousin's *visit?*"

"Now Danny," Lovina purred softly in a conciliatory tone, "don't be upset. It's not what you think. Cousin Lena . . ."

He cut her off abruptly. "Cousin Lena's already told me that she's *movin'* to Shipshewana, and there's a cart on the station platform overflowin' with her baggage to prove that fact. It will take the rest of the day to transfer all her earthly possessions here." As he scolded, Lovina began chewing her lower lip, effectively redirecting Danny's focus to her full, pouty mouth. He wished she'd stop doing that.

"But she's not moving in with us permanently, Danny. When the girls go home at the end of the month Lena's going with them, and she has plans to be in her own place before next year."

Danny figured there was more to this story than what Lovina was telling him. "What kind of plans would make it possible for her to get her own place? How does she expect to support herself?"

Lovina began fiddling with a wavy strand of honey blond hair, that had mysteriously escaped her prayer cap, winding the silky, golden lock around her finger. She was still chewing that lip, which had reddened to the color of cherries, and swollen to a tantalizing plumpness. Danny knew perfectly well what she was up to. She was deliberately trying to distract him, . . . *and he thought it might be working.* Well, two could play this game.

"You haven't explained how Lena plans to make it on her own."

After giving a melodramatic sigh, Lovina took a chest expanding breath, and pulled her shoulders back. "Lena's hoping to marry, and have a family."

Whatever crazy explanation he'd been expecting, this wasn't it. "You're joking! The woman is about to overtake the mid-century mark. It seems a little late in the day to be lookin' for a husband, to say nothin' of startin' a family! Tell me, Lovina, does your cousin have her sights zeroed in on any particular target, or is she just aimin' to cull the herd of one of its old and weak?"

Propping a hand on her hip, Lovina commenced a subtle swaying motion. There was more lip nibbling, and hair twisting, with the fluttering of her thick black eyelashes thrown in for good measure.

Danny was immovable. "I'm waiting, Lovina."

"Oh, all right, if you insist on all the details! Lena's taken a real shine to a widower she worked for in Ohio. A family man left with eight children still at home. When she found out where he'd disappeared to, she followed him here."

He couldn't believe his ears. "Do you mean to say she's stalkin' the man? Lord have mercy on the poor fella! Lovina, why didn't you just tell me the truth to begin with?"

She looked down, her voice a little shaky. "Well, it's no secret that you don't especially *like* Lena." A solitary tear sparkled on his wife's rosy cheek.

Danny couldn't abide a woman's tears, especially Lovina's. "Now, that's not true," he objected. "I don't *dislike* her. Although I do think she's kinda scary. What's the real reason for keepin' me in the dark? You can tell me."

Lovina gave an impressive demonstration of moistening her lush lips with the tip of her tongue. "I thought you'd be angry with me for inviting her to stay with us," she whispered, risking a tearful glance at Danny's face.

"That's nonsense, Lovina," he protested sternly, but by then the single tear had been joined by others, and Danny began to panic. "Now, now don't cry. Do you honestly think I could ever be really angry with you? Even now?"

He made the fatal mistake of letting his guard down, and was immediately ambushed by the seductive gaze she turned on him from those incredibly large, sapphire blue eyes.

"Well," he stammered, "well, Lovina, what do you have to say?"

"I say, . . . you talk too much, Danny."

He had no choice but to pull her into his arms, to prove he was capable of more than talk.

Days later, Danny reflected that it might not be such an inconvenience to have Lena around after all. She was a natural born pied piper, drawing the children to her with songs, stories, and even bird calls. They couldn't get enough of her. The woods and meadows rang with laughter and the joy of discovery, as Lena led her band of followers on one escapade after another. She kept the Byler boys busy, hunting arrowheads, fishing, wading in the creek and tree climbing. Even Eli had forsaken his former hero, trailing after this unlikely enchantress. Little Felty was Lena's special pet, carried aloft on her shoulders everywhere she went.

Danny had to admit he felt kinda sorry for Lena when he thought about how life had treated her. He was mulling over the poor hand Lovina's cousin had been dealt, when his missus walked into the room.

Lovina asked, "What's got you looking like you've lost your last friend?"

"I was just thinkin' about Lena. Say, you never told me the name of the man she followed here."

"His name is Moses Zook."

A mischievous smile spread over Danny's face as he stood and laid an arm across Lovina's shoulder. "You don't say? Well, we're goin' to do everything in our power to help your second cousin, once removed, bag her prey!"

Chapter 27

In spite of Dat's warning, the exchange of messages continued unabated, thanks to Danny's help. "You're early today," John said, taking the book eagerly from Danny. "I didn't expect to see you until later."

"Well, it's this blasted heat. I thought I'd get an early start before the temperature ramps up. I hope we get a break from this heat sometime soon."

"You and me, both. So, how's it going with Looney Lena?"

"Things couldn't be better, John. You know, it was wrong of me to ever repeat that old nickname. I've developed a whole new appreciation for Lovina's cousin, and I think it's high time you met her. Why don't you come to supper tonight?"

"Danny, I have a sneaking suspicion this is more than an invitation to supper. It's clear there's something on your mind, so you might as well come out with it."

"All right, I'll tell you the whole story. As it turns out, I'd been misinformed about the nature of Cousin Lena's visit. It was only after pickin' her up at the train station that I learned Lena was movin' to Shipshewana. Lovina just called it a *visit*, to get around old Danny Boy. The plain truth is that Lena's come to our neck of the woods in pursuit of a husband. Her unsuspectin' prey is a widower from Ohio, by the name of Moses Zook. Lena had cared for his wife, and eight children too, during the last year of the poor woman's life. After his wife's death, Mose packed up his family, leavin' Ohio for a new start in Indiana, without sparin' so much as a 'fare thee well' for Lena. It wasn't long after she returned from Pennsylvania that she tracked him down to Shipshewana, in order to set her traplines.

"Somehow, Dat got wind of this newly-arrived widower,

and assumed he'd be lookin' for a wife, and stepmother for his children. After meeting the man at a horse sale, Dat took a likin' to him, and was inspired to play matchmaker. The long and short of it is that Dat invited Mose Zook and his children to supper this Friday night. There's nothing in the world that would make the old man happier than to see Katie married to an Amishman."

John had been pacing while listening to Danny. Now he made a fist with his right hand, slamming it into his left palm. "That's enough! I don't want to hear anymore. Abe has left us no choice but to elope as soon as possible."

"Now hold your horses, John. I can see how you'd feel that way, but the timin' is all wrong for elopin' right now. You and Katie both agreed that a wedding in November would suit you best. By then the harvest and field work will be finished, and you'll have everything in order at your cabin. Katie will be able to take leave of Mamm in good conscience, knowin' she'd eased her burden of puttin' all in readiness for the winter. Mose is no threat. He only needs to be reminded that there's someone much better for him than Katie."

"Someone, for instance, like Lovina's cousin?"

"Exactly."

"If Lena suits him so well, why did he leave her behind in Ohio?"

"Maybe Mose don't know what he wants right now. The man's still grievin' the loss of his wife. Just be at our place tonight at mealtime, and bring Isabel along with you."

Lena had grown used to the look of astonishment registering on the faces of people seeing her for the first time. From her elevation of five feet, eleven inches in her stockings, blending in with the crowd was something Lena could only dream about. It was beyond her control that without even trying to, she captured everyone's attention. To her credit, she never slouched, walked with hunched shoulders, or bent her knees in an effort to diminish her height. Her posture was ramrod-straight, and her demeanor, full of confidence. She reasoned that

God must have known what he was doing when he made her tall as a tree, and she'd learned to live with it. Invariably, Lena's acceptance of what set her apart from most women, had the effect of putting folks at ease around her.

At John's first sight of Lovina's lofty cousin, he'd instinctively reacted with a low whistle, one note up, and one note down, signaling his amazement. This boyish response underwent a transformation to a coughing fit after Isabel helpfully applied a sharp elbow to her brother's diaphragm, saving him from further embarrassment in the commission of this faux pas.

Isabel's reaction to Lena, was one of open admiration. *Here*, she thought, *was a woman who knew her own worth and capabilities.* Isabel detected an uncommon grace, and beauty of spirit about Lena, despite the somber clothes hanging unflatteringly off the Amish spinster's spare frame.

After supper, the others went outside, leaving Lena and Isabel to wash and dry the dishes. Lena talked about the time she'd spent with the Zook family. "It was a bittersweet time for me. My old friend, Mary, was slowly failing, and yet we shared many precious moments together. I was grateful for the opportunity to render all the care and comfort that were within my power to give. During that year, I came to love her children as if they were my own, and I know they loved me, too. After Mary passed, I offered to stay on as Mose's housekeeper, but he flatly refused to even consider it. We'd always gotten on well with each other, so I was surprised when he said it wouldn't be proper for me to be a member of his household as hired help. His rejection of my offer so affected me, that I ran out of his house, fleeing to Ephrata, Pennsylvania to visit a cousin. Mose and the children were gone when I returned to Sugarcreek several weeks later. My brother, Menno, told me the family had moved to Indiana."

Isabel looked at Lena in awe. "How did you ever find the courage to follow them here?"

"Maybe it's not courage at all, maybe it's pure foolishness, but I'm going to find out, and not spend the rest of my life wondering. After praying for guidance, I felt compelled to follow Mose."

"When do you think you'll see him, Lena?"

"I expect it will be Saturday."

Lovina entered the kitchen just then. "What will be Saturday?"

"Mose and his family coming over to break bread with us," her cousin answered.

"That's right," Lovina confirmed. "Dat has invited them over for supper on Friday night. He's insisting Katie put on a big spread to impress Mose. We'll have to plan something really special if we're going to beat Katie's cooking."

Lena objected. "Now that would be a miscalculation where Mose is concerned. He's a man of simple tastes, and likes his food plain, nothing fancy. Give him a choice between an apple off the tree, or a piece of pie and he'll go for the apple every time. Besides, these dog days of summer put a damper on everyone's appetite for big meals."

"That's true," Isabel agreed, "and there's nothing so uncomfortable as cooking over a hot stove this time of year."

Lovina added, "the farmers aren't looking for an end to this heat wave anytime soon, either. This weather reminds me of a saying one of my old uncles used to quote. *It's hotter than a two-fisted billy goat eatin' grasshoppers!* Now what do you make of that? Do billy goats even eat grasshoppers?"

"I've never heard that one before," Isabel remarked, drawing the conversation back to the Ohio widower. "Lena, what else can you tell me about Mose and his family?"

"Where shall I begin? Well, Mose grew up in Sugarcreek, same as me, and his folks belonged to the same church district as mine. The other school children called us 'The Scarecrows,' because we were both tall and spindly, all loose-limbed knees and elbows. Back then, I was just another one of the boys, and I hunted, fished, explored, and scuffled with the best of them. The only time I didn't tag along was when they were of a mind to go skinny-dipping. Mose and I were best friends for a while, until he discovered girls, then it was like I didn't exist anymore. He and Mary had fifteen children in the thirty years they were married. Of course, some of the older ones have started their own families, but Mose still has eight at home. Before she died, Mary told me it would be the biggest comfort to her, if Mose and I were to marry when she was gone." Lena blushed, "I don't know if she said any such thing to him, but I believe he needs me, and goodness knows, I want to be needed by him."

As Lovina listened, she felt empathy for the plight of her cousin, and then an impish light shone in her eyes. "I've just been thinking about the meal Katie will be fixing for Mose on Friday. You know, even the most capable cook among us has experienced that occasional catastrophe in the kitchen. The bread won't rise, the milk turns sour, too much salt in the soup, not enough sugar in the pie, . . . you get the idea. There's any number of mishaps that can ruin a good supper, and those things *will* happen from time to time."

Lena was quick to respond. "If you're suggesting sabotage, I don't like that idea, not one little bit. It's deceitful and underhanded, to say nothing of being wasteful."

"Now, don't get all stirred up. I was only pointing out that sometimes bad things happen, not that they're *going* to." Lovina spoke reassuringly, while crossing her fingers behind her back.

Isabel changed the subject. "Lena, what dress are you going to wear Saturday?"

"I haven't given that any thought. Every one of my dresses is the same, except for color. Most are black, but I do have a dark brown one, and a blue one, too. Why do you ask?"

"You share the same flawless complexion with Lovina, and I imagine your blue dress would really show your eyes off to their best advantage. Would you try it on for me?"

"I suppose I could, if you want me to."

After Lena modeled the dress, Isabel asked for a needle and thread, and followed the spinster back upstairs. A few strategic alterations made the fit of the garment much more flattering to Lena's figure. Lovina showed her approval of Isabel's work by making such a fuss that Lena felt self-conscious. Just then, John and Danny walked in, carrying the two youngest boys who'd succumbed to the effort of trying to keep up with their brothers. The men stopped in their tracks at the sight of Lena, looking almost like a rosy-cheeked schoolgirl.

"Well, I declare," Danny said appreciatively, "aren't you a picture?"

Lena's blush deepened at the flattery, and she hung her head in embarrassment. Reaching out, she took Felty from Danny's arms. "Here, let me put this little one to bed."

John passed Eli to Lovina. "We should be going. Thank you for the tasty supper. Are you ready, Belle?"

Getting to her feet, Isabel said, Thanks for your hospitality, Danny. Please thank Lovina and Lena for us."

Summer's long twilight was just beginning as the evening star appeared. Fireflies danced over the fields on either side of the road, and crickets filled the night with their noisy chirping as John and Isabel journeyed home to Scottsburg. Both were preoccupied with their own thoughts, not feeling the need for idle talk, and completely at ease in each other's company.

Alone at last, after dropping Isabel off at the farmhouse and stabling Blaze, John settled back in his chair to read Katie's letter. Instead of the usual salutation, Katie had written another poem.

The Fault with Time

There is a fault with time, you know,
When we're apart the moments go
So slowly that it does appear

A single day is like a year.

Hours pass in tedious pace,
The clock's hand falters on its face,
And bell that marks the passing time
Has fallen silent and does not chime.

The weeks and months, in frozen state,
Must a warming thaw await,
Until your coming brings the sun,
Then all of time will quickly run.

Chapter 28

It was hours before dawn, and too early to get out of bed, when Katie gave up all hope of sleep. There was no use thinking daylight would bring any relief from this sweltering heat wave. She might as well stop wishing for a miracle, it was time to be about her business. If she started baking now, maybe the pies would be finished before the worst of the day's heat. It was going to be a real scorcher, that much was for certain.

For days, Mamm had tried to reason with Dat about his insistence to serve their guests a heavy meal in the hot house. She pointed out the dulling effects that stifling heat imposes on appetites and digestion, suggesting it might be better to change the supper menu to something simpler. Wouldn't a picnic outside under the trees, be a better idea? Every attempt to persuade her husband with logic and rational thinking, fell on deaf ears. Abe was unyielding, holding staunchly to his opinions, which he was convinced were always right.

By noon, both Katie and Mamm were drenched with sweat. There wasn't the faintest stirring of a breeze through the windows to offer any relief from the oppressive heat and humidity. Soon Dat's voice was heard, calling out for his dinner. Mamm put together a plate of cold leftovers and delivered it to him. The sight of Abe, relaxing against the trunk of a large tree, and fanning himself with his straw hat, only added to Mamm's irritation.

When he finished, Katie was sent to collect the empty plate. She found Dat dozing, arms crossed atop his ample belly, head bent forward and long beard covering his chest. That position couldn't be comfortable, and he'd probably have a crick in his neck when he woke up. Still, she hesitated to disturb him. As they say, *it's best to let sleeping dogs lie*. She lingered briefly in the shade of the old chestnut, listening to the leaves rustling overhead. This was bliss! The temperature in the shade felt cooler than the air in the kitchen by at least twenty degrees. As much as she'd like to rest, there was still work to do inside. Katie bent to pick up the dirty dish, and when she straightened, Dat was looking straight at her.

"Katie, you better fix up before Mose and his family get here. It wouldn't do for you to make a bad impression now. Your face is all red blotches, and your hair's coming undone. For a fact, you look kind of wrung out."

The afternoon hours passed slowly while Abe waited anxiously for his guests. They arrived promptly at a quarter to five. After the horse was watered, and tied to a hitching rail, Abe showed the Zook family into the house. Mamm and Katie stood side by side, ready to welcome their visitors.

Mose introduced his eight children, beginning with Cletus, the oldest son, and ending with Esther, a toddler of two. Dat directed everyone to find a seat around the long table, that was groaning under the weight of a typical thresher's dinner: fried chicken, beef and noodles, mashed potatoes with gravy, dressing, green beans, stewed tomatoes, and biscuits. Several pies were lined up on the sideboard. Mose felt stuffed, just looking at all that food. After a silent prayer, Abe began passing large platters and bowls around, urging everyone to help themselves, and take plenty.

Mose put modest portions on his plate, addressing Mamm. "You shouldn't have gone to all this trouble for us. We seldom indulge in such extravagance, especially in the summer, and it must have been miserable laboring in a hot kitchen all day."

Abe quickly answered for Barbara. "It was no trouble at all. In fact, Katie's the one who prepared the meal. She's a real good cook, if I say so myself. Are you sure you took enough, Mose? Or, maybe you're saving plenty of room for dessert? That's always a good idea. I happen to know there are apple, and fresh peach pies."

Mose paused a moment to wipe beads of sweat from his forehead. "I have more than enough, Abe. Thanks all the same."

The back of Katie's neck was clammy under the drooping weight of her hair, and she felt queasy at the sight and smell of all that food spread out across the table. It didn't help matters that Cletus, seated directly across from her, kept staring insolently at her with his mouth open. Chewing large forkfuls of beef and noodles proved no hindrance to his gaping observation. She tried to divert her eyes as he devoured a couple of fried chicken legs, followed by the noisy licking of his fingers. Katie was repelled by the young man's rude attention and poor table manners, but Dat was oblivious to everything, except the wooing and winning of Moses Zook for his next son-in-law. Katie prayed the earth would open and swallow her whole as Dat began enumerating her good points.

"In addition to being a good cook and housekeeper, Katie's got experience with anything that needs doing on a farm. Past the recklessness of rumspringa, yet still young enough to be biddable, she's just the right age for settling down to life as a wife and mother. And speaking of motherhood, Katie comes of good strong childbearing stock. Just take a look at Barbara. She was never down more than a day after the birth of every one of our children. She's stout and solid as they come, and dependable as a prize brood mare."

Barbara gasped, as Katie witnessed hurt and anger flashing across Mamm's face, before she was distracted by the loud crack of finger snapping from across the table. Of all the nerve! Cletus was winking at her, a leering smile on his greasy face! She dropped her fork, shot to her feet and ran outside.

The children had grown listless and drowsy in the stale, heavy air. When Mamm offered to take them to the shaded backyard, they jumped at the chance to escape. Mose was sincerely grateful for Mamm's suggestion, uncomfortably aware of the heat and tension in the room. Cletus wondered aloud if

Katie would be interested in a buggy ride, and tagged along after the others.

Abe was inwardly congratulating himself that he'd done his utmost to promote Katie's desirability as Mose's future missus. Now that they were alone, it was time to get down to brass tacks. He cleared his throat. "So, Mose, what do you say? Will Katie do?"

Mose was shocked by the presumptuous nature of Abe's question. "If you're asking if she'll do for a wife, I'm not sure that's for me to say."

"Well, who then if not you?"

Folding his napkin and laying it over the uneaten food on his plate, Mose took a deep breath. "Let me just say, Abe, you Indiana folks sure do things differently from our people in Ohio. If I'm taking your meaning right, you want to negotiate some kind of marriage contract for your daughter. Where I come from, we let the young folks manage their own affairs in such matters, and since Cletus and Katie have just met, it seems too early to be thinking about a wedding if you ask me."

"Cletus? I'm talking about a new wife for you! No offense, Mose, but your boy seems entirely too immature for Katie."

"Is that so? Well, given time he'll grow out of his immaturity as we all do, but being impulsive and flighty, . . . now that's altogether different. Women don't usually outgrow those tendencies."

Abe's temper flared. "Are you insinuating that Katie wouldn't be an obedient and submissive wife?"

Moping his brow again, Mose felt rivulets of sweat trickling down his back to dampen his shirt. "Those are *your* words, Abe. There must be some reason they came to mind. Anyway, I think it's time for me to take my family home."

Barbara overheard this last statement as she walked in on the end of their contentious conversation. "There's no need to rush off, Mose. I was just going to serve pie."

"Maybe another time. Thank you for your hospitality, Barbara. Good day."

Before she could ask what had happened, Abe demanded to know where Katie was.

"That Cletus Zook was pestering her, and she needed to get away for a while. I said she could walk over to Danny and Lovina's house. Do you feel all right, Abe? You look flushed and sweaty."

Glaring at her, Abe ground his teeth. "What do you expect? It's hot as blue blazes in here!"

Watching him storm angrily out to the barn, Barbara shook her head.

"Lord, please bring that man to his senses soon, or he'll be the death of me."

The old Byler farmstead, now Danny and Lovina's home, appeared to be deserted when Katie walked up the drive. There was no sign of life anywhere around the place. On a hunch, Katie skirted the house, following a footpath through the woods. The noise of children frolicking and splashing drew her on closer to the creek. The extreme heat seemed to lessen with every step in that direction. Just before the final bend, where she'd become visible to anyone watching, Katie stepped off the trail and hid in a thicket of rhododendrons, to spy unseen on the merrymakers. Lovina and Lena were seated on a blanket, the two youngest boys napping between them. The older ones were cooling off in the shallows while Danny prepared to test the rope he'd secured to a sturdy, overhanging branch. A big splash from his drop into the deepest part of the flowing water evoked cheers from the onlookers.

Katie found it impossible to keep from smiling, although she managed to suppress the urge to give way to a fit of giggling that would have revealed her hiding place. The next moment she was weeping, her vision blurred by tears. Katie took several deep breaths to keep from sobbing aloud. What was there to cry about? She had only witnessed a loving family enjoying time together, that's all. And she so wanted that kind of life with John. Dat was making things at home so difficult lately. She wiped her eyes and mentally scolded, *just look at you, Katie Byler, feeling sorry for yourself and crying like a baby. You ought to be ashamed.*

Any further admonition she was going to preach at herself was cut short as a pair of strong, wet arms encircled and tossed her over a shoulder, as if she weighed nothing more than a bag of meal.

"Danny! Put me down, what do you think you're doing?"

Ignoring her protests, he carried her to the water's edge. "Boys, look who I found hiding in the bushes! What shall we do with her?"

The wriggling pack of male cubs was merciless. Lusty choruses of "throw her in, throw her in," filled the air.

"No, Danny, don't," Katie begged, kicking her legs.

When he shrugged indifferently, she challenged his advantage. "You wouldn't dare!"

Lovina got to her feet, and Lena stood next to her. Katie caught her sister-in-law's eye and shouted. "Lovina, please help me!"

"Danny," Lovina waved her arm, getting her husband's attention. Then, she gave an emphatic thumbs down. "Throw her in, she needs to cool off!"

He stepped off the bank obediently. "Make way, boys!" They cleared a space in the center of the stream as he waded up to his thighs, dumping his furiously flailing sister into the water. She came up spitting, sputtering, . . . and laughing! Then, her nephews moved in, splashing her repeatedly, as if she wasn't already soaked to the skin.

Danny had returned to dry ground to watch in amusement, when a flurry of movement caught his eye. Lena was cannon-balling into the watery fray. "Hey, four against one isn't fair! Take heart, Katie, the cavalry's comin'!"

The boys screamed their delight at the appearance of a fresh adversary, and a watery battle was waged until Katie and

Lena subdued the youngsters, herding them out of the creek. Lovina met them with an armload of towels she'd brought from the house.

"You look like a pack of drowned rats," she laughed! "Now, everybody back to the house to get into dry clothes."

Danny scanned the gathering thunder clouds forming in the upper atmosphere. "Hurry now, I don't like the look of that sky!"

Chapter 29

Mother Nature unleashed her fury, hurtling bolts of blinding light, and throwing thunderous tantrums. When she'd finally worn herself out, tears of rain watered the land. The new day wore a fresh scent, redolent of Eden reborn. The old folks noticed a spring in their step, and rather than lamenting the trials of age, they suddenly felt equal to the challenge of inspiring the next generation.

Katie was determined to dawdle on her way home, not ready to return to Dat's house after having spent a joyous evening with Danny and Lovina's family. She heard a buggy approaching as she reached the end of the drive, and waited to avoid being passed on the road. Without raising her head, she casually waved the driver on while she waited. When the buggy halted alongside her, she glanced up in confusion.

"Hey pretty miss, can I give you a ride?"

"John!" She grasped his outstretched hand, springing up onto the seat beside him. "What are you doing here?"

His answer was to cover her lips with a kiss that set her heart racing. "I've come to steal you away. Any objections?"

A familiar male voice exclaimed. "Mercy Sakes! What you don't see in broad daylight these days!"

Covering her face with her hands, Katie quickly slid to the far side of the buggy's bench. Suffering no such reticence himself, John expressed his objection to this most unwelcome interruption.

"Danny! You're always lurking somewhere in the background, and turning up where you're not wanted."

"And where should I be? I live here!"

"Well, why don't you try getting lost once? Can't you see I've found the girl of my dreams?"

"Oh, I can see all right, and just what do you want me to tell the dream girl's dat if he comes round, lookin' for her?"

"I'm sure you'll think of something." John slapped the reins against his horse's back, and left Danny at the side of the road, splattered with mud from the buggy's wheels.

Katie wondered briefly about where John was taking her, but she didn't really care. All she wanted was to be with the man she loved. Slipping an arm around her waist, he pulled her closer to his side. She obligingly rested her arm on his back, and began kneading the tense muscles in his neck. He pushed back against the pressure of her fingers while reveling in her touch. If he'd been a cat, he would have purred.

"Am I distracting you, John?"

"If you only knew," he said with a rueful laugh. "I couldn't sleep last night for thinking about you, and I made up my mind nothing was going to stop me from seeing you this morning. A couple of times yesterday afternoon I was tempted to bust up the little welcome party for Moses Zook."

"How did you know about that," Katie asked in surprise? "Wait! I can guess. Of course, Danny told you."

John nodded. "So, do I need to challenge this guy to a duel or something? If he's any kind of man at all, I imagine he's madly in love with you by now."

She heard the tone of his voice harden, and saw the muscles along his forearm contract. Katie couldn't waste such a perfect opportunity to try John's patience. "A duel?" She pretended for a moment to seriously consider the idea. "Well, Mose doesn't exactly strike me as the dueling type. Besides, the fifth commandment, *thou shalt not kill*, is taken very seriously among our people. So, pistols at ten paces is definitely out of the question. Now, possibly a fistfight would be acceptable, and might even give you an advantage. Danny said they used to call you 'Ditcher' in the old days, although you were much younger then. Well anyway, there's no need to rush into any sort of contest between you and Mose. We never did get around to discussing marriage yesterday."

Turning his head to look at her, John read the mischief in her dancing eyes. "You rascal, I see you share your brother's inclination for teasing. Just take warning, I might put you to the test one of these days to see if you can take as good as you give. Especially for insinuating that I'm past the prime of my manhood! I'm only too willing to dispel that erroneous notion." He prefaced his next remark with a roguish wink. "I think you'll find my best years lie ahead. But, back to your dat's grand matchmaking scheme. Tell me how his plans played out yesterday."

Katie told him, describing the scene and the Zook family in such detail John almost felt like he'd been there. A fly on the wall.

"Of course," she sighed, "the suffocating heat alone made the whole occasion nearly unbearable. Everyone just picked at the food on their plates. The only ones with any appetite at all were Dat, and Cletus, that's Mose Zook's oldest son," she clarified, giving an involuntary shudder. "I don't believe Mose would even have accepted the supper invitation in the first place, if he'd known he was going to be subjected to Dat's not very subtle attempts to rope him into marrying me. Dat pursued this goal with such dogged determination that both Mamm and I were humiliated."

"We weren't halfway through the meal before the younger children started drooping, wilting like wild flowers in a parched land. My heart went out to them, and then Mamm came to their rescue. She took the children outside, and settled them under a shady tree, bringing apples and a jug of cool water from the spring house. I would have gone with her, but for the warning look Dat sent my way. In any case, the final straw for me was being gawked at by Cletus. He was horrid! That's when I pushed myself back from the table and ran away. I honestly have no idea what happened after I left."

John sympathized with Katie's ordeal, but also

recognized the silver lining she had overlooked. "Katie honey, don't you see? Everything that went wrong, actually works in our favor."

"What?"

"I'd be willing to bet that after yesterday's encounter with your dat, it's not very likely Mose will be wanting Abe Byler for his father-in-law. And as for that incorrigible Cletus Zook, it sounds like someone needs to teach him some manners. I'm happy to volunteer for the job."

At the county line, John turned his rig back toward Danny's house. "Have you heard about the Scottsburg Grange Fair? It going to be held on the last Saturday in September. Prizes will be awarded for the judging of all kinds of livestock, garden produce, and agricultural crops. Lots of folks come just for the horse-pulling contest. Other events are scheduled too. I'm trying to persuade Isabel to enter the pie baking event. There are games, races, and storytelling circles for the children. Something for everyone. A bonfire, and square dancing will cap off the evening. Jake Evans from the general store tells me it's not to be missed. Folks flood into Scottsburg from all around to attend the fair."

Katie was caught up in John's enthusiasm. "It sounds like lots of fun. Are you going?"

"On one condition, if you'll come with me."

She wanted to respond with a resounding, *yes, of course, I'll go with you*, but something held her back. "Well, I wish I could, but how can I? People would wonder what an Amish girl was doing at such a worldly entertainment, especially with an Englisher bachelor. And, I've never danced, and wouldn't even know where to begin. Oh, John, I'm sorry, . . ." She couldn't go on, knowing she was disappointing him.

They had traveled to the entrance of a small graveyard, bordered by farms and cow pastures. John turned through the gates of Forest Grove Cemetery, stopping at a hitching rail. "Give me your hand, Katie. There's something I want to show you."

He didn't say a word during the time it took to lead her past several rows of gravestones. The way her small soft hand lay in his as they walked, reminded him of other times. Occasions when one of his sisters had taken his hand, trusting his strength to help them navigate some rocky terrain. John had hoped Katie would have that same confidence, that assurance of his care and protection. But now he was prone to wonder if their decision to marry on November tenth had been made in haste. If Katie couldn't even commit to spending a day with him at the fair, would she really have the courage to marry him two months from now?

He stopped in front of a small white headstone, a forlorn little lamb in *bas relief* at its top. Positioning Katie in front of him, John placed his hands on her shoulders, and rested his chin for a moment on her head.

After reading the engraved words, Katie lifted a hand to lovingly stroke the lamb. Then, she broke her silence. "You had a brother? I am sorry, John. I never knew. Were you old enough to remember him?"

"I was four when Alfred was born, and almost eight when he was taken from us. I remember him very well. Mother used to say he was her best baby, happy from the very first. There is no sound in all the world so joyful as a baby's laughter, and as long as I live, I'll never forget his. I loved to make him laugh by making funny faces at him. When he grew older, he was my constant companion, copying everything I did. Then he was stricken with a sudden fever that resisted all efforts to bring it down. Alfie died three days later. After watching his casket being lowered into the ground, I was a different boy. Despite my folks trying to help me understand his death, the belief had already taken root in me that I should have been able to protect my little brother, to save him. Katie, I'd hoped that someday one of our sons would bear his name."

John felt Katie trembling under his hands as she began crying softly. Enfolding her tenderly within his arms, he continued. "I became increasingly more protective of my sisters. Henry and Edward thought they were home free when they got father's blessing to marry Musetta and Rose Ellen, but they still had to pass muster by me, and I wasn't easy on them. Things weren't so simple with Isabel, she was always a free spirit, and consequently, more vulnerable. Even though Friedrich's dead, I still worry about her and the children. You see, Katie, I'll always take care of the ones I love, especially you."

She turned to face him. "I love you too, John."

"I'm sure you believe that, Katie, but do you trust me?"

"How can you ask, John? Of course, I trust you."

He lightly caressed her cheek while searching the fathomless brown depths of her eyes. "I believe it would be best if we postponed our wedding."

Katie stepped back, disbelief on her face. "No! How can you say such a thing?"

"Katie, I'm not sure you understand how much your life will change if you become my wife. I believe with my whole heart we're meant to be together, but maybe we're rushing into something we ought to approach more slowly. I don't want you to have any regrets later. My circumvention of a proper courtship has robbed us of the time we need to really get to know each other. I want to learn everything about you, and for you to know all there is to know about me, and my family. That's why I wanted you to see Alfie's grave. He is a part of who I am, and when we marry, everything each of us brings to our union will become part of the other.

"It's time to take you home. Right about now, your dat is probably wondering where you are. He may never change his mind about me, but he's going to know I believe in doing things the right way."

Abe *was* watching for Katie, and he made it clear how he felt about seeing her in John's company. "Get out of that buggy, Katie! What do you want here, John Hartman?"

"I'm glad you asked, Abe. You can expect to be seeing a

lot more of me in the coming weeks and months, when I begin formally calling on your daughter. It will be my pleasure to get better acquainted with you, and Katie's Mamm. You may even change your mind about me."

Abe puffed up like a banty rooster. "You might have lost your mind, John, but I haven't lost mine. Coming back here will only be a waste of your time."

John helped Katie out of the buggy, handing her down to her father. "Well, it's my time to waste, Abe. I'll see you next Friday."

The drive home provided plenty of time for John to mull over his actions of the morning. The bravado and bluster he'd imbued himself with earlier had vanished, and it occurred to him that he just might have made the biggest mistake of his life. He didn't know quite what had come over him this morning. What had he been thinking? And, what must Katie be thinking? She hadn't spoken a word to him since they'd left the cemetery. Not that anyone could blame her. He'd made a presumptuous decision about delaying their wedding, without giving her the courtesy of expressing an opinion on the subject. And then, just like that, to announce he was taking her home. Finally, there was his boldness with her father. Did he really believe he could change Abe Byler's mind about him?

Katie didn't know what to think. She tried to engage with Mamm's lively chatter as they canned peach preserves, but found herself distracted by troubling doubts. Had John completely changed his mind about marrying her? Was this postponement just a step toward his calling the whole thing off? No, she couldn't believe that, not after the way he'd kissed her this morning, unless that had been a good-bye kiss. Katie was certain a bond had been cemented between them when John opened up about the little brother he'd lost. Or, had she been mistaken?

Chapter 30

Though it wasn't even noon, some of the Zook children were already complaining about not feeling well. They argued for staying home tonight. Mose sympathized with them. He didn't particularly feel like having dinner with any more members of the Byler family either. There was nothing in his past experience to compare with the unpleasantness of last night. Had he known Abe's motives beforehand, he would have declined the invitation in the first place. To think it was all about trying to pair him up with Abe's youngest daughter. That realization set Mose back on his heels!

Then, of course, there was that outrageous performance by Cletus. Well, he'd been called to account for his insolence when they got home. That boy had never wanted to come to Indiana, and now Mose was regretting his insistence on it. Perhaps, he'd send Cletus back to Ohio to live with one of the boy's older brothers.

Thankfully, last night's storm had dispelled the heat and humidity, leaving in its wake fresh air and milder temperatures. As for what this afternoon and evening held in store? He could only hope for the best. Mose took comfort in the fact that Danny and Lovina had half a dozen youngsters. Undoubtedly, the presence of these other children would give his own the opportunity to make some new friends. The trials of the past year had been hard on his family, and he knew they were all struggling with grief, in spite of the assurance that their loss was heaven's gain. He was certain that even now, his Mary was with the saints in Glory, no longer suffering in body or subject to the woes and sorrows of this world. Of course, her passing wasn't the only loss the Zook family had endured.

During the last year of his wife's illness, Lena Kauffman,

an old school friend, had cared for Mary with the affection one might have shown a beloved sister. When Lena wasn't at Mary's bedside, she was looking after the household, and lovingly caring for his children. It was plain to Mose that the youngsters had grown very fond of Lena. And, then Lena was gone too, and the fault was all his.

Mary had seen the truth, and named it to him before Mose had been able to fully grasp it himself. He'd felt both guilt and shame when he finally admitted that Mary was right. Tender feelings for Lena had stolen into his heart. Truthfully, it had surprised him. He'd never meant to fall in love with her. The silence of the moment he and Mary shared after his confession, seemed to stretch into hours. He recalled the memory clearly. The windows in their bedroom had been covered for months, dimming the light so Mary's eyes wouldn't be pained by the brightness, and because she was always cold, the room was kept warmer than usual. He'd been jolted by the iciness of the fingers Mary lay on his, but he instinctively covered them to transfer the heat radiating from his always warm hands to her cold ones. Mose had wanted to lie down and hold her in his arms, but she was so frail he was afraid of hurting her, afraid he'd already hurt her with his words. He needn't have worried his mind. She laughed quietly at his distress, before absolving him of any imagined wrongdoing. Mary assured Mose that the last, unresolved burden weighing on her heart, would be eased if he and Lena would raise the children together in a loving home. Mary made him promise that he would be happy, and not mourn. He kissed her then, and she fell asleep, passing sometime in the night to her eternal rest.

A promise easily made is sometimes harder to keep, and Mose broke his the very next day. He mourned his wife of thirty years with genuine grief and tears, finding himself adrift in her absence. If it hadn't been for Lena holding his family together during the weeks it had taken him to get his bearings, he didn't know what would have become of them. Mose never told Lena how much her faithfulness, and compassion for his family meant to him, and he berated himself for completely botching the conversation that resulted in her abrupt disappearance from Sugarcreek after Mary's death. Without meaning to do so, he'd given Lena the idea that she was no longer needed, or wanted, when she asked about remaining with the family as his housekeeper. He remembered saying something to the effect that having her living in his household as an unmarried woman, would be inappropriate. He'd meant it wouldn't be appropriate because of his feelings for her, but it had come out all wrong. She hadn't waited to hear more, and that was the last he'd seen of her. No one seemed to know where she'd gone. When Lena didn't return after several weeks, Mose decided to put the past behind him, and move to Indiana for a fresh start. He had acted impulsively, uprooting and moving his family hundreds of miles away from their old home. Though he hadn't realized it at the time, he was running away from the aftermath of Mary's death, as well as Lena's disappearance. Maybe it wasn't too late to go back to Ohio. But first, the invitation he'd accepted for a meal with the Danny Byler family had to be honored.

They were greeted by an enthusiastic quartet of boys, pausing in the middle of a no-holds-barred version of tag. The Byler lads urged the new arrivals to join the game, . . . and be quick about it! Mose barely had time to stop before his four youngest sons leaped from the buggy, eager to answer the call to action. Danny met Mose at the hitching rail, offering his hand. "Welcome, Moses. We are looking forward to getting better acquainted with you and your family. It seems that our boys have plowed on ahead of us in that regard."

"Thank you for having us. Your gesture of friendship is appreciated. We're still getting to know folks around here." While Mose was speaking, Cletus arrived in the second buggy with the rest of the family. After stepping down from the buggy, they flanked their dat. "Danny, let me introduce my son, Cletus, and my daughters, Amanda and Maggie, aged fifteen and thirteen. My youngest is two-year-old Esther, the little sleepyhead in Maggie's arms."

Danny spied his nieces coming across the yard to greet the visitors. "Sarah and Veronica, will you take these young people around to the picnic area? And, show Maggie where she can lay Esther down." The teens needed no further encouragement. They formed an easy alliance, moving away in a tight knot, absorbed in animated conversation with each other. Even Cletus, who had planned to go home after delivering his sisters, quickly tied his buggy to the rail and ran to catch up with the girls.

When Mose started walking in the direction of the house, Danny held him back. "I heard how things went at my dat's yesterday, and I'd just like to say, I'm sorry. I hope you won't hold it against him."

Mose's response hinted at his wry sense of humor. "I'm not surprised to learn that the account of Abe's failed matchmaking attempt has already traveled up and down the Amish grapevine. Apparently, Ohio's gossip trail has its equal in Indiana. Our people will certainly never need that newfangled telephone contraption."

The ringing of the dinner bell interrupted further conversation. It was the signal to let everyone know it was time to find a seat at one of the long tables. Before Danny and Mose reached the backyard, the easygoing atmosphere of the gathering shifted into one of concern, evidenced by the hubbub of raised voices calling for Esther. The two men jogged the last several yards into the midst of the group. "Where's Esther," Mose asked? When Amanda and Maggie both tried to answer at the same time, he held up a hand. "One at a time, girls. What happened, Amanda?"

The worried girl was wringing her hands, "we left her sleeping on the quilt under that tree, and now she's disappeared." Maggie added, "she was there only minutes ago, and none of us saw her leave."

Mose scanned the area. "She can't have gone far. Let's split up and start searching." Suddenly he froze, as if he'd seen a ghost.

A chorus of jubilant voices exclaimed. "Lena! Look Dat, it's Lena, and Esther!" The Zook siblings nearly crushed the smiling woman in their eagerness to embrace her, oblivious to the paralysis of their parent.

After disentangling herself from the hugs of the children, Lena made a beeline for the man she'd been seeking since they'd parted in Ohio. "Did you lose someone, Mose?"

He held her eyes, even as Lena handed Esther over into his arms. "I sincerely hope not, Lena. Maybe we can talk later?"

"I'd like that," she answered, walking away to help Lovina carry food to the tables. Mose was encouraged when Lena seated herself across from him, settling in between Maggie and Amanda. The spread was a feast for his eyes, and a meal exactly to his taste. Ripe, sliced tomatoes, corn on the cob, freshly baked bread, and grilled panfish. Lena's fingerprints were all over the menu, and there was no doubt she'd had a hand in preparing the meal. A sweet, juicy watermelon was the perfect dessert. After supper, an impromptu seed-spitting contest was organized by the boys, and provided some light-hearted entertainment for everyone. Veronica and Sarah rose to the occasion, dispatching all challengers to emerge the champions. The boys were good sports about losing the competition, and quickly convened an all-male wrestling match.

Lovina offered to watch Esther, if Mose wished to ask Lena to go walking with him. Shy as a boy who'd never spoken to a girl before, he nodded his thanks and went in search of Lena. She had taken his breath away when she'd come walking toward him earlier, carrying Esther. Now that they were alone, he couldn't think how to start up a conversation with her. Neither of them had anything much to say as they started down the path to the creek. Walking in silence until they could hear the murmur of the water, Mose captured her hand. "Lena, I regret the way we parted in Ohio. I believe there's been a misunderstanding between us."

"Well, I daresay you're right about that, Mose. I keep thinking about when I asked to remain on as your housekeeper after Mary died. You said it wouldn't be proper, because I was a spinster. Frankly, I don't understand why that should be a problem. There's nothing unusual about widowed men having live-in house help. We've been friends a long time now, and I thought we'd always gotten along well with each other. You know I care deeply for your children, and I know the feeling is mutual. With the sole responsibility for so many youngsters still at home, you've got to admit you need someone to help carry that burden. Forgive my boldness for saying so, Mose, but I believe that 'someone' is me."

He pulled Lena over to a fallen log, where they sat, and shared with each other all that was in their hearts. By the time they returned to the gathering, dusk had fallen and they joined the others to gaze at a star-filled sky with shining eyes.

Chapter 31

Country folk could detect a subtle shift in the seasons, even before the dog days of August completely loosened their hold on the advancing year. When the calendar's page turned to September, children were sent off to school, most with a shiny, red apple in hand for the teacher. These were heaped in a deep, wooden bowl on Miss Baxter's desk until they nearly spilled over the top. She greeted returning scholars with a smile, and new pupils with a little hug of encouragement, promising that everyone would find a surprise on their desk the following day. The older ones knew what they could expect to see – a cinnamon-spiced, baked apple square, wrapped neatly in thin paper. It was Miss Baxter's first lesson of each school year: *life is always sweeter when you share what you have with others.*

With the children back at their studies, women began to feel a sense of urgency to pick and preserve the last of the garden's prolific yield. Such diverse methods as canning, pickling, air-drying, and cold storage were all employed to stock home pantries for the long winter. Root cellars were bursting with bushels and barrels of potatoes, cabbages, and winter squash, as well as apples, pears and nuts. The men too, were caught up in the final gathering in of crops to provide for their animals over the coming winter. Soon the fields would be filled with corn shocks, and cribs bulging with dried ears of corn. Lofts were heaped with fragrant hay, and fodder was stored in silos.

As autumn progressed, the verdant green of summer yielded to muted hues of russet, brightened with accents of scarlet, plum, and yellow. The first kiss of frost magically transformed the tannic bite of unripe persimmons into sweet ambrosia, rich and honey-like on the tongue. These native fruits were eagerly gathered from under the trees where they fell, if the opossums, racoons, and other wildlife that favored them hadn't amassed them first. Usually after a hard frost, somewhere around the middle of October, hogs would be butchered, hams hung in smokehouses, and fall hunting parties organized.

In spite of the seasonal hustle and bustle, Katie looked forward to these golden, transitional months. This year, in particular, she was thankful for the work that kept her hands busy, and her mind too occupied to dwell on the unsatisfactory turn John's courtship of her had taken in recent weeks. Since declaring his intention to openly court her at Dat's house, they'd had no opportunity to converse in private, let alone spend unchaperoned time together. Katie understood that John's aim was to ultimately win Abe's respect, if not his blessing. She had cautioned him that this strategy was doomed to fail, but her warning was ignored, and Katie recognized a trait John and her father shared in common. They were both as stubborn as mules. Every Friday without fail, John arrived at the Byler home early in the morning, full of optimism, and the determination to cultivate Abe's favor by easing the older man's workload.

Abe refused John's help on the first Friday, insisting he didn't need it, though his aching joints and sore muscles told him differently. The next week, John's offer of free labor was begrudgingly accepted. Whatever work needed doing, no matter how demanding, John tackled it with all his might. Katie knew he was working doubly hard at home to spare his own father the added burden of being a man short on Fridays during the busy harvest season.

In the spring, as was his custom, Abe had sown mangelwurzel in a large field next to the road. Now, the time had come to pick and process these large-rooted beets, grown for winter livestock feed. While hauling a full load to the barnyard for packing into feedbags, an agitated swarm of bees flew over Abe's team in an undulating wave, spooking the team. While swatting at the insects, he lost control and was violently pitched from the wagon seat as the pair of Belgians tore through the barnyard, and off down the road. By some miracle Abe suffered no broken bones, but he was sporting plenty of scrapes and bruises, a few bee stings, and strained muscles in both arms. Walking with a pronounced limp after struggling to his feet, he refused to admit any injury to his leg. John had run after the team, following the trail of scattered beets to find the pair a mile down the road, safe and sound in the custody of a neighboring farmer.

Over her husband's loud objections, Barbara sent Katie in search of an Amish healer to assess Abe's injuries, and begin treatment. When Bennie Schrock arrived, he performed a thorough examination, and quickly prescribed at least two days of bed rest. The bee stings along Abe's forearms had raised red, swelling welts. While removing the stingers, Bennie asked Barbara to make a poultice of comfrey leaves to draw out the venom. For muscle aches and soreness, he ordered repeated applications of his own specially compounded liniment. The final blow to Abe's pride was the placing of leeches on the swelling bruises ranged over his face.

While Abe was being treated, John was dispatched to get Danny. The two of them could hear Abe's belligerent bellowing even before they entered the house. "I will not stay in bed! There is work waiting, and I've always said hard work never hurt anyone. If it doesn't kill you, it will make you stronger!"

Barbara tried in vain to reason with him. "Abe, you're not a young man anymore. You must allow yourself time to heal. The work will get done, or it will be waiting for you when you are better."

Entering the room, Danny forestalled further argument. "Calm down, Dat, there's no need to raise such a ruckus. Between John and me, everything will be taken care of around here. The more rest you get now, the sooner you'll be back to work. I'll be here early tomorrow for the mornin' chores."

Abe protested, "I don't need to be coddled like some kind of invalid." His words lost some of their effect as a deep groan involuntarily escaped his lips as he attempted to raise himself to a sitting position.

Beckoning Barbara to follow him downstairs for a private word, the healer produced a brown glass bottle from his bag. "A spoonful of this tonic in a glass of tepid water will help Abe sleep through the night. I'll be back on Monday to see how he's faring."

Abe was not the easiest patient to care for, and in no time at all, he had Barbara run ragged, hurrying upstairs and down in response to his calls and complaints throughout the afternoon. Apparently, Abe's injuries hadn't adversely affected his appetite, so Barbara served him an early supper. She decided after collecting dirty dishes from his room around five o'clock, that she'd had about all she could handle for one day. Calling it close enough to bedtime for a dose from the brown bottle, Barbara prepared the tonic. Over the many years Barbara had been married to Abe, experience had taught her what proper dosing was for her husband. *If a little was good, more was better.* She stirred two, generous tablespoons of the pungent liquid into his water glass. Within fifteen minutes after downing his medicine, he was snoring loudly. It was sweet music to her ears.

At Katie's urging, Danny and John stayed for the supper she'd prepared. Afterwards, Danny excused himself to go home, but John said he would stay overnight, bedding down with the horses. That way, he could put in at least a half-day's work before returning home tomorrow. When he couldn't be talked out of it, Barbara offered him a room upstairs, but he insisted a blanket in the barn was all he needed.

"Suit yourself then," Barbara said, rising from the table. "I'm just about give out myself, and think I'll go to bed early. See you both in the morning. Katie, when you've finished in the kitchen, get a quilt from the upstairs cupboard for John, and don't keep him up, he needs his sleep, too."

John began clearing the dishes from the table, but Katie shooed him away, sending him out to look after Blaze. "I'll be out soon, and then we can talk for a while." When the kitchen was in order, Katie spared a few minutes at the washstand in her room to freshen up before folding a quilt over her arm, and carrying a lighted lantern outside. There was still light enough to see by, though it was fading quickly, and would be darker in the barn. The horses nickered softly at her approach, and she was surprised John wasn't waiting for her. Walking softly past each stall, she reached an empty box at the end of the passage. Katie peeked in to discover John sleeping soundly on a bed of fresh straw. With all the weariness and tension of the day erased from his face, he looked more like a boy than a man as he lay there. A feeling of tenderness welled up inside her as she covered him with the quilt. Asking God to give John rest, Katie closed the barn door behind her and walked back to the house through the falling darkness.

The scrambled eggs had just finished cooking, when John and Danny jostled each other through the doorway into the kitchen. They'd been busy with chores for more than an hour, and were ready to make short work of the hearty breakfast Barbara had set out on the table. The plan for the day was to finish harvesting the field of mangels, and then pack them into used feed sacks. After a few weeks of aging, the beetroots would be stored in the ground, insulated by a mound of straw. Eager to get started, John swallowed the last of his coffee. "Where's Katie this morning, sleeping in?"

Barbara rolled her eyes at the thought. "Not that girl! She's been up for hours, and left some time ago for reinforcements. She should be back with volunteers any minute now."

Just then the sound of voices drifted in through the window. Assembled in the yard was a willing crew, waiting to be put to work. Peering out, Danny saw his two oldest boys, and Lena, standing beside Katie. He looked at John. "What are we waitin' for, Ditcher? Let's get those beets in!"

Everyone was assigned a job, and the system ran like

clockwork. Amos, Ben and Lena, caught and stacked the large beets that John and Danny pulled and tossed up into the wagon. Katie drove the wagon forward through the field, pausing to help catch and stack the mangels, too. By the time the dinner bell rang, the wagon was loaded and ready to be moved to the barnyard. After a break for the noon meal, the harvesters rested in the shade for half an hour, waiting for further instructions.

Danny reckoned that Lena and the boys should return home, and figured John probably wanted to be on his way back to Scottsburg. "Katie and I will chop off the beet leaves and begin filling sacks with the roots."

Lena and the boys didn't wait around for any change of plans, but John wasn't ready to be dismissed so easily. "I'll stay for a while yet."

Danny plucked John's hat from off his head, sailing it out into the yard. "Some people don't know when they're gettin' a lucky break."

Jumping to her feet, Katie sprinted off to retrieve the hat, unaware that John was trailing after her until he spoke. "You didn't need to run after that."

She handed the hat to him, "I don't mind. If I sit too long doing nothing, it makes me yawn."

"Yeah, I know the feeling. I am sorry we missed our chance to talk last night. I just couldn't keep my eyes open." Glancing around to make sure no one was watching, John pulled her close and whispered in her ear, "I miss you more than you can imagine."

The sensation of his breath and warm lips on her skin made her feel light-headed. She clutched at his sleeve to keep her balance. "I've missed you, too, John. Won't you reconsider postponing our marriage?"

"Katie, I do reconsider it each and every day, but I still believe I have to stay this course. Try to trust me on this, Katie. Can you do that?"

She managed a not very convincing nod, and leaning

against him, rested her forehead under his chin.

Chapter 32

Bennie returned on Monday to find that Abe's cuts and bruises were healing, but his patient's temperament had gotten worse. Well aware of the Amishman's reputation for stubbornness, the healer was surprised that the man had actually confined himself to bed for the prescribed two days. Expecting Abe to throw off the covers and leap from his bed when Bennie made the suggestion that it was time to ease back into routine chores, he'd been stumped by Abe's reaction. After asking whether or not Abe felt ready to get back to work, the only response Bennie received was a weak shrug from his patient, as if it was a matter of complete indifference to him. Attempts to draw Abe into conversation failed when he closed his eyes, feigning sleep. This wasn't like Abe Byler.

Though he was being ignored, Bennie sat quietly, continuing to observe his patient, and the surroundings. Abe's breathing was regular, his color was good, and the room was comfortable in every respect. Barbara had reported that her husband's appetite had suffered at all, and he was sleeping through the night. As the healer sat at Abe's bedside, he listened intently, tuning into sounds inside and outside the house. What he heard was the typical noise of housework, the neighing of horses in the paddock, and the pleasant murmuration of laughter and small talk coming from women busy in the garden. Everything seemed to be as it should be, except here in this silent room.

He confronted Barbara in the kitchen. "Abe should be chomping at the bit to get up. I don't know what his problem is, but the time for rest is over, he needs to start moving to get his strength back. See what you can do with him, he's not listening to me. Look for me on Friday, but send word if I'm needed before then."

Barbara had bobbed her head meekly, while biting her tongue to keep from answering Bennie in a tone she'd have to repent of later. Bennie may not know what her husband needed, but she certainly did. Abe could use a swift kick in the pants! He was moping, feeling left out, and sorry for himself. She decided to allow him one more day of grace, and if he still hadn't come around, Barbara was going to start administering some healthy doses of castor oil. He'd be getting himself out of bed then, whether he wanted to or not!

Fortunately, Abe was granted a reprieve from this purgative treatment by way of a letter Danny picked up at the post office that very afternoon. Finding Mamm in the kitchen, he handed it over to her. She noted the return address. "We haven't heard from the folks back in Somerset for several months. I hope everyone is well." Breaking the seal, she opened the envelope and read the message aloud that was written in a spidery hand:

Dear Brother,

I pray this letter finds you, Barbara, and all your family well. Has it really been two years since we saw you last? How time flies! It still seems like only yesterday that you and your bride set out for Indiana as newlyweds so many years ago.

Those of us in Somerset are planning a family reunion here the last weekend in September for the children and descendants of Christian and Anna Byler. If you have no reason to rush back to Shipshewana, consider staying a while after the reunion and we'll have a long, overdue visit. We're all getting on in years, and I don't need to remind you that five of us have already passed on since our folks died. Don't you agree we should spend time together again, before it's too late? Please come, and bring as many of your children as possible.

With love, your sister,
Catherine Byler Miller

"Well, well," Barbara mused. "I think this reunion, and a change of scenery could be just what your dat needs."

"Do you think he'll consider making the trip," Danny asked?

"There's only one way to find out. Carry this letter up to him, while I start dinner."

Abe betrayed absolutely no interest in the letter, and when Danny talked about the state of affairs on the farm, his father turned his head away. Clearly Abe was in no mood for a little friendly chit chat. Danny left the letter on the bedside table, and thought that for two cents he'd slam the door on his way out of the room.

"Mamm, how do you do it? You must have the patience of a saint to put up with his cantankerousness."

"I'm no saint, Danny, just tryin' to do my best. Did he read the letter?"

"He wouldn't even touch it."

"Well, mark my words, he won't be able to resist it for long."

It is possible that Abe intended to ignore the epistle from Somerset, but just as Barbara predicted, curiosity got the better of him and he pulled the carefully folded paper out of its envelope. While reading his sister's invitation, Abe began to mentally calculate the ages of his surviving siblings. Catherine would be seventy-two next month, John had just turned sixty-nine, and Abe himself wasn't far behind at sixty-eight. Their little brother, Christian, had recently celebrated his sixty-sixth birthday. How was that even possible? Already, one of Abe's brothers and four of his sisters had passed away, the most recent being Lydia. She was the youngest, and died two years ago. One never knew who would be next. This reunion could very well be the last chance he'd ever have to see his remaining sister and brothers. Sitting up, he swung his legs over the side of the bed, hollering for Barbara before his feet hit the floor. Making all the necessary arrangements to assemble and transport the number of people Abe was envisioning for a trip of four hundred miles would be no small undertaking. He better get Barbara on the job right away!

By the time the dust settled a week later, friends had been lined up to care for the livestock, and Barbara had managed to coordinate all the travel plans. They would be making the journey by train. Danny argued for staying behind to look after the farm, but was overruled by Dat's insistence that *all* his children go. Jonas, the youngest of Abe and Barbara's boys, was the only one excused due to extenuating circumstances. He and his wife were expecting a baby any day.

Upon arriving in Somerset, the individual Byler families were parceled out among relatives for the duration of their visit. Abe, Barbara and Katie lodged with Catharine and her husband, David. After the reunion, everyone stayed over for church on Sunday, and prepared to depart the following day for Indiana. Everyone that is, except for Abe and Barbara. They were extending their visit for an indefinite period of time. Dat agreed that Katie could stay with Peter and Betsy in Clear Springs until he and Mamm returned. When she asked when that might be, Abe replied, "you'll see us when we get back."

As far as reunions go, this one had been a grand success, with plenty of food, stories, games, laughter, and hijinks. Abe, and his siblings spent hours talking over old times, setting aside petty differences, and forgiving some long-held grudges. They shared the experience of getting better acquainted with each other's families, frequently amazed at the similar physical characteristics, and personalities of their children. The second generation of cousins quickly formed friendships, based on common interests, as well as their familial connection. Katie had been especially delighted to encounter a kindred spirit in the person of her first cousin, Lizzie Otto. The girls were inseparable, until reluctantly parting at the train station on Monday morning. They pledged to keep in touch. On the west bound journey, the Byler children remarked to each other that Dat looked at least ten years younger.

Back in Clear Springs, Katie couldn't stop thinking about the Scottsburg Grange Fair, now less than two weeks away. She'd been hatching a scheme to surprise John, one that would require some help to successfully pull off. Katie knew just the person for the job. Before leaving Somerset, she'd mailed a first-class letter to Isabel, laying out the details of her plan. She didn't have to wait long after arriving in Clear Springs for a response. Peter was soon on his way to collect Isabel, who'd agreed to stay with them for a few days, in order to play the fairy godmother to Katie's Cinderella.

The final day of the fair dawned with that golden, Indian Summer light that could almost persuade the staunchest Calvinist to believe in magic, but John was impervious to its spell. He had lost all enthusiasm for attending the event after he'd invited Katie, and been rebuffed. His heart just wasn't in going, especially since he had originally hoped to be squiring Katie around on his arm. As far as he was concerned, the whole idea of attending the fair had been shelved, but Belle was unrelenting in her pleading with him to escort her and the children. He knew if she didn't give up pestering him soon, the only way he would be rid of her was to do her bidding.

As if reading his mind, she resorted to the shameful tactic of laying a little guilt on her brother. "After all, John, it was *your* idea that I enter the pie baking contest, and now that I have, the least you can do is be there for the judging."

She had scored a bull's eye with that argument. He *had* encouraged her to compete in this event, and realized he couldn't live with himself if she thought for one moment that he'd let her down.

"All right, quit badgering me. I'll take you and the children."

The pie baking contest was scheduled for late morning, and the building was packed with contestants, and their supporters. The winners would be selected from a field of twenty entrants, by a panel of five judges. Apple pies dominated the submissions, followed by peach, blueberry, rhubarb, pear, custard, and one Concord Grape pie. Five entries were quickly eliminated on the basis of being under-baked, or burned. Seven more fell short in the flavor category, judged too sweet, too tart, or just lacking in flavor altogether. The critical flaky crust test resulted in the rejection of four more contenders. The Dutch apple, spiced pear, Concord Grape, and custard pies, emerged as the surviving finalists. After several minutes of repeated tasting and consultation, the judges came to a unanimous decision about the final ranking of the winners. Their spokesman, Mr. Mason, faced the crowd with a fistful of ribbons. "In fourth place, earning an Honorable Mention, is Mrs. Birdie Beckett for her egg custard pie." The crowd applauded politely, as a dour-faced woman snatched the yellow ribbon from Mr. Mason's hand, and stalked away. A few titters were heard from the back of the room, and the judge continued. "Third place is awarded to Miss Millie Miller for her Dutch apple pie." A plump young woman, overcome with excitement, abandoned all decorum while accepting the white ribbon, planting a loud buss on Mr. Mason's cheek. Laughter and wolf whistles erupted as the red-faced judge attempted to regain his composure.

As the judging progressed, the force with which Isabel was clasping John's hand increased almost to the point of pain. She was holding her breath as they waited on the next pronouncement. "Our second-place winner," Mr. Mason declared, "is Mrs. Isabel Bachman for her spiced pear pie. As Isabel rushed forward to accept her prize, the judge cautiously held out the red ribbon, stretching his arm to its limit, as if to ward off any further, unwanted advances. Not to be outdone by his exaggerated gesture, Isabel halted an arm's length from the judge, and much to the amusement of the onlookers, made a great show of reaching out to grasp the ribbon with the very tips of her fingers.

Acknowledging the crowd's laughter and applause, Isabel bowed graciously, and returned to her seat where John congratulated his sister on her prize, . . . and performance.

"And, now," Mr. Mason said, "it's obvious the baker of this indescribably delicious, and unusual, Concord Grape pie, is our blue-ribbon winner. Please come and get your prize, Miss Katie Byler."

John thought his ears were playing tricks on him, but when he gave Belle a sideways glance, she couldn't hide a guilty grin. John looked for Katie, but didn't see her anywhere, only a lovely young woman, the very picture of understated elegance, moving with great poise toward Mr. Mason. At last, the pieces of the puzzle fit together. His mother had only told him Isabel was visiting a friend when he'd raised the question of her whereabouts earlier in the week. Which was the truth, as far as it went. The *friend* had been none other than Katie, and it was evident from the admiring appraisals aimed in her direction that Isabel's fashion sense, and skill as a talented seamstress, were as sharp as ever. Paying particular attention to the perfect execution of details, Isabel had designed a high-necked, ivory shirtwaist, featuring a lace yoke, from which soft folds of loosely shirred linen fell to the hipline. The blouse was belted snugly, with a braided, satin cord over a fitted, plaid skirt. Katie's hair had been arranged in the latest style, providing the perfect, crowning touch. She hardly looked like herself, and John felt rather uncertain about how to address such a graceful creature when she approached him, her eyes asking a question only he could answer.

"Well, do you like it, John?" A nervous timbre in her voice betrayed some insecurity.

He leaned close to whisper his answer for her ears alone, and whatever he said, it left her blushing.

Young Johnny, having just identified this mystery lady, broke the spell by throwing his arms around Katie's skirt, Eliza copied her brother in the embrace. "Katie! Congratulations on the blue ribbon! Can we have a piece of your pie?"

"That's a wonderful idea, Johnny. Come along with me, there are tables set up for the winners, and their guests."

The little group sat around the table clearly marked, *Reserved for 1st Place Winner.* Its centerpiece was the winning entry. Isabel joined the party with her pear pie in hand, just as the elder Hartmans arrived.

John greeted his parents. "If I'd known you were coming, we could have all fit into one buggy."

"Yes, that's true," his mother agreed, "but this way you, Katie, and Isabel can stay for the evening's festivities."

After a picnic lunch, the family spent the rest of the afternoon wandering around the various exhibits, and visiting livestock pens to view the champions in each category, from the humblest barnyard fowl, to the most magnificent horses. In the children's area, they found storytellers, magicians, and games. Johnny recognized one of his classmates, and the two boys became partners in the three-legged sack race. They won by skillfully managing to navigate through an obstacle field of fallen competitors. Eliza was mesmerized by the jugglers and puppets, and had to be lured away with the promise of ice cream.

The organizers provided plenty of attractions for the teens and adults, too. An old woman in the guise of a gypsy fortune teller, tempted folks to learn what the future held for them by promising to read their palms, all for the bargain price of 15 cents. Several kissing booths were strategically situated around the grounds for the purpose of raising funds for next year's fair. As evidenced by the long lines, there was no shortage of men eager to contribute to the cause. One of the most popular kissers was the apple-cheeked, third-place finisher in the pie baking contest. Word soon spread that Mr. Mason was one of the biggest donors of the day, having already patronized Miss Miller's booth five times. A portrait photographer had set up his wagon, and was doing a lively trade capturing images for posterity. John insisted Katie have her picture made, saying it would be a lasting commemoration of the day. The photographer said he would let

John know when he might collect the finished portrait from his studio. Walking away from the wagon, John happened to see the Reverend Franklin Bailey, and his haughty daughter, Hildy, heading in their direction. Pulling Katie into a quick about-face, the pair ran into Jake Evans, nearly knocking the shopkeeper over.

"Sorry, Jake! I didn't see you. Are you alright?"

"No harm done, John. You're looking well, and who is your young lady?"

"This is Katie Byler. Don't you remember seeing her in your store?"

"Well, the name is familiar, . . ." John could see the wheels turning in Jake's head as he tried to put a face to the name. After taking a closer look at Katie, Jake's eyes popped open wide. "Well, the butterfly has emerged from its cocoon! Nice to see you again, young lady. Those uppity girls that were so mean to you this summer should see you now. Are you staying for the dance tonight?"

Katie stole a glance at her smiling escort. "I'd love to, if John will consent to be my partner."

Taking her hand for Jake and the whole world to see, he said, "nothing in this world would make me happier."

Chapter 33

In a tree bordered clearing outside the grange hall, a platform of wood planks had been fashioned into a dance floor. Hanging from posts and tree branches, lanterns created an atmosphere of gaiety. A little band of musicians was tuning their instruments in an out of the way corner. Most of them were locals, like the farmers and shopkeepers ready to lead their wives and sweethearts through the steps of a square dance. An Irish fiddler passing through on his way to Chicago, was the only outsider performing with the group. After several dance sets, the band switched over to a livelier tempo. The jigs and reels emanating from Seamus Kelley's fiddle seemed to vibrate through the very bones of those in the crowd, lifting them off their feet, to dance with unrestrained abandon. The experience of being whirled around the floor in John's strong arms, exceeded all of Katie's expectations.

Taking a break to catch their breath, they went inside the hall for refreshments, where John's sister and other women, were busy serving cider and doughnuts. Seeing them, Isabel tilted her head in the direction of an empty table, following after with mugs of cider.

"Well, how was the dancing," she asked, placing a drink in front of each of them?

John paused to quench his thirst. "Katie was amazing, I can't believe she hasn't been dancing her whole life."

"You have Belle to thank for that, John," Katie confessed. "She taught me the basic steps. I'm not what you would call a natural, but with you as my partner, dancing was like second nature to me."

John raised his mug to salute Katie, and his sister. "I'm proud of you both." After draining his cider, he looked around the room. "Have you seen anyone you know, Belle?"

"No, well just a few folks. I have noticed a man staring at me all night. He looks vaguely familiar, but I'm sure he's not anyone I know."

"Really?" John's protective instincts instantly went on high alert. "Where is he?"

He's leaning against the far wall, behind you, . . . no, don't look. Oh dear, he's coming this way!"

John rose to his feet, turning to shield the girls behind him, and to confront the approaching man. Almost at once, his shoulders relaxed and he exhaled a sigh of relief. "Isaac, my friend! It's good to see you again."

The two men shook hands, and John made the introductions. "Isaac, this is my fiancée, Miss Katie Byler, and my sister, Mrs. Isabel Bachman. Ladies, meet Mr. Isaac Lehman."

Katie fancied she detected a trace of disappointment pass over Isaac's face when John prefaced Isabel's name with the title, *missus*, but at the same time her own head was spinning with his public reference to their engagement. She felt her heart beating in her throat.

Isaac made a neat, gentlemanly bow. "I am honored to make the acquaintance of two such lovely ladies." He turned back to John. "Congratulations! I wish you and Miss Byler every happiness in your marriage."

"Thank you, Isaac."

"Mr. Lehman," Isabel asked, "how did you and my brother come to be acquainted with each other?"

"We met through a mutual friend. Jake Evans and I are both members of the Scottsburg Grange, and we've been encouraging John to join ever since he moved here."

John admitted as much. "I fully intend to do that one of these days. Tell us more about the organization."

Happy to oblige, Isaac expounded on the merits and benefits of the Grange. He was really warming to his subject when it became clear to him that he'd somehow lost his audience.

John's attention had shifted to the beautiful Katie Byler, who was likewise enraptured with her admirer. Mrs. Bachman looked bored, or restless, and Isaac wondered if he'd suddenly become invisible.

Moments later, Isabel stood. "Please excuse me, Mr. Lehman. It looks like the dishwasher could use some help. It was very nice to meet you."

Isaac rose by reflex. "I assure you the pleasure is all mine, Mrs. Bachman."

As Isabel began walking away, an afterthought occurred to her and she turned, posing a question to her brother. "You'll find me when you're ready to leave, John?"

Though absorbed in an intimate tête-à-tête with Katie, John acknowledged Isabel's query with a casual wave of his hand, signaling that he'd gotten the message. At the same time, it was impressed on Isaac that *two is company, and three's a crowd.* Following Isabel's lead, he found a reason to excuse himself.

After several minutes, a shrill whistle captured everyone's attention. It was announced that the bonfire would be kindled in a quarter of an hour. People began streaming outside to find good seats. It was the quintessential, autumnal night. The Hunter's Moon hung overhead in its waning, crescent phase, reminiscent of a harvesting scythe. The wind was dead calm, and the air cool when the tepee-shaped stack of logs was ignited. Flames licked upwards, illuminating scores of happy faces encircling the fire. Someone began singing an old favorite, and soon other voices joined in, filling the air with harmonious melody. The night was made for lovers, and a sense of timelessness enveloped John and Katie, lost in the magic of the firelight, the music, and each other.

On the way to Peter and Betsy's house, Blaze was allowed to set his own pace, and when the horse halted, neither of his passengers made any move to disembark. Even after Blaze tossed his head and stomped impatiently, John delayed, not wanting the evening to end. "Katie, you can't imagine what this day has

221

meant to me. I was so proud of you when your name was called as winner of the pie baking contest. You fooled me though; I almost didn't recognize my Amish sweetheart."

"Your sister helped me with the dress, and she's going to give me other patterns, too. There is so much I have to learn about fitting into your world, but I want you to know that I am ready to leave my old way of life behind for our future together."

Two things happened simultaneously as Katie finished speaking. She and John both realized to their horror that they'd forgotten Isabel, leaving her behind at the fair. At the same time, a strong wind blew in from the southwest, bringing with it a deluge. They sprinted to the house between driving bands of rain. John opened the door and quickly pushed Katie inside, out of the wet.

Cursing under his breath, he drove Blaze as hard as he dared, back to the grange hall.

As Isabel began looking around for John, she noticed the size of the crowd was dwindling rapidly. It had been two hours since she'd left John and Katie at the table. The bonfire was dying down to embers, and the hour was growing late. A feeling of uneasiness was growing every minute while she searched for her brother. Isabel's arms were folded over her waist. Her bearing radiated a sense of vulnerability, and when a man in close proximity to her shoulder addressed her by name, Isabel nearly jumped out of her skin. "Mrs. Bachman? I don't mean to startle you but I couldn't help noticing you standing here, giving every appearance of a damsel in distress. Is anything wrong?"

Isabel's right hand moved involuntarily to the base of her throat, as she took a quick breath. "Oh! Mr. Lehman! It's just that I seem to have lost track of my brother. He is supposed to be taking me home. Have you, by chance, seen him?"

"I saw John and Miss Byler at the bonfire over an hour ago, but not since then. There's Jake Evans. Let's ask him if he knows where we might find them."

She gratefully took the arm he offered her for support,

and walked with Isaac across the room to consult Jake. What the storekeeper told her was not reassuring.

"Yes, I saw John. He and Miss Byler left quite a while ago, heading in the direction of Clear Springs." Isabel's lips compressed tightly together in a straight line, and Jake surmised what had happened. "I'm guessing it slipped John's mind that he was meant to take you along, but no cause for alarm. There's bound to be someone going your way. In fact, if I remember correctly, Mr. Lehman owns a farm on Union Road, just a short distance from your folks. I'm sure your brother would have no objections to his escorting you home. Now, if you'll excuse me, there's one of my customers, and I must have a word with him before he gets away. You both have a good evening."

After Jake left them, Isabel arched an eyebrow at Isaac. "I am sorry, Mr. Lehman. It looks like you're stuck with me."

He objected. "There is no reason to apologize, I am glad to be of assistance. It's the least I can do for my friend."

Once in the buggy, he said. "Just by way of clarification, Mrs. Bachman. If I seemed at all hesitant to see you home before Jake made the suggestion, it's only that I didn't wish to compromise your reputation. Being in the company of a man other than your husband, might be fodder for the gossip mills. I hope it won't be a problem for you."

Despite knowing that Isaac had just given her the perfect opportunity to put his mind at rest on the matter of her marital status, Isabel found she simply couldn't bring herself to blurt out that her husband was dead.

Their homeward journey had just gotten well underway, when a sudden downpour turned the secondary road into a muddy quagmire. Their progress was slowed considerably until they reached the main thoroughfare. Isabel openly admired Isaac's sure-footed horse, and his skill as a driver. These compliments breached the awkward silence that had settled between them. As they conversed on various subjects, they discovered they shared similar interests, especially creative pursuits. When Isabel said she loved growing flowers, and arranging floral centerpieces, Isaac confessed his love of gardening, and painting still-life compositions. "Perhaps, Mrs. Bachman, you might consent to fashion an arrangement for me to capture on canvas?"

"I'd consider that small payment for coming to my rescue tonight, Mr. Lehman."

"Please, feel at liberty to call me Isaac. Every time I hear you say, *Mr. Lehman,* I feel like the ghostly presence of my father is hovering about. He always did say he'd come back to haunt me." This last remark was delivered with a wink and a smile, letting her know he was teasing about his father being a spook.

Appreciating his quirky sense of humor, Isabel laughed. "Then you must call me Isabel. John neglected to tell you that I am a widow. My children and I have been living with my parents since Mr. Bachman died in March of this year."

"Oh, I am so sorry, I didn't know. I hope my thoughtless remarks alluding to a *ghostly presence* didn't offend you."

"No offense taken, Isaac. It makes me believe your father was the kind of man who didn't take life too seriously, and enjoyed a good joke at his own expense."

"You have him pegged to a T. He left me with many fond memories, and I miss him every day. But, how are you and the children getting on? Tell me about them."

Isaac listened attentively as Isabel talked about Johnny and Eliza. He felt he had a pretty good picture of them in his mind when she'd finished. "They sound like wonderful children, Isabel. I'd like to meet them someday."

Isabel hadn't realized how quickly time had passed, while giving candid, and entertaining accounts of her children's forays into mischief. With a start, she saw that Isaac's horse was nearing the drive. "Here we are. I see a lamp has been left burning for me. Thank you for seeing me home." Before he could help her down, she gathered her skirts and jumped, landing neatly on the kitchen stoop. She flashed a smile, and waved. "Good-bye,

Isaac."

Returning the smile, he lifted his hat. "Goodnight, Isabel," adding to himself. "Goodnight, but if I have anything to say about it, it isn't good-bye."

John missed Isaac by only thirty minutes, but it was long enough for Isabel to embellish the whole tale of being left behind at the fair. Her theatrical nature kicked in as she got wound up. "I was humiliated!"

"You were embarrassed," her mother corrected. "Don't confuse the two. Now, all's well that ends well, and most importantly, you got safely home. Who *was* the good Samaritan who came to your rescue?"

"His name is Isaac Lehman, he's actually a neighbor, and a friend of John's. Thank goodness Isaac was there. I don't know what got into that brother of mine tonight, he's never done anything like this before, and he's going to get an earful from me when I see him." Isabel flounced upstairs.

As John expected, his mother was waiting for him when he rushed into the kitchen. "Belle? Is she here, is she all right? I unintentionally left her behind at the grange. When I returned, she was gone, and there was no one else around."

"There's no need to worry, John. Isabel is here. Your friend, Isaac Lehman, brought her home about half an hour ago. As for your sister being all right? She's madder than a wet hen, but I expect she just might get over being angry at you by morning. Now it's time you went to bed, John. If you don't get to sleep soon, the sun will be up before you are." Ignoring her own advice, Susanna Hartman sat alone with her private contemplations, taking note of the fact that children never outgrow their need for a mother.

Chapter 34

John had already milked the cow, and turned her out to pasture before the sun crested the horizon. Setting the pail of fresh milk next to the sink, he found his breakfast waiting for him, but if he was going to be on time for Sunday worship, there wasn't a moment to spare for a second cup of coffee. He still clung to the fellowship of believers at the little Vistula church, although his parents had transferred their membership to a local parish. Belle and her children had been accompanying him lately, but this morning there was no sign of them, and he was disappointed to be going alone.

Feeling terrible about stranding his sister at the grange hall last night, John couldn't blame her for being angry with him. He would do everything he could to make things right with Belle. Raking the litter of dried, withered blossoms and wilted foliage from her many flower beds should go a long way toward restoring him to her good graces. Then, there was that new plot to dig for the dozens of tulip bulbs she wanted to get in the ground before the first hard freeze. If all these efforts failed, he would reorganize the garden shed, making room for the potting bench she wanted.

Satisfied with this plan, John's thoughts turned to Katie. On the drive to church, he recalled what Jake Evans had said after recognizing her at the grange last night, 'the butterfly has emerged from its cocoon.' Katie had always been beautiful in John's eyes, but the world was full of people who would not see beyond someone's outward appearance. On more than one occasion John had overheard derogatory remarks about the Amish, based on the peculiar, old-fashioned attire they wore, and their strict rules. It was no wonder that the sect was adamant about maintaining some separation with those outside their faith.

Personally, he'd grown up admiring his Amish neighbors, and considered many to be his friends. But despite the high esteem he held for them, he knew he could never make the leap required for a conversion to their faith. He'd never heard of a non-Amish person making the transition to becoming Amish. Was such a thing even possible?

While pondering this question, John thought about Katie's determination and courage, making such a radical change for him. At times, it must feel like she's stepping off a cliff into thin air. Katie had to know that deviating from the traditional Amish dress, could not, and would not, be overlooked by the church. Yet, she was risking it all for him as she moved closer and closer to the point of no return.

At the church, John greeted a small knot of men lingering outside the doors, before he joined the parishioners filling the pews in the sanctuary. He had just taken his seat when Reverend Smith invited everyone to stand for the opening prayer, and first hymn. Echoes of the pastor's 'Amen' filled the sanctuary as the organist began working the pedals to inflate the bellows of the pump organ. The chords coming from the instrument cued the worshipers to lift their voices in praise. Standing behind the pulpit, the old minister offered a message of love and grace to the congregation. For John, beginning each week with church set the tone for the coming days. It was the only way he could imagine spending Sunday mornings, and soon Katie would be at his side to share all of this with him. At the conclusion of the service, he felt at peace, prepared for the unknown challenges ahead, and inspired to love his neighbors. To quote Robert Browning, "God's in his Heaven, All's right with the world!"

The whole Hartman clan usually gathered at James and Susanna's on Sunday afternoons. There was no prior planning involved, it just happened spontaneously. As he'd anticipated, John saw two familiar buggies tied to the hitching rail when he returned home. His brothers-in-law, Henry Kline and Ed Carson, had finished placing tables, chairs, and benches around the yard.

Anticipating the usual, Sunday afternoon game, they were now checking out the horseshoe pitch. Johnny, Eliza and their cousins played happily together, racing from one end of the yard to the other until they were all red-faced and panting.

John went immediately in search of Belle, finding her in the kitchen, which was a hive of activity. His mother and sisters were preparing the big Sunday dinner, and catching up on the latest news. When Musetta and Rose Ellen caught sight of John in the doorway, their eyes shot daggers in his direction. *If looks could kill, he'd be a dead man.* Obviously, they'd heard all about last night, and now he was in big trouble with all his sisters. Belle's back was to him when he entered the room, but now she turned, and the kitchen's usual welcoming ambience plummeted to a sub-zero chill.

Why is it, he sighed, *that sometimes it's easier to love your neighbors, than your own family?* Taking a deep breath, he strode intentionally across the room to face the sister he'd offended.

"Belle, I don't blame you for being angry with me. Forgetting you at the grange was inexcusable, and I won't insult you by suggesting there is any acceptable excuse for what happened. Although I don't deserve it, Belle, won't you forgive me? You know neither of us will be happy until we're reconciled. How about it?"

John's apology was spoken so humbly and sincerely that Belle's heart melted. Embracing him, tears filled her eyes. "Of course, I forgive you," she said, adding a stipulation. "Just don't let it happen again!"

After everyone had eaten too much, the children returned to their play, and the dirty plates were put to soak in the big dishpan. Susanna and her daughters retired to the parlor for a full quarter hour's rest, before cleaning the kitchen. As John was preparing to join his father and brothers-in-law in a horseshoe pitching contest, a buggy pulled into the drive.

Recognizing Isaac Lehman, he waved him over toward the hitching rail. "Isaac! Your timing is nothing, if not providential. Now I can thank you personally for bringing Belle home last night. I consider myself in your debt. If there is any way I can ever repay you, just say the word. Won't you stay for a while?"

"Thank you, John, but I can't today. Anyway, it looks like you have a houseful already. I just stopped by to return a glove your sister dropped in my buggy last night. She's probably wondering where she lost it." Isaac didn't mention that he had reverently tucked the glove into his vest pocket, and only minutes ago won a hard-fought battle with himself about whether to give it back to its rightful owner, or keep it close to his heart.

"It's only the family here," John assured Isaac, "so you must stay. Belle will be happy to see you, and the glove, again."

Unable to refuse the invitation, Isaac fell into step with John. "That's the second time you called her Belle."

"What?"

"I thought your sister's name was Isabel."

"Oh, yes. Yes, Isabel *is* her given name. I'm the only one who calls her Belle. I suppose it's a holdover from childhood."

John's admission prompted Isaac to share a brief history of his own family, which consisted now of only two brothers and three sisters since their parents died. His siblings had all married years ago, and moved west to Illinois. John was interested to learn more about Isaac, but this was not the best time or place for that conversation. He did however, make a conscious decision to attend the next grange meeting with his neighbor, come rain or shine.

The aroma of freshly brewed coffee drew John and Isaac up the back steps and into the kitchen. Susanna and her girls were setting pies out, ready to be cut and served later for dessert. Glancing up when the door opened, Isabel caught sight of John's friend, and tried ineffectually, to smooth back a few stray tendrils of hair that persisted in framing her face with curls. She nervously wiped her hands on the gingham apron that covered her dress. After introductions, John explained that Isaac had come to return Isabel's glove. Musetta and Rose Ellen watched with growing interest as a very becoming blush spread over their older sister's face.

Susanna Hartman extended her hand to Isaac, giving Isabel a moment to compose herself. "Mr. Lehman, I am glad to meet you. Thank you for seeing Isabel safely home last night."

"I am honored to meet you, Mrs. Hartman. It was my pleasure to be of some small service to your family." After acknowledging Isabel's sisters with a courteous nod, Isaac looked directly at her.

Forgetting proper etiquette, Isabel curtsied to their visitor, as if she'd just returned from London to visit the Queen. *What was she doing? She'd never done such a thing before! Had she lost her senses?*

An audible intake of breath was heard as Musetta and Rose Ellen locked eyes, and felt compelled to clasp each other's hands. Susanna Hartman was the only one who didn't seem surprised at the chemistry charging the atmosphere, and in that moment, John realized that for Belle and Isaac, the other occupants of the room had ceased to exist.

Responding in kind to Isabel's old-world curtsey, Isaac bowed gallantly while ceremoniously withdrawing the glove from his pocket. When he offered it to Isabel, their fingers touched and sparked with physical electricity. Then their neighbor departed, walking to his buggy in a trance-like state before driving away.

Isabel discovered that she needed to remind herself to breathe. Released from a spell of silence, the two younger girls flocked to their sister, asking questions and demanding answers. Observing a smug expression on his mother's face, John followed her out into the yard.

"What do you know about this, Mother?"

"Only what my intuition is telling me. That Isaac is a good man, and maybe now Isabel might be more understanding about how you could have forgotten her last night."

"Well, he's moving a little too fast in my opinion."

"John," she patted his shoulder, "I hope I'm still around when young men start showing up to court your daughters."

Not inclined to dwell on that distant possibility just yet, John decided it was past time to pitch horseshoes and engage in some rational discourse with his own kind.

Katie had lain awake for hours after John brought her home, reliving the thrills and romance of being with him at the fair. If it hadn't been for leaving Isabel without a ride, the evening would have been perfect. She drifted off to sleep at last, dreaming of the life that awaited her with John.

After waking in her old room at Peter and Betsy's house, Katie came downstairs dressed once again in her Amish clothes. They didn't seem to fit her as comfortably as they had before. She was grateful there was no church scheduled for their district today, as she seriously doubted whether she would have been able to stay awake during the three-hour service.

After suffering through several rapturously delivered accounts of Katie's big night, Peter finally fled to the barn, seeking some privacy in which to read the paper. Katie had been describing to Betsy every detail of her time at the fair, beginning with the pie baking contest and ending with the bonfire. Peter had heard enough. Even though the whole scheme had been known to him from the beginning, it'd still been a shock to see his sister-in-law dressed like an English woman. While conveying her to the grange last night, as inconspicuously as possible, he'd actually felt uncomfortable, like he was in the company of some fine lady. He and Betsy counted themselves among those happy to see John and Katie coming together as a couple, although they knew that there would inevitably be a day of reckoning. A disquieting sense that the other shoe was about to drop, made itself known in Peter's mind.

Betsy was preparing a covered dish for their ailing neighbor, when Joshua's mewling cries escalated into squalls of distress. The four-month-old was cutting teeth and he was clearly miserable. Sending Betsy off on her mission of mercy, Katie ran upstairs to comfort her nephew. She cuddled Josh close and after several minutes of dandling him against her shoulder, he fell into an exhausted sleep. Crossing her fingers, she laid him down in the cradle as quietly as possible. After tiptoeing to the kitchen, Katie attacked the soapy dishes in the sink. A sudden, sharp rapping on the back door startled her and a wet plate slipped from her fingers, breaking on the floor. Seconds later, Joshua's wailing filled the house. Perturbed by this unwelcome intrusion, Katie jerked open the door, and came face to face with Bishop Yoder from Shipshewana, Indiana.

Chapter 35

Deep in his own thoughts, Abe Byler sat alone on the rustic bench in David and Catherine Miller's backyard, unconsciously turning the hat in his hands round and round. Who could have imagined that less than four weeks after the reunion, his brother Joseph would be dead? It was a painful reminder to Abe of his own mortality, and the importance of not putting things off, especially where estranged relationships were concerned. He reflected on every conversation they'd shared during what neither of them knew to be the final days they would have together. A bone of contention had existed between the brothers for years, each one stubbornly clinging to the opposing view he'd held with regard to certain interpretations of scripture. From his recently acquired perspective of grieving brother, the question of who was right and who was wrong, didn't seem to matter much anymore. Abe was thankful he and Joseph had finally agreed to allow each other the liberty of having different opinions, but he regretted the wasted years they'd spent judging each other.

Of course, he and Barbara had stayed for the funeral, and on through the next week, until forced at last to acknowledge that postponing their departure date only increased the risk that bad weather might impede their return home. Snow often commenced in Somerset County by the end of October, and frequently lasted through April. If they wanted to lessen their chances of being snowbound, it was best to go while they could.

Regardless of that fact, something he couldn't put his finger on, was making this goodbye a difficult one for Abe. These old stomping grounds had stirred up memories of untold hours spent exploring the woods, streams, and higher elevations of Elk Lick Township, and further afield into the Lower Turkeyfoot region. He had roamed this area for weeks in the summer of 1860, before finally putting his footloose days aside to marry Barbara, and move to Indiana. Yet, even the passage of four decades was not enough to diminish the pull of this place on him, any more than a man could blot out the memory of his first love.

So, why was he finding it so hard to leave? He'd changed the trajectory of his life long ago, when he and his new bride turned their backs on Pennsylvania to strike out on their own. Without any conscious effort on his part, a heavy sigh pushed past his slightly parted lips. Only then, in his peripheral vision, did he catch sight of a figure approaching. If he'd known someone was watching him, he might have taken care to school his face into an inscrutable mask. Turning for a better view, Abe recognized Catherine, and slid over to make room for her on the bench.

She playfully mussed his hair before taking a seat beside him. "Abe, you look like you've been caught with your hand in the cookie jar. Show me your palms, little brother, so I can check for crumbs," she teased.

He couldn't help chuckling while obediently holding out his hands for inspection. Catherine always could make him laugh. She was one of those rare individuals who lifted the spirits of everyone she encountered.

"Something's troubling you, Abe. Do you want to talk about it?"

He responded with a self-deprecating attempt at humor that sounded phony, even to his own ears. "Oh, I'm just feeling my age, I guess, – never expected to be a nostalgic old fool, but being back in Somerset has made me sentimental about the past. That chapter of my life is over, and I think it's a waste of time to dwell on it. Don't you agree?"

"If you really want to know what I think, Abe, I'll tell you. Shall I?"

She was serious. He'd been expecting a droll comeback that would release his pent-up tension and leave them both grinning, but there was something in her voice he'd never heard before, and it made him wary, yet hopeful at the same time.

After a moment, he nodded and gave her his undivided attention.

"I think viewing our life as a simple timeline with fixed starting and stopping points is a mistake. That approach robs us of the fuller appreciation of its mystery. Our lives overlap with those before us, and those coming after, like stitches on a knitting needle, building on each other to create something bigger than ourselves. As long as we live on this earth, the past is a part of us, and when we're gone, it lives on through our children. But I suspect there's more on your mind, than reminiscing about days gone by. Before Katie left with the others, I noticed an expression on your face every time you looked at her – like she was slipping through your fingers, and you were powerless to hold on to her."

Abe's reaction was like that of someone being surprised by the unexpected appearance of a ghost. Catherine had seen through him as if he were as transparent as glass. He had forgotten what an uncanny ability his sister possessed for divining what was at the root of a matter. It was a relief finally, to unburden himself about the conflict raging in his heart. She listened thoughtfully while he made all the firmly established, and accepted, arguments against an Amish person marrying someone outside the faith. Encouraged by the repeated, affirming nods of her head, he said. "So, you agree I'm right to follow my principles."

"Of course, Abe. There was never a question about that, and it's obvious you did what you thought right when you married Barbara."

"What? No," he protested, agitated that Catherine hadn't been paying attention. "I'm talking about my forbidding Katie to marry an Englisher! What did you think I was talking about?"

Catherine paused, allowing Abe to calm down. "Well, naturally I thought you were referring to a decision that was yours to make, not a choice belonging to someone else." She let that sink in for a minute, before going on.

"In my mind, Abe, I still see you just as you were more than forty years ago. Strong, capable, a young man seeing endless possibilities ahead, brimming with the confidence that you'd navigate every turn along the road, and make all the right decisions." She laid her hand on his shoulder. "You really haven't changed so much, my dear brother, you are still strong, capable and confident."

It didn't escape his notice that she had omitted the word, *young.*"

She cleared her throat, "I believe we should cherish the past, live in the present, face the future, and love, unconditionally." Using his shoulder as a prop, she eased herself to a standing position. "Supper will be ready soon." Catherine was already walking away, but stopped and turned. "One more thing, Abe. Don't be sorry for the loss of your youth, it can be replaced with something even better."

He was curious. "And, what would that be?"

"Did you ever stop to think that when we were young, we had all the answers? It's only in later years that the trials and disappointments we've experienced cause us to question almost everything we thought we knew. If you allow them to, Abe, those questions can lead to an open heart and mind that will give wisdom a place in which to abide."

Watching Catherine wind her way back to the house, he thought about what she'd said, and recalled random fragments of Ecclesiastes, Chapter 3:

To everything there is a season, and a time to every purpose under heaven:

A time to be born, and a time to die . . .

A time to get, and a time to lose . . .

A time to rend, and a time to sew . . .

That which hath been is now; and that which is to be hath already been . . .

Abe thought it was time to go home.

Danny was waiting for them at the station. What had been a clear, bright day only hours earlier, was quickly growing darker as billowing thunderheads scudded across the sky, obscuring the sun. The temperature was dropping quickly, and Barbara shivered as she maneuvered into the buggy's rear seat, squeezing in alongside their bags. Abe noticed the horse holding his neck braced tensely in an upward position, eyes wide and nostrils flaring as he scented the approaching storm. The set of Danny's face, as Abe settled onto the seat beside him, warned of bad news to come.

Racing the storm home, Danny tried to prepare his folks for the gossip that was traveling at lightning speed along the Amish grapevine. He said that Peter and Betsy had brought Katie home from Clear Springs three days ago. She had been in a bad way, visibly shaken. Pausing to reconsider the bluntness of what he'd just said without sufficient explanation, Danny started over at the beginning, exercising the permission Katie had granted him to speak for her. Now, he told them everything, relating in detail how Katie had conspired with John Hartman's sister to surprise John at the fair. She had dressed in English clothes, worn her hair in a modern style, without a covering, and worst of all, she had danced. Granted, it was a scandalous thing for an Amish girl to do, but Danny defended her, and said he did not believe her behavior warranted the swift and severe retribution it had garnered. Someone, whose identity was unknown, had recognized her at the fair with John, and tattled to Bishop Yoder. The very next day she was confronted by the bishop, and accused of being a wicked woman. He'd warned her that her very soul was in danger. If she didn't break it off with John; repent, and join the church, she was surrendering herself to the devil, and would burn in hell for eternity. Peter, who'd been in the barn during this confrontation, hurried to the house after hearing a man's voice raised in anger. He opened the door in time to witness Katie telling the bishop that her salvation was between herself, and her God. The man was so inflamed that he slapped her with enough force to leave the imprint of his hand on her cheek. Before he could raise his hand to her again, Peter lifted the bishop off his feet and threw him outside. When she returned, Betsy found her husband pacing the floor, as Katie sat crying in the rocker. Peter wanted to go for John, but Katie had forbidden him, fearful of what John might do. Instead, she insisted they take her home to Shipshewana, to wait for her parents' return.

Danny halted the horse at the kitchen door, trying to calm the high-strung animal with a gentle, steadying voice. Barbara was desperate to get out of the buggy and comfort her daughter, but Abe reached back, caressing the side of her face with his hand.

"Please Barbara, give me a few minutes alone with her."

The oil lamp was turned so low that neither father, nor daughter, could clearly delineate the other standing at opposite ends of the room. Katie turned the wick up and their eyes adjusted to the light. Her face was streaked with tears, and her voice was raspy. "Dat, I never meant to cause you pain, but I can't be sorry for loving John. I'll always love him."

Letting his actions speak louder than any words, Abe opened his arms wide, and Katie flew into the refuge of her father's embrace. She had been afraid of hurting him, and he of losing her, but their fears evaporated as they held each other. After releasing her to Mamm, Dat took Danny aside to speak to him privately.

"This is just between us, do you understand? I am going to see Bishop Yoder first thing tomorrow morning, and then I'm going to Michigan to call on John."

It was not yet daybreak when Abe reached the Yoder farm, and as one would expect, the man was in the barn at this hour, milking his cows. Foregoing his usual respectful greeting, Abe confronted Yoder, suggesting that if he wanted to hit someone, he should pick on a man his own size, instead of a girl.

The bishop cowered in the face of this challenge, and a heavy thud echoed off the barn walls before Abe stalked out and drove away, heading north. Filling his lungs with clean, sharp air, he was invigorated by the simple act of breathing. Though he'd never been to the Hartman home before, Abe estimated his arrival for midmorning based on Danny's directions. There was plenty of time to take in the scenery, and think about what he was going to do.

Breezing through the kitchen door with Eliza in tow, Isabel pulled up short, noticing the best cloth laid out carefully on the table, and coffee brewing on the stove. "You're expecting company," she said, making it a statement, rather than a question as her mother emerged from the pantry with a plate of raisin scones.

"Yes, he should be here any minute now. It's actually someone to see your brother, so we'll just make the visitor welcome until John returns from town."

"Who's coming," Isabel asked?

The sound of buggy wheels on the drive rendered the question moot. Susanna greeted Abe at the hitching rail and invited him inside, as Eliza was sent in search of her grandfather.

Abe tried to politely decline Susanna's hospitality. "I don't mean to intrude on your day, my business here is with John."

"Yes," she nodded, "he's on an errand, and should be returning soon. Come in and have some coffee while you wait."

Despite his resolve to maintain some distance between himself and this family, Abe couldn't refuse the invitation without being rude. He sat and accepted some coffee. As James walked into the room with Eliza riding on his shoulders, she boasted proudly that she'd tracked him down to the outhouse. Laughter rippled round the table, and Isabel made a pretense of scolding her daughter for talking too much. Abe noticed how easily conversation flowed back and forth between family members, and soon he himself was caught up in horse talk with

James.

At first, John mistook the buggy tied to the rail for Danny's, but a second look corrected that assumption. It wasn't Deacon in the traces connecting the harness to the rig. *That gelding,* he thought, *seemed familiar though, in fact, it looked an awful lot like one of Abe's driving horses.* He tucked a flat package under his jacket and went inside.

Isabel saw it first, the edge of a parcel peeking out from the place where it had been concealed. She called out excitedly. "He got it!" A feeling of anticipation seemed to come from the rest of the family as well. Isabel persisted, "have you opened it yet? Let us see it."

John ignored her, and went directly to Abe, offering his hand. "How are you, Abe? This is a surprise. Is everything all right at your place?"

"I'm fine," he said responding to John's initial inquiry, while disregarding the second. "I wonder if you could spare me a few minutes of your time this morning? No hurry though, it's obvious there's something under your coat that your family is anxious to see. I can wait."

John stalled, "I don't want to hold you up."

"I'm sure Abe would be interested to see what you have, too," his mother volunteered helpfully, or not.

Left with no alternative but to comply, John carefully withdrew and opened the package, laying its contents on the table between Isabel and Abe, while the others jockeyed into a position to look over their shoulders. Exclamations of admiration filled the room, but Abe remained puzzled as to why Susanna thought he'd have any interest in this image. *Was he supposed to know this person?* Intently studying the cabinet photograph, he was nearly rocked back when he suddenly recognized Katie's face looking straight at him. He couldn't deny that she was beautiful in those fancy clothes. What she wasn't – was Amish, but she was still his daughter.

Abe raised his eyes to meet John's. "I've been hearing a

lot about this cabin of yours, I'd like to see it. Would you show it to me?"

They walked the worn trail in silence for several minutes, until Abe was certain they were out of anyone's earshot. Then he told John, word for word, what Danny had reported about Katie being found out for attending the fair with him. He watched the young man beside him stiffen, and clench his fists when he described the bishop's vicious reprimand of Katie.

Abe rubbed his right hand as if it was troubling him. "I had a few things to say to the old bishop when I called on him earlier this morning."

John glanced at Abe's hand, noticing the scraped and swollen knuckles. "You didn't," he asked incredulously?

"I think it was the first time in my life I wanted to use my hands for violence on another person." This was said almost pridefully, and John was surprised to feel a surge of solidarity with Katie's father. "Thank God," the Amishman continued, "I diverted my aim at the last moment, and pummeled the barn's wall instead."

After inspecting the cabin, inside and out, Abe commented favorably on the quality of John's repairs and his improvements to the structure. "I see only one thing missing."

"What's that," John asked, wanting to know what he'd overlooked?

"You need a wife, son, and I'm giving you my blessing to marry Katie. It's time the two of you started making wedding plans."

Chapter 36

News traveled fast, and when word leaked out that John and Katie planned to marry on November tenth, there was no shortage of unsolicited advice and offers of assistance made to the couple. Everyone it seemed, wanted to lend a hand. Female relatives on both sides had been quick to offer ideas about what the bride should wear, who the attendants should be, where the event should take place, what kind of cake should be baked, . . . and so on. For their part, the men's reactions alternated between back thumping congratulations, the occasional ribald joke, and warnings about getting permanently shackled with a ball and chain. It was however, the threats of a wedding night visitation that caused John to lose the most sleep. Personally, he considered the old Scots-Irish custom of giving the newly wedded couple a shivaree to be a rude prank, regardless of the fact that as a younger man he'd spared little sympathy for other grooms. John could attest as a former participant, that it was much more fun being on the giving, rather than receiving, end of this indignity.

Katie found making plans to be a bittersweet experience. From the moment she'd accepted John's proposal, it was understood that the Amish tradition of an all-day wedding celebration would be forfeited. The Amish celebration of a marriage typically began in the morning with a lengthy sermon, and culminated with vows taken before the assembly of family and friends. Around midday, when the service was concluded, a large meal would be served. Singing, games and socializing would fill the hours between the noon dinner, and evening supper. It was an occasion everyone in the Amish community looked forward to with eager anticipation.

Understandably, Katie felt a pang of loss, knowing she would never experience this time-honored custom, although she didn't admit any of this to John. She consoled herself with the knowledge that it was the groom that would make this day the happiest of her life, not the accouterments that usually went along with the event. She had no regrets about saying yes to John Hartman. He was the man she loved, and the one at whose side she wanted to be for the rest of her life.

The bestowal of Abe's blessing on their marriage had eliminated the necessity of an elopement, but his consent brought with it some other considerations. If the wedding was held at the Vistula church, Katie's family would feel out of place, but having the ceremony at either of their parents' homes might be construed as favoritism. As a compromise, and out of respect for the feelings of both families, John and Katie opted for a private, civil ceremony at the Lagrange County courthouse. They were persuaded to agree to a family dinner following the official sanction of their marriage, with both sets of parents involved in the organizing of the dinner to be held at Danny and Lovina's home. Time was running out to accomplish the necessary preparations, and all available hands were put to work on one project or another. The loan of extra tables and chairs was arranged, and a major housecleaning undertaken two days before the appointed date. All of Katie's possessions, with the exception of her wedding clothes, had been packed up and delivered to the little cabin on the Hartman farm earlier that week.

On the big day an army of women invaded the household before dawn to begin cooking. Susanna and Isabel brought dozens of homemade cinnamon rolls. The first of many pots of coffee were brewed for the family and other early arrivals.

Katie was still in bed when Barbara fixed a breakfast tray to carry up to the prospective bride. The girl had slept very little during the previous night, her mind spinning with all that had transpired in the last thirteen months. She'd been riding a wave of emotions since falling for John, and now at last, they were about to become husband and wife. Sometime in the wee hours, Katie fell into a fitful sleep from nervous exhaustion.

Barbara knocked softly and entered the room, only to be arrested at the sight of her daughter, . . . her baby, oblivious to the world. Katie's face in repose was one of trusting innocence. There was so much of life this girl had yet to learn. Tears welled up in Barbara's eyes and she thought to herself, *it is going to be hard to let this one go. Not that seeing the others leave home had been easy. It was never easy, but Katie had chosen a very different life from the rest of her children.* Barbara sniffled and fought against tears, growing impatient with her sentimental musings. *Get on with it now, woman, the coffee is getting cold.*

She set the tray down a little noisily on the bedside table. "Good morning, sleepyhead. You'd better get up, unless you've changed your mind about marrying John today."

Katie's eyes popped open and she sat bolt upright. "What did you say? What day is it, Mamm?"

"It's your wedding day. I've brought you something to eat." Impulsively, Barbara hugged Katie and kissed her cheek. "When you're ready, we'll go to Danny's. Isabel is already there to help you dress."

Barbara closed the door behind her, leaving Katie alone. Warming her fingers around the steaming mug, the words, "when you're ready," played over in her mind. *Was she ready?* The answer came without hesitation. *She could hardly wait!*

Yet when the time came to submit to Isabel's ministrations, the symbolism didn't escape Katie that she would enter the dressing chamber in her plain Amish clothes, and leave wearing distinctly different garments. Today all the official aspects of her identity would change: her name, marital status and place of residence. No longer would she be known as Katie Byler. Instead, she would be Mrs. John Hartman of Scottsburg, Michigan. She thought abstractly that this mystical transformation might be compared in part to what the church taught about baptism. The dying to self to be raised into something new. Katie thought about this. Like all married women, she would take her husband's name, but she wasn't

244

about to bury the essence of who she was, and always had been. For one panic-stricken moment Katie wondered just how much of herself John might expect her to forsake. Then her anxiety vanished. She knew he loved her just as she was.

It had been a blow to Isabel that she wasn't allowed to design an extravagant bridal ensemble for the occasion, but the couple had made it clear they didn't want their nuptials to be a showy affair. To soften the disappointment, Isabel was granted the privilege of dressing Katie from the skin out for the occasion. Knowing there wouldn't be any mirrors in the starkly appointed bedroom of the Amish home, Isabel had brought along a hand mirror, to prop up on the chest of drawers.

After Katie disrobed, Isabel commenced the dressing process with a set of silk underclothes, a special gift to this girl who would soon be her sister by marriage. The bride-to-be flushed pink at the sight of herself in the mirror wearing these delicate things. The beauty and intricacy of the details used to construct the chemise, corset and petticoat surprised Katie. After all, the fine tucking and lace wouldn't be visible after she was dressed, and who was going to see this feminine frippery anyway? As the answer dawned, Katie felt light-headed, and swayed slightly, before dropping into a chair to keep from fainting. Isabel waved smelling salts under Katie's nose, prompting the girl to take shallow whiffs until her head cleared.

The ivory shirtwaist Katie had worn to the fair was now paired with a fitted jacket and matching skirt, the soft gray of a dove's breast. After styling Katie's hair, Isabel satisfied her own desire for extravagance by dabbing just a touch of French perfume behind Katie's ears. The *pièce de résistance* of the finished outfit was the high-crowned velvet hat, adorned with the merest whisper of a veil that fell gracefully over Katie's features to the middle of her slender throat.

John was pacing impatiently, his back to the others when the rhythmic thrum of activity that filled the room suddenly stilled. Turning around he saw at once where everyone's attention had been drawn. Katie stood halfway down the stairs, pausing in her descent. Looking up, he caught the gleam of her dark eyes, slightly obscured behind sheer gossamer silk.

It was ten o'clock when they arrived at the Clerk's office to obtain the marriage license. Once the paperwork was completed, the couple was shown into an adjoining room where the Justice of the Peace presided over a simple ceremony. They repeated their vows to each other, and then the officiant asked if there was a ring. Katie had not expected one, and was overcome when John slipped a heavy gold band over the third finger of her left hand. A chaste, public kiss followed, and they were duly pronounced husband and wife.

They were within a mile of the Byler farm when John's attention was captured by a group of men on horseback blocking the road ahead of them. Katie tensed beside him. "What is it you think they're after?"

He pulled on the reins, slowing the buggy to a halt as masked riders thundered toward them, yelling and raising a cloud of dust. John clasped Katie's hands, trying to reassure her with a low whisper. "Don't be afraid, you will be perfectly fine. It's only me they're after." There was no time for him to say more before the riotous band bore down on them. One of the men leaped from his horse while others muscled John from his seat, forcing him to mount the steed left riderless by the man who'd vacated the saddle. Katie's last sight of John was the unnerving spectacle of her new husband surrounded by a gang of disreputable looking characters, forcing him away. She was frightened as the man who'd stayed behind took John's place at her side. Fear quickly turned to anger when he pulled the kerchief down to reveal his identity.

"Isaac Lehman! Who are those men, and where are they taking John?"

"Now Katie, they're only some of his friends. Trust me, it's all just some harmless fun. Your husband won't suffer any permanent damage, and he'll be back soon."

She crossed her arms and sputtered, "friends? They didn't look very friendly to me!"

Scooting away from Isaac, Katie seethed in silence for the passing of what seemed like hours but was in reality closer to thirty minutes. The pounding of hoof beats announced the men's return. John climbed back into the buggy, looking a little worse for wear, and slightly rumpled. After the assailants had ridden away, Katie assessed her husband's condition with a raised brow, deciding she deserved an answer. "What was that all about?"

Before answering, John pulled Katie into his arms, giving her a deep, prolonged kiss that tasted strongly of distilled spirits, and not the medicinal kind. She was quite breathless when he released her.

"That, my love, was the ransom price to ensure our wedding night is not interrupted by a bunch of rowdies. We better hurry now to the dinner."

A crowd had gathered outside the Danny Byler house to greet the newlyweds. Katie noticed among those lining the drive, a certain scruffiness in the appearance of several male guests, including her brother Danny, Peter Christner, Jake Evans, and both of John's brothers-in-law. Taking a closer look, she was sure a swelling on Danny's cheek suggested the blooming of a bruise. Despite having grown up with brothers, she would never understand what possible enjoyment males derived from physically accosting each other.

The afternoon was growing late, and there were twelve miles of travel ahead when John and Katie finally got away, to head toward home. It had been a long day. All the hours on the road, the celebration with family, and her sleepless night were catching up with Katie. She yawned as John drove past the cabin, going on to unhitch and secure Blaze in the little stable. Someone had left an oil lamp burning inside so they wouldn't have to enter a darkened house. At the door, John swept Katie off her feet and carried her over the threshold. Liking the feel of her in his arms, he took his time before releasing her. They hung their outer wraps on the hall tree. Then John lowered himself to one knee in front of the fireplace, raking the embers, and adding logs to ensure the fire would last the night. Katie shivered while hovering over him to capture some of the fire's warmth. As John prepared to stand, a cascade of soft silkiness tumbled around him. Katie had unpinned her hair and let it fall. Turning as he got to his feet, John buried his hands in the luxuriant dark tresses and pulled Katie to him. Holding her gaze, he saw that her eyes were smoky with desire. She wrapped her arms around his neck, kissing him with a passion that left him wanting more. Her lips were soft and warm against his as Katie whispered, "take me to bed, husband."

Squinting, she woke to sunlight slanting through the window as it illuminated a trail of clothing scattered across the floor from the door to the four-poster bed. The lovers lay nestled together under the quilts, neither wearing a stitch between them. Katie warmed with the memory of last night, and stole a glance across the pillow to see if John was awake. His deep, even breathing told her he wasn't. It was impossible not to think about how he had tenderly and patiently loved her. She couldn't say whether or not this was what every bride experienced when a marriage was consummated, but it had irrevocably expanded her limited understanding of lovemaking.

Again, Katie eyed the clothes that needed picking up. Well, she was a wife now, and she was going to be a good one. Quietly concentrating on slipping out of the cozy warmth without disturbing her husband, Katie was suddenly pulled tightly back against John's body as he nuzzled her neck. "That can wait until later."

Spent by the sweet demands of their love, Katie had fallen asleep in her husband's arms, allowing time for John to contemplate his love for this woman, and all that she meant to him. He had dreamed for so long of having her in his bed, imagining that by claiming her body she would be his, but he'd been fooled on that account. It was only now he knew himself to be completely at her mercy, and helpless to do anything except obey her slightest wish. Katie had yet to figure that out for herself.

Chapter 37

Awakened by a rude, repeated knocking on the door, John surfaced slowly to a state of semi-consciousness. His head pounded in time with each blow that shattered the peace and quiet. Coming fully awake, he viewed his surroundings with confusion. It must be midmorning, if he was to believe the light from the window, but what was more bewildering was the fact that he was alone in bed. Where was his wife? The room had been tidied up, and the only clothing in sight was a pair of his pants and a shirt, folded neatly on a chair. That blasted knocking hadn't abated, if anything the tempo and volume were increasing. Shrugging into his clothes, John hurried from the room to see who was demanding entry.

Jerking the door open he found Belle on the other side, a smirk of amusement on her face.

"John! I'm shocked to find you just getting out of bed at this hour. Are you sick, or something? You look – well, you look awful! Maybe being married to someone so much younger doesn't agree with you." Belle pushed past him, eyes searching. "And, just where is Mrs. Hartman this morning?"

Before the question hanging in the air between John and his sister could be addressed, the back door swung open to admit Katie, windblown and dazzling with roses in her cheeks and a radiant smile on her face. She quickly crossed the room to stand close by John's side.

"Good morning, Isabel. Won't you join us? I'm just getting ready to put breakfast on the table."

"Thank you, Katie, but not today. We ate hours ago. I'm delivering an invitation from mother for supper tonight. Will we see you later then?"

Katie looked to John for the answer, and after a moment,

he grudgingly nodded at Isabel. Satisfied that her mission was accomplished, she departed with an impish wink. John and Katie spent the rest of the day alone, not answering the door, or venturing from the cabin until the dinner bell summoned them to the farmhouse.

It was a small group seated around the Hartman table. The immediate family was present and accounted for, but there was one surprising addition. Isaac Lehman was seated directly across from Isabel. He explained his presence to the newlyweds by saying he'd only stopped by to deliver a gift for them, and had been prevailed upon to accept Susanna's hospitality. John's welcome was sincere and hearty. Katie's greeting was less enthusiastic.

After the meal, the party moved to the parlor, Isaac excusing himself briefly, before returning with a rectangular package he'd retrieved from a corner of the dining room. He presented the gift to Katie with an air of formality. After removing the wrapping to reveal an artistic rendering of the old homestead cabin, any animosity she'd harbored against Isaac for participating in John's abduction yesterday was forgotten. Painted in a striking contrast of somber and bright hues, the sensitive execution of the subject perfectly captured a sense of the cabin's warmth and welcome, as well as the implied promise of contented domesticity. Katie's reaction was immediate and emotional. Tears filled her eyes and she hid her face on John's chest. "It's our home! Thank you, Isaac, it's beautiful!"

Everyone was so effusive in their praise of the artist that Isaac, who was humble by nature, became self-conscious to the point of being uncomfortable. "I really must be going home, it's getting late." Isaac's comment about the lateness of the hour tempted John to issue a similar statement, but he calculated by doing so his real motivation would be obvious. Truly, he wanted nothing more than to be alone with Katie in the privacy of their own bedroom. If only he could find a way to discreetly extricate them from his family. *Patience is a virtue,* he reminded himself, and settled back in his chair to wait. The murmur of a conversation between his wife, mother, and sister as they dealt with the aftermath of the evening meal, could be heard from the kitchen. *Did women never run out of things to say to each other?* A half hour dragged by, during which Johnny and Eliza became restless and began bickering with each other. A loud snoring from his dozing paterfamilias reverberated like thunder around the room, and set John's teeth on edge.

He tried to immerse himself in the latest edition of *The Scottsburg Sentinel*, but he couldn't seem to concentrate on the newspaper. It was becoming increasingly uncomfortable for John to suppress the urgent desire he felt to be in private circumstances with his wife. Deciding after several more interminable minutes to take matters into his own hand, John snatched up the painting, along with Katie's shawl, and advanced boldly into the bastion of feminine occupation. Assuming an authoritative, husbandly manner, he flung the shawl over Katie's shoulders. "It's time to go home, dear. I just can't wait any longer to see how this painting will look over the fireplace." She was not blind to the yearning look in his eyes, and as the door closed behind them, they set off chasing one another down the woodland path to the cabin.

A good part of the next day was spent combining Katie's belongings into their household effects, for she had not come empty-handed to the marriage. Like most girls raised in an Amish home, Katie's cedar chest had occupied a focal point during her adolescence, serving as the repository for items deemed necessary to future housekeeping. An assortment of crockery, treenware, and kitchen utensils was soon unpacked and put away on shelves, and in cupboards. In addition to the contents of the chest, the Byler family had been generous with gifts of foodstuffs to stock the couple's larder with everything from dried apple slices to smoked hams. Likewise, the contents of the linen press were enlarged by the addition of several quilts, some goose-down pillows, Hudson Bay blankets, and utilitarian muslin pieces.

Finally, Isaac Lehman's painting was displayed in pride of place over the mantelpiece, where it could be admired by all.

From all appearances, the house was outfitted with everything necessary to the art and function of homemaking. It seemed that nothing had been overlooked, until one glaring omission was discovered the morning a mouse startled Katie in the root cellar as she was filling her apron with potatoes. A shriek of surprise brought John running, and though the unwelcome vermin had already disappeared, nothing would satisfy Katie until she was promised they could get a cat that very day. An impromptu visit to the Byler farm was undertaken for the express purpose of adopting Pittypat, the cunning mouser *par excellence,* into their family.

The comfortable routine of sitting before the fire each evening was soon established. Pittypat alternately purred and slept on the hearth rug while Katie's knitting needles clicked softly. John usually read aloud, or he might serenade his wife with a song played on the mandolin. Sometimes Johnny and Eliza were allowed to stay over on a Friday night, enjoying popcorn and cider before being tucked into a cozy trundle bed in the loft. The cheerful, little abode attracted other company as well. Isaac and Isabel, especially, became regular visitors. In-laws and friends came from near and far, eager to call on John and Katie before the north winds sweeping in from Canada made the journey of many miles an ill-advised venture.

Thanksgiving was celebrated in Indiana with the Bylers, followed by a sense of escalating excitement for the coming Christmas holiday. Katie spent hours with Isabel and Susanna in the matriarch's kitchen, learning some of her mother-in-law's recipes. The women busied themselves with holiday baking, and soon tins of cookies, fruitcakes, and crocks of mincemeat lined several shelves in the pantry. The house was filled with irresistible aromas, enticing men and children alike to pass through the kitchen on regular forays, seeking an oven fresh morsel that might be filched from a cooling rack. As much as Katie enjoyed this time with her mother-in-law and Isabel in the big farmhouse, she was always eager to return to the little cabin and her husband.

John made a trip to the general store for some last-minute shopping the week before Santa was expected to arrive. While he waited to settle with Jake, the shopkeeper produced a letter from the mail he was sorting. On the envelope a familiar return address identified the sender from Shipshewana. John could hardly wait to get home so he and Katie could open it together. It proved to be the announcement they had been waiting for, though it contained an unexpected surprise. The newest addition to Danny and Lovina's family of rough and tumble boys was a baby girl. The tone of the correspondence suggested that Gemma Byler had, without any effort at all, managed to wrap her father securely round her little finger. Katie was excited over the arrival of a new niece and could hardly wait to get her hands on Gemma, but John advised patience. The almanac's predictions for a cold, snowy winter didn't bode well for travel, and Katie reluctantly agreed. John knew she was disappointed and was sure he had just the remedy to lift her spirits.

"Now go to the bedroom, Katie, and stay there until I call you to come out – no fair peeking, all right?"

"Why? Am I being punished," she asked with a naughty smile, and flirtatiously batted her eyelashes at him?

Distracted by the obvious implication of her question, John contemplated several scenarios playing out in his mind, at least one of which involved spanking. He was considering acting on this impulse when the sound of childish laughter preceded a knocking on the door. Already adept at reading her husband's mind, Katie laughed at his predicament, and he gave her a dark look in return, as she swept past him to admit Johnny and Eliza. The children spilled into the room, talking excitedly over one another.

"Uncle John, Aunt Katie," Johnny said, "there's a tree on your porch! And . . ."

"And boxes, too," Eliza completed the sentence!

Despite their inopportune timing, John welcomed the children enthusiastically. "Well, you'd better come in then, and help us trim our Christmas tree. Johnny and I will handle the heavy work and Eliza can help Aunt Katie pop some corn for stringing."

Decorating for the holiday was a new experience for Katie. Christmas in the Amish community was not celebrated with trees and tinsel, and she couldn't help marveling at the transformation taking place right before her eyes. Fragrant evergreen garlands soon graced the mantel and framed the windows. While adorning the tree with strands of popped corn and cranberries, a perfect little bird's nest was discovered tucked among the pine boughs. Enchanted at this find, Katie insisted the nest remain in its place. Then it was time to hang the gingerbread men, brought by Johnny and Eliza. These were strategically hung on the tips of branches. While the few cookies that had been damaged in transport were put on a plate to be served with hot chocolate, another knock sounded on the door. Isabel and Isaac had come to walk the children home, but were easily persuaded to stay for some refreshments. Her sister-in-law handed Katie a soft package wrapped in paper. Upon opening it Katie found an assortment of crocheted lace snowflakes, and immediately found a place for them on the tree. They provided a lovely counterpoint to the garlands and gingerbread ornaments already there.

After their visitors had departed, Katie admired her first Christmas tree, praising John. "I've never seen anything so beautiful. Thank you, it's perfect."

"Well, I'm not sure," he said, pretending to find fault with the tree, "something seems to be missing. Sit here by the fire, close your eyes, . . . and don't open them until I say you can look." He delivered this admonition in an authoritative tone.

"I don't think I'm very good at minding you," Katie giggled, "but I'll try."

She listened as his footsteps moved away from her. There

were more sounds: paper rustling, the creaking of a chair supporting John's weight as he stood on it, then sharp, hammer blows before he stepped down. Katie couldn't imagine what he was doing and was dying to know.

With eyes tightly shut, she felt him take her hand. "All right, you can look now."

There at the very top of the tree was a beautiful crystal star. She caught her breath and placed a hand at her heart. "The star of Bethlehem! It *is* perfect now. But what were you pounding?"

John resisted pointing it out, wanting her to find the object for herself. Her gaze traveled around the room, and over the ceiling beams, coming to rest on a little bundle of bright greenery with white berries, tied with a red ribbon, and suspended from a nail.

Katie walked over to study the unusual hanging plant. "What is it?"

"I'm glad you asked," John said, and introduced her to the Christmas tradition of kissing under the mistletoe.

"So," Katie asked when she could breathe again, "if a couple stands under the mistletoe, they must kiss?"

"Yes, that's the custom."

"Why didn't you have it in place when Isaac and Isabel were here?"

"I don't think they need any encouragement from us," John answered. "If Isaac wants to kiss Belle, let him get his own mistletoe."

In the darkness before dawn, John and Katie woke to a hushed silence, and the unmistakable luminous quality of light that denotes a heavy snowfall. This implication was confirmed when they looked out the window to see that the stark, winter landscape of yesterday had been magicked into a scene of enchantment. A fresh, thickly laid carpet of pure white covered the ground, sparkling like diamonds in the moonlight. Resembling burly sentinels standing at attention, the conifers bore up valiantly under the tremendous burden of snow with which they were laden. Their deciduous cousins were elegant and spare; black trunks and branches lined with a tracery of pristine icing. As the couple gazed in awe, a small herd of deer emerged from the woods, moving closer to the cabin searching for twigs to browse. On an impulse, John quickly began dressing. He called back over his shoulder while dashing out the door.

"Hurry Katie. Put on your warmest things. I'll be back for you in about twenty minutes."

She didn't waste time wondering what John was up to, though she had a strong suspicion, and was excited at the prospect. By the time she'd finished garbing herself in layers of warm clothes and covering her head with scarves and mufflers, the jingling of bells broke the dark stillness. When she stepped through the front door, John was waiting to help her into a lovely, old sleigh, and then they were off. The horses pulled the small cutter effortlessly across snow-covered fields, uphill and down. Katie could almost believe they were flying through time and space. Feeling her nestle closer to his side, John looked down at her, and knew he had never been happier. Neither of them would ever forget this spur of the moment moonlit ride that had carried them into an enchanted wonderland.

At daybreak, crimson cardinals crisscrossed the space in front of the hitching rail, creating brilliant bursts of color and motion as John reined the horses to a stop at the door. Katie climbed out of the sleigh, blowing a kiss in his direction. "I'll have breakfast ready when you get back, John."

John's fingers were freezing when he entwined them around the steaming cup of coffee Katie had set before him. His heart was full with the satisfaction of having delighted his wife with a spontaneous adventure. John loved just looking at her, and he looked at her now, standing at the stove with her back to him, oblivious to his study of her every curve and line. At least he thought she was unaware of his adoring gaze, until Katie carefully moved the skillet off the heat and turned around to meet his eyes. The desire he read in the intensity of her expression brought him to his feet as she approached. Taking his cold hands in her warm ones, she led him to their bedroom. Breakfast was delayed, but John didn't mind at all. In fact, he decided that settling into married life was easier than falling off a log, and infinitely more satisfying. Resolving not to take his good fortune for granted, John began and ended every day thanking God for the incomparable blessing of Katie Byler Hartman, his wife.

Chapter 38

Following on the heels of a frigid, snowy start to the new year, the January thaw arrived in the middle of the month with temperatures approaching a balmy, sixty degrees. Taking advantage of this unseasonably warm weather, John and Katie headed for the Shipshewana countryside on a sunny, Saturday morning. When they reached their destination, Katie could only conclude from the unusual state of quietness and inactivity, that the place was deserted. There were no boys tearing around in perpetual motion accompanied by whoops and hollers. It could only mean one thing. The Danny Byler family must be away. Disappointed to find no signs of anyone about, John and Katie were preparing to drive over to her folks when the front door opened, and ten-year-old Amos walked sedately out to greet them.

Katie grew alarmed at his restrained demeanor. "Is something wrong, Amos? Where are your brothers, your folks? Why is everything so quiet around here?"

Amos answered in a hushed voice. "It's Gemma. We have to be quiet so she can take a nap."

Katie studied this neat, well-mannered youngster intently. "Who *are* you, and what have you done with my nephew?"

The boy was confused and it showed plainly on his face, "I don't understand what you mean, Aunt Katie."

John spoke up, "It's all right, Amos. Your aunt just thinks you're acting older than your age, growing up too fast. We'd better go in and meet this little sister of yours."

Katie had fully expected to see Danny come strutting out of the house, thumbs hooked under his suspenders with a wide grin plastered across his face, like he had on every other occasion of showing off a new baby. Something was very different this time. Following Amos into the house, they saw the rest of the boys sitting quietly around the big table, drawing pictures on paper. It felt to John and Katie like they'd walked into a library.

Danny acknowledged them with a restrained nod, but there was no sign of Katie's sister-in-law, or the baby. Now Katie's curiosity was tinged with apprehension. "Where is Lovina?"

Danny placed a finger over his lips, cautioning Katie in an exaggerated whisper to lower her voice before he answered her question. "Shhh! She's upstairs putting Gemma down for a nap."

Her brother then began nervously wringing his hands, and Katie felt a sense of foreboding. "Oh Danny! What's wrong? Is it the baby? Is Gemma sick?"

Footsteps sounded loudly on the stair treads. "There isn't a thing in the world wrong with that baby, except that she has the misfortune to have a lunatic for a father!"

This declaration caused an immediate reaction from the Byler boys. Six heads swiveled as one, and twelve eyes fastened on the head of their family. Lovina continued, "the day is too beautiful to waste, sons. Get your jackets on and go outside to play – just be sure to keep an eye on Felty."

"Not too loud now," Danny admonished in a whisper as they passed him, racing through the door in their haste to be released from captivity.

Before slamming the door behind them, Lovina contradicted her husband's edict. "Hey boys, why don't you see who can yell the loudest? Make all the noise you want."

"Lovina, shush!" Danny scolded, "you're going to wake Gemma."

"Gemma doesn't even need a nap right now, and you're spoiling that girl," Lovina objected loudly. Her frustration was obvious.

Already by this time John and Katie were feeling distinctly ill at ease, as well as in the way. Then, an ear-splitting wail from the nursery effectively interrupted the contentious exchange they'd been witnessing.

"Now see what you've done," Danny accused, while taking the steps two at a time!

Lovina banged the coffeepot on the stove, and pointed John and Katie toward the table. "Sit! And don't even think about leaving. I'm making some coffee – unless John has a flask of something stronger hidden in his pocket."

"Surely you're not thinking Danny needs a shot of whiskey," Katie asked in disbelief?

"I don't know what *he* needs, but he's just about to drive me to drink," Lovina said. "I have never seen him behave like this in all my life. He is constantly fussing over, and coddling that baby like nobody's business. The farmwork is largely being left up to the boys because Danny's worried to distraction about Gemma. If she makes the littlest squeak, or breathes too softly, he drops everything to pick her up. The rest of us have to tiptoe around here like somebody's dyin'. You know her lungs may never develop properly if she's not allowed to cry like other babies."

John stood to comfort Lovina with a pat on her back, "I think you can put your mind at ease about that. It seems to me her lungs are in pretty good, working order."

"And, what would you know about anything," Lovina snapped, before dissolving into tears?

John watched in stunned amazement as Katie rolled up her sleeves and took charge of the situation.

"Don't cry Lovina. I'm here now and everything's going to be all right. Set yourself down in a comfortable chair and take it easy."

"John, you check on the boys, and see if there are any chores that need doing in the barn. I'll send Danny out directly."

Without waiting for a response, Katie marched upstairs, leaving John to wonder if she had any inkling of the trouble her interference might cause. Then, leaving her to suffer the consequences, he went outside as ordered. There wasn't much time to speculate on what kind of trouble might be brewing, before Danny came into the barn to find John holding Felty, while overseeing the boys feed and groom the horses.

"My apologies, John. I'm sorry you found us in such a state today. It's been an adjustment, gettin' used to havin' a baby girl in the house."

"And why is that, Danny? You've had plenty of babies before, and a baby's a baby after all. I mean, it can't make that much difference whether it's a boy or girl at this age. What's got you acting so strangely? You're not the old devil-may-care Danny we're all used to."

"I know, I know, and it's hard to explain what's happened. I'm thinkin' maybe Dat put a hex on me. Back in August during a disagreement, he said I'd never grow up until I had a daughter, and understood the God-given responsibility fathers must assume for them. That thought kinda came back to haunt me when Gemma was born. Seems like all I've been doin' since then is worryin' about how to raise a girl."

John couldn't recollect even one time when his old friend admitted to having any doubts about his capabilities before. "I don't know what to say."

"That's all right, Ditcher," Danny said with a wink, "your wife had plenty to say on the subject. She reminded me of a few facts I'd forgotten. Like who the strongest people on God's green earth are – namely women; includin' my wife, mother and sisters, in particular, who've done more than their fair share of raisin' children, and takin' care of us menfolk. Yeah, my baby sister gave me a real tongue-lashin' and I guess I had it comin'. The only thing I can say is, *you got your hands full with that one*. Oh yeah, and dinner's ready."

Katie spent the rest of the afternoon with Gemma in her arms, gazing adoringly into her niece's bright eyes. Twice John had to call her name in order to tell her they needed to start for home. It wasn't until he lightly touched Katie's shoulder that she became aware of his presence.

"I'm sorry, John. Did you say something?"

John caressed her smooth cheek with the back of a finger. "I said it's about time to leave – and I don't think we can take Gemma with us."

A soft laugh was the prelude to Katie's reply. "I see I'll have to be more careful with my thoughts, now that I know I'm married to a mind reader."

As aunt to a large number of nieces and nephews, it had always tugged at Katie's heart after cradling the latest newborn, when the time came to hand the warm, little bundle back. Once again, she felt bereft, and her arms empty after surrendering the baby to Lovina. Someday, she thought, there will be a baby in my arms that no one can take away. She and John said goodbye and put on their wraps. As the horse drawn buggy conveyed them closer to Michigan, Katie introduced the subject of Danny's strange behavior, and her confrontation of him.

"Did Danny tell you I gave him my two-cents worth about acting like Gemma was a porcelain doll? Maybe, I shouldn't have, but his being so protective of her was affecting everyone in the family – and not in a good way either."

John admitted, "well, he said you didn't hold anything back. By the way, did he mention why he'd been acting that way? What Dat said to him in August?"

"No," she shook her head, "I guess I didn't give him much of a chance to say anything."

"Well, I'll say a word or two in Danny's defense then, if you don't mind?" John turned toward her, his raised eyebrow asking her indulgence.

"Please go ahead," she said, "I'm eager to hear what you have to say that might excuse his behavior."

"Katie," he sought to clarify, "it's not about excusing his actions, only explaining his intentions, that's all. The thing is, Dat laid a weighty mandate on Danny when he charged him with special responsibilities fathers have for their daughters. Of course, all children need guidance and instruction, but boys are easier, less trouble in some respects, although visits to the woodshed may be more frequent. But, according to Abe Byler, because girls are especially vulnerable to being adversely influenced, or taken advantage of, they require more oversight and protection."

An indignant snort from the passenger's side of the seat diverted John's attention away from the road to his wife. Her brow was furrowed, and the plump, lower lip of her kissable mouth was thrust out in a pout of unmistakable disapproval. They traveled several miles without speaking, during which time it occurred to him that he must have said something to upset Katie, and he was sure she'd let him know what it was, sooner or later.

She held her tongue until after they got home, and John had taken care of Blaze. Then she took a deep breath. "Of everything that came out of your mouth on the way home, the one thing I agree with is that boys often have more 'hands-on' experience in the woodshed than most girls require. But if you think boys are easier and less trouble, you didn't grow up with my five brothers! It's my opinion that what you call a father's special responsibility for his daughters, only results in less independence for them. I believe women are every bit as capable as men. In fact, most men rely on women far more than they realize, or are willing to admit."

"Whoa, Turtledove," John cooed, "I didn't mean to ruffle your feathers. I was just stating how your father framed his position to Danny. You don't need to convince me about the capabilities of the female of the species. Let's agree not to allow other people's problems to come between us, okay?"

Katie thought for a moment before answering. "As long as you understand that I'll freely speak my mind when we have a disagreement."

"I would expect nothing less. Is there anything more you want to know?"

"Just one thing. What else did Danny say?"

"He said I was going to have my hands full with you."

She opened her mouth to protest, but John silenced her with a kiss, and she allowed herself to be pulled into his strong arms.

Chapter 39

Winter returned with a vengeance at the beginning of February, bringing road travel to a grinding halt. Farmers spent hours every day shoveling through several feet of snow in order to reach their livestock in barns and pens. And, when the blizzard persisted for two days straight, the men had to repeat this backbreaking labor again and again. Shopkeepers and townspeople were similarly engaged in the monumental task of clearing walkways for anyone finding it necessary to get out. These footpaths soon resembled trenches bordered by towering marble walls.

Most folks, country or city, simply had no choice but to hunker down and wait out the weather. Mother Nature delivered this mess, and she would remove it, eventually. Known for being resourceful, Midwesterners prided themselves on being prepared to deal with the season's hardships. Their woodpiles loomed large with a ready supply of firewood for heating and cooking. Pantries and root cellars were filled with preserved food: dried, canned, smoked or salted, as well as fruits and vegetables held in cold storage.

Truly, the inconvenience of being snowbound didn't mean much of an imposition, unless you wished to travel any distance beyond your immediate neighborhood. Isabel had just such a wish, and being thwarted in the fulfillment of that desire was causing her anguish over the welfare of someone she cared for a great deal. Maxwell Reid's health had been declining over the past few months. It was only a year ago that her friend and former landlord had been well enough to undertake an arduous journey south to spend the winter in Florida. After his return last Spring, Isabel and the children visited Maxwell at least twice every month until the recent, heavy snowfall disrupted their schedule.

Isabel was worried. The old gentleman had looked quite ill the last time they'd seen him. His complexion was cast in a translucent gray pallor, and the fact that he was in pain was plain to see on his face. For fear of tiring Maxwell, Isabel had insisted on cutting their last visit short. When they said goodbye, the grasp with which he held her hand was stronger than she would have thought possible, considering his condition. His voice was strong too, when he told her he loved her like she was his own daughter. Isabel kissed his forehead then, her tears falling on his cheeks before she could stop them. She gathered Johnny and Eliza close to his bedside, and they prayed that Mr. Reid might get well. They were eager to see him again as soon as the roads were passable.

After the blizzard had blown itself out, Isabel gave up trying to keep Johnny inside. Neither of the children had been allowed to leave the house during the worst of the weather, and everyone had grown tired of the boy's repeated pleas to go outside. Games, stories and other indoor amusements were no match for the allure of the silent and strangely altered world that beckoned beyond the snow-covered windows. Johnny expressed worry about how his dog was faring in the barn, despite his grandfather's assurances that Rex was snug and comfortable bedding down with the cows. At last Isabel's father agreed to keep an eye on the boy while he attended to chores, and so Isabel relented, bundling Johnny up in layers of coats and scarves against loud protests that he couldn't move.

Those claims were proven false by the muffled thud of snowballs pelting the shed door. Before long, the frequency with which these missiles were hitting their mark suggested to Isabel that reinforcements had arrived. To confirm as much she peeked through a kitchen window, and spied Isaac at Johnny's side, fully engaged in the battle. Fortunately, James Hartman was able to cross the line of fire without incident and reach the warmth and safety of the kitchen. After shedding his coat, he sank into the chair closest to the blazing kitchen range while Susanna knelt to remove her husband's boots.

Involuntary shivering coursed through his body, and he stuttered, "it's c-c-c-colder than a miser's heart out there! I t-t-told those two they better come inside and get warm."

On cue, the back door opened admitting Johnny and Isaac, along with a strong gust of arctic air. The boy's cheeks were apple-red, and icy cold to the touch, but his smile was bright and cheery. He happily accepted one of the mugs of hot cocoa his grandmother was ladling from a large kettle on the stove. Susanna gestured Isaac toward the wood-burner, "get yourself out of that coat, and sit over here where it's warm."

Isabel stood behind Isaac, raising her hands and resting them on his shoulders to receive the well-worn Mackinaw jacket. The slight weight of her touch was transmitted through the heavy wool, and he would have liked to linger under its warmth, but he shrugged free of the garment, and her hands.

While sipping his hot chocolate, their neighbor enjoyed listening to the family talk easily together, and whenever his opinion was solicited Isaac obliged with an appropriate comment to advance the conversation. Having grown accustomed to living alone, Isaac hadn't realized what he'd been missing until experiencing the inclusivity granted him by this family. He felt comfortable here, accepted and at home, and he didn't want to leave. But he had things to do and the longer he stayed the harder it would be to say goodbye. None of them were making it easy for him, either. James hinted strongly that he'd not enjoyed a good game of backgammon since before John got married. The children wanted him to show them how to make shadow animals on the wall. Susanna asked him to stay for dinner, and the temptation to accept was almost irresistible. Isabel was the lone holdout, saying nothing he could interpret as encouragement for him to stay. He went on his way and the house was quieter after he left.

When the big clock struck three a.m., Isabel threw off her

blankets, deciding she may as well get up and make herself a cup of tea. An oil lamp's glow shone out from the kitchen to let her know she wouldn't be alone. Steam was rising from the teakettle and her mother was placing cups and saucers on the kitchen table.

Isabel extinguished the flame on the candlestick in her hand, and set it down carefully. "Why are you up so early, Mother?"

Susanna smiled, acknowledging Isabel's appearance, "I thought you might want to talk about what's troubling you. If I had to guess, I'd say it was our neighbor."

Isabel could have denied it, but Susanna's precognition, especially where her children were concerned, ruled out the possibility that she would believe a lie, no matter how well crafted.

"Yes, all right," Isabel reluctantly admitted, "Isaac is a big part of it, but not all. Along with the rest of the county, he believes that my husband is dead, and what troubles me is that we don't know for certain what happened at the mill on the day of the accident. We only know the shoes John received from the undertaker could not possibly have belonged to Friedrich. In good conscience, I cannot allow Isaac to continue believing something that may not be true, can I?"

"No," her mother agreed, "not if you truly care about him. He deserves to know of our suspicions, and about how Friedrich mistreated you and the children. It's clear Isaac cares for you, and I don't believe his feelings will be altered by what we know – or don't know."

Isabel was doubtful, "maybe not, but it might change the way other folks look at things. He shouldn't be seen with someone who has a complicated history that could reflect badly on him."

"Don't underestimate Isaac, he's not so superficial as to be too concerned about what people may think." Susanna took a moment, choosing her next words carefully. "Have you considered consulting a lawyer? I know the thought of divorce is repugnant, but if it were proven that Friedrich is alive, and willfully abandoned you and the children while faking his death, perhaps it would be best to pursue that course of legal action. No court in the land would find you responsible for the breakdown of your marriage under those circumstances."

Isabel was on her feet before her mother finished speaking. "Never – my children will never suffer the shame of having a mother who is a divorcée! Except for a respectable reputation, there is precious little else I can give them."

The clatter of a teacup landing forcefully in its saucer drew Isabel's attention back to the table. "I won't sit quietly by and hear you talk like that. Johnny and Eliza couldn't have a better mother. You've given them everything. They are happy and healthy, living in a home where they are safe and loved."

"All thanks to you and father for taking us in. The few dollars I occasionally earn sewing and making alterations amounts to almost nothing. There is no possible way I could support myself and the children on my own."

Susanna embraced her daughter. "Our home is your home, Isabel. It's a blessing to have you with us. Don't ever doubt that you and the children are wanted here, and if it's any comfort, I believe everything will be fine in the end. Now go back upstairs and try to sleep a while longer."

The idea of drifting off to sleep was a nice thought, but Isabel's mind was right now occupied by two, very different men. The specter of Friedrich Bachman rose up to taunt her, and the slightest possibility that he was alive and could show up without warning was more than enough to frighten her. It was an awful thing to admit, but she hoped he really was dead. After the "accident," when an official death certificate had been issued for Friedrich, Isabel had gradually found herself again, restored once more to the person she was before the abuse and trauma she'd sustained during her marriage. The children too, had blossomed in their father's absence. The nightmares that used to torment

Johnny in his sleep had lessened, and then just stopped. Eliza's fearful, clinging demeanor had also ceased.

For a while, Isaac's presence in her life had vanquished Friedrich's ghost to the outer limits of her consciousness, making Isabel believe that true love and happiness were nearly within her grasp. Both her folks liked him, and he was one of John's most trusted friends. More to the point, Isaac had recently made his feelings clear to her, saying he would wait patiently for an answer. She dreamed about having Isaac for a husband, but knew in her heart that until the question was resolved once and for all about whether Friedrich was alive, there was no way she could give the man she loved the answer he wanted. It was time for a heart-to-heart talk with Isaac.

Chapter 40

"We need to talk!"

John barely had time to register who was brushing past him after he opened the door. It wasn't like Isaac to barge in without waiting for an invitation. What could have happened to cause the man to forego his usual, exemplary manners? Perching on a chair in front of the hearth, elbows on his knees and head in his hands, Isaac was the picture of a dejected lover.

The sound of footsteps coming down from the loft, alerted John that Katie was about to enter what could be an unpredictable scene, and he rushed over to head her off before she blithely greeted their unexpected guest. Steering her into the bedroom, he whispered something in her ear before returning to Isaac. Moments later, clad now in a long coat, Katie announced that she was going out, and would be back later. John waited until the door closed behind her.

"All right, Isaac, you want to talk? Let's talk."

When Isaac raised his head, John saw hurt and anger on his face. "I should have stuck with my gut. I should have known it was all too good to be true."

"What are you talking about? Did you and Belle have a fight?"

Isaac responded with a question of his own. "Do you remember when you introduced your sister to me at the Grange Fair? You used the word *missus*, and I accepted that designation at face value. I wasn't happy to learn she was married, but I accepted it. Then later that night when I drove her home, she told me you'd neglected to mention that her husband had been killed. So, I thought she was a widow, and you all let me believe it too. Isabel and I began seeing each other, and your parents seemed to encourage the deepening relationship between the two of us. Everyone made me feel like one of the family. Now, after telling Isabel she's the only woman in the world for me, I am given to understand that her husband may not be dead after all."

It was clear Isaac was even more agitated as he shot to his feet, confronting John face to face. "And, to answer your question – no, your sister and I did not have a fight. The very thought is an affront to me. My feelings for her are such that I would never want to hurt her, no matter what. But I do feel betrayed, and not only by Isabel, but by you, too. Tell me, John, is this deception your idea of how to treat a friend?"

It was meant to be a rhetorical question, intended as Isaac's parting shot, before he walked out in anger.

Only John wasn't having it. He grabbed hold of Isaac's arm, preventing his departure. "We're not finished talking until I say we're done." Isaac pulled free of John's hold. After gauging each other's strength with several hard shoves, both reached the conclusion that they were pretty evenly matched. The shoving contest progressed to the throwing of punches that each man was able to block without a single blow finding its mark. The sparring left them panting, and John stepped away to consider what Katie might have to say if he beat Isaac up in her house. About the same time, Isaac figured whipping Isabel's brother wouldn't make him look any too good in her eyes, either.

By means of some telepathic communication, an unspoken truce was called. John waved Isaac over to a chair at the kitchen table while he teased a bottle from its hiding place at the back of a cupboard, and handed it to Isaac.

"Elderberry Tonic," Isaac read while John plunked tumblers down on the tabletop?

"It's my mother's elderberry wine, labeled tonic so as not to offend Katie's prejudices against what she considers strong drink. On occasion, my mother prescribes it when quick tempers threaten to overrule sound judgment." John opened the bottle and poured. "Shall we raise a glass to reason?"

"To reason," Isaac repeated before swallowing a

mouthful and giving the wine his approval with a thumbs-up. "Go ahead, I'm listening."

"Well," John said, "according to the official record, Friedrich *is* dead. What would happen if he should show up to dispute that fact is anyone's guess. We only began to suspect he may have been involved in murder and faking his death after examining the shoes that the undertaker claimed were Friedrich's. I even went to the county sheriff with our concerns, but without some hard evidence to back up my suspicions, no argument I made could persuade him to investigate."

"I see," Isaac said. "Well, she's not willing to marry me until she knows for certain that Friedrich is dead. What do you think, John? Is he dead, or still alive?"

"That is the question, isn't it? To be honest, my sketchy knowledge of the "accident" and my instincts tell me that unless he's run afoul of some bad characters, he is still alive, and he could be anywhere. My mother shares this same intuition. She suggested that Belle consult a lawyer for a clearer understanding of the law in this case, but she's afraid. The way I see it Isaac, there's not much any of us can do right now. Belle just needs some time to figure things out."

"The man must be a monster, a real scoundrel. If he ever crosses paths with me, he'll regret it. What does he look like, anyway?"

Attempting to give a verbal description, John suddenly remembered something and excused himself. He returned minutes later, handing a photogravure to Isaac.

"This was produced about nine years ago, but it will at least give you an idea of Friedrich's appearance."

It was a wedding picture, and Isaac had to cover Isabel's figure with his hand in order to study the man at her side. "May I borrow this?"

"You're welcome to. It was found in some things Belle had thrown out, and while I detest Friedrich, I couldn't abide the thought of my sister's lovely image being discarded."

"Thank you, I'll return it soon. I'm going to do as you advise, John, and leave Isabel alone for a while. I'm sorry for the way I acted today. Still friends?"

"Of course, Isaac. Stop by whenever you feel like it, you're always welcome at my hearth."

With his hand on the door, Isaac turned back. "I'm assuming Katie went to see Isabel after I arrived. Do you think she might have said anything about my being here?"

John looked his friend in the eye. "I think you can count on it."

Katie found her sister-in-law in the parlor, dabbing at her puffy eyes with a damp handkerchief. "I thought you might want some company. May I join you?"

"If you want to, though I probably won't be very good company today. I tried to talk to Isaac earlier, and it didn't end well. Is he at your place?"

"Well, he was there when I left. John shooed me out just after Isaac arrived."

"Did he send you here to check on me?"

"You know John, he's always concerned about you. So, here I am to cheer you up. My mamm used to say the best way to get your mind off your troubles is to keep your hands busy. I have an idea. New snow is the best thing there is to clean and freshen carpets. Let's take all the rugs outside, lay them right side down and let the children stomp on them while we sweep and mop the floors. Then, the carpets can be hung over the clothesline, and flogged with a carpet beater until all the dirt and snow is out, or our arms are sore, whichever comes first."

Isabel looked unconvinced. "Don't you think a little tea and sympathy would be better?"

"Maybe later. Trust me, by the time we're finished with this little chore, you will have forgotten about anything that's bothering you."

Katie was right. The fresh air and hard work raised Isabel's spirits in spite of herself. It would be hard for anyone to foster a morose attitude with the sun shining, temperatures rising and birds filling the air with song. Johnny and Eliza enjoyed tramping all over the rugs, and then had fun making a family of snowmen. Afterwards, when the house was put back in order, Katie noted with relief that Isabel was in a greatly improved frame of mind.

When the afternoon shadows began to lengthen, John came looking for Katie. She was happy when he agreed to their staying for supper with the family. In spite of her cheery smile and glowing complexion, John could see his wife was tired from the exertions of the day, and insisted they leave immediately after the meal.

Wanting to divert her thoughts from Isaac, Isabel tried to read, but laid the book aside when her eyes wouldn't stay open. She didn't know when she'd fallen asleep, or what it was that woke her. The house was quiet, and the room dark, save for the reflected glow of starlight outside her window. It was just enough to illuminate a man's shadowy figure standing at the foot of her bed. At any other time, Isabel would have screamed. Logic dictated that she should be frightened, but she sensed the man's presence was not threatening. Then he spoke, whether audibly or in her mind she didn't know, but his words were clear to her just the same.

"My dear girl, I couldn't leave without saying goodbye and seeing you one last time. Hold onto your faith, and all will be well. The angels are watching over you."

Isabel's next conscious thought was that a new day had dawned, and she could hear her mother stirring in the kitchen. Now she must get up, and help with the breakfast preparations. She sat up, dangling her feet over the side of the bed as she looked around the room. The vivid details of last night's dream refused to fade. It had seemed so very real. As she considered this strange aberration, her attention was suddenly riveted on a neatly folded piece of linen, lying on the night stand. The monogrammed initials 'MBR' seemed to pulsate in her vision. As

Isabel picked up Maxwell's handkerchief with trembling hands, something small and shiny fell to the floor with a metallic ping. She gasped, and slid from the bed in a faint.

Isabel gradually became aware of a voice, seemingly originating from far away. It was calling her name. "Isabel! Isabel! Wake up. What happened? Did you fall?"

"I don't know. I don't remember, but he was here, Mother. Maxwell Reid was here, and now he's gone. He's gone forever."

Susanna listened intently as her daughter recounted the strange dream, and recognized it at once for what it was, a materialization of Mr. Reid's departing spirit.

"I believe you've experienced something quite special and rare, Isabel. Sometimes it happens that a person's attachment to a loved one is so strong they cannot pass from one dimension of time to the next without saying goodbye. It seems that Maxwell felt compelled to comfort you, even while he was dying." Spying the little key on the floor, Susanna picked it up, and held it out to Isabel on her open palm. "Where did this come from?"

"It fell out of Maxwell's handkerchief. I have no idea what it opens."

"My advice Isabel, is to put that key in a safe place. I have a feeling you'll find out soon enough what secrets it may unlock."

Chapter 41

Exactly one week after Maxwell's funeral, an envelope addressed to Mrs. Friedrich Bachman, in care of Mr. James Hartman, was conveyed by special courier to the Hartman farm. Isabel eyed the official looking mail warily, before breaking the seal. It was from the law firm of Redfern and St. Clair in Centreville, Michigan.

Mrs. Friedrich Bachman,

This letter will serve as notification that in my client's last will and testament, you have been designated one of the beneficiaries. Your presence is requested for a reading of Mr. Maxwell Reid's will on Monday, March 12, 1900, at 10 o'clock a.m. in the offices of Redfern and St. Clair, Attorneys at Law.

Respectfully,
Phineas Redfern, and Bartholomew St. Clair, Esquires.

Her parents were pleased at the prospect of some good news for their daughter. Isabel had surely had more than her share of troubles in the past, and deserved a brighter future.

"Aren't you excited, Isabel," her father asked? "The suspense must be unbearable."

"Oh Father, you sound like a child at Christmas. I suspect Mr. Reid has made a small bequest to Johnny and Eliza. It would be just like him to do that. He was always so fond of the children. In any event, I'm sure you'll find out I was right, when you escort me to the reading of the will."

Exactly at ten o'clock A.M. on the appointed day, Isabel and her father were among a select few gathered around the conference room's large table at the prestigious law firm in Centreville. Mr. Redfern opened the proceedings by sharing a truncated version of Mr. Reid's life.

Maxwell Benjamin Reid had been born in England to a prominent, well-to-do couple. After emigrating to the United States, he parlayed a substantial, family inheritance into even greater wealth. Mr. Reid personally oversaw the building of a magnificent house for his American bride, and to satisfy her inclination for whimsy, allowed her to give their estate the fanciful name of Bramble Briar Lodge. Mr. Reid's happiness proved to be fleeting when his young wife was mortally injured in a horse-riding accident and died. He was left sorrowing and brokenhearted. Ultimately, Maxwell turned his grief to good purpose and spent the rest of his life supporting those benevolent causes whose mission was to remedy the plight of those suffering the pain and hardship of poverty.

Several charitable organizations were named in his will as well as a handful of individuals. Mr. Reid's former resident housekeeper, Mrs. Violet Markham, was to receive a furnished house and twelve thousand dollars. Virgil Brown, the faithful groom and driver, inherited a small rural holding that included a cottage on some acreage, and the sum of ten thousand dollars. Mrs. Isabel Bachman's inheritance was fifteen thousand dollars, and a number of crates already on the way to her parents' home in Scottsburg, Michigan. The remainder of Maxwell's estate would become the property of the county, with the stipulation that the residence would be used to house and care for the aged and infirm.

James glanced at his daughter's bloodless face, realizing Isabel had been taken completely by surprise at the scope of this bequest. A tray, holding a bottle of sherry and glasses, was carried into the room to toast the beneficiaries' good fortune. After taking a swallow, Belle felt better, but remained convinced that this was all a mistake.

"Isabel, I know this is a little premature, but have you

given any thought to what you're going to do with the money," her father asked while helping his daughter into the buggy?

"Oh, my goodness, no! I don't know what to think, Father, or where to begin." She held the envelope containing the bank draft tightly in her gloved hands. "It's too big a responsibility for me. What am I going to do with all this money?"

James answered her. "It's not necessary to make any big decisions right now. In fact, it's not advisable. Take all the time you need to think this through. My first suggestion would be to deposit the draft with a reputable bank, as soon as possible. If you like, we can call on my banker before we go home. Secondly, I believe it would be wise, at least for the time being, to keep the existence of this money secret from everyone, except your mother, and John, if you wish to confide in him."

Isabel readily agreed to her father's recommendations, and they went immediately to the bank. When informed of the unfair prohibition denying women the right to have bank accounts in their own names, she rebelled inwardly, but had no choice in the matter. The bank draft was deposited in a new account under James Hartman's name, listing him as custodian of the funds for his daughter.

It was decided mutually between the two of them, that one hundred dollars should be kept at home, locked in her father's strongbox. Just the idea of that money, hard cash at hand, was almost beyond imagining. By virtue of hard work, and frugal living, the Hartman family had always managed to get by well enough. Their financial philosophy had been to make do, or do without. Only after she'd married Friedrich, had Isabel known what it was like to go hungry whenever he gambled away his earnings. For the first time in her life, Isabel began to think about what possibilities this inheritance could mean to Johnny, Eliza, and herself. It was all of a sudden exhilarating to comprehend that she could change the lives and fortunes of her whole family.

Upon arriving home, the sight of a wagon loaded with

crates parked outside the kitchen door, drove all other thoughts from Isabel's mind. Arms akimbo, Susanna Hartman looked on in amazement while Rex growled and barked a warning at the strangers on his turf.

"What is all of this, and where are we supposed to put it," Susanna asked, trying to keep the children from getting trampled underfoot by the men unloading the wagon?

James, helping Isabel down from the buggy, yelled to make his voice heard. "Put everything in the dining room for now. It will get sorted out later."

Having been alerted by the dog's frantic barking, John and Katie came hurrying from the woods to learn the reason for Rex's warning. Sizing up the situation, John quickly lent a hand with the crates, and Katie led Johnny and Eliza around to the front porch where they could watch without being in the way. The children's curiosity continued to mount, and they began to wonder if there just might be something of interest in that pile of boxes that would appeal to a boy or girl. Susanna took up her post in the kitchen, while Isabel joined her children and Katie as they observed the long procession moving into the house.

It was past dinnertime when the wagon, emptied of its load, finally left. Susanna prepared an early supper to compensate for the missed noon meal, and for once everyone was quiet. After saying a brief blessing, James suggested they all refrain from talking until after the meal, when Isabel would have something to share with the family.

Everyone gathered in the parlor, and Isabel repeated what Mr. Redfern had revealed about Mr. Reid's early life, and his desire to help the less fortunate. She explained that Bramble Briar Lodge, where she and the children had spent many happy hours with Mr. Reid, was going to become a home and refuge for the ill and elderly that had no other place to go. She reminded Johnny and Eliza they must always be thankful to have known such a wonderful person, who'd cared so much for them. By now, Johnny had held his curiosity in check as long as he could, and was in danger of bursting from excitement. Without waiting for permission to speak, he asked.

"Are all those cartons in the dining room from Mr. Reid?"

"Yes Johnny, they are, and before you ask what's in them, I'm too tired to find out tonight. Perhaps Uncle John can help me pick out just a couple of boxes we can open to satisfy your insatiable desire to learn if there is anything for you. The rest will wait until tomorrow."

The perimeter of the dining room was lined with boxes, stacked more than halfway to the ceiling. Isabel hardly knew where to begin but John reassured her with an understanding smile, and promptly picked up the two large crates he'd earlier set off to the side of the fireplace.

"This should make you feel better, Belle. I noticed these were the only ones labeled, one for Johnny, and the other for Eliza."

Isabel took a closer look and recognized Mr. Reid's handwriting. Raising her eyes heavenward she whispered. "Thank you, Maxwell."

Watching the delight on her children's faces after they opened the crates, erased Isabel's earlier fatigue. An extravagantly expensive, imported train set appeared, pulled piece by piece from the box until the floor around Johnny was littered with tracks, and all kinds of train cars, from the engine to the caboose. Eliza was so mesmerized watching her brother that she had to be reminded to unpack her own present. It was a deluxe Victorian dollhouse, outfitted with furnishings, a large family, and servants. After an hour that passed much too quickly for the children, Isabel tucked them into bed, returning to the parlor and her family waiting there.

It was then, after securing promises of secrecy from those present, that Isabel revealed the details of her inheritance from Mr. Reid. The reactions from her mother, brother and sister-in-law were exactly what she had known they would be – genuine happiness for her new found fortune, and assurances that the knowledge of this windfall would be held in the strictest confidence.

"I am so happy for you, Belle," John said, hugging his sister tightly! "It was wonderful of Mr. Reid to remember you and the children with such generosity."

Katie was the next to embrace Isabel. "I'm overjoyed for you too. And, if you need someone to look after Johnny and Eliza while you're sorting through everything, please let me help. I'll be glad to keep them occupied."

"Thank you, Katie, that would be such a great help to me. I have too much to think about now."

"We are all ready to help in any way we can," Susanna said. "Just don't rush into any big decisions, dear. You have plenty of time."

Early the next morning, Isabel and her parents began opening crates, starting at the top and working their way down, layer by layer. Susanna suggested making an inventory as they discovered the contents of each box, volunteering to act as scribe. Making herself comfortable at one end of the long table, she arranged ink, paper and pens within easy reach. It very quickly became obvious that Mr. Reid had been a passionate collector of specimens from the natural world, everything from fossils to seashells. These had been carefully labeled and beautifully displayed in sealed frames. Dozens of boxes contained souvenirs from Maxwell's world travels. By noon they were ready to call it quits for the day when John walked in, whistling at the piles stacked neatly at the end of the table opposite his mother.

"These are incredible, Belle," he said, admiring a collection of moths! "What are you going to do with them?"

"They're yours, if you want them," she replied. "I don't know what Mr. Reid could have been thinking when he left them to me."

"If he left no specific instructions, Belle, I'm sure he trusted you to see that these items would go where they'd be most appreciated. Have you thought about contacting a museum?"

"That's a wonderful idea, John! Would you look into that possibility for me? This is turning into a much bigger job than I could ever have imagined."

"Of course, I'll help, and I'm anxious to see what else you've discovered. Do you remember when I visited the World's Columbian Exposition in Chicago, six or seven years ago? Only a year later, a natural history museum opened there, and I've been wanting to check it out ever since. Perhaps that would be a good place to start on the hunt for a permanent home for this collection. But first things first," John said, "Katie's in the kitchen fixing something to eat, and I don't know about the rest of you, but I'm starving."

Chapter 42

The tedious job of opening, and cataloging the contents of the crates was accomplished in less than two weeks. Thanks in great part to Katie assuming responsibility for all the household tasks at the farmhouse. A few boxes that appeared to hold personal belongings were set aside for Isabel's later perusal, but most of what was unpacked looked to be items that really should be put on public display. John composed a letter to the museum in Chicago, asking if they might have any interest in this material. The inquiry was drafted and posted before the beginning of April.

All signs were pointing to an early spring this year. In the marsh, Red-winged blackbirds swayed atop last year's cattails, their unmistakable trilling vocalizations dominating the songs of other harbingers of the season. The promise of new life was manifest everywhere, as wild creatures and domesticated livestock produced the next generation. Newborn lambs were soon frolicking among Susanna's small flock of Southdown sheep amid a rolling, green pasture.

Farm families felt the pace of work quicken as the year picked up momentum. The planting and tending of crops and gardens consumed time in ever increasing increments, building toward the final climax of harvest. It was a familiar, reassuring cycle that varied little from year to year.

Isaac had been minding his own business for weeks, giving Isabel a wide berth while fighting the impulse to call on her. He was thankful that work kept him busy, even if it didn't keep Isabel from his thoughts. Like all the local growers, he'd been occupied from dawn to dusk with the never-ending demands of farming, until a broken equipment part necessitated an unplanned trip to town. The blacksmith promised to make a replacement within an hour, and Isaac headed over to the general store to kill some time while he waited.

Jake Evans swapped tidbits of gossip with Isaac before selling him a newspaper, and turning his attention to another customer. Settling back in a chair, Isaac previewed a new feature about local culture and society. The column had been written by someone with the unlikely name of Miss Brunhilda Ophelia Bailey. The headline read:

From Rags to Riches
by Brunhilda Ophelia Bailey

A Cinderella Story, which begs sharing with one and all, has come to the attention of this reporter. Some details vary from the original fairytale, but the reader may still find the facts in this version entertaining.

I have it on good authority from sources within the legal community that the widowed Mrs. Friedrich Bachman, formerly known as Isabel Hartman, has come into a considerable fortune, courtesy of the recently departed Maxwell Reid of Vistula, Indiana.

In his Last Will and Testament, Mr. Reid, a well-known philanthropist, endowed several charities with sizeable monetary gifts to continue the benevolent work of these organizations. He also amply rewarded his household staff, providing for each one in his will. Truly, no fault can be found with these bequests, but one does wonder what the nature of Mrs. Bachman's relationship to the deceased must have been to warrant such generosity from him?

I remind myself it is not Christian to tell tales or spread rumors, even in the face of evidence suggesting that the widow in question, had at one time been a nonpaying tenant of her benefactor.

Everyone must arrive at their own conclusions. That is all for now, dear readers. Farewell until next week.

Isaac approached the counter, determined to get as many copies as possible out of circulation. "Jake, are these all the papers you have?"

"Yes, they're hot off the press, no more than an hour ago. The first one I sold today was to you."

"Good! I'll take the rest of them. You don't have more in the back room, do you?"

"No, that's my full order, but I have some regulars that come in every week for a paper. How about you leave me at least two?"

"How about I pay you double for the whole lot?"

Jake rubbed his chin. "Guess if I said 'No,' I'd be proving the old adage that says two fools meet when one party offers more for something than it's worth, *and* the other party turns him down. For twice the money, you're welcome to all the papers. Always good doing business with you, Isaac."

"See you around, Jake."

In the little homestead cabin, day was drawing to a close. John and Katie had put aside their cares to fully enjoy this time together in front of the hearth. The subtle aroma of burning pine logs perfumed the air, and the quiet atmosphere was punctuated by an occasional sizzling as resinous vapors from within the wood were released by the fire.

His feet resting on the ottoman, John felt the tension in his shoulders ease, but his pleasure in this peaceful repose evaporated with a loud knocking on the door.

"Don't answer that," he begged Katie as she rose from her chair. "Let's pretend we're not home."

Incessant tapping on the window drew their attention. "Hey! Let me in!"

"Stay where you are, John," Katie said. "I'm already on my feet. Hold your horses, Isaac. We hear you."

Bursting through the door, Isaac took a paper from the bundle in his arms and threw it on John's lap. "Page 2, left side – read it."

Katie stood reading over John's shoulder. After finishing, she covered her mouth in shock. John's face turned red and he struck the arm of the chair with his fist.

"Where did you get these," he demanded?

Isaac explained how he happened to be at Jake's store, picking up a newspaper while there. "Before leaving, I took all he had so I could destroy them. Then I thought you'd probably want to see the pack of lies this woman is spreading. How can she get away with this? There can't be a shred of truth in here."

"Put that pile of trash beside the fireplace, Isaac. We'll burn them later. In the meantime, have a seat and I'll tell you the whole story."

Excusing herself, Katie went to the kitchen to brew a pot of strong coffee. It looked like none of them were going to get any sleep tonight. So much for promising Isabel they would honor her privacy and keep the news of her windfall quiet. It didn't take much imagining on Katie's part to know how her sister-in-law was going to feel when she learned of this column. She would be devastated. What kind of person would make such hurtful and false insinuations about Isabel and Mr. Reid?

Katie overheard the end of the conversation between her husband and his friend.

"So," Isaac said, "it *is* true. The part about Isabel inheriting a fortune, I mean."

"Yes," John admitted. "That is true, but it's not something the family wanted everyone to know. This publicity will likely expose Belle to all the wrong kinds of attention. I have no doubt father will want to talk with Phineas Redfern tomorrow. The specifics of Mr. Reid's will should never have been made public. If I have anything to say about it, Miss Bailey will no longer be writing a society column, and the newspaper will print an apology, and a retraction, although for all intents and purposes, the damage is already done."

Preparing to leave, Isaac stood and held out his hand. "Let me know if there's anything I can do to help, John, and give your sister my regards."

"Wait a minute, Isaac. Have you spoken to Belle lately?"

"No, I've been making myself scarce, just like you suggested. Isabel hasn't reached out to me, and it's doubtful she ever will now. I'm sure she can do far better than a poor farmer. Just tell her I'll always be there for her if she needs a friend."

John burned all the papers except for one, which he carried to the farmhouse early the following morning. Isabel was inconsolable after she saw the story, escaping to her room with a terrible headache. His father's reaction was just what John had predicted, and soon they were sitting in the attorney's office. Mr. Redfern had already gotten wind of the slanderous piece, and was not surprised to learn the Hartman men were requesting a meeting with him.

"Gentlemen, I assure you we will get to the bottom of this. Miss Bailey, and the publisher of The Scottsburg Sentinel will pay dearly for such irresponsible and damaging accusations. Furthermore, I am very interested to discover the source of Miss Bailey's information. It goes without saying that every precaution should be taken to ensure the safety of your family, especially where Isabel and her children are concerned. I'll call at your home in two days, if not sooner, to bring everyone up to date on the case."

A degree of satisfaction was provided by the paper's retraction and apology. Even better was the announcement that the offending column had been discontinued. There was no mention of the reporter, but Jake heard Miss Bailey had run off with a law clerk. A young man formerly employed at the offices of Redfern and St. Clair.

Finding her world turned topsy-turvy, Isabel began to feel like a prisoner in her parents' home. Stonemasons were hired to lay up a boundary wall around the house and stable yard. This extreme measure was taken to discourage would-be robbers, and the unwelcome suitors who'd already begun showing up to court the wealthy widow. James took to sleeping with a loaded pistol handy to his reach, and a shotgun tucked into the corner beside the bedroom door. Johnny's collie, Rex, maintained watch outside for any threat to his young master's family. A large gate installed at the end of the drive was kept locked at night.

John rejected the offer made by his father to include the cabin and surrounding area within the confines of the stone walls, preferring to trust to his own methods. It took some convincing to win Katie over to the idea of a dog, but she finally gave in when John promised to find a canine that could coexist peacefully with Pittypat. Until such a creature might be found, John kept his rifle on a gun rack beside the cabin door.

By far, the worst consequence of Miss Bailey's spiteful story, was the formation of a bitter rift within the Hartman family. Reading about their older sister's good fortune in the local paper was an unexpected revelation for Musetta and Rose Ellen. They'd never kept secrets from each other before. The women's husbands succeeded in throwing fuel on the fire when they began recounting all the ways everyone had pulled together to help Isabel and her children after Friedrich's death. They wondered how much it had cost their father-in-law to build what amounted to a virtual compound, effectively shutting out his other daughters. The slightest suggestion of favoritism had been enough to destroy the lines of open communication between the families of the two youngest daughters, and everyone else. It's hard to say how long this estrangement might have lasted, but for a tragedy that befell the family.

Susanna had known at once that something was wrong. She felt weak, and had no feeling on the left side of her face. The arm on that side of her body was useless, too. When she tried to stand, her legs crumpled beneath her and she fell heavily to the floor. The ability to think and talk coherently, deserted Susanna. The fear and confusion she experienced was frightening.

John was sent for the doctor. After a thorough examination, the physician reached his diagnosis. Susanna had been stricken with apoplexy. She would need complete bed rest, indefinitely. Betrayed by her own body, Susanna faced something she feared more than death -- being pronounced an invalid. She tried to make sense of the word, but in her compromised state, it was beyond her comprehension. *Invalid, in valid, without validity, unacceptable.* Now she was angry, agitated, and trying to summon the strength to fight this thing when the administering of a sedative quenched that will to fight.

In the face of a real crisis, the true perspective about what was important came into focus. Everyone volunteered to help with Susanna's care. Both Musetta and Rose Ellen offered to devote one day every week to care for their mother. After working together to establish a schedule, Isabel asked her sisters to join her in the parlor. Attempting to repair the misunderstanding between them, Isabel apologized for neglecting to inform them personally of Mr. Reid's bequest. She explained that after the paper's column was published, there had hardly been time for her to grasp its far-reaching consequences. Isabel also revealed that not a penny of James and Susanna's money had been spent on the wall, or other protective measures taken at the farm. Musetta and Rose Ellen were ashamed to have judged Isabel so harshly, and then they were speechless when Isabel disclosed that she was sharing a portion of her inheritance with each of her siblings, and their parents.

Chapter 43

It would be an exaggeration out of all proportion, to compare the Hartman family's time of testing to the Old Testament trials of Job. But there could be no question that two events, each independent of the other, had dramatically altered the circumstances in which the family presently found itself. Isabel's unexpected windfall and the prospect of everyone reaping some financial benefit as a result, seemed to promise a level of security previously unknown to the Hartmans. By contrast, Susanna's stroke served to illustrate that wealth is not the universal panacea to all of life's misfortunes. Everyone in the family had been affected by the necessity of caring for the highly regarded matriarch. This was especially true for Isabel and Katie. The two shared round-the-clock nursing duties, in addition to all the household chores. James, finding it more than he could stand to be away from his beloved wife, ceded management of the farm into John's capable hands. The elder Hartman took on the responsibility for the family's vegetable plot, allowing him closer proximity to the house, and Susanna. For the sake of convenience, John and Katie locked up the little cabin and moved temporarily into the farmhouse.

During this period of domestic upheaval, one especially bright spot proved a blessing. A positive response to the letter John had written to the natural history museum was received. Near the end of April, a small team of curators arrived to evaluate the collections amassed by Maxwell Reid. They were suitably impressed, and offered to buy whatever Isabel was willing to sell. An agreement was reached, and Isabel earmarked the money from the museum's acquisitions, for the benefit of widows and orphans of workers, who'd been killed while employed at local mills. She donated generously to other causes, too. While grateful for the opportunity to ease the suffering of others, Isabel would happily have relinquished all her wealth to see her own mother's health restored. Susanna's condition improved slightly, though she'd not regained use of her left arm, and attempts to walk with a cane were unsuccessful. The impediment of not being able to express herself with lucidity, caused Susanna the most consternation of all.

As days, and then weeks passed with hardly any noticeable progress, discouragement and fatigue threatened to win the battle being waged for Susanna's recovery. Isabel and Katie had been tireless in administering every therapy they could think of to stimulate her body and mind. Massage, herbal concoctions, words of loving encouragement, and visits from family had all been faithfully put to use. The prayers of family and many friends were also offered daily. Despite all these efforts, Susanna began to deceive herself into thinking that she had outlived her usefulness, and was now only a burden to those she loved. Despondent and withdrawn, she had no wish to go on living.

It was Musetta's turn to help with her mother's care, and she was running late. James and Isabel had an appointment at the bank, and couldn't delay their departure any longer. Katie assured them there was no reason for concern, dismissing their worries about leaving her short-handed, and waved them on their way. Eliza was a willing little helper, and Johnny would be around after he returned from carrying fresh water to the workers in the field. Hand in hand, Katie and Eliza climbed the stairs to the bedroom.

Katie managed by herself, to get Susanna out of the bed, and settled into her wheelchair. Whether it was the effort of lifting her mother-in-law, or something else, Katie became dizzy and fainted, striking her head on the corner of the night stand as she fell. Eyes wide with fear, the little girl looked at her aunt, unmoving on the floor, and began to cry.

Garbled attempts at speech issued from Susanna's throat.

Clutching at Eliza's shoulder with her right hand, she mumbled something over and over, before Eliza finally understood. "Go help. Get John." Rushing from the room as fast as her legs could carry her, the child ran blindly. Flying through the kitchen door she nearly collided with Isaac as he was coming up the steps. Delivering her message with quavering sobs, Eliza pointed the way to the bedroom, and Isaac sprinted upwards, the little girl at his heels. Kneeling beside Katie, he observed that her breathing was steady, but she was unconscious and didn't respond when he called her name. She was also bleeding from a gash on her head. Lifting Katie to the bed, he found a piece cloth nearby, which he folded and pressed against the injury.

He called to the child. "Eliza honey, come here. Can you be a brave girl and hold this over the cut on Aunt Katie's head?"

She nodded, coming to him at once. Isaac showed her how to apply pressure with her hands on top of the cloth.

Distressed at her inability to help, Susanna was moaning and waving her arm aimlessly. Taking a moment to squeeze the woman's hand, he tried to comfort her. "Don't worry, I'll be back in a minute. Will you be all right?"

After she nodded, Isaac ran from the room. Seconds later the dinner bell was clanging erratically. Rex, who'd recognized Isaac earlier as a friend, hadn't sounded a warning then, but sensing the alarm now rolling off the man in waves, the dog began to bark for all he was worth. Isaac willed John to hurry as he continued to give the rope several more pulls before returning to his friend's wife.

Eliza had been a trooper, staying steadfastly at her post while staunching the flow of blood. As he lowered himself to one knee beside the little girl, Isaac rewarded her with a big smile.

"Good work, Eliza. I'm proud of you."

Katie's eyelids fluttered open, and she stared in confusion at Isaac. Before she could ask what had happened, heavy footsteps pounding up the stairway announced John's arrival. Hearing the bell, he'd braced himself for bad news about his mother, but when he entered the room, he saw her seated in the wheelchair. Then his eyes traveled to the bed where he saw his Katie, a bloody cloth next to her head on the pillow. He rushed to her side.

"Katie, darling, what happened?" John asked, his voice breaking with worry. He stroked her hair while examining the cut on her forehead.

"I must have fallen, John – I'm sorry to be such a bother."

Noticing Susanna's mounting anxiety, Isaac rolled her chair closer to Katie, allowing the two women to clasp hands. For the first time since he'd come on the scene, Isaac noticed that James and Isabel were absent. "Are you on your own here, John?"

"It looks like it. Musetta must be late. Father and Belle had errands in town.

"What can I do to help? Shall I go for the doctor?"

John and Katie both answered at the same time, one 'yes,' the other 'no.'

Isaac didn't wait around for détente to be achieved between the disagreeing parties, but rode directly to Scottsburg. After sending the doctor on his way to the farm, Isaac was lucky to catch James and Isabel just as they were leaving the bank. Informing the two of Katie's injury, he considered returning with them, but there was a prior engagement that required his attention on the seedier side of town.

Stopping outside a tavern on the banks of the St. Joseph River, Isaac hesitated a moment before entering. He was never certain whether or not he'd make it out alive when he came here. The structure, built precariously above the water seemed to be in the process of sliding into the river. It was a ramshackle affair, built of cast-off materials, and boards obviously salvaged from some burn pile. A sign, bearing the image of a crudely drawn mug of beer, was nailed haphazardly above the open door. The bar, which ran the length of the room was already crowded with men when Isaac found an empty table in a corner. It was pay day at the mills, and many of the workers here would blow through their week's wages before stumbling home to confront a weary wife and hungry children. The man Isaac was expecting hadn't shown up yet, but he would. While waiting, Isaac ordered two beers. Shortly after the bottles were plunked down, an old fellow with rheumy eyes limped over to sit across from Isaac. Neither of them said a word until after the newcomer had slaked his thirst, draining the bottle closest to him. When he eyed the second one, and began reaching for it, Isaac stopped him. "Tell me what you know. Have you seen him?"

After nodding to confirm that he had seen the individual in question, the man was prompted to relate specific details. "Are you sure it was him?"

"As sure as my name's Burt Clarke."

Isaac had no way of knowing whether the name was an alias or not, but carried on with his questioning. "Did he look like the drawing I gave you, Burt?"

"The spittin' image, 'cept he's aged some. I saw him just a couple of days ago at another waterin' hole outside of town. He were braggin' about comin' into a whole load of money soon."

Satisfied after gleaning a few more details from his informant, Isaac slid the untouched bottle across the table, to within his companion's reach, and dropped a handful of coins. "Thanks, Burt. Get yourself something to eat."

Before reining his mount eastward along the old Chicago Trail, Isaac paused a moment to pull a much-handled paper from his pocket. Smoothing out the creases to study his drawing, he addressed the image of the man he was pursuing. "No good hiding any longer. Now, I've got you."

Doctor Caldwell said the cut on Katie's head was no real cause for alarm. It wouldn't even require stitching up, although a barely visible scar might result. He was more interested in determining what had caused her to faint. Checking vital signs and observing Katie's overall appearance, the doctor made note of the fact that she appeared to be in good health, except for exhibiting signs of fatigue. He addressed John. "Would you mind stepping out of the room for a few minutes?"

It might have been phrased as a question, but the doctor wasn't offering him a choice. To avoid upsetting Katie, John complied as graciously as possible.

After several minutes alone with his patient, Doctor Caldwell asked her. "Why haven't you told your husband yet?"

Katie leaned back against the headboard, wringing her hands. "I was going to, but with his mother's stroke and everything else, it seemed like he had more than enough cares on his mind. I didn't want him to worry about me."

"Mrs. Hartman, I assure you this is just the news he needs to hear right now. Take good care of yourself, and I'll be out to check on you in a month."

Closing the door quietly behind him, the doctor motioned John to the far end of the hall, raising a hand to silence the younger man's questions before they could be asked. "No worries, John. Your wife is fine, but she's going to need more rest for a while." Laying his hand on John's shoulder, he squeezed and gave a congratulatory wink. "Katie has something to tell you. Now I'm going to look in on your mother."

Musetta had matters firmly in hand by the time James and Isabel returned home. Shooing them out of the kitchen, she said the family would be called to the table as soon as dinner was ready. In the meantime, they'd find Susanna comfortably ensconced in the parlor with Johnny and Eliza keeping her company. The farmhands had been fed an hour ago and were back in the field. John had remained upstairs with Katie, after the doctor's departure. Word hadn't trickled down to Musetta about the nature of her sister-in-law's condition, and she was very concerned. If this was what she could expect in the way of excitement upon arriving late, Musetta vowed it would never happen again.

John had been called to the table for dinner, but hadn't

responded. The family was just preparing to say grace when he appeared in the doorway of the dining room, cradling Katie in his arms. There was no need for questions, or a big announcement. The beaming faces of the happy couple said it all.

Chapter 44

The celebration taking place around the table, was interrupted by Rex's barking, and the sound of someone knocking at the door. Isabel jumped up, pardoning herself as she went to see who was calling. The smile on her face froze when she saw who was standing on the other side of the threshold. Before there was even time to react, she was pulled against her will into a smothering embrace.

"My darling," he gushed. "I've missed you, and have so much to tell you."

On the verge of hysteria, Isabel screamed while struggling to free herself.

John raced to his sister's defense, unaware that his young nephew had followed in his steps.

"Friedrich! What are *you* doing here? Aren't you supposed to be dead? The coroner filed a death certificate with your name on it."

"Dead? There's obviously been a terrible misunderstanding, John. I can explain everything."

A timid voice broke into the conversation. "Daddie?"

"Johnny," the man exclaimed, extending a hand toward the boy! "Yes, it's me, son. Come here and let me hold you."

All of a sudden, a familiar pair of hands rested heavily on Johnny's shoulders, and the boy heard his grandfather say that Aunt Katie needed him right away. Almost with a sense of relief, the child obeyed, turning away from the man he remembered rather vaguely as his father.

"Leave here at once, Friedrich," James ordered, "and if you know what's good for you, you'll stay away from my family."

"Excuse me, but did you say *your* family, James? I hate to contradict you, but Isabel is still my legal wife, and the children are mine, too. Now wouldn't it be better if we all sat down like civilized people, and you can hear what I have to say?"

Trembling fearfully, Isabel clung to John as he answered the unwelcome intruder. "Friedrich, you are not taking Belle and the children away from here."

"I have no intentions of forcing anyone to do anything. All I ask is that Isabel give me a chance to explain what really happened during the accident at the mill. Is that so unreasonable? When I've said my piece, I'll leave." Friedrich crossed his heart, "I promise!"

To prevent Susanna from becoming distressed by Friedrich's appearance, she was moved upstairs. Katie kept watch at her mother-in-law's bedside, while the youngsters played quietly nearby.

In the parlor, James, Isabel, and John presented a united front against Friedrich, allowing him the opportunity to speak. Rising to the occasion, Friedrich began by presenting a fantastical account of the events that occurred on the day of the fatal accident at the mill. In his version, he'd been leading a new man to the cutting shed when a bundle of logs fell from overhead, striking him, and mortally injuring the other worker. According to his story, Friedrich suffered a hard, glancing blow to the head during the incident, resulting in a total loss of memory. Unable to understand what had happened, he staggered away from the scene and lay unconscious in a nearby field for hours. When Ivan Johnson, a reclusive old trapper found him, Friedrich didn't even know his own name. Johnson took him in and nursed him back to health. The better part of a year passed and gradually his memories began to resurface. As luck would have it, one day he picked up a discarded newspaper, and read about Mr. Reid's death. When he saw Mrs. Friedrich Bachman mentioned in the article, her image instantly appeared in his mind and every forgotten detail about their life together came flooding back. It was a shock when Friedrich learned he'd been pronounced dead, realizing the unknown victim had been mistakenly identified as himself.

John listened closely as Friedrich, in a meek and humble voice, spun his tragic tale. There was no way he, or his father, was swallowing this story, but he wasn't so sure about Belle. She was a tenderhearted soul, and had always been an easy mark. He looked over at his sister. She sat with arms crossed, gazing at the floor while avoiding eye contact with her husband. John was encouraged to see a stubborn set to the line of her jaw.

Ramping up his performance, Friedrich portrayed himself as the innocent casualty of unfortunate circumstances. He would never have knowingly walked away from his wife and children, and all he wanted was to be reunited with his family, to take care of them.

"As I recall," James interjected, "the way in which you cared for my daughter and grandchildren left a lot to be desired. Your past treatment of them could only be characterized as abusive."

"I've changed, Father Hartman. It's clear you and John have some doubts on that score, but I'd like to hear what my wife has to say. Isabel, don't you believe it is God's plan that we honor our marriage vows? That our children be raised in a home with both of their parents?"

At some point in Friedrich's narrative, Isabel's struggle to retain her composure began to falter. Having arrived freshly shaved and shorn, her Friedrich's overpowering cologne emitted a sickening stench that nauseated her. As he droned on, the subtly condescending tone of her husband's voice morphed into the deafening buzz of bees in Isabel's ears, and she felt the blood in her veins turn to ice. All she wanted was for him stop talking, and leave.

Isabel raised her head to look Friedrich squarely in the eye. "Talk is cheap. How do you propose to support us? Has Mr. Gosling reinstated you to your former position at the mill? Do you have a place to live?"

Shrugging aside her questions as though they were

inconsequential, he said. "Well of course, I have a plan. I always have a plan. A lucrative business opportunity has been dropped in my lap. It should pay off handsomely after an initial investment, and I already have my eye on a suitable property. Trust me, Isabel, you won't be sorry. This is our chance to start over again on the right foot."

Isabel's patience had been exhausted long ago. "Tell me, Friedrich, do you have the financial means to pursue your plan?"

He assumed a casual pose, draping his arm along the high, curved back of the settee. "Isabel, you know very well we have the inheritance from Maxwell Reid."

A palpable sense of outrage coursed between the Hartmans, not unlike a current of electricity.

Isabel protested. "That money was given to me, Friedrich. No part of it belongs to you."

A low, humorless laugh escaped his lips as he inwardly congratulated himself on the stellar performance he'd just given. "It's a pity I missed you at the bank today. By producing irrefutable proof that your husband is not dead, I was able to replace your father's name on the account with my own. And, I recently discovered a very interesting fact about property laws in Michigan. Married women are allowed to own, and manage property and assets in their own name, *only* during the incapacity of their husband. But as you can see, Isabel, I am hardly incapacitated."

John felt his hackles rise and resisted the urge to lunge at Friedrich. "You abandoned your family, deserted them! How can you even claim to be Isabel's husband under those circumstances?"

"For your benefit, my good brother-in-law," Friedrich answered in a patronizing manner, "I am more than willing to enumerate the documentation I provided to the bank president. In addition to my physical appearance as a living person, I had a sworn statement from the good Samaritan who cared for me, attestations from a doctor, and several others verifying my identity. And, I saved the best evidence for last -- the record of my marriage to your sister."

"You won't get away with this despicable scheme," John vowed. "We'll see you in court!"

"As you wish, John. I don't want to drag lawyers into this business, but if it comes to that, I have the best lawyers and witnesses that money can buy. I warn you not to interfere in my personal affairs, the law is on my side. But let's not end the evening on a discordant note. Since the hour is growing late, I won't impose myself on you all any longer. I will return tomorrow morning at ten o'clock to collect my wife and children. That will give Isabel ample time to pack a few bags. If she and the children are not ready when I arrive, I'll go to the sheriff."

Isabel's face blanched. "Friedrich, you have the money now, what could you possibly want with us?"

"I have my reasons. Chief among them is the fact that married men are generally viewed as more respectable, and as such are accorded a higher level of gravitas among their fellows. With my ambitious aspirations, it's important I give every appearance of being upright and honorable. You might say a wife and children go a long way to complete that picture. In any event, I intend to have custody of my children, with or without you. As long as you don't meddle with my handling of things, you're welcome to stay with us. You are, after all still quite lovely to look at, and may be of some ornamental use to me."

Rising unhurriedly, Friedrich said. "Don't bother getting up, I can see myself out. Until tomorrow then. You'll be ready when I arrive, my dear?"

Isabel could hardly believe what she was hearing. Her world was collapsing around her!

John wracked his brain for any solution to this unimaginable calamity. Was Friedrich bluffing? He'd been surprised the man was insistent on taking Johnny, Eliza, and Belle, especially after getting his hands on the money. But he'd not been surprised that Friedrich had gone to the trouble of researching his legal options. The wiliest criminals quickly learn to bend the law to their own benefit. John considered that if they resisted his brother-in-law's demands, the consequences might be even more dire for Isabel and the children in the long run.

In a corner of the room, James conferred quietly with Isabel while Friedrich looked on, a gloating smirk on his face. He could barely contain his glee.

Isabel fought back tears as she conceded defeat. "All right Friedrich, we'll be ready, but I want to know where you are taking us."

"I figured you'd see things my way. For the record, we'll be staying at the finest hotel on the southeast shore of Lake Michigan. It's all first class all the way from now on. Good night and sweet dreams, Isabel."

Swaggering past his wife's father and brother, Friedrich left through the front door.

Isabel fought against opening her eyes. As long as she kept them closed, she could almost pretend this was just a bad dream. But it wasn't a dream, and she hadn't been able to sleep at all last night. Her mind had envisioned one scenario after another, each one worse than the one before. Finally, she'd gotten up and lit a lamp. There by the door, were the bags she'd hastily packed last night, one for the children and one for herself. She had left the hardest task for morning. Isabel must tell her children that their father was taking them all away to live with him. The best she could do was to put on a brave face and help them adapt to the uncertain future ahead. She determined to set the example, submitting as gracefully as possible to the circumstances in which she found herself.

Waking the children with an air of excitement she didn't feel, Isabel told them they were about to embark on a great adventure. As they'd learned last night, their father was alive, and he was coming for them this morning. At least for a while, they would be living in a grand hotel. Eliza was willing to accept this new development, as long as her doll, Sally, would be making the trip with them. Johnny was less eager, remembering his relief last night when Grandfather had sent him out of the room, away from his father.

Stripping the linens from the bed, Isabel tucked four sealed envelopes under the pillow, confident they'd be found and delivered after she was gone.

Chapter 45

How could yesterday have held so much joy? And so much sorrow? That was what Katie asked herself after Isabel and the children left with Friedrich. The whole family was crushed by this latest turn of events, and Katie's tears came close to breaking her husband's heart. James consoled Susanna as she absorbed the news about Isabel and the children. He'd assured her. "We're not giving up without a fight. John and I are going to Mr. Redfern's office at once. There must be something that can be done."

Unable to dispel the eerie silence of the house, Katie resorted to her usual method of dealing with adversity – she got to work. Gathering dirty clothes together for laundering, Katie entered Isabel's now deserted bedroom. It was impossible to believe she was gone. Most of her clothes and personal things were still here. Would she be returning for the rest of her belongings? Katie found the bedclothes already stripped, and heaped in a pile at the foot of the bed. She added them to her growing bundle, and plumped the pillows to fluff up the goose down filling. Four sealed envelopes lay exposed on the mattress. After slipping them into the pocket of her apron, Katie found she could no longer bear the feeling of sadness that lingered in the room.

When Musetta arrived, she found Katie scrubbing a pair of heavily soiled dungarees on a large washboard. After asking where Isabel and the children were, Katie spilled the whole story of what had happened yesterday after Musetta left. This most pragmatic of Katie's sisters-in-law, enveloped her in a quick, reassuring hug before picking up a basket of wet, newly washed clothes. On her way to the clothesline, Musetta called over her shoulder. "Leave the rest of the wash for me, Katie. You should rest for a while. I'll check on Mother after this load is hung up to dry."

Telling herself she'd only lay down for a moment, Katie woke later to discover she'd slept until mid-afternoon. She was ravenous. When her sister-in-law walked through the door carrying a tray, Katie hopped briskly out of bed. "I don't need to be waited on, Musetta. I'll eat in the kitchen. And anyway, those clothes are probably ready to come off the line."

"All done. The clothes are dry, folded and ready to be put away. Now eat your lunch. If you don't want it here, carry it into Mother's room. I know she would be glad to see you."

Katie acted on the suggestion, and the women sat without talking. Clearly Susanna was concerned over Isabel and her children, but she wasn't falling apart. She definitely had her wits about her, and exuded a calm resolve. For the first time since her stroke, Susanna was determined to recover. She was needed now, more than ever.

When John and his father returned from town wearing long, solemn faces, the family gathered in Susanna's room to hear the outcome of their consultation with Mr. Redfern. It wasn't good. The lawyer confirmed Friedrich's assertion that he was exercising his lawful rights as a husband and father. No one broke the silence that followed, until Katie's hand dropped despondently onto her lap, and a muffled crackling caused every head to turn in her direction.

"I forgot," she exclaimed! "I found letters Isabel left for us." Pulling the envelopes from her pocket, Katie handed them to John who distributed them all around, with a single exception. The one addressed to Isaac was laid aside for later. Every message began the same way: *Please pray for me and the children.* After that admonition, Isabel had penned some personal remarks for each recipient, and expressed her profound gratitude for the faithful love of her family. Then she revealed that certain packages in her chifforobe had been marked to identify the intended receiver for each one. Lastly, Isabel urged everyone not to worry for her, but to trust God as she herself intended to do.

James immediately led the family in prayer as they joined hands and bowed their heads. Sustained by their faith, the family managed to endure the nightmare of passing that first evening, not knowing how Isabel and the children were faring.

It had been approaching twilight when they'd pulled up to the hotel's porte-cochère. Isabel discovered Friedrich hadn't exaggerated about the extravagance of their accommodations. He had arranged adjoining suites, one for himself, the other for Isabel and the children. Only halfway through a light supper, Johnny started yawning and Eliza's head began nodding. When Isabel suggested it was well past the children's bedtime, Friedrich willingly agreed. Exhibiting unexpected tenderness, he carried his sleeping daughter to the bed prepared for her, and wished Isabel and Johnny each a goodnight before closing the door behind him. A welcome relief washed over Isabel when it became clear to her that she was not expected to share her husband's bed tonight. She sincerely hoped Friedrich had no intentions of resuming conjugal relations with her any time soon.

The next morning, startled by giggling and a soft kiss landing on her cheek, Isabel's eyelids flew open to the sweet faces of her children.

"We're hungry, Mama," Johnny said. "What are we going to eat?"

"That's a good question, Johnny. Let's all get dressed and see what plans your father has for breakfast."

As it turned out they didn't have to wait long for an answer. Upon entering the hallway, they encountered a smartly dressed man wheeling a cart in their direction. The man greeted her. "Good day to you, Mrs. Bachman. Before he left, your husband ordered breakfast to be delivered to your suite. It's my pleasure to serve you this morning."

Retracing their steps, Isabel, Johnny and Eliza sat at a small table while being served like royalty. Though the food and service were excellent, Isabel felt like a fish out of water. She suspected this special treatment was all part of Friedrich's larger plan to win her and the children over to his side. With some reluctance she acknowledged that as the children's father he was entitled to have a relationship with them, but she mistrusted his motives. To her knowledge, Friedrich had never been known to do anything for anyone, without expecting something in return.

Their attendant had almost finished clearing away the dishes when Isabel addressed him. "Thank you, Sir. I don't believe you gave me your name earlier, but I appreciate your taking care of us this morning."

"You are very welcome, Ma'am. You may call me Spencer. Though I have been engaged to primarily serve as Mr. Bachman's personal valet, I am also charged with looking after his family until he secures a lady's maid for you, and a governess for the children." Handing her a handwritten paper, Spencer continued, "your husband has prepared a list of things he's planned for you today. He expresses regret that he was unable to discuss any of this with you in advance, but he's inviting you to have dinner with him this evening. He will call for you at seven thirty. If there's nothing else, Ma'am, I will see you later this morning."

"Spencer," Isabel stopped him. "What is Mr. Bachman doing today?"

"He has a full day of business meetings scheduled, though I am not at liberty to disclose any of the particulars to you."

She tried the door leading to Friedrich's suite out of curiosity, and found it locked. Then she glanced at the agenda her husband had organized for her. An appointment at the finest ladies' apparel shop in town was first on the list. A notation had been made that Spencer would be her escort, and one of the hotel maids would be minding the children. She breathed out an exasperated sigh. Experience told her it would be a waste of time to resist Friedrich's wishes.

Maeve, the girl secured to watch Johnny and Eliza, was a recent Irish immigrant with a face as fresh as a daisy, and an irrepressibly cheerful personality. Isabel's intuition told her she need have no qualms about leaving her children in this young woman's care. The childish laughter greeting her upon returning to the suite after shopping, proved her trust had been well placed. It served to lift her spirits as well. Spencer, juggling the tower of boxes and parcels filling his arms, followed in Isabel's train. After divesting himself of this burden, he left his mistress to attend to the unpacking on her own.

"Tell me what you did while I was gone," Isabel asked the children?

Johnny excitedly related that Maeve had taken them to a park on the beach, and shown them how to build sand castles. Then, they shared a picnic lunch. They looked windblown, sun-kissed, and very happy. After hours in the sun and fresh air, the youngsters were ready for an early night, and fell into bed before Maeve had finished helping Isabel dress for dinner. At exactly seven thirty, a soft rapping on the door announced Friedrich's arrival. Isabel wondered if he would just let himself in, but he waited to be granted admittance. Once inside, he spent an inordinately long time appraising her dress with a critical eye, requesting that she spin around so he could view her appearance from all sides. Complimenting her on the fashionable gown, he proceeded to disarm her then with a warm smile as he withdrew a jeweler's box from his inside pocket and opened it. "Here is a token of my affection, if you'll have it." A gold ring, set with the largest diamond Isabel had ever seen, sparkled brilliantly in the light from the chandelier.

When she hesitated, he asked, "doesn't a man have the right to lavish nice things on his own wife?"

Relenting, she wondered if this is how it felt to fall into a trap.

"Now," he said with satisfaction, "I will be the envy of every man in the hotel."

Indeed, their grand entrance into the newly redecorated dining room was met with some envious glances. The maitre d'hôtel personally escorted them to the best table in the house. Friedrich ordered champagne for everyone, inviting their fellow diners to raise a glass to his long-awaited reunion with the lovely Mrs. Bachman, his wife. Isabel had almost forgotten how charming her husband could be, when he wanted. A number of the hotel guests stopped by their table to offer congratulations, introduce themselves, and wish the couple an enjoyable stay. By the end of the evening, Isabel was a little unsteady on her feet after several glasses of wine. Bracing herself on Friedrich's arm, she managed to arrive at the entrance to her suite without becoming completely unbalanced. Amused at her instability, Friedrich whispered something in her ear that created a flush to spread from her head to her toes. When she vehemently shook her head to indicate a negative reply, he merely laughed and said. "I can wait."

Already aware of a throbbing at her temples, Isabel felt ill. She had intended to take only a sip of champagne but had emptied her glass – at least twice. Friedrich had been attentive, well-mannered and engaging, but she still didn't trust him. Isabel knew she was holding herself back, but why? For heaven's sake, the man was her husband. That fact was impossible to deny. She remembered being swept off her feet when they'd first met, dazzled by his attractiveness and sophistication. It was later, when the facade fell away, and the heavy drinking and carousing began, that she had bitterly regretted her decision to marry him. There was no way out then, and there was no way out now. She had vowed for better or worse, and she couldn't exactly say which this was, but that was irrelevant. He was her husband, and Isaac must be uprooted from her heart, to make room for Friedrich.

Chapter 46

It was the last thing in the world John wanted to do, but he couldn't put it off any longer. Not fifteen minutes ago, he had observed Isaac riding along the road on his way home. Tucking the letter inside his shirt, and settling himself in the saddle, he reined Blaze toward the Lehman farm. Isaac had been excited to see him.

"John, wait until you hear. I've been asking around and have gotten reports that Friedrich is back in the area, boasting about his plans to come into a fortune. If you ask me, the man is up to something, and it can't be good."

Instead of an answering flash of indignation, John shoved his hands deeper into his pockets, and hung his head. This reaction from his friend left Isaac perplexed. "Well, what's up? Don't you have anything to say?"

"Isaac, there's no easy way to say this. Friedrich showed up at our folks' place two days ago, and . . .," John's nerve failed him.

"And what? Spit it out. What are you trying to say?"

"He made good on his boast about the money, but that's not the worst of it. Friedrich has Belle, and the children, too."

John had prepared himself to be on the receiving end of an angry outburst, or a blue streak of murderous oaths, or a mean right hook to his jaw, but none of these things happened. It was worse than anything he could have imagined.

With a deadly seething calm, Isaac demanded to know how all of this had come to be, and John told him. When he'd finished, John laid a hand on Isaac's shoulder. "Would you like to sit and talk?"

Isaac broke free of John's hand, and replied through clenched teeth. "What I would like is for you to remove your hand, and leave me alone." Remembering the letter in his pocket, John offered it to Isaac. "Belle left this for you."

The envelope was wrenched from his hand, then savagely ripped into pieces and thrown on the ground. The slamming of the door rang in John's ears as he rode away.

Back at the stable, John dismounted, and was about to remove Blaze's tack when he felt a pair of comforting arms winding around him. "I guess I don't have to ask how it went with Isaac?"

John stepped away from the horse, pulling Katie into his embrace. "Am I so easy to read?"

"Only to me, I think," she said. "And, I had a pretty good idea about what kind of hornet's nest you might run into. In some ways, you and Isaac are very much alike."

"How so?"

"You both love deeply."

"Katie, I can't even let myself imagine what Isaac is feeling right now."

"I know, John. It seems unfair that we're so happy when others are in despair. How do you think Isaac will come to terms with losing Isabel?"

"God only knows. I sure don't."

Isaac managed, by exerting all the willpower he possessed, to restrain himself until after John had ridden out of sight. He knew he'd behaved badly toward his best friend, but he'd sooner take a beating than accept pity. Cursing the light breeze that was whipping up the shreds of Isabel's message, Isaac raced out of the kitchen to gather the scraps of paper before they were scattered to the four winds. It was a painstaking process to reassemble Isabel's message, but at last he had the whole of it.

Dear Isaac,

Please pray for me and the children, even as I will keep you in my prayers.

I've always heard it said, "be careful what you ask for . . . .." In hindsight, that is a warning I wish I had heeded, since now I know the answer to whether or not my husband lives, and all my hopes for a happy future with you have been dashed. The law upholds a man's rights over his wife and children, and while the option of my leaving him does exist, such a decision would put my future with Johnny and Eliza in jeopardy. It is unthinkable to risk being forbidden to see my children. I am left with no choice, but to submit to my fate.

Though it must remain unfulfilled, never doubt my love for you. My deepest regret is for whatever pain and sorrow you may feel at receiving this news.

Your Isabel

So, this was it. This was goodbye. There was not a thing he could do to change Isabel's circumstances. It was out of his hands, and suddenly Isaac felt an urgent need to get away from here, someplace far, far away, and an idea began to take shape in his mind.

The month of June was drawing to its close before anyone at the Hartman home heard from Isaac. Rex, ever vigilant, announced the arrival of someone outside the gate one evening after supper. Katie had been throwing dishwater on the flower bed when she recognized Isaac at the end of the drive. Raising her index finger to let him know she'd be with him in a minute, she rinsed the empty dishpan, and leaned it against the hand pump to drain.

Isaac couldn't help noticing a certain glow about her features, and the unmistakable little rounded belly that betrayed her condition.

After unlatching the gate, Katie embraced him in a sisterly hug. "We've missed you, Isaac. John's been hoping you'd stop by. Come up to the house with me."

He walked at her side, leading his horse, which he tied to a hitching post near the kitchen door.

"Look who's here," Katie called out!

In the parlor, James rose from his seat to greet Isaac, and Susanna reached up with her right hand, pulling him down to plant a kiss on his cheek. There was a brief moment of awkwardness and uncertainty, when John stood to extend his hand. Isaac began to reciprocate in the same manner, but a mutual compulsion turned the handshake into a fierce, manly embrace. Isaac swallowed hard, and said, "I'm sorry, John. Will you forgive me?"

"There's nothing to forgive, Isaac. Please sit with us."

"I'll get some coffee," Katie volunteered.

"I'll help," Susanna said, leaning on her cane for support as she slowly got to her feet.

Isaac watched the women leave the room, arm in arm. "Your mother's recovery is nothing short of miraculous. It gives me hope to see an answer to prayer."

John smiled. "I've learned that powerful forces are unleashed when determined women are in league with the Almighty. Katie has worked tirelessly to help my mother achieve the results you just witnessed. Neither one of them are quitters. There's a lesson in that for all of us, I think."

James leaned forward, making eye contact with their neighbor. "How are you getting on, Isaac? I hope you know you're like a second son to Susanna and me."

Nodding in the affirmative, Isaac got straight to the point of his visit. It would be easier to say with the women out of the room. "I wanted to let you folks know that I'm going away for a while, probably a year at the least. Arrangements have been made for a tenant farmer and his family to stay at my place, and manage everything in my absence. The Harpers are fine people, and will make good neighbors for you."

This unexpected announcement caught John and his father by off-guard, leaving them both speechless for a moment. John was the first to recover. "Where are you going?"

"I'm going to Illinois, to visit my brothers and sisters. It's been some years since we've seen each other, and after they tire of putting up with me, I'll travel farther west. Montana maybe."

"When are you leaving," James asked?

"Tomorrow morning, on the train bound for Chicago. Here," he said handing John a scrap of paper, "I'll be staying with my oldest brother. Write to this address should you need to reach me for any reason. Now, I think I'll just slip out the front way, and loop back around to get my horse before the women return. Please tell Susanna and Katie goodbye for me, I cannot endure another sad parting."

John walked with Isaac down the drive to wish his hurting friend godspeed on his journey. After the gate closed between them, Isaac mounted his horse and turned to John with a grin.

"I'll just say congratulations before I go. I couldn't help but notice that Katie's in the family way. I am happy for you both."

"Thanks Isaac. We'll be waiting for your return. May God go with you."

Where are you, *God? Are you there, or have you forsaken me?* Isabel instantly rebuked the thought. She knew in her heart that God hadn't abandoned her, even though her prayers seemed to rise no higher than the ceiling. All the time they'd been here, she and the children had suffered no abuse at Friedrich's hands. Their needs had all been met, with one exception. He had strictly forbidden any contact with her family.

If only she could escape this pointless existence. At least it was pointless from her perspective. Isabel woke every morning to the feeling of Déjà vu. Another day, just like the one before, spent in the company of women with whom she shared nothing in common, except the status of being married to men with money. The ladies whiled away the hours playing whist, attending highbrow lectures, or indulging in frivolous luncheons while the husbands engaged in business. Children were customarily relegated to the care of governesses, and rarely seen. Isabel was relieved to know that Maeve, of whom she'd grown very fond, had been permanently hired to look after Johnny and Eliza.

The pinnacles of social competition took place during the

evenings, when she and Friedrich were invited to one palatial estate or another for dinner and dancing. Critical eyes sought out every infraction of what was considered acceptable attire, and should someone's couture be found wanting, word of that violation spread like wildfire. This standard held true for proper deportment as well. One faux pas was enough to make the offender the subject of gossip for days.

Friedrich was a natural when it came to mingling with this crowd. In his desire to emulate the most powerful men, he drank, and wagered to excess. Flirting outrageously with the preeminent matrons, he whispered sweet flattery in their ears while whirling them around the dance floor. For her part, Isabel despised hobnobbing with these people, but it was what Friedrich expected of her, and so she complied. She endured without complaint, the slavering attentions of men who took inappropriate pleasure in getting their hands on her. Friedrich didn't seem to mind, as long as her beauty and style elevated his status among those from whom he sought approval. As long as she made him look good, he placed no other demands on her. She knew he spent lavishly to ensure she always wore the most fashionable and expensive gowns, and she wondered how much of the money he'd already exhausted. After overhearing a conversation between Friedrich and one of his partners, Isabel had grown alarmed by the unbelievable amount her husband had invested in a risky venture.

He'd also decided against purchasing an existing home, and was engaged in negotiations with builders to construct an ostentatious mansion. The family would continue to reside at the hotel until his grand residence was built. When Friedrich proposed sending Johnny to a private military academy, Isabel put her foot down.

"Friedrich, he doesn't need the structure of a military school. He and Eliza need a father in their lives. You barely know them. They are bored, and growing ill-tempered. This is no place in which to raise children."

"They have more now than ever before, every plaything they could want."

"Please Friedrich, can you not spare them any of your time and attention? We could get away by ourselves, maybe picnic on the bluffs above the lake." The sincerity in her voice softened his heart.

"All right, just this once."

The bracing wind blowing across the lake tempered the heat of the day, and inspired comparisons of the billowy white clouds in the sky, to an armada of white-sailed ships running along a deep blue sea. The atmosphere was paradoxically exhilarating, and calming at the same time. Friedrich couldn't remember the last time he'd lain on his back, doing nothing but feeling the warming rays of sun penetrate his body. The children had actually been delighted when he'd played a game of tag with them. They'd run until they grew tired, collapsing in a heap on the blanket. Johnny stretched out, covering his eyes with a hat, and Eliza nestled close to her father before falling asleep. Isabel reclined on her side; head propped on one hand as she read a book. Friedrich exchanged a long look with her, thinking for the first time that maybe he already had everything he wanted. Then he dozed off.

Isabel's frantic scream roused him, and he easily overtook her while they raced to the edge of the bluff. In pursuit of the butterflies she was chasing, Eliza was running too near the precipice, unaware of the danger so close at hand. Friedrich literally snatched her from midair before she could fall, swinging her back to Isabel, but his momentum was such that he could not save himself. He plummeted over the edge. Johnny, arriving in time to see his father disappear, had dropped to his knees beside his mother. From the crowd of bystanders gathering at the scene, a few men cautiously made their way down the steep slope. One of them was a medical student. It seemed like hours before he reappeared, commanding the onlookers to make room for those assuming the role of recovery workers. Leading Isabel and the children to a secluded spot, he told her that after tumbling to the bottom, her husband had struck his head against a half-buried anchor. The young man put his arms around Isabel's heaving shoulders. "Ma'am, I am so very sorry. Your husband's neck was broken upon impact. There was nothing anyone could do."

Chapter 47

Although the sun wouldn't crest the horizon for an hour yet, the light had already begun to change. It was at first, an almost imperceptible transition. Aurora, or first light, is an ethereal interval when the sleeper wakens, but waits for the veil of night to be drawn aside, revealing what is there, but has been hidden in the darkness.

Through the soft glow, John regarded Katie as she slumbered peacefully at his side. Quietly adoring her, he marveled at her resilience, her seemingly inexhaustible reserves of energy, and her caring heart as big as the whole world. If it were possible to sum up all that is good in heaven and on earth, he reckoned the result might approximate a fair description of Katie Byler Hartman.

John splayed his hand across the contoured expanse concealing the mystery that was their unborn child, silently expressing gratitude for his blessings. At once he was rewarded by a yet-unknown someone, pushing strongly back against his palm. Katie smiled sweetly in her sleep, and by reflex placed a hand on top of John's. He was just about to kiss the smile on her lips when he heard the slow shuffling of his mother's footsteps halt outside their bedroom. Slipping from under the covers, he opened the door to admit her before she could knock.

"John," she said, clearly distressed. "It's Isabel! You must get to the telegraph office right away."

Before he could say anything, Katie was at his side, as if taking form out of thin air. "I'll start breakfast, and then I'll pack a bag for you." Shrugging into a robe, she helped Susanna downstairs, leaving her husband to dress.

John bolted his breakfast, and found Father waiting in the buggy. Within minutes of arriving at the telegraph office, a message came in over the wire and was decoded for him. John immediately dictated a reply to the sender and went straight to the railway station to buy a ticket for the next train to South Haven.

While waiting for James to return with word of whatever catastrophe had befallen Isabel, Katie listened to Susanna declare she hadn't experienced such a strong premonition for a long time. The jolt of knowing that Isabel needed their help had literally rocked her frame, and almost caused her to topple over. Katie hugged her mother-in-law. "John will take care of everything, there's no cause for worry now."

The force of Belle rushing into her brother's arms nearly landed both of them on the floor. Then Johnny and Eliza attached themselves to their uncle with no intention of being pried loose. Coherent conversation was impossible for several minutes.

Later that night, John listened to Belle as she related the events of the past few months. Friedrich's final selfless act, imparted to Belle the hope that her wayward husband may have achieved a measure of redemption in the end. She shared with John how faith had sustained her through this time of testing. John hoped Belle's faith would remain steadfast, not telling her that Isaac wouldn't be around to greet them when they returned. She would find out soon enough.

It required four days, with Spencer's able assistance, to sort out and settle Friedrich's immediate debts and obligations. Estimating that more than half of the money may have disappeared, John advised Belle to retain Mr. Redfern, and let the lawyer untangle the intricately twisted and shady details of her late husband's business affairs. For the second and last time, John made funeral arrangements for Friedrich. On this occasion there was no doubt about the identity of the deceased. Friedrich's body had been shipped ahead to the undertaker. Spencer was compensated for his services, and dismissed to seek a new position elsewhere. Maeve's wages, along with a gratuity, were handed over to the girl, but she had lingered, making herself useful to Belle.

At last, the day for departure arrived. The hotel bill, which had been staggering, was paid in full, and John's sister and her children were all packed and at the station. John noticed that their party's number had increased by one, but he wasn't surprised. Claiming that Maeve had become indispensable to her, Belle insisted the girl accompany them. John suspected it was more likely that Belle had grown fond of the Irish lass, who'd bravely crossed the ocean by herself to find a new life in a new land.

Katie had not been idle during John's absence. Furiously dusting and cleaning the walls, corners and floors of every room in the farmhouse had kept her busy. Disregarding Susanna's entreaties to rest, and not overexert herself, Katie continued to carry out the second phase of her plan. When she learned that Isabel was returning with a helper, Katie's determination to be reinstalled in the cabin by the time John returned, grew stronger. Stray dust and overlooked cobwebs were subjected to a cleaning frenzy. She told herself it would be wonderful for the two of them to once again enjoy time alone, but the overriding motivation was her desire to give birth in their own, little cabin. Whether aware of the fact or not, Katie was in the throes of a maternal nesting instinct.

Excited cries rang out from the kitchen stoop, as James drove the crowded buggy up to the door. Running excitedly between the horses' hooves, Rex barked his own special welcome to Johnny. There was a good deal of commotion with everyone hugging everyone else. Maeve stood off to one side, trying to be invisible until Katie pulled her into their midst. After the luggage was unloaded and the horses stabled, the family reunion continued inside the house, where Isabel introduced the easy-going Irish lass.

After the mayhem subsided, John was sidetracked by Katie pulling him insistently toward the woodland path.

"It's this way, or have you forgotten already," she teased? "There's no room in the big house for the two of us, let alone a baby. I've moved us back to our honeymoon hideaway."

His answering smile was just what she'd been hoping for, although he couldn't resist a reprimand. "You shouldn't have done all this by yourself. Didn't the doctor say you should stay off your feet as much as possible?"

Katie ignored the question as she reached out to depress the door latch, but John stopped her. "I believe it's customary for the groom to carry the bride over the threshold."

She snickered, "I'm afraid you'll find the bride a good deal heavier this time."

Lifting her easily with an exaggerated grunt for effect, he said, "still light as a feather."

The next morning when Katie began to rise, John pushed her back onto the pillow. "Where do you think you're going?"

"I thought I'd fix breakfast for the folks, and then come right back to get ours."

"You stay put, Little Lady. Isabel and Maeve can manage very well without your help, and I'll take over getting our meals while you rest for a few days."

"What? This is news to me. I didn't know you could cook!"

"I admit it's a closely guarded secret, but Susanna Hartman would have considered it a grievous failure on her part if she'd neglected schooling me in basic cookery. Now, how do you like your eggs?"

It wasn't long before John was reminded that it was impossible to make Katie do something she didn't want to do, and he soon tired of chasing her back to bed. They strolled to the farmhouse in the afternoon and spent the evening with family. Belle and the children had made themselves at home, and except for Maeve's presence, it was like they'd never been away. Over the next few days, life resumed its normal, predictable routine for the beginning of harvest season.

The Harpers stopped by to deliver a surplus of garden bounty, and share the latest news from their landlord. This was how Isabel learned that Isaac had rented out the farm, and was wandering around the country. His quest to find where he belonged had carried him as far west as Fort Benton, Montana. Belle's eyes grew wide at this news, and she gave John a look that conveyed her desire to have a private word with him at the first opportunity.

That afternoon, John and Belle talked in the garden. In a manner he hoped was both gentle and forthright, he explained his decision to delay telling her about Isaac. The timing had been all wrong, until now. John would have felt like he was meddling if he'd had this discussion with Belle when he first saw her after Friedrich's death. If it was meant for Belle and Isaac to get together, it would happen without his help or interference. Surprisingly, Belle accepted her brother's rationalization, saying she was contented to leave the matter in God's hands.

Anticipating the imminent arrival of the newest Hartman, preparations had been put in place and there was nothing left to do but wait, and wait, and wait some more. The doctor said it could be any time now, but the baby would come when it was ready.

Katie wasn't good at waiting. She didn't like finding herself in a situation beyond her control. She didn't like it at all. After a long night of tossing and turning, she woke early on All Hallows Eve, feeling that something was different. The thought of food held no appeal for her, and she turned up her nose at the tray John brought into the bedroom. She was restless, unable to find a comfortable position, and just about that time she became aware of a dull ache, radiating from her back, around to her belly. The pain was like a constricting band, encircling her lower abdomen. John consulted with Belle and his mother. Susanna confirmed what they'd all suspected, Katie was in the early stages of labor. Out of an abundance of caution, John's mother proposed sending for the doctor.

"Katie, you're a healthy young woman, and it's not likely you'll have any complications, but since this is your first baby, I believe the doctor should be informed that your labor has commenced."

"No," Katie objected. "I don't want the doctor. I want you and Isabel. I'm comfortable with you. Please . . . ," she begged.

"Overruled" John said firmly. "I'm going for the doctor."

Fate ruled in Katie's favor, decreeing the matter of whether the doctor would, or would not, attend the birth to be moot. He was indisposed on an urgent call, and not expected back until morning at the soonest.

Day passed, and darkness fell. Katie's labor had progressed beyond mere discomfort to the point of real pain, and she gained a new appreciation for what women had endured since time immemorial to bring life into the world. There were times when Katie wanted badly to scream, but she resisted the impulse, reasoning that if she lost control now, what would she do when she could stand it no longer?

John paced for hours outside the room, wishing that Isaac had been here to keep him company in this unending purgatory. He was tense, expecting at any moment to hear Katie cry out in pain, but he didn't hear much of anything. Only the quiet droning of women's low voices, imparting encouragement, reassurance and comfort. A subtle change in the voices alerted him to a seismic shift occurring in the next room. Loud and regular panting overrode the sound of voices, before all noise was drowned out by the blessed, outraged mewling of a newborn. Mercifully, Belle slipped out to put his mind at ease about Katie and the baby. She hugged him tightly around his neck., "Katie is just fine, and so is the baby. Give us a few minutes and then you can come in." Turning back before returning to her post, she flashed a big smile at her brother. "Congratulations, John."

The very moment the newborn was laid against her chest, Katie fell madly in love with the helpless, little mite pressed close to her. After mother and child were sponged off and made presentable, Susanna and Belle left the room, allowing John to enter.

Katie was radiant, more beautiful than he'd ever seen her. Her eyes lingered on his before she lowered them once again to the snugly wrapped bundle in her arms. "Your Papa has come to meet you, little one."

John put all the feeling he couldn't find expression for, in the kiss applied passionately to her lips. Cradling the baby in his arms, he asked, "is it a boy, or a girl?"

Katie laughed, "does it matter?"

"Not at all, but it might have some bearing on what name we choose."

"It's a boy, John. Our first son, our first child."

He situated himself on the bed beside her where they could both look into the pair of eyes looking back at them.

"Are you saying you'd actually go through all this again, Katie? I don't know if my heart can take any more."

Caressing their son's downy head, Katie said. "Oh John, darling, this is only the beginning."

Made in the USA
Monee, IL
26 September 2023